"ARE YOU GOING TO
FEED ON ME TONIGHT?"

"It depends."

"On what?"

"On you." His gaze moved over her, lingering on her lips, the swell of her breasts beneath the white silk shirt. "I'll leave you alone tonight in exchange for one kiss, freely given."

"A kiss?" Was he kidding? How could he think about kissing at a time like this?

Gideon nodded. It had been a long time since he'd had a woman. He could have compelled those the witch brought him. He could have taken them by force. Neither option appealed to him. Nor had any of the women. But this one . . . there was something about her that intrigued him like no other. "So, what do you say?"

She eyed him warily. "How do I know you'll stop with a kiss?"

He shrugged. "I guess you'll just have to trust me . . ."

Other titles available by Amanda Ashley

A WHISPER OF ETERNITY

AFTER SUNDOWN

DEAD PERFECT

DEAD SEXY

DESIRE AFTER DARK

NIGHT'S KISS

NIGHT'S MASTER

NIGHT'S PLEASURE

NIGHT'S TOUCH

IMMORTAL SINS

EVERLASTING KISS

EVERLASTING DESIRE

BOUND BY NIGHT

BOUND BY BLOOD

HIS DARK EMBRACE

Published by Kensington Publishing Corporation

Desire The Night

AMANDA ASHLEY

ZEBRA BOOKS
KENSINGTON PUBLISHING CORP.
http://www.kensingtonbooks.com

ZEBRA BOOKS are published by

Kensington Publishing Corp.
119 West 40th Street
New York, NY 10018

All Kensington titles, imprints, and distributed lines are available at special quantity discounts for bulk purchases for sales
promotion, premiums, fund-raising, educational, or institu-
tional use.

Special book excerpts or customized printings can also be
created to fit specific needs. For details, write or phone the
office of the Kensington Special Sales Manager: Attn.: Special Sales Department. Kensington Publishing Corp., 119 West
40th Street, New York, NY 10018. Phone: 1-800-221-2647.

Zebra and the Z logo Reg. U.S. Pat. & TM Off.

ISBN-13: 978-1-4201-2134-6
ISBN-10: 1-4201-2134-0

First Printing: September 2012

10 9 8 7 6 5 4 3 2 1

Printed in the United States of America

To my critique group—
Carol Amato, Molly Dillon,
Judith McAllister,
and
Mart Shaughnessy.

I couldn't do it without you.

Prologue

Gideon Marquet stared into the darkness, his limbs aching from the weight of the heavy silver chains that shackled his ankles to the thick cement wall behind him. His body felt like it was burning from the inside out, causing his veins to shrink, while his skin grew painfully tight with the need for sustenance.

So long since he had fed.

So long since his thirst had been satisfied.

His eyes narrowed as a tall woman appeared in the basement. Clad in a shimmering white robe trimmed in white fur, she looked like an angel when, in truth, she was anything but.

The hem of her velvet robe made a soft, swishing noise as she drew closer, then knelt outside the cell. Verah.

Gideon groaned inwardly as she picked up the slender, silver-bladed dagger that rested beside a golden jewel-encrusted goblet on a low wooden table. His body tensed as she began to chant, her voice soft, almost hypnotic. He winced as she reached between the bars and dragged the blade across his right thigh. Lifting the goblet, she held it under the wound to collect the dark red blood that leaked from the long, shallow gash. When the goblet was half-full, she made a similar cut in his left thigh, chanting all the while. When the cup was full, she left the cellar.

She returned a short time later.

Gideon sat up a little straighter, his fangs extending as the cell door opened and a woman clad in a wrinkled brown dress was pushed inside. She fell to the floor, crying out as she scraped her knees on the cold cement. His hands clenched as the warm, sweet coppery scent of her blood filled his nostrils.

Blind with panic, the woman scrambled to her feet and ran to the iron-barred door.

"Please!" she cried, her hands fisting around the bars. "Let me out! Please, oh, please, let me out of here!"

But her frantic plea fell on deaf ears.

His prey sobbed hysterically as Verah turned and left the basement.

With her only hope gone, the woman darted to a far corner of the cell, her back pressed against the bars, her arms wrapped tightly around her waist. Tears flooded her cheeks as she murmured, "Please, don't."

But all he heard was the frantic beating of her heart, the whisper-soft sound of the blood flowing through her veins.

"Please." She fell to her knees, hands raised in supplication.

But that wouldn't save her.

Nothing could save her now.

It was feeding time.

Chapter 1

Gideon stirred, then awoke with an oath on his lips. Another day lost in oblivion, another night in hell. If he could have ended his own existence, he would gladly have done so long ago.

Sitting up, he cursed the witch who had captured him, the enchantment that had blinded him to her true identity, his insatiable lust for blood, the heavy silver chains that rendered him powerless.

Damn.

He glanced at the dark-haired woman curled up on the floor beside him. Her breathing was shallow and erratic, her hair and clothing disheveled. How many women had he killed since this nightmare began? He tried to resist the siren call of their blood, but in the end, no matter how he tried to fight it, he always surrendered to the hunger that burned through him, relentless, impossible to ignore. He felt a twinge of regret for this, his latest victim. She was middle-aged, married with four children, and doomed to die by his hand.

He clenched his fists as remorse gnawed at him. Regret had become his constant companion, along with an intense hatred for the witch who kept him in captivity, who bled him and starved him to the point of death, until whatever scrap of humanity or mercy remained within him was erased by a hunger too excruciating to deny.

The woman stirred, her eyes growing wide with fear when she saw him staring down at her.

"No, please." She scooted away from him, but there was nowhere for her to go, nowhere to hide.

No escape for either of them.

Resting his head against the wall behind him, Gideon closed his eyes, his thoughts drifting back in time, back to the night he met Verah. . . .

He had gone into the city in search of prey, but all thought of feeding had vanished when he entered a seedy nightclub and saw a woman dancing in the middle of a crowd of cheering men. She had been beautiful beyond compare, her movements as sinuous as silk as she dipped and swayed to the pulsing beat of the music. Like every other man in the place, Gideon had been caught in her spell, mesmerized by the veiled promise lurking in the depths of her sea-green eyes.

When she smiled at him, he was lost.

When she invited him to her house, he had no thought to refuse.

When he asked her name, she laughed softly, then took him by the hand and led him out of the tavern and down a narrow winding road that led to a large two-story house. Once inside, she locked the door with a flourish, then led him into her bedroom where she had indulged his every fantasy.

When he awoke the next night, he was in chains, the beautiful woman was gone, and an emaciated, gray-haired hag was collecting his blood in a jewel-encrusted gold cup. He had been imprisoned in this wretched cage ever since, held captive by strong silver chains that drained his strength and weakened his preternatural powers.

It hadn't taken him long to figure out what was going on. The woman who had beguiled him was a witch who had cloaked her ugliness in the guise of a young siren. She had been searching the world over for a vampire and Gideon had walked blindly into her trap. With his blood, Verah had regained her youth and beauty and now she sold his blood to anyone who could pay the price. Some paid in cash, some in gold, and some in humankind, hence the females that were brought to him from time to time.

Gideon glanced at the woman cowering beside him. When Verah had first brought her to him, she had been robust, her blue eyes bright, her fair skin luminous. Now, she was pale, her eyes sunken and shadowed with fear, her hair stringy and unkempt. The witch brought the woman water once a day, but no food. Why waste sustenance on one who was doomed?

Gideon swore softly. He didn't want to hurt the woman or deprive her children of their mother, but sooner or later the urge to feed would become uncontrollable, the pain of resisting excruciating. Even now, the frightened pounding of her heart stirred his instinct to hunt. The scent of her blood flowed warm and red in her veins, promising instant relief from the agony that engulfed him.

Sooner or later, he would have to feed, and when he did, he would take it all. Perhaps it would have been more merciful to have killed the woman the first night Verah had brought her to him instead of letting her linger, her dread growing as she waited for him to strike.

In an effort to resist the inevitable, he rested his head on his bent knees and closed his eyes. How long had he been imprisoned in this place? A year? Two? He had lost track of the time. There were no windows in the cellar, no way of knowing whether it was summer or winter. The floor beneath him was always cold.

He closed his mind to the woman sobbing beside him. Women. They had ever been the cause of his troubles, from the mother who had abandoned him when he was thirteen to the treacherous female who had stolen his mortal life and turned him into a monster.

Verah was simply another in a long line of women he had foolishly trusted. Morbidly, he considered the fact that she would most likely be the last.

A deep breath carried the scent of the poor doomed creature who shared his prison. She was destined to die, whether by his hand or Verah's.

He groaned softly as pain clawed at his vitals. He had spent the last five nights resisting the urge to feed on the woman. Each evening, the agony inside him burned hotter, brighter, like a fire that could not be quenched. His fangs ached, his veins were shriveling, starved for nourishment, for relief. Relief that lay curled up in a tight ball on the far side of the cell. He could feel her watching him surreptitiously, taste her fear as she waited for him to sink his fangs into her throat.

The hunger growling inside urged him to take her, to put an end to the physical torment that racked his body and the mental anguish that tormented the woman.

Muttering, "Forgive me," he dragged her into his embrace and put both of them out of their misery.

Chapter 2

Kiya Alissano spoke softly to the frightened dog quivering on the examination table. The Rottweiler stilled immediately, its liquid brown eyes suddenly filled with trust instead of fear.

"I don't know how you do it, Kay," Wanda Sandusky said. "I tried to calm that monster down for ten minutes with no success. One word from you, and voilà! She's practically asleep."

"I guess I just have a way with animals," Kay said, scratching the dog's head. And it was true. From the time she had been a little girl, animals had trusted her—dogs, cats, birds, deer, squirrels, horses, even snakes. They never ran from her, never showed any fear which, all things considered, was pretty strange. It was a definite advantage in her job, though.

"A way? Girl, it's more like magic." Wanda glanced at her watch. "Since you don't need any help in here, I'm going to lunch. I told my mom I'd meet her over at the mall around noon if I could get away."

Kay nodded. Wanda wasn't only a co-worker, but her best friend. "Bring me back a Coke, will you?"

"Sure thing," Wanda called over her shoulder as she closed the door behind her.

Kay stared after her friend, wishing she and her mother shared the kind of relationship that Wanda and her mother had. Wanda went out to lunch with her mother every week or so. They went shopping together and texted back and forth and did a dozen other fun things. Of course, it wasn't Dorothy's fault that she and Kay didn't do fun things together. Her father rarely let her mother leave the compound. It still amazed Kay that he had agreed to let her go away for a year.

She looked up when Dr. Saltzman entered the examination room a few moments later. He was a tall, good-looking man with a plump, red-haired wife and six red-headed kids.

He shook his head when he saw the Rot lying quietly on the table.

"I see you've worked your Indian magic again," he said, pulling on a pair of gloves. "I don't know what I'd do without you."

Kay continued stroking the dog's head, occasionally whispering to the animal in Lakota, while the vet performed his examination. The Rottweiler had been hit by a car and had been brought in bleeding from several cuts. One leg and several ribs were broken. The Rot had been reasonably calm until they carried it into the examination room and then it had bared its teeth, growling and snapping at anyone who came close until Kay entered the room.

"We'll need to sedate her to set that leg and bind up her ribs," the vet said, preparing a shot to anesthetize the dog. "Keep talking to her."

Kay nodded. "There, now," she murmured, still stroking the Rot's head. "Dr. Saltzman will have you fixed up in no time at all."

"So, what shall we do tonight?" Wanda asked as they left the office that evening. "Do you want to go to a movie?"

"Not tonight," Kay said. "I have something to do."

"A date?" Wanda asked, waggling her eyebrows.

"No, nothing like that. How was lunch with your mom?"

"Don't try to change the subject," Wanda admonished with a shake of her head. "It's that monthly thing, isn't it? You're planning to take tomorrow off, aren't you?" Wanda poked Kay lightly on the shoulder. "Sooner or later, I'm going to find out what you're up to."

"Believe me, I wish I could tell you," Kay confessed, digging her keys out of her handbag. "But I can't. I'll see you on Friday."

"All right, girlfriend."

Kay sighed as she unlocked the car and slid behind the wheel. She would love to tell Wanda why she had to take off one day a month, but it was never going to happen. She was bound by the law of the pack not to reveal their secrets, and the truth of what they were was the most tightly guarded secret of all. The penalty for disclosing it to humans was severe, and that applied to Kay, too. Being the daughter of the Shadow Pack's Alpha wouldn't grant her any special privileges or immunity if she violated pack laws.

As far as the wolves were concerned, there was only one law—the law of the pack—and they all seemed perfectly happy to obey it. Why wasn't she? Why couldn't she obey without question? Conform to pack hierarchy without a qualm? Be content to do as she was told and live within the pack boundaries? Why couldn't she be who her father wanted her to be? Was it so wrong to want to make her own decisions, decide where she wanted to live, who she wanted to marry?

At home, she broiled a chicken for dinner and washed it down with a glass of wine, hoping the chardonnay would calm her nerves. Too restless to sit still, she dusted and vacuumed, cleaned the oven, scrubbed the floor. And all the while, she could feel the wolf prowling inside her, waiting impatiently to get out.

In the morning, she called Dr. Saltzman and told him she

needed the day off, then she ate a quick breakfast, packed an overnight bag, and drove to her favorite haunt in the sacred *Paha Sapa*, the Black Hills of South Dakota.

Ancient tribal elders Sitting Bull, Crazy Horse, and Red Cloud had walked these hills and valleys in days long gone. They had sought visions on the tops of the mountains, hunted the buffalo on the plains, defeated Custer in a battle still discussed by red man and white alike. Sitting Bull had called the tribes together in a last, desperate attempt to defeat the whites so they could keep the Hills and protect their way of life. She often wondered what life would have been like if the Indians had won their fight.

The Hills were a magical place, filled with beauty and mystery, a vast expanse of pine-covered mountains with trees that were so dark a green that they looked black from a distance. The perfect spot for her monthly retreat from the world.

Wrapped in a fluffy yellow towel, Kay stood in a lush valley deep in the heart of the Black Hills watching the moon rise. It called to her, causing her whole body to quiver in anticipation.

The transformation came in a flood of physical sensations—the realigning of bones and muscle, the change in temperature as a thick pelt sprouted from her skin, the sudden acuity in her senses, the feel of the earth beneath the sensitive pads of her feet.

Lifting her head, she howled at the moon. How often had she wished she could transform more than once a month, that she could experience the wonder and freedom of this moment whenever she desired? She had often dreamed of being an Alpha, like her father, able to transform at will, to have his unlimited power and authority, to give orders instead of having to take them. But there was no use in wishing for what could never be.

With a shake of her head, she broke into a ground-eating run, yipping with pleasure as she bounded effortlessly over rocks and brush. She reveled in the sense of invincibility that filled her as she raced along.

She hadn't gone far when a jackrabbit exploded from its cover.

With a short bark, the werewolf gave chase, reveling in the sting of the wind in her face, the myriad scents that assailed her nostrils from every side, the sheer joy of the hunt.

The unfortunate rabbit never had a chance.

Chapter 3

Verah reclined upon a bed covered with soft furs, a large bowl of exotic fruit at her fingertips, while a pair of handsome male servants hovered nearby, waiting to do her bidding. Her familiar, Rama, stretched out beside her, purring softly.

Verah knew that some of her fellow witches thought her lifestyle a bit on the eccentric side because she preferred to wear long skirts and peasant blouses instead of more modern garb. When they commented on the way she dressed, or remarked that they thought some of her magic was primitive, she merely smiled and told them she had an old soul. Far older than any of them knew or suspected.

There were all kinds of witches, and many forms of magic—some witches were born with it, some learned the craft from another witch. In rare cases, the magical arts were bestowed on some lucky soul as a gift. There was earth magic and water magic, fire magic, and magic wrought by the wind. Verah had inherited her magic from her mother, but she had wanted more power, more knowledge, and so she had sought out the old Navajo shaman who had instructed her mother. Yanaba was respected and feared by his own people, though none dared call him a witch to his face.

Verah had often considered telling the old witch about the

magical properties in Gideon's blood, but whenever she started to do so, some inner voice warned her that such knowledge should not be shared with anyone else.

Verah smiled as she glanced at the two photographs standing side by side on the nightstand. One showed an old woman with stringy gray hair, wrinkled skin mottled with age spots, sunken eyes, and yellow teeth. The other was of a young woman with thick pale blond hair, porcelainlike skin without a spot or blemish, and bright green eyes—a beautiful woman in the prime of her life.

She gazed into the small gold-framed mirror standing on the nightstand on the opposite side of the bed, and the image of the beautiful young woman smiled back at her.

"Ah, Rama," Verah murmured, stroking the cat's head. "Hard to believe both photographs are of me, isn't it?"

Before Gideon, Verah had rarely left her house, too ashamed of her appearance to let anyone see her. Always vain about her looks, she had shunned her cronies when her beauty began to fade, had veiled her face or covered her ugliness beneath a magical spell on the few occasions when she'd had to leave the house.

She smiled as she thought of the handsome nightwalker imprisoned in her basement. She owed her restored well-being to him. His blood nourished her inside and out, gifting her with increased health and strength. And youth. She ran her fingertips over her cheek. The skin was soft and firm and baby smooth. Gone were the ugly wrinkles and discolorations of age, the hideous liver spots on her hands.

She had the vampire blood spell found in one of her mother's ancient grimoires to thank for her renewed youth. When Verah had first read the spell, she had dismissed it as nonsense. Surely something so quick and easy could not be effective. But as age had continued to take its toll on her youth and her beauty, as her body began to break down, she had gone in search of a vampire. No easy task, she mused, remembering how long it had taken her to find one. The fact that he was young and handsome had been a nice bonus.

Determined to put the age-old spell to the test, she had located the requisite golden chalice, filled it with the required amount of fresh vampire blood, and chanted the necessary words before drinking from the cup. The taste had been vile. Not knowing what to expect she had been amazed by the results, which had been immediate and undeniable.

Best of all, Gideon was virtually immortal. He would serve her purpose, willing or not, for as long as she wished, and that would be a good, long time.

The changes in her appearance were quickly noted by her acquaintances. Verah ascribed it to a miracle elixir she had stumbled upon, the ingredients which were, of course, tightly guarded.

Word of her miraculous elixir spread across the Internet like wildfire and soon wealthy women were ordering it online, willing to pay whatever she asked for a bottle of the remarkable tonic that was guaranteed to shave ten years or more off of a woman's appearance.

Of course, Verah couldn't let it be known to anyone—mortal or witch—that she had a vampire in her basement, or that, combined with the spell she had found, it could guarantee good health and long life indefinitely. Vampires were notoriously hard to find. And witches notoriously clever. She couldn't take a chance on someone spiriting Gideon away. After some consideration, she tore the spell out of the grimoire and burned it, thereby assuring that no one else would ever duplicate it.

She accepted credit cards from mortals, but demanded payment in humankind from witches and wizards.

After all, she had to provide suitable nourishment for the handsome vampire chained in the cellar.

Chapter 4

Kay stifled a yawn as she finished filling the food and water dishes for the dogs and cats—and one bad-tempered ferret—that would be spending the weekend at the clinic. A pretty little cocker spaniel, who'd had some surgery earlier in the day, whined when Kay closed the cage door.

"You'll be better soon, Blackie," Kay said, scratching the dog's ears. "I'll see you Monday."

Leaving the kennel, she grabbed her sweater, then waited by the door for Wanda, who was shutting down the computer.

"I'm starving," Kay said. "Let's go grab some dinner at Conklin's. I'm in the mood for a good steak." She always had a healthy appetite, and never more so than right before the full moon. Hard to believe it was almost that time again.

"Sounds good to me," Wanda said. "I'm going to go home and change first. I'll meet you there in twenty minutes."

"Okay. And then we can go to my place for dessert. I made an apple pie."

"You make a mean apple pie," Wanda remarked, licking the last of the crumbs from her lips.

"There's more."

"Don't tempt me." Wanda put her plate on the coffee table. "So, what shall we do tonight?"

"I don't know." Kay glanced at the new paperback waiting for her on the end table. "It's been a long week, and . . ."

Wanda followed her gaze, then shook her head. "Oh no, you don't. I know exactly what you're thinking, and you can put it out of your head right now. It's the weekend, girlfriend, time to kick up our heels."

Kay shook her head. "I know what *you're* thinking, too. And you can just forget it. I'm not going to that nightclub. We can go to a movie or bowling or whatever, but no nightclubs. I don't party and I don't sleep around and that's all the guys who go to places like The Roan Horse are interested in."

"How do you know that?" Wanda demanded, arms akimbo. "You've never even been there."

"I've heard stories about that place." Kay regarded Wanda's appearance. With her spiked blond hair, black lipstick, black sweater, and skintight pants, Wanda looked like an escapee from a horror movie, but it was all the rage now. Kay had tried the Goth look once, but it wasn't for her.

"Do you believe everything you hear?" Wanda asked.

"Not everything," Kay admitted, but there were more strange things in heaven and on Earth than Wanda knew.

"Come on," Wanda said impatiently. "Let's at least check it out. It'll do you good to get out of the house. You've been moping around here long enough."

She had good reason to mope, Kay thought glumly. In just a few months, her father was going to announce her engagement to Victor Rinaldi, a man who was, in Kay's opinion, an arrogant ass.

Wanda tapped her fingers on the arm of the sofa. "If you don't like the club, we'll leave and go to the movies."

"You promise?" Kay asked, her resolve weakening.

"Yes, now hurry up and change and let's go."

Tired of arguing, Kay hurried into her bedroom. Shrugging out of her jeans and sweater, she pulled on a long-sleeved white silk shirt, a short black skirt, black leggings, and a pair of knee-high black boots that had cost her a month's pay and were worth every penny.

Wanda grinned when Kay returned to the living room. "You'll knock 'em dead."

"Yeah, right."

"Cheer up, girlfriend. Maybe a little firewater will put a sparkle in your eye and a spring in your step."

Kay rolled her eyes at the firewater reference. Wanda didn't do it often, but every now and then she couldn't resist making a remark about Kay's Lakota heritage.

Wanda moved toward the door, then paused and glanced over her shoulder. "You coming or not?"

"All right, paleface," Kay said with an exaggerated air of resignation. "Let's get it over with."

Wanda was right, Kay thought as they climbed into Wanda's red Jetta and drove to the club. She might as well go out and have a good time while she could.

It was Friday night and The Roan Horse was rockin'. Located within driving distance of several small towns, it was a magnet for singles—mostly young Lakota and Cheyenne males. Kay shook her head as she crossed the threshold. It was too crowded, too noisy, and after one glance at the occupants, she knew coming here had been a mistake.

She tugged on Wanda's sleeve. "All right, I'm ready to go."

"Are you kidding me? We just got here. We haven't even had a drink yet. Any chance I can talk you into something stronger than a virgin piña colada tonight?"

Kay shook her head. She'd gotten drunk only once, on a single martini, and once was enough. She didn't know if it was her werewolf blood, her Lakota blood, or a combination of the two, but she had no tolerance for liquor.

"I'll see if I can find us a table," she said, thinking that what she really needed to find was another friend, someone who liked country music and old movies. Wanda was always into the next new thing, no matter what it was.

Trevor stood at the bar, his gaze drifting over the crowd. He didn't know what he was doing here tonight. Friday night was date night, even at The Roan Horse, a bad time for what he had in mind. He was thinking of calling it a lost cause and going home when two females entered the club. The blonde with the spiked hair had a worldly air about her that would likely make her hard to charm. But the black-haired one . . . she looked perfect. Innocent. Gullible.

When the blonde headed for the bar, Trevor made his move. Pasting a benign smile on his face, he walked past the dark-haired one, accidentally bumping her arm. "Excuse me," he said, flashing an easy grin.

"No problem," she said with a friendly smile. "There's quite a crowd here tonight."

He nodded. "My name's Trevor Clark."

"Kay Alissano."

"I don't suppose you'd care to dance?"

"Of course she would," the blonde said, coming up behind them, a drink in each hand. "Go on, girlfriend, have a little fun for a change."

The girl, Kay, glared at her friend, but allowed him to lead her onto the dance floor.

All too easy, he thought. He asked her about herself, her family, and when the dance was over, he urged her to have a drink with him.

Kay glanced at Wanda, who was out on the dance floor, practically glued to her partner. No help there. She regarded

Trevor thoughtfully. He was tall and good-looking, with a winning smile, short brown hair and brown eyes.

"One drink," she agreed, taking a place at an empty table. After all, what could it hurt? "A virgin piña colada, please."

Trevor smiled as he made his way to the bar. One drink was all it would take.

Returning to the table, he handed a glass to Kay, then lifted his own. "A toast," he said. "To new beginnings."

It was the last thing Kay remembered until she woke up in hell.

Hell smelled like urine. And even though Kay knew it was only her imagination running wild, it also smelled like blood. And death.

She didn't open her eyes. If she kept them closed, she could pretend she was trapped in a remarkably vivid nightmare. She could pretend she was sleeping in her own bed even though she knew she was lying on something hard and cold and damp, like cement.

She could pretend that she was alone, when she knew she wasn't.

Warily, she opened her eyelids a crack. And found herself staring at a man with shaggy black hair, skin so pale it was almost translucent, and dark gray eyes that burned into hers like hot coals.

Kay shuddered. Maybe she really was in hell. Because the creature hunkered down across from her was either the devil incarnate. Or a vampire.

Either way, she was as good as dead.

Gideon's nostrils twitched as he inhaled the female's scent. She smelled of perfume and fear and something he knew instinctively was a drug of some kind, which explained how she had come to be here. But it was another scent that lay beneath the rest that had him frowning. She smelled . . . feral.

The enticing scent of her blood, the rapid beating of her heart, overshadowed everything else. It had been over a month since his last kill. The woman's nearness freshened his hunger and he reached for her, his gaze drawn to the pulse throbbing in the hollow of her throat.

She scrabbled backward, but there was nowhere for her to go. In a move too swift for human eyes to follow, he grabbed her ankle and drew her slowly, inexorably, toward him.

She lashed out at him, her eyes wild with fear, her nails leaving long, bloody furrows down his arm and across his cheek.

His hand tightened on her ankle, his predatory instincts sharpened by her struggles.

As though realizing that, she went suddenly still.

"There's no escape for you." His voice was deep, quiet, and edged with regret. "I can kill you now, quickly, or drain you a little at a time."

"You won't like the way I taste," she warned. "I can promise you that."

"I'm past caring."

"How long have you been here?" If she could just keep him talking, she might be able to make him think about something besides killing her.

"How long?" He shook his head. "I don't know."

It couldn't be very long, she thought, since he didn't have a beard and his hair wasn't overly long.

"My beard doesn't grow," he said. "Neither does my hair."

"Why not?" She stared at him, suddenly realizing she hadn't spoken the thought aloud. "How did you know what I was thinking?"

He pressed his forefinger to his temple. "Vampire."

It was disconcerting, knowing he could read her mind, but before she could think overly much about it, he began to stroke her ankle, his thumb moving lazily back and forth, back and forth. Even through her leggings, his touch sent a shiver down her spine. It took her a moment to realize her boots were gone. Why would someone take her boots? And why was she worrying about that when a monster had hold of her leg?

He cocked his head. "What year is it?"

"Two thousand and twelve."

"Has it only been three years, then?" he muttered. "It seems longer."

Monster or not, Kay couldn't help feeling sorry for him as she glanced around the cell. There was no bed, no blanket, nothing but a cold stone floor, iron bars, and damp cement walls. A small table stood just out of reach on the other side of the bars. She shuddered. How had he endured being locked up in this place for three years without going mad? But that was the least of her concerns. Right now, she wondered if she was going to survive until sunrise.

With the speed of a striking snake, his hand curled around her forearm and he dragged her closer.

"I'm sorry," he muttered, his voice gruff.

"Please, don't."

He closed his eyes for a moment. If he hadn't been a vampire, she might have thought he was praying. More likely, he was saying grace, she thought with morbid humor.

She glanced around the cell again, looking for something she could use as a weapon, but there was nothing save for a dim lightbulb that hung from a knotted cord outside the cell.

And then he was looking at her through those hellish red eyes.

"I'm sorry," he said again, and folding her into his embrace, he pulled her shirt collar aside and bent his head to her neck.

Kay shuddered when she felt the sharp prick of his fangs against her skin. It was useless to fight, she knew. He was larger, stronger, deadly, but her instinct for survival quickly took over. She pulled his hair and scratched his face. Her nails left bloody furrows down his pale cheeks. She sank her teeth into his arm, and lashed out with her feet. All to no avail. It was like trying to punch her way through a brick wall.

Winded from her struggles, growing weak from the loss of blood, she closed her eyes and waited for death. And then a strange thing happened. As soon as she stopped fighting him, her fear slipped away. There was no pain as he drank from her, only a sense of pleasure that was oddly sensual.

It was her last thought before she drifted away into oblivion.

Gideon gazed at the woman in his arms. She was lovely. Her hair, Indian straight and black, fell past her shoulders, her inky lashes were thick and long. Her complexion was pale now, but her cheeks had been rosy before he drank from her, her skin the color of pale copper. Her eyes were a warm golden brown. She had been right about one thing: He hadn't liked the taste of her blood. It was strong, bitter. Had he not needed nourishment so badly, he would have spit it out after the first swallow. Had it not been for the sour taste, he would have drained her dry; instead, he had taken only enough to take the edge off his hunger.

He eased her down onto the floor, oddly reluctant to let her go.

Standing, he paced the narrow cell from one end to the other. He had been a vampire for three hundred and sixty years. Wasted years, he thought, looking back through the corridors of time. True, he had traveled the world many times over, seen countries and kings rise and fall, but what had he ever accomplished? Nothing. Lisiana had bequeathed him a long life, but she had robbed him of the chance to have a home and a family. Tied to no one, he had lived like a vagabond, always on the move, drifting through the centuries, leaving no mark of his passing.

Of course, he'd had little incentive. In the beginning, hunger overrode every other desire, every other need. For a time, he had indulged his every whim. He had taken what he wanted, heedless of the consequences to others. He wasn't particularly proud of his behavior back then, but being a vampire had put him outside the law. Clothing and carriages, horses and homes, gold and wine and women. He had used his preternatural power to take them all, and blamed Lisiana. She had stolen much more than that from him. Didn't he deserve to get even?

Eventually, he grew weary of such a life. Without realizing it, he had accumulated a good amount of money, which had enabled him to buy lairs in London and Paris, in Madrid and Portugal.

And then he had come to the New World. And ended up here, in what was, for all intents and purposes, a prison. Considering how he had spent his existence, perhaps it was where he belonged.

Swearing under his breath, he shook off his maudlin thoughts.

He paced back and forth, never tiring, until he sensed the sun's rising, and then he stretched out on the floor and closed his eyes.

Once, he had dreaded the beginning of each new day, hated the darkness that dragged him down into nothingness. But that was before Verah had trapped him. Where he had once dreaded the darkness, he now welcomed it as his only escape from reality.

Chapter 5

Verah stood outside the cell, her brow furrowing as she stared at the captives sleeping on the floor. The vampire had one arm around the girl's waist, almost as if he was trying to protect her.

The girl had been here for the last two days and nights. Verah tapped her fingertips against her lips. She had thought to find the female dead by now, since Gideon had not fed in quite some time.

Verah glanced at the goblet in her hand. She rarely bled the vampire during the day, mainly because he was trapped in sleep and therefore immune to the pain and humiliation. Where was the fun in that? But she had just received a rush order from an old friend.

A wave of her hand unlocked the cell and she stepped inside, her skirts rustling over the cement. She never entered the cell at night. Weak or not, shackled or not, he was still a vampire. Only a fool would underestimate him. And she was not a fool.

Since he wore only enough to cover his loins, it was easy to find a place to bleed him. Chanting softly, she made a quick incision in his thigh. Dark red blood flowed from the cut into the goblet.

She stood when the goblet was full. There was no need to bandage the wound. Vampires healed quickly from all but the most severe wounds. Even in his weakened condition, the cut in his thigh was already little more than a faint pink line. It would be gone before she left the basement.

It wasn't until she started toward the door that she noticed the female was awake and watching her, a look of horror on her face.

"Do not bother to ask for your freedom," Verah said before the girl could speak. "You will never see daylight again."

With that, Verah stepped out of the cell, locked the door behind her, and left the basement.

Kay stared after the fair-haired woman who had so casually sliced into the vampire's leg and drained his blood. What did she do with it? Surely she didn't drink it. The mere idea made Kay gag. Perhaps she used it in casting spells.

Kay glanced at the vampire. His arm was curled around her waist, trapping her in place. Asleep, he didn't look so frightening. His features were strong and masculine; some might even think him handsome. His cheeks, so pale when she had first seen him, had a hint of color this morning, no doubt due to the blood he had taken from her. She noticed that the wound in his thigh had already healed, leaving no trace of a scar.

She had never seen a vampire before. She had heard of them, read about them, but she hadn't really believed they existed. Kay lifted a hand to her neck. She knew differently now.

Almost as frightening as the realization that vampires existed was her certainty that the fair-haired woman was a witch, and a black witch at that. Unlike white witches, black witches were evil creatures who drew their power from the pain and fear of others.

It took considerable effort to lift the vampire's arm so she could slip away. Rising, she noticed the dark brown splotches on the cement. Dried blood, she thought, grimacing. Would her life's blood be the next to stain the floor?

Kay straightened her clothing, ran a hand through her hair. She was hungry and thirsty. And more frightened than she cared to admit.

With nothing to occupy her time, the hours ahead seemed endless. She slept and woke and slept again, her dreams filled with eyes that blazed red as hellfire in the gloomy cell.

When next she woke, those eyes, calm and gray now, were watching her.

Gideon sat up, bracing his back against the wall. He scowled when he caught Verah's scent. "She was here?"

"The witch?"

"You know what she is?"

Kay nodded. "She bled you while you slept."

"She does that from time to time."

Sitting up, Kay scooted to the far side of the cell. "What does she use it for?"

"She drinks it. It keeps her young and vibrant."

"Really? Couldn't she just cast some kind of illusion and get the same effect? It would be a lot easier, and a whole lot less disgusting than drinking blood."

"An illusion only works on the outside. My blood not only keeps her looking young, it gives her the inner strength and vitality of youth."

"Ah."

"Yeah. And what she doesn't use, she sells to others, claiming it has magical healing properties."

"Does it?"

"I don't know if works for others. It certainly works for her."

Kay frowned as her stomach growled loudly, reminding her that she hadn't eaten in days. "I don't suppose she's going to feed me?"

"Probably not. She's never bothered to feed any of the others."

"The others . . . how long . . . ?" She swallowed the bile rising in her throat. "How long did they last?"

"A few days, perhaps a week, depending on how often the witch steals my blood, and how much she takes."

Feeling suddenly cold all over, Kay rubbed her hands up and down her arms. A few more days, perhaps a week.

"I'm sorry," Gideon said quietly.

"It's not your fault."

He frowned at her.

She made a vague gesture with her hand. "You're a vampire. You're only doing what comes naturally."

He stared at her a moment, and then he grinned. "You are a most unusual woman, Kiya Marie Alissano."

"How do you know my name?"

"I'm a vampire," he answered, as if that explained everything.

"Most people call me Kay."

"Do they? I think I prefer Kiya."

She shrugged. What difference did it make what he called her? "Do you have a name?"

"Gideon Marquet."

"Have you been a vampire very long?"

"A few hundred years. How did you wind up here?" She wasn't like any of the other women the witch had brought him. The others had all been helpless, poor, down on their luck. Mostly women who would not be missed. Judging from this girl's appearance—well-kept hair and nails, designer clothes— she came from a different class of people. Someone, somewhere, would be looking for her, though they would never find her, living or dead.

"I went to a nightclub with a friend of mine. I think someone must have drugged me." She shuddered with the memory.

"When I woke up, I was here." She was shivering now. She wrapped her arms around her bent knees and drew them up to her chest. "Are you going to feed on me tonight?"

"It depends."

"On what?"

"On you." His gaze moved over her, lingering on her lips, the swell of her breasts beneath the white silk shirt. "I'll leave you alone tonight in exchange for one kiss, freely given."

"A kiss?" Was he kidding? How could he think about kissing at a time like this?

Gideon nodded. It had been a long time since he'd had a woman. He could have compelled those the witch brought him. He could have taken them by force. Neither option appealed to him. Nor had any of the women. But this one . . . there was something about her that intrigued him like no other. "So, what do you say?"

She eyed him warily. "How do I know you'll stop with a kiss?"

He shrugged. "I guess you'll just have to trust me."

"Trust a hungry vampire? Yeah, right."

"Is that a no?"

"Hmm." He was a good-looking guy. Cleaned up and well fed, he was probably devastating. "One kiss," she said, and scooted closer to him. "No tongue."

He grinned, his shackles rattling as he reached for her. She could feel the power in his arms as he embraced her. For stretched seconds, he simply held her, his gaze locked on hers. She felt a tingle of awareness bloom inside her as his hand moved up and down her spine, then slid over her shoulder to stroke the edge of her breast.

She started to push him away when he claimed her lips with his, and all thought of protest—indeed, all thought, period—vanished as his mouth closed over hers. She hadn't expected to enjoy his kiss. He was a vampire, after all, but his kiss was like nothing she had ever known. Her fingers tangled in the hair at his nape as she drew him closer, suddenly inexplicably hungry for the press of his body against hers.

She moaned softly when he took his mouth from hers, sighed as he rained kisses along the length of her neck. Lost in a maelstrom of sensual pleasure, she was scarcely aware that he had bitten her until, with a choked cry, he pushed her away, then retreated to the other side of the cell.

Kay blinked at him, confused and suddenly light-headed. And then, seeing the red in his eyes, the single drop of crimson at the corner of his lower lip, she realized what he had done. "You said you wouldn't feed on me."

"I'm a vampire," he said, his voice faintly mocking. "I was only doing what comes naturally."

She glared at him when she realized he was repeating what she had said earlier.

"I'm sorry," he said quietly, then cocked his head to one side. "What are you?"

"What do you mean?"

"Your blood. It isn't human."

She didn't deny it.

He rubbed a thoughtful hand across his jaw. "It isn't vampire."

"No."

"I don't believe in fairies or trolls and you're too pretty to be a zombie. So, what are you?"

Kay stared at him, wondering what he would do, what he would say, if she told him the truth. She considered a lie, then shrugged. Maybe it would save her. If not, she would be no worse off than she was before. "I'm a werewolf."

For the first time since he'd been imprisoned, Gideon laughed. The sound echoed off the walls and the ceiling, sounding totally out of place within the squalid confines of the cell.

Kay stared at him, perplexed. "You think that's funny?"

He blew out a breath. "Don't you?"

"There's nothing funny about being a werewolf, or turning fanged and furry when the moon is full, or spending the night in the woods once a month so I don't hurt anyone, or . . . stop laughing!"

"Don't you see? You're our way out."

"How do you figure that?"

"Werewolves are supposed to be strong, aren't they? The next time the moon is full, you can break down the door and get us the hell out of here." It would have been easy for him to do just that if it wasn't for the silver chains that rendered him almost powerless. "Can't you?"

"I don't know. I've never tried to do anything like that."

"But you're strong when you've changed? Stronger than normal, right?"

She nodded. It was a strength she had never fully tested, much to her father's disgust and her aunt's disappointment.

"Can you control when you change? Or is it involuntary?"

"Totally involuntary. It happens the first night of the full moon whether I want it to or not." Why did she sound so defensive? She loved being in her wolf form.

"So, do you go totally wolf, or are you aware of what you're doing? Do you remember it the next day?"

"Yes, I'm still me inside. I can understand what people are saying. And I remember everything that happens, everything I do."

He dragged his hand across his jaw. "When's the next full moon?"

"In three days."

"Damn," he muttered. "Locked up with a werewolf." He shook his head, then grinned at her. "It'll be interesting to see which one of us survives."

Chapter 6

Kay studied the vampire sleeping beside her. The fact that he was asleep meant that the sun was up. *How long until sundown?* she wondered. How much longer could she go without food? Without water? Even now, her stomach was cramping painfully. She had never been this hungry, or this thirsty. How long did it take to starve to death? Would she survive long enough to find out? Could Gideon resist the urge to feed for another two days so they could put his escape plan into effect? Was she strong enough to break down an iron-barred door? She had to be, she thought glumly, because if she couldn't do it, she was as good as dead.

Cheerful thoughts, she mused, but it was hard to remain upbeat in this morbid place. The smell of urine and fear and unwashed bodies hung heavy in the air. The endless gloom and lack of sunshine was disheartening. Add to that the disquieting knowledge that her cellmate was a vampire and a girl could get depressed mighty fast. How slowly the hours passed when one had nothing to do but contemplate one's own death!

She ran her hand over her skirt. Like her shirt, it was badly wrinkled. She would have traded her brand-new Prada pumps for a change of underwear and five minutes in a hot shower with a bar of lavender soap and a bottle of shampoo.

"Stop wishing," she muttered. "It ain't gonna happen."

Her father had warned her that leaving the pack would be dangerous, but Kay had insisted she wanted to live on her own for one year. She wished now she had listened to her father and stayed home where she belonged, even though it meant that she would now be engaged to Victor Rinaldi. Of course, all things considered, life with Victor was looking pretty good right about now.

In an effort to distract herself from her surroundings and her dismal future, she concentrated on Gideon again. No doubt about it, he was an extremely attractive man with his long black hair and deep gray eyes, not to mention his quirky sense of humor, which she found endearing.

Suddenly overcome with an irrational need to touch him, she sifted her fingers through his hair, ran her fingertips along his sculpted cheekbones, then lowered her hand to trace the width of his shoulders, the rock-hard planes of his chest and flat belly.

He never stirred. Was he really dead while he slept, or merely trapped in the darkness, aware of what went on around him, but unable to respond? She couldn't begin to imagine what it would be like to be sucked down into oblivion with every sunrise. True, she was compelled to change into a wolf when the moon was full, but it was something she enjoyed. And it was only one night a month. Unlike movies and books, she didn't turn into a ravening monster that killed everything that crossed her path, although deer and rabbits were fair game.

There were advantages to being a werewolf, though she was only half wolf. Even in her human form, her senses were sharper than those of mere mortals. Werewolves aged more slowly than humans, and healed more quickly.

Rising, she paced the floor. Gideon's plan had to work. It was bad enough being caged as a human; she had no idea what effect it would have on her in her wolf form. During the full moon, she had always been in the wild, free to run and hunt to her heart's content. Who knew how she would react if she couldn't escape? She had never attacked anyone before, but then, she had never been in close quarters with a human—or a vampire—when the moon was full.

She paced until her legs ached and then she sank down on the floor and buried her face in her hands. She was hungry, so hungry. And thirsty . . .

Ever so slowly, she lifted her head and stared at Gideon. He drank from her to sustain his life. What if she drank from him?

The mere idea turned her stomach. It was one thing to eat raw meat in her wolf form, quite another to sink her human teeth into mortal—well, almost mortal—flesh.

Her stomach growled loudly. With a low groan, she curled up on the hard, cold floor and cried herself to sleep.

Warmth, pressing against his side. The scent of blood and woman. Not yet fully awake, Gideon was still aware that Kay was lying beside him, her head pillowed on his shoulder, one of her legs flung over his.

Slowly, he slid his hand along her side, lingering at the warm swell of her breast beneath his palm. Three years since he had lain with a woman. Three long years of abstinence. Vampires were sensual creatures by nature. With their preternatural senses, everything was enhanced—taste, smell, touch. Especially touch. He groaned softly, remembering how soft and sweet her lips had been. Turning his head, he captured her mouth with his, felt his desire roar to life.

Tamping down his hunger, he drew back, frowning when he noticed how pale she looked, how shallow her breathing, how irregular her heartbeat. She hadn't had anything to eat or drink since Verah had brought her here; last night he had taken more than he should have, which had weakened her still more.

"Kiya?" He shook her lightly. "Kiya, wake up."

Her eyelids fluttered open, her gaze unfocused. "Mark?"

"No." Dammit, he knew he had taken too much. And who the hell was Mark? "It's me. Gideon."

She blinked at him. "Gideon?"

Cursing under his breath, he bit into his wrist, then held the wound to her lips. "Drink this."

She wanted to refuse, but she was so thirsty. And there was nothing else. She forced down a swallow, gagged, and turned her head to the side.

"Look at me, Kiya." He captured her gaze with his own. "What's your favorite drink?"

"Hot chocolate with a dash of cinnamon and lots of whipped cream on top."

"Okay, that's what this is, and it's the best you've ever had, hot and sweet. Drink now. You need it."

When he held his wrist to her lips again, she drank willingly. When he took his arm away, she asked for more.

"That's all for now," he said, gathering her into his arms. "Go back to sleep."

Her eyelids fluttered down, and she slept.

"Damn." Gideon stroked her hair, bemused by his feelings for this woman. In the three years he had been here, he had never offered his blood to any of his prey. It had grieved him to take their lives, but it was theirs or his, and his sense of self-preservation would not be ignored or denied.

But this woman . . . Kiya. She was different, and it wasn't just because she was a werewolf.

The witch's appearance at the cell door put a stop to his musings.

Verah lifted one brow when she saw the girl cradled in his arms. "Like this one, do you?" she asked with a leer.

He shrugged. "Her blood pleases me."

"And yet she still lives."

"I decided to savor it while I could. It was a long time between meals last time."

The witch looked thoughtful. "I suppose I could prolong her life, since she pleases you."

It took all his self-control to keep his surprise from showing on his face. In all the weeks and months he had been here, she had never done him a kindness.

He grimaced as she reached into the voluminous pocket of her robe and withdrew her silver-bladed dagger and jewel-encrusted goblet.

She looked at him, one brow raised, until he shifted Kay to one side and shoved his right arm through the bars. He clenched his jaw as she made a long shallow gash in his forearm, felt his anger grow as his blood flowed into the goblet, although he didn't miss the irony of a mortal taking vampire blood.

When the goblet was full, Verah wiped the blade on a scrap of cloth, then dropped the dagger into her pocket. "I'll send someone with food and water for the girl."

Looking perplexed, she stared at him a moment.

Gideon stared back. If she was waiting for a thank-you, it would be a hell of a long time coming.

Kay woke feeling strange and with a bad taste in her mouth. But all that was forgotten when she opened her eyes and found herself nestled in Gideon's arms.

She glanced around, as if uncertain of her surroundings. "What happened?"

"You were hungry. I gave you something to drink."

"Something? Like . . . ?" Revulsion flashed in her eyes. She had tasted his blood, but only one taste, but she no longer felt weak or dizzy. Comprehension dawned with a jolt and she shook her head in denial. "You compelled me, didn't you?"

"You needed nourishment, and it's all I've got."

"But . . . you drank from me! And now you've given me your blood. . . ." She bounded out of his arms and fled to the far side of the cell. "Am I going to become a vampire now? Is that even possible? I'm a werewolf!"

"Calm down, Kiya. You're no different than you were before."

"How can that be?"

"I'd have to drain you to the point of death and then give you my blood to turn you. And like you said, you're a were-wolf. It probably wouldn't work anyway."

Slightly mollified, she slid down on the floor across from him, her back propped against the bars. He had given her his blood. No wonder she had a bad taste in her mouth.

At least she wasn't hungry anymore.

Was he? How often did he have to feed?

"Normally, once a week or so," he said, replying to her unspoken question.

She felt her cheeks grow warm. "Do you read all my thoughts?"

He shrugged. "Not all. Who's Mark?" He held up his hand. "I didn't read your mind. You said his name when you were sort of out of it."

"He was my brother."

"Was?"

"He's dead, killed by a bounty hunter."

"I'm sorry."

Blinking back her tears, Kay buried her face in her hands. Mark had been two years her senior and she had adored him. They had been playing in the woods one night when the moon was full. Mark had been bragging that he would be able to run with the pack the following month.

* * *

"No, you won't," she said. "You have to be thirteen to shift, and you're only twelve."

"Wanna bet?" he crowed. "Watch this!"

The words had barely been spoken when he changed from human to wolf and back to human again.

"That's fantastic," she cried, clapping her hands. "Do it again!"

She had watched, happy for him, as he changed back and forth to amuse her. He would be Alpha someday; only Alphas could change at will. He was still in his wolf form when three men burst into the clearing.

Before Mark could shift back to human, before Kay could beg them to go away, one of the men killed her brother.

Her scream of denial alerted her father and several members of the pack, who came running.

The three hunters didn't have a chance. She had watched in horror as they were caught and killed. And eaten, leaving no trace.

A rattle of chains told her Gideon was moving toward her. She looked up, startled to find him so close. She thought he was going to feed on her and for a moment, she hoped he would drain her dry and put her out of her misery. She was surprised when he slipped his arm around her shoulders and drew her close.

"I'm sorry about your brother," he murmured, stroking her hair. "It's hard to lose those you love."

"You've probably lost a lot of people," she said, sniffing.

"Yeah, but only a few I really cared about. So, you're not married, or anything?"

"No." She blew out a sigh. "That's not entirely true. I'm engaged to be engaged."

"What the hell does that mean?"

"My father has chosen a mate for me. He's going to announce our betrothal when I go back home."

"You don't sound very happy about it."

"Victor Rinaldi is the most conceited, arrogant male I've ever known."

"So, why are you marrying him?"

"Three reasons. My father loves Victor like the son he lost. Victor's father and mine have been friends for over fifty years. And Victor's father is Alpha of the Green Mountain Pack. Their territory borders ours, and my marriage to Victor will make both packs stronger and more secure."

"Don't you have any say in the matter?"

"No." She looked up at him. "Do vampires get married?"

"Some do."

"But not you?"

"Nope. Never found a woman I wanted to spend more than a few days with."

"Do you really think we'll get out of here?"

He looked at her, his gaze sliding along the length of her neck, lingering on the pulse throbbing in the hollow of her throat. "For your sake, I sure as hell hope so."

Chapter 7

Dorothy Alissano fidgeted with her apron while listening to one side of the phone conversation her husband was having with Kiya's employer. It was bad news: She knew it. David Saltzman had never called them before.

"What is it?" she asked when Russell ended the call. "What's wrong?"

"Kiya is missing."

"Missing?" Dorothy felt the blood drain from her face as she dropped into one of the kitchen chairs. "What do you mean, missing?"

"She didn't report to work on Monday, and Saltzman hasn't heard from her since. Her friend, Wanda, said the last time she saw Kiya was at some nightclub. She thinks Kiya went home with a man she met there."

Dorothy shook her head. "Kiya wouldn't do that. She would never go off with a stranger."

"Maybe you don't know our daughter as well as well as you think you do."

"I know her a hell of a lot better than you do!" Dorothy folded her arms over her chest, worry for her daughter unleashing words she had never dared speak aloud. "You've never loved her. Never forgiven me for being unable to give you a son to take Mark's place."

Complications from Kiya's birth had made it impossible for Dorothy to have another child.

Russell's eyes narrowed ominously. "Watch your tongue, *mitawicu.*"

Dorothy bit down on her lower lip, a sudden stab of fear making her tremble. In all their married life, she had never dared talk back to him. Her husband was not only an alpha male, he was an Alpha werewolf, accustomed to being obeyed without question.

"It's true, isn't it?" she whispered. "You wish Victor was your son. You love him more than you love your own daughter."

He didn't deny it. "I'm going to make some phone calls, see if anyone has heard anything about Kiya."

Dorothy held her tears in check until he left the room, then she buried her face in her hands and let the tears flow. Not being able to give Russell another son had created a gulf between them that could not be crossed. For Dorothy, it was a pain that had never healed. And yet, in spite of the bitterness between them, she loved him still.

Wiping her eyes on her apron, she let her thoughts drift back in time, remembering how it had been in the beginning. . . .

She had been walking home from a girlfriend's house one evening when a large dog attacked her. She had fallen to the ground and curled into a ball, her arms folded over her head, screaming bloody murder, but no one had come to her aid and then, seemingly from out of thin air, a man had appeared. He spoke to the hound in a language Dorothy didn't understand and the dog had whimpered and run off with its tail between its legs.

"Are you all right?" the man asked.

She had been too scared to speak, too frightened by the blood running down her arms and leg to think coherently.

He had looked undecided for a moment, then swept her

into his arms and carried her to the hospital located several blocks away. In the emergency room, she had begged him not to leave her alone, so he had lied to the nurse, saying he was her husband. He had stayed at her side, holding her hand, while they bandaged her arms and stitched the nasty bite in her leg. When they left the hospital, Russell had called for a cab and taken her home.

Dorothy had been afraid she would never see him again, but when the cab pulled to a stop in front of her house, he had surprised her by asking if he could call on her the next night.

They dated for several months and she fell head over heels in love with him. He was tall and dark and in some ways, a total mystery to her. She was fascinated by his Indian heritage, by his bearing, which was almost regal. To her, he seemed like Rhett Butler and Superman all rolled into one.

Things seemed perfect, until she found out she was pregnant. She had been afraid to tell her parents, afraid to tell Russell, but it was a secret she couldn't hide forever. He wasn't happy about the pregnancy. Neither was his family— a family she had never met. She had thought it strange that he never took her home to meet his parents—until he did.

Her first thought upon viewing the compound where he lived was that it looked like a prison; later, it became one, at least for her. She learned a lot about Russell that night, including the fact that he was a full-blooded Lakota Indian and that Russell Alissano wasn't his real name. He had been born Nagin Luta, which meant Red Shadow. The Lakota believed names had power and his tribal name was used only by loved ones and members of the immediate family.

His parents had not made her feel welcome. Russell's father, Sake Sapa, who went by the name Charles Alissano, insisted she have an abortion immediately. Dorothy had been too afraid of the man to tell him no to his face, but later, when she was alone with Russell, she told him she didn't want an abortion and that nothing he could say would change her mind.

He didn't say anything for several, nerve-racking moments.

Fighting back tears, she had waited for him to say he never wanted to see her again. But, once again, he surprised her. Instead of leaving, he had proposed to her. They eloped the next night.

Her parents weren't pleased.

Russell's father never forgave him for marrying a white woman.

Dorothy sighed. She had loved her son, she loved her daughter, but sometimes she couldn't help thinking they would have all been better off if Russell had never come to her aid that fateful night.

Chapter 8

Kay stood in a corner of the cell, her hands fisted around the bars, staring blankly at the far wall.

Earlier, a man had brought her a covered tray and slid it under the narrow gap between the bottom of the cell door and the floor. When she'd uncovered the tray, she found a roast beef sandwich, a can of root beer, and a bottle of water. She had devoured the sandwich in four bites, drained the can in a few quick swallows, and wished for more.

She had sipped the water throughout the day.

But it wasn't food or water that occupied her thoughts now. There was only one more night until the full moon. Already, she could feel the change starting within her, the tension, the flutter of anticipation.

In the past, she had gone into the wilderness the night before the change occurred, away from people and civilization, where she was free to run and hunt without fear of discovery.

Her wolf had never been caged up, never been confined in a small space.

In such close quarters, would she feel the need to attack Gideon? Would he have to kill her to defend himself? Which one of them was the stronger? How would she live with herself if she destroyed him?

She turned away from the bars and began to pace the cell. In her wolf form, she had razor-sharp teeth and claws and increased physical strength. Gideon also had sharp teeth and great strength. In addition, she knew he had preternatural powers she lacked, plus he had the ability to read her mind. Would he be able to read her thoughts when she was in her wolf form? If so, that would be a decided disadvantage for her; he would know what she intended to do before she did it.

With a sigh, she sank down on the floor. Hugging her bent knees to her chest, she rested her forehead on her arms and closed her eyes. How lonely the days were with no one to talk to and nothing to do but contemplate an uncertain future. How long the nights were when she sat with Gideon, wondering if every breath would be her last.

Her only hope was that, in her wolf form, she would be strong enough to break down the cell door, defeat the witch, and escape before the unthinkable happened and she killed Gideon. Or he killed her.

She glanced over her shoulder to where he lay sleeping. For the first time, she wondered if she should try to kill him before he killed her. But she couldn't do it.

She had never killed anyone.

He stirred and she quickly put all such thoughts out of her mind.

But not quick enough.

"I wouldn't try it if I were you," he said mildly.

"Try what?"

He sat up, one brow arched in wry amusement. "It isn't safe to attack a vampire at rest," he said. "Most of us are able to sense danger and rouse long enough to defend ourselves."

"Thanks, I'll keep that in mind." She sat cross-legged on

the floor, facing him. And then she frowned. "Why don't you wake up when the witch takes your blood?"

He lifted one shoulder and let it fall. "I would, if she intended to kill me." He leaned forward, nostrils twitching. "You smell like meat."

"The witch sent me a sandwich earlier."

Gideon regarded her a moment before asking, "What was your life like, before this?"

"Pretty ordinary, actually, except for the werewolf thing. I went to work during the week, relaxed on the weekends. I hung out with my best friend, Wanda." She shrugged. "Nothing special."

"Is Wanda a werewolf, too?"

"No."

"Does she know what you are?"

Kay shook her head. She had shared a lot of things with Wanda, but telling her best friend she turned into a wolf once a month hadn't been one of them.

"I thought werewolves were pack animals."

"We are, but I wanted to live on my own for a year, and after a lot of arguments with my father, he finally agreed. What about you? What did you do before"—she waved a hand, indicating the cell—"this?"

"Whatever the hell I wanted." He tugged against the chains that bound his ankles, cussing mightily as the silver burned deeper into his skin. "Dammit!" he snarled.

Kay recoiled as his lips peeled back, revealing his fangs.

The anger drained out of him as quickly as it had risen and he slumped back against the wall, his jaw clenched against the fresh wave of pain caused by tugging against his shackles.

Kay wrapped her arms around her waist as her stomach growled loudly. One sandwich and a can of soda was hardly enough to make up for all the meals she had missed. She looked up, meeting Gideon's gaze.

"I can ease your pain, if you want."

"You mean by giving me more of your blood?"

He shrugged. "I'd rather give it to you than have Verah take it."

Kay bit down on her lower lip, thinking about his offer. She knew he had hypnotized her into drinking from him before, but she had no memory of it. Still, she grimaced at the idea.

"I can make you think it's hot chocolate with whipped cream on top."

"Is that how you made me drink it the last time?"

He nodded.

And still she hesitated.

"You'll need all your strength for tomorrow night," Gideon reminded her.

He was right, darn it. The way she felt now, she couldn't fight her way out of a paper bag, let alone break down a door made of iron bars.

Gathering her courage, she scooted to Gideon's side.

Gideon took a deep breath as Kay's nearness slammed into him. His fangs lengthened in response to her fear. The scent of her blood called to his hunger. It took all of his considerable willpower to keep from sinking his fangs into her soft flesh. Instead, he spoke to her mind, bending her will to his, implanting the suggestion that she was drinking a cup of her favorite hot chocolate as he bit into his wrist, then held it to her lips.

When he released his hold on her mind, she looked up at him, her gaze slightly unfocused. And then she tilted her head to the side. "Turnabout is fair play."

"Not much point in giving you my blood if I take it back."

"You'll need your strength, too."

He considered it a moment, then drew her into his arms and

gently brushed a lock of hair away from her neck. Keeping a tight rein on his self-control, he said, "I only need a little."

Hands clenched, heart pounding with trepidation, Kay again tilted her head to the side, granting him access to her throat. What if he didn't—couldn't—stop? Well, she thought fatalistically, one way or another, she would soon be out of this place.

"Relax," he murmured.

"Easier said than done," she muttered, and closed her eyes as he bent his head to her neck.

Later, when she lay asleep in his arms, Gideon stared into the darkness, his fingertips absently stroking her cheek as he imagined what it would be like to share a cell with a werewolf.

In all his long life, he had never encountered one. He had heard of them, of course—who hadn't? They were usually depicted as ravening monsters who couldn't control themselves and killed indiscriminately when the moon was full. Occasionally, they were depicted as social creatures, loyal to their pack, able to change at will and live ordinary lives.

Kay, it seemed, fell somewhere in between the two. She had no control over the change but she apparently lived an otherwise normal life save for those nights when the moon was full.

And it would be full tomorrow night.

Kay woke with a start. Sitting up, she stretched her arms over her head. A glance to her right showed Gideon was asleep. So, the sun was still up. Although she had no idea how long it was before the moon's rising, she could feel the anxiety growing within her as her body anticipated the change. Had she been home, she would have called her boss and told him she was taking a sick day—something he allowed his employees to do from time to time—then she would have packed a bag and driven up into the Black Hills.

Closing her eyes, she visualized the Hills—an isolated mountain range that ran from South Dakota to Wyoming, a place of towering pines and craggy bluffs and clear, crystal streams and lakes. The Hills were a werewolf's paradise, inhabited as they were by a wide variety of prey—buffalo, mountain goats, bighorn sheep, elk, and white-tailed deer. An added plus were the miles of wide-open spaces where she could run to her heart's content.

Filled with nervous tension, she began to pace the floor. Pausing briefly, she picked up the bottle of water that had been left for her sometime during the day. After rinsing away the bad taste in her mouth, she drained the bottle, then resumed pacing, back and forth across the narrow space.

Gideon hovered on the brink of awareness. Though only half awake, he felt the vibration of Kay's footsteps as she restlessly paced the floor, smelled her growing apprehension as the sun slipped over the horizon. Only hours left until the moon took command of the sky.

Between one thought and the next, he was wide-awake and alert. Jackknifing into a sitting position, he tilted his head back and sniffed the air.

"Dammit!" He rose fluidly to his feet. "She's coming." He had known that was a possibility, but since the witch had recently taken his blood, he had hoped they could make their escape without her being the wiser.

Without conscious thought, Kay moved to stand behind Gideon.

Verah appeared moments later. Clad in a leopard-skin jumpsuit, her long pale blond hair pulled back in a tail, she looked like a wild animal on the prowl.

She smiled a predatory smile as she waved her silver-bladed knife in one hand and the golden goblet in the other. "Guess what time it is?" she purred.

"So soon?" Gideon's jaw clenched tight. How often had she sliced into his flesh with that accursed knife? Each cut seared his skin like hellfire.

"Word is spreading." Greed glittered in the witch's eyes. "I am now getting a thousand dollars for a single vial of your blood."

He glared at her. There was undoubtedly some spell she could cast that would make her wealthy. Unfortunately for him, wealth was not her motive for keeping him imprisoned. She enjoyed the sense of power it gave her to hold a vampire captive. She enjoyed inflicting pain. But it was vanity that played the most important role. Without his blood, she would quickly revert to her true appearance—an aged hag with stringy gray hair, sunken rheumy eyes, and skin as dry and wrinkled as old parchment.

The witch tapped the blade against her cheek. "Hold out your arm," she said impatiently.

"Go to hell!"

"Do not make me come in there," Verah said, her eyes narrowing ominously.

Gideon snorted. "What are you gonna do, witch? Drain me dry? Well, do your worst. I'm tired of being your fountain of youth."

The moon was rising. Even if he hadn't been able to feel it on his own, he would have known it from the shudder that rippled through Kay, the sudden confusion in her thoughts.

Verah unlocked the cell door with a wave of her hand.

A low growl rose in Kay's throat.

Verah paused at the feral sound, her attention focusing for the first time on the woman partially hidden behind the vampire.

There was a ripple of preternatural power, the sound of tearing cloth followed by a sharp cry somewhere between a groan and a howl.

Verah's eyes grew wide as the woman's form shimmered

and then, between one heartbeat and the next, the woman was gone and a long-legged wolf with coal-black hair and bright brown eyes stood in her place.

With a hiss of disbelief, Verah jumped backward and slammed the cell door. She stared at the wolf for several disbelieving moments, then vanished from the basement.

Gideon swore softly. There would be hell to pay now, but even as the thought crossed his mind, the wolf took one of the chains that bound him between its teeth and with a mighty tug, pulled the bolt out of the wall. She did the same with the other shackle, then launched herself at the cell door, striking it full force with her shoulder, once, twice, and the door flew off its hinges. There was an unearthly screech as the metal skidded across the concrete.

The wolf looked up at him, tail wagging, then turned and trotted out of the cell toward the basement door.

Gideon followed her up the stairs, the chains still fastened to his ankles rattling with every step.

To his surprise, they didn't encounter anyone when they emerged from the basement. The wolf made a sharp left when she crossed the threshold and then, without a moment's hesitation, she jumped through the first open window she came to.

With a shake of his head, Gideon followed her. Gunshots chased him over the sill. He winced as a bullet grazed his shoulder, cursed under his breath when the next shot hit the wolf. With a high-pitched whine, she tumbled end over end and lay still.

Without slowing, Gideon scooped the wolf into his arms and ran on. If it hadn't been for the silver that drained his power, he would have transported them to one of his lairs. As it was, all he could do was keep running.

When he came to an abandoned building some miles later, he kicked in the door and ducked inside. Pausing, he scanned the dusky interior. From the looks of the place, it had once been a warehouse. Pulling an oil-stained drop cloth from a counter, he spread it on the floor, then lowered the wolf onto it. A quick search turned up a hacksaw; moments later, he was free of the shackles he had worn for the last three years.

A door at the far end of the building opened into an office where he found a couple of shop towels. He wet the cloths in the adjoining bathroom, then returned to the wolf's side. Kneeling, he wiped the blood from her fur, his fingers probing the wound until he found the slug lodged in her back leg. Grateful that she was unconscious, he slid two fingers into the nasty hole and extracted the slug. He hissed when the misshapen chunk of silver burned his fingers. Had it found a vital organ, it would have killed her.

Lifting Kiya the wolf into his arms, he willed the two of them to his lair on the outskirts of Phoenix. It was his least favorite place to stay, but his powers were weak, and it was the closest.

Chapter 9

Verah slapped the young man standing before her. The sound echoed through the living room. "You missed?" She slapped him again, harder. "I do not pay you to miss!"

"I'm sorry, Mistress."

"I do not want apologies!" Muttering an incantation, she placed her hand over the man's mouth. "Be gone."

The man opened his mouth, but no sound emerged. Suddenly mute, he stared at her in horror.

"Be gone!" she snarled, "lest I turn you into a toad."

Face pale, eyes wide with fright, he hurried from her presence.

"Stupid fool!" Verah stormed from one end of the room to the other. Angry with her own stupidity for not realizing the woman had been two-natured, she had lashed out at the boy.

Picking up a large crystal vase, she hurled it against the wall, then took a deep breath. The werewolf was of no consequence. But Gideon . . . she needed him and she intended to get him back, no matter the cost. Vampires were hard to find and harder still to manipulate.

The fact that his blood added to her wealth was merely an additional bonus.

That his blood kept her young and vibrant made him indispensable. She had several vials stored in a cool place, but the shelf life was remarkably short, a fact she found odd, given that vampires themselves were nearly immortal.

She had to find him, and soon, before his blood grew rancid.

Before her beauty began to fade.

And if she couldn't find him, what then?

In a rage, she stormed down the stairs to her workroom, where she gathered up several books and placed them on her worktable. Settling on a high stool, she carefully opened the first grimoire. The parchment was old and yellow, disintegrating in some places.

Rama jumped up on the table, his keen yellow eyes watching intently as Verah perused the pages.

"There must be a spell or an incantation in one of these books that will work as well as his blood," she muttered. "There has to be!"

An hour later, she closed the ancient text, and reached for another. It had taken her mother a lifetime to collect these moldy old tomes. Surely one of them possessed the spell she needed.

When none of the grimoires yielded the information she sought, she contacted Yanaba. But the Navajo shaman who had helped Verah refine her magic and gifted her with the wisdom of his years had no answers for her.

Verah blew out a breath of exasperation. If Yanaba didn't have the answer, maybe the spell she was looking for didn't exist.

Chapter 10

Victor Rinaldi listened attentively to the conversation taking place between his father and Russell Alissano. It concerned Kiya's disappearance, of course. Damn the girl. Even when she wasn't here, she was nothing but trouble. He was under no illusions about her feelings for him. No doubt she had run off in an attempt to avoid their upcoming engagement.

Well, she could run far and wide, but she wouldn't be able to hide for long. Her old man was bound to sniff her out sooner or later. For his part, Victor hoped it would be sooner so he could get this marriage over with and move on.

He was tired of pretending to be smitten with Alissano's daughter, but he was determined to play the game of lovesick suitor to the end. The reward would make it all worthwhile.

His people had lived in the shadows for too long. It was time for the werewolves to shed their veneer of humanity and take their proper place in the world—right at the top of the food chain.

Chapter 11

Gideon's Phoenix lair was located in a ground-floor apartment. There had originally been two barred windows facing the street, but with the owner's approval, Gideon had had them plastered over with the understanding that, when he moved out, he would restore the windows. He had also replaced the flimsy wooden door with one of reinforced steel and installed a pair of the best dead bolts money could buy. His rent and utilities were paid ten years in advance, assuring that he had electricity and running water whenever he chose to return. The same was true of the other places he maintained here in the States. The lair in New York City was far more lavish than this one. The same was true of his place in Tennessee.

Materializing in the bedroom, he lowered the wolf onto the mattress. Was she out for the rest of the night? If not, how would she react when she awoke in a strange place? Would she remember who he was before she tried to rip his throat out?

He regarded her a moment, thinking that, wolf or woman, she was something to see. Her fur was as black as midnight, her ears small and pointed, her body trim and compact but well muscled. Quite a package, he mused, in whatever form she was in.

Maybe some night he would change into his wolf form and they could run the hills together.

Chuckling softly, he went into the bathroom and closed the door. After removing the filthy rags he had worn for the last three years, he stepped into the shower and turned the water on full blast. Damn, but it felt good! Closing his eyes, he stood under the spray and let the hot water sluice over his head and body. He hadn't had the luxury of a real bath since Verah captured him. Whenever his stink got to be more than she could stand, she had turned a hose on him.

He stayed in the shower a good forty minutes, washing his hair and scrubbing away the stink of captivity.

When he returned to the bedroom, a towel wrapped around his hips, the wolf was still out of it. He figured she would likely sleep through the night after all they'd been through.

Moving to the dresser, he pulled on a T-shirt and a pair of gray sweatpants, then stretched out on the bed beside the wolf. He needed to feed but it didn't seem wise to leave her here, alone, on the off chance she might wake up. For a moment, he contemplated taking a few sips of her blood, but the thought of getting a mouthful of fur quickly soured him on that idea.

Turning onto his side, he stroked her head. Her fur was soft and warm. Touching her was soothing somehow. Closing his eyes, he slipped into oblivion, clean and at peace for the first time in years.

Kay woke with a start, surprised to find herself lying naked in a strange bed with Gideon, in a room she didn't recognize. How had they gotten here? And where was here? The last thing she remembered was a searing pain in her flank. When she touched her leg, there was no wound, but that didn't surprise her. Most injuries healed overnight, although in her case, serious injuries sometimes took a little longer, since she was only half werewolf.

She wrinkled her nose. The room smelled musty, as if no one had lived in it for a very long time. Of course, if this was Gideon's home, it had been unoccupied for at least three years, which would account for the smell, and the thick layer of dust on the nightstand.

Sitting up, she glanced around, wondering if there was anything to eat in the place. Considering who lived here, she doubted it. And even if there happened to be a stray loaf of bread or a package of lunch meat lying around, after sitting on a shelf for three years, it certainly wouldn't be edible.

Swinging her legs over the edge of the bed, she went into the bathroom and closed the door.

It had only been a few days since she had showered, but it seemed longer. She washed her body twice and her hair three times before she felt clean.

Wrapped in a towel, she returned to the bedroom. A glance at Gideon showed he was still sleeping soundly. She bit down on her lower lip for a moment before moving to the mahogany dresser against the far wall. Rummaging through the drawers, she found a short-sleeved navy T-shirt and a pair of sweatpants similar to the ones he was wearing. The pants were miles too big and too long, but better than nothing. She used a belt she found in the closet to keep them up, rolled the cuffs so she wouldn't trip, and left the bedroom to do a little exploring.

The living room was sparsely furnished with little more than a dark leather sofa, a rectangular coffee table made of distressed oak, and a large bookcase filled with books, magazines, and a bronze statue of a tiger, all covered with dust. A state-of-the-art flat-screen TV hung over the fireplace. The fourth room was the kitchen. The cupboards were empty. There was no stove, only a small white refrigerator, also dusty. She stared at it, grimacing as she pictured the inside filled with bags of old blood.

Going back into the living room, she dropped down on the sofa, displacing little puffs of dust. She needed something to eat. Unfortunately, she had no cell phone with which to order anything and no money to pay for it anyway. And no idea where she was. For all she knew, she could be in the middle of Timbuktu. She regarded the TV for a moment. Gideon had been away for three years. What were the odds that the electricity was still on? Only one way to find out. Taking the remote from the coffee table, she hit the on switch, pleased to discover that the TV had power and the batteries in the remote weren't dead. She was relieved to see a familiar news program. At least she was still in the country.

She tapped her fingertips on the arm of the sofa, wondering if Gideon kept any money in the house, and if so, where? She spent several useless minutes trying to imagine where a vampire might keep a few dollars stashed and then went looking—there was nothing in the dresser but T-shirts, socks, and underwear, and nothing in the closet but pants and shirts and shoes.

When she looked in the nightstand beside the bed, she found a brown leather wallet. Hunger overrode guilt, and she looked inside, hoping to find a few dollars. What she found was several hundred in twenties and fifties.

Taking two twenties, she put the wallet back, closed the drawer, and headed for the front door, only to pause, her hand on the knob.

She didn't have a key. If she went out, and the door locked behind her, she wouldn't be able to get back in.

If she left the door open . . . she bit down on the inside of her lower lip. She couldn't expose Gideon to a risk like that. It was unlikely that anyone was looking for him, or would expect him to be here after being away for so long. Still . . . she chewed on her thumbnail, her stomach growling loudly all the while. It would be hours until he woke. Darn it. She was stuck in here until sundown.

With a sigh of exasperation, she plucked a book from the

shelf and blew off the dust, thinking it was too bad she couldn't eat the pages.

Gideon woke with the setting of the sun. A glance to the left showed he was alone in bed. So, where was Kay? Sitting up, he sniffed the air, felt himself relaxing when he heard the faint sound of her breathing from the other room.

Throwing back the covers, he got out of bed and padded barefooted into the living room to find his houseguest curled up on the sofa. She looked incredibly young lying there, her lips slightly parted, her cheek pillowed on her hand, her hair spread around her face like a cloud of ebony silk.

When he took a step toward her, she jerked upright.

"I thought you were asleep," he said.

"I'm starving."

"Sorry. Come on, I'll take you out to dinner."

"I don't have anything to wear."

His gaze moved over her. With her hair falling loose over her shoulders and clad in his T-shirt and sweats, she looked like a little girl playing dress-up in her father's clothes. "We'll stop on the way and buy you something."

"I can't go out looking like this."

"Sure you can. Let me put on a pair of jeans and we'll go. There's a mall down the street."

Huffing a sigh of exasperation, she muttered, "Sure, you get to change," but he was already gone.

He returned a few minutes later wearing a pair of jeans, boots, and a leather jacket over a T-shirt. "Ready?"

She glanced at her bare feet, grimaced, and said, "Let's just go."

He sketched a bow. "After you."

With a shake of her head, she preceded him out of the apartment.

She was too hungry to spend much time shopping. In

the department store, she picked out a pair of jeans, a yellow sweater, and a pair of flip-flops, quickly changed clothes in the dressing room, and was ready to go.

Passing through the shoe department, Gideon insisted Kay try on a pair of black suede Gucci boots to replace the ones Verah had taken.

"You don't have to do that," Kay said. "It's not your fault that witch is a thief."

"But it's my fault you were there."

She couldn't argue with that. She sat down while the clerk went to get the boots in her size.

Kay gasped when she saw the price tag. Seven hundred dollars. "These are way too expensive," she said. They were far nicer and considerably more costly than the ones Verah had stolen.

"I can afford it," Gideon said. "If you don't like these, pick out something else."

"These are fine," Kay said. How could you go wrong with Gucci?

He nodded at a display table, then told the clerk, "We'll take that matching bag, too."

When she started to protest, Gideon shushed her with a look.

After they left the store, he stuffed a handful of greenbacks into her new purse. "Mad money," he muttered. "Just in case. So, what are you in the mood for?"

"A steak and fries."

"I like a woman who knows what she wants," Gideon said, grinning.

Twenty minutes later, she was sitting across from Gideon in a swanky steakhouse.

"I think we're a little underdressed," Kay remarked, glancing around. Most of the men wore suits or sports jackets, the majority of the women wore dresses and heels.

"Are you kidding? Your boots probably cost more than most of the dresses these women are wearing."

She couldn't argue with that.

When the waitress came, Kay ordered the biggest steak the place had to offer—rare, please—fries, and a glass of iced tea. Gideon ordered a glass of dry red wine.

"Do you ever miss eating?" Kay asked when the waitress left to turn in their order.

"Not anymore." He leaned back, one arm draped over the back of the booth. "So, what are you gonna do now?"

"I don't know. Go home, I guess."

"Where's home?"

"Custer, South Dakota."

"Are you serious? What the hell are you doing there?" He shook his head, and then laughed. "Couldn't you find a smaller town?"

She looked at him as if he wasn't too bright. "I like it because it *is* a small town. Not a lot of people. And it's close to the Black Hills."

"Ah. Lots of game and plenty of wide-open spaces."

"You've been there?"

"Honey, I've been everywhere."

Of course he had, she thought. "So, where are we now?"

"Phoenix."

"Phoenix!" How did she get so far from home? "What are we doing here?"

"I maintain a couple of residences around the country. This one was the closest to Verah's place."

Kay considered that a moment. "So, where does the witch live?"

"Some little no-name town in New Mexico."

"New Mexico!" Kay exclaimed. She knew she had been drugged when she went nightclubbing with Wanda, but she'd had no idea her kidnapper had taken her so far away from home.

Gideon leaned forward, his arms crossed on the table. "I don't think I thanked you for getting me out of that hellhole."

"My pleasure. So, what are *you* going to do now?"

"Stay away from witches," he answered with a wry grin.

"Me, too." She spread her napkin in her lap, her expression thoughtful. "My boss must be wondering where I am. I've never missed a day without calling in. Which reminds me, I'm going to have to get a new cell phone. Wanda's probably worried sick, and angry because I haven't shown up at work."

"What kind of work do you do?"

"I'm a veterinary assistant and part-time receptionist."

"Makes sense. Who better to work with the fanged and furry than a werewolf?"

"Very funny." Kay sat back when the waitress arrived with their order. It took all her self-control to keep from pouncing on the thick slice of prime rib.

"You sure that's dead?" Gideon asked, gesturing at her steak. "Wouldn't surprise me if it got up and walked away."

Kay stuck her tongue out at him.

Smiling, Gideon sipped his wine.

In no time at all, she had devoured the steak and fries.

"Do you want another one?" he asked, wondering where she had put that enormous slab of meat. To look at her, you'd think she hardly ate at all.

"I was hungry," she replied defensively. "After all, I haven't had a decent meal in days."

"I know. So, do you want another one?"

When she nodded, Gideon waved the waitress over.

"Yes, sir," she said. "What can I get for you?"

"I'd like another glass of wine," he said. "And another steak for the lady." He grinned at the astonished expression on the waitress's face as she jotted it down.

"Right away, sir," she said, and hurried away.

"She must think I'm a . . . a . . . I don't know what," Kay muttered.

"The way she took off, I'm thinking she was afraid she might be the next course."

Kay glared at him.

Gideon laughed softly, amused by her embarrassment. She was something else, he thought—a werewolf who blushed like a schoolgirl. He hadn't been this enchanted by a woman in a long time, nor wanted one as badly. It surprised him to realize he was going to miss her when she was gone.

When they left the restaurant, Gideon suggested they take a walk, and Kay agreed.

She took a deep breath, inhaling the fresh clear air. Even though she had been imprisoned for only a few days, it seemed much longer.

They walked in silence for a few minutes before Gideon said, "I guess you're in a hurry to go home."

"Well, sure," she said. "I mean, I have a job and . . . why do you ask?"

"I was kinda hoping you'd stick around for a while."

Kay's heart skipped a beat. "Oh?"

He shrugged. "I feel like I owe you a good time, you know? Or at least a new cell phone."

"You don't have to buy me anything else."

"Didn't we already have this conversation?"

She arched one brow. "Just because you can afford it doesn't mean I want you spending your money on me."

"Listen, Kiya, money's the least of my problems. What do you say? Can you hang around for a few days?"

"I don't know," she said with a saucy grin. "When you buy me that new phone, I'll call my boss and see what he says."

As it turned out, Kay had three weeks vacation coming. It took some fancy footwork on her part to explain why she hadn't come in to work or called. In the end, she wasn't sure Dr. Saltzman believed she'd been in a car accident and spent the missing days in a hospital with amnesia. The tone of his voice seemed to imply that he suspected her of indulging in a casual fling, but he finally agreed she could take her vacation early, minus the days she had missed.

Kay's second call was to Wanda.

"So, where have you been?" Wanda asked. "Last time I saw you, you were dancing with that good-looking guy at the club. Have you been with him all this time? And why didn't you call me?"

Kay took a deep breath. What on earth was she going to say? She looked at Gideon, and then she knew.

"I've been with a good-looking guy, but not the one you saw me with. Listen, I'm taking my vacation now. Would you water my plants and collect my mail until I get home?"

"Sure, but . . ."

"I have to go. He's waiting for me. I'll tell you all about it when I see you," she promised, and hung up before Wanda could ask any more questions.

"Is that other 'good-looking guy' me?" Gideon asked with a wicked grin.

"Oh, get over yourself," Kay said. She slipped her new iPhone—apparently Gideon bought nothing but the best, whether it was boots, bags, or phones—into her new handbag, then looked up at him. "So, you've got me for two weeks, give or take a day," she said with a saucy grin. "Now what?"

Gideon rubbed a hand across his jaw as he considered her question. Two weeks. Not a vast amount of time in his world, he mused. Nevertheless, she was lovely. She was desirable. And he wanted her.

"Now what?" he drawled. "How about this?" And so saying, he drew her into his arms and covered her mouth with his.

There was nothing tentative about his kiss, nothing gentle, or tender. It was a bold declaration of his intentions. He figured if she was willing, she would kiss him back, and if she wasn't, he was prepared for a good hard slap.

She tensed in his arms and for a moment, Gideon thought he had misjudged the undeniably potent attraction between them, but then, with a little sigh, she wrapped her arms around his waist and melted into his embrace.

Holding her close, Gideon willed them to his lair in New York City, which was located in a renovated loft on the top floor of a ballet studio.

Still enfolded in Gideon's arms, Kay looked up at him, her brow furrowed. "What just happened? Where are we?"

"My lair in the Big Apple."

"New York?" She glanced around, her eyes widening as she took in her surroundings.

If his place in Phoenix had been sparse, this one was magnificent—from the polished parquet floors to the luxurious velvet draperies at the barred windows. A pair of deep burgundy sofas faced each other across a glass-topped coffee table in front of a large white marble fireplace. Abstract paintings adorned two of the walls, a flat-screen TV took up most of the third. A narrow curio cabinet held an assortment of antique weapons.

"This place is amazing."

"It should be, for what I paid for it." He kissed the tip of her nose. "Wanna see the rest?"

"Sure."

Setting her on her feet, he led the way into a room paneled in dark oak. A forest-green carpet covered the floor, matching drapes hung at the barred, single window. A pair of floor-to-ceiling bookcases stood on either side of the window. Brass figurines of mounted knights and dragons were scattered among the numerous volumes on the shelves. A life-sized wooden Indian, complete with warbonnet and lance, stood in the far corner. A large desk, which held only a laptop computer, dominated the room. She noted the small white refrigerator located beside the desk. No need to ask what that was for.

"I take it you read a lot," Kay remarked, glancing at the bookcases.

Gideon nodded. "You could say that."

"And the wooden Indian?"

"I picked it up cheap at an antique store that was going out of business. Are you offended by it?"

"No, just curious."

"Guess I've always had a thing for Indians," he said with a wink.

"You're just saying that."

"No. I spent a couple of months with a small tribe of Cherokee back in the late 1700s. Nice people."

"Hmm." Her gaze drifted back to the bookcases. His taste was eclectic, she thought as she perused the titles. There were several plays by Shakespeare, poetry by Blake and Yeats, novels by Tolstoy and Kipling, King and Koontz and Clancy, and, to her amusement, the works of Stephenie Meyer.

Grinning inwardly, she followed him down a carpeted hallway that ended in a bedroom that would have held her entire apartment. The walls were a clean, crisp white, the bedspread and drapes a deep wine red. Carpet that must have been two inches thick muffled her footsteps as she moved around the room. The biggest bed she had ever seen stood against the far wall, flanked by a pair of ebony nightstands. A matching entertainment center held a TV and dozens of DVDs. Most of the wall across from the bed was taken up by a fireplace with a raised marble hearth.

A bathroom appointed in marble and gold-veined tile adjoined the bedroom.

Kay shook her head. "I've never seen anything like this. Did you decorate the place yourself?"

He snorted. "Hardly. I hired a fancy decorator who charged me a ridiculous amount of money for this layout."

"Well, it was worth it."

Coming up behind her, Gideon slid his arms around Kay's waist and nuzzled the side of her neck. "How would you like to try out the bed?"

"Not on our first date," she answered primly. "I'd like to be romanced first."

"Romanced, huh?" He nipped the tender skin just beneath her earlobe. "I'll see what I can do."

Chapter 12

Later that night, after Kay had gone to bed, Gideon left the house to go hunting. New York City was one of his favorite hunting grounds. No matter the time of night, prey was never hard to find, whether it was some drunken bum down on his luck, a world-weary hooker trolling for one last trick before calling it a night, or some small-town tourist foolish enough to go out alone after midnight.

Gideon strolled along Broadway, past Times Square. In the early sixties and seventies, this part of the city had been a red light district, but these days it was more family-oriented. Moving on, he came to that part of Broadway known as the Great White Way, so named for the millions of lights of theater marquees and billboards. Most of the theaters were dark now. He glanced at the marquees—*The Lion King, Wicked,* and the ubiquitous *Phantom of the Opera,* which he had seen perhaps a dozen times.

His hunger quickened when he spied a young couple looking at the posters in front of a theater. On cat-quiet feet, he moved up behind them. Speaking to their minds, he commanded them to follow him.

Faces slack, expressions blank, they trailed behind him as he moved toward the deep shadows near the theater doors.

He took the male quickly, the female more slowly, his whole being focused on the woman in his arms, the scent of her hair and skin, the warmth of her blood quenching his thirst. Her blood was sweeter than Kay's. Even so, he wished it was Kay he held in his embrace, Kay's blood easing his hunger.

After satisfying his thirst, he wiped the incident from the couple's minds and sent them, none the wiser, on their way.

Hands shoved in his pockets, Gideon turned for home. So, Kiya the werewolf wanted to be romanced, did she? He grinned at the idea and then, with that thought in mind, he headed for the mall located in the heart of the city. It was closed at this hour, but that wasn't a problem for him. The owner was a friend. And a vampire.

On waking, Kay stretched her arms over her head, and then froze as she realized she was in a strange bed in a strange room, and that she wasn't alone. It took her a moment to remember where she was, and who was lying beside her.

Turning onto her side, she regarded the sleeping vampire. He was bare to the waist, revealing a broad chest, wide shoulders, and six-pack abs that would have made any male model jealous. She realized, abruptly, that he wasn't breathing. When she touched his arm, he didn't move. She worried her lower lip with her teeth. Maybe vampires really were dead when they slept. A creepy thought, that, sharing a bed with a dead man, even one as roguishly handsome and sexy as Gideon Marquet.

And with that in mind, she practically jumped out of the bed, only then noticing the flowers set around the room—vases of red roses and pink carnations occupied every flat surface save for the dresser, which held a large white box and two shoe boxes. Her name was scrawled across the box tops in a bold hand. Opening the largest box, she found two pairs of jeans, a pink T-shirt, a couple of sweaters, and three

changes of underwear, all the right size. The first shoe box
held a pair of strappy black sandals; the second, a pair of
white sneakers.

She ran her hand over a pair of silky black bikini panties,
wondering how he had known what size she wore. But she
didn't care. She selected an aqua sweater and a pair of jeans
and carried them, along with a bra and panties, into the bathroom, and closed the door behind her.

There were more flowers in the bathroom—roses, again—
along with a new toothbrush, toothpaste, a hairbrush, and a
comb. Heaven bless the man for his thoughtfulness.

With a shake of her head, she dropped her dirty clothes on
the floor and placed the clean ones on the counter. When she
opened the shower door, she found a bottle of shampoo, a new
bar of soap, a pretty pink washcloth, and a single red rose.

Who knew vampires had such a romantic streak? Stepping
into the shower, she wondered what other surprises the day
might bring.

Additional gifts, flowers, and treats arrived all day long.
Shortly after she finished her shower, a waiter from a nearby
restaurant knocked on the door bearing her breakfast on a silver
tray, along with a single red rose in a delicate crystal vase.

Kay smiled, thinking how sweet it had been for Gideon to
order her something to eat.

A full-body massage came an hour later, followed by a
manicure and a pedicure.

As the manicurist was leaving, lunch arrived, accompanied by another red rose.

She had barely finished eating when there was another
knock on the door. She opened it to find several personal
shoppers from Bloomingdale's standing in the hallway. After
introducing themselves, they laid out a wide array of cloth-

ing for her consideration—everything from dresses to pants, shoes to hats, nightgowns to slippers.

Reluctant at first, Kay soon got into the spirit of things. She chose a couple of casual dresses by Tahari and Calvin Klein, jeans and T-shirts by Guess, shoes by Ferragamo, a handbag by DKNY, a nightgown and robe by Natori. As Kay signed the receipt, she hoped Gideon had been serious when he said money was the least of his problems, because she had just spent a small fortune.

The sun was setting when the ladies from Bloomingdale's packed up the rejects, thanked her profusely, and left the apartment.

Kay was standing at the window, gazing at the darkening skyline, when Gideon ghosted up behind her. Slipping his arms around her waist, he drew her against him. "How was your day?"

"Wonderful. Thank you." She turned in his arms and smiled up at him. "I hope you really are rich."

His gaze moved over her. "Whatever that outfit cost, it was worth it. You look terrific." *Better than terrific,* he thought with an admiring glance. A sleeveless black dress made of some clingy material outlined every delectable curve. A pair of black, sling-back pumps did wonderful things for her legs, which were long and shapely.

"I should look fantastic, considering the small fortune this little black dress cost you."

He laughed softly. "You're right. You do look fantastic."

"So do you." Her gaze moved over him. He looked gorgeous in a dark green, long-sleeved shirt, a pair of khaki pants with a crease that looked sharp enough to cut steel, and black leather boots. "It was very thoughtful of you, sending all those clothes over, but really, something a little less expensive would have served just as well."

"Nothing but the best for my lady werewolf," he said with

a shrug. "Besides, it's only money, and if you don't spend it, what am I gonna do with it?"

"Well, I'll be more than happy to spend it for you, since you have so little regard for it. Where did you come by it all, anyway?"

He lifted one shoulder in a negligent shrug. "In the beginning, I pilfered what I needed from the rich. But then, as I got richer, I invested it. And now . . ." He made a vague gesture with his hand. "Now, I have more than I need." He grinned at her. "And finally, someone to spend it on."

"'Pilfered'? Now there's a word you don't hear every day."

"True."

"How long have you been a vampire?"

"Three hundred and sixty years, give or take a decade or two." His hands spanned her waist, his thumbs lightly stroking back and forth. "In answer to your next question, I was turned when I was twenty-seven by an ancient vampire who had grown weary of living but who didn't want her very old, very powerful blood, to go to waste."

"So, she turned you against your will?"

"Most assuredly. For someone so ancient, there was little substance to her," he recalled. "Or so it seemed. But she was a lot stronger than she looked. I tried to fight her off, but she held me down easily. 'I'm going to give you a wondrous gift,' she said, and then she buried her fangs in my throat. When it was done, she took me to her home and told me what I needed to know to survive.

"It was near dawn when Lisiana told me good-bye. When I asked where she was going, she told me she was over a thousand years old and she was tired of living. 'I'm going out to meet the sun,' she said. 'Do what you wish with the house. Keep it, sell it, burn it down.'" He paused a moment. "Before I could ask her anything else, she was gone. When I woke up that night, I was a vampire. I never saw her again."

Kay stared up at him. It was an incredible tale, she thought, and then she grinned. "You seem to be a magnet for older women. What are you doing with me?"

Gideon threw back his head and laughed. "Damned if I know."

Moving to the sofa, Kay sat down and crossed her legs. "You seem to like being a vampire."

"No sense being miserable over something that can't be changed," he said, sitting beside her. But the truth was, once he'd gotten over the fear and the shock, he did like it. "What about you? You like being a werewolf?"

She tossed his words back at him. "'No sense being miserable over something that can't be changed.' I was born this way."

"So, basically, when the moon's full, you turn furry."

She nodded.

"How does it usually affect you? You didn't go all Lon Chaney the other night and start killing everything on two legs, so I'm assuming you have at least some control."

"Yes. I've never had the overpowering urge to go on any kind of killing spree, although"—a faint blush heated her cheeks—"I feel the need to hunt, but only deer or rabbits and the occasional squirrel."

He stretched his arm along the back of the sofa, his fingers lightly stroking her bare shoulder. Her skin was soft, and warm, and baby smooth. "So, are all werewolves as benign as you are?"

"The civilized ones. I've heard there are a few who go totally feral and kill anything they come across, but, thankfully, I've never met one."

He mulled that over a moment before asking, "If you bite someone, do they turn fanged and furry?"

"No. That only works with vampires. Werewolves are born, not made."

He grinned wryly. What would happen, he wondered, if a very old vampire tried to turn a very young werewolf?

* * *

During the next week, Kay gradually changed her sleeping habits so that instead of sleeping until eight or nine in the morning, she slept until one or two in the afternoon, which meant she ate breakfast about the time she would normally have been eating lunch, which she skipped altogether. Gideon took her out to dinner except when he needed to feed. On those nights, she dined alone, and then they spent the rest of the evening together.

Kay had never been to New York before and each night brought a new adventure. One evening, after dining at the Savoy, he took her to the top of the Empire State Building. She had stared in awe at the bird's-eye view of the city spread out below. The next night, they went walking through Central Park, and even though the Conservatory Gardens were closed, Gideon whisked her inside for a private tour, and then he transported them to the Bronx Zoo, which was also closed.

"Not much to see," she remarked as they passed exhibit after exhibit of sleeping lions, tigers, bears, camels, zebras, elephants, and monkeys.

"I guess the animals need their beauty rest," he replied, grinning as they paused to watch a pair of sleeping pandas.

"They aren't the only ones," Kay said, yawning behind her hand.

"Don't tell me you're tired?"

"A little."

A moment later, she was in his car, with no memory of how she had gotten there. "I wish I could do that," she exclaimed. "How does it work?"

He shrugged. "I'm not sure. I just think of where I'd like to be and I'm there, and so is anyone I happen to be touching— or holding—at the time. Pretty cool, huh?"

"Very."

The next night, he presented her with two tickets to the *Phantom of the Opera*.

It was the most amazing play she had ever seen. Sitting in the front row, she was close enough to see the actors' facial expressions, to feel the flames when one of the actors lit the footlights. She lost herself in the play, totally caught up in the Phantom's anguish as he told Christine good-bye. Gideon obligingly offered her his handkerchief so she could dry her tears.

She was still crying when they left the theater.

"Hey," he chided with a smile, "it was just a play."

"But it was so sad! How could she leave him like that when he loved her so much?"

Gideon snorted. "Are you serious? Did you really expect her to give up a life of ease with a rich, handsome count to live in a drafty old cellar with a disfigured madman?"

"I would have. He needed her. The count didn't. Raoul could have had his pick of other women."

"The phantom was a murderer."

Muttering, "I think the pot's calling the kettle black." Kay thrust his handkerchief at him.

Gideon arched one brow. "Is that so? Just what are you accusing me of?"

"Nothing. I mean, you *are* a vampire. I just assumed . . . oh, never mind."

He came to a stop, turning her to face him. "You're right," he said quietly. "I've killed a lot of people in my time."

She bit down on her lower lip, her gaze not quite meeting his. "I'm sorry. I didn't mean . . ."

"It's all right, Kiya. I'm not making excuses for what I've done, but that was before I learned I didn't have to kill to survive. Since then, I haven't killed anyone who wasn't trying to kill me."

He started walking again and she hurried to keep up. "I believe you."

"There was a lot of vampire hunting going on back in the early seventeenth and eighteenth centuries," he remarked. "Lots of superstitious nonsense back then. Witch hunts. Vampire hunters. A lot of innocent people died."

She knew about that. She had read about the Salem witch hunts in school, had done additional research online. Now and then, she had overheard her father talking about ancestors who had been killed before the werewolf community went underground.

"Vampires have always gotten a bum rap," Gideon said. "Back in the old days, anytime there was an illness no one could explain, or the hens stopped laying, or the cow dried up, the old men in the village would start looking for a vampire. And sure enough, sooner or later they'd find some poor soul who looked a little pale, or who was a stranger just passing through, and the next thing you knew, it was 'off with his head.' Sometimes they accused whole families."

"That's terrible."

He shrugged. "People were a lot more superstitious back then, a lot more ignorant than we are today. Uncontrollable weather, unexplained deaths, insane behavior—the culprit had to be a vampire. It was probably the same for werewolves, wasn't it?"

They were at the car now. Gideon held the door for her, then walked around the front and slid behind the wheel.

"Not so much," Kay said, fastening her seatbelt. "We've managed to keep a low profile. No one believes in werewolves anymore," she said. "Partly because vampires were getting all the notoriety for a while there. Then, too, there aren't so many of us. We rarely go off on our own, and we're bound to do whatever our Alpha says. There are only five packs left in the United States and all the Alphas have agreed not to do anything that would draw undue attention to the double-natured."

"Where does your pack makes its home?"

"Jackson, Wyoming."

"More open spaces," he mused. There would be good hunting in Yellowstone and the National Elk Refuge.

Kay nodded.

"So, do you like living on your own, away from the pack?"

"Probably more than I should." She bit down on her lower lip. "I'm going to miss my freedom when I go back."

"Then don't go."

"I'm afraid I don't have much choice."

"Pack law and all that, I guess."

"That's part of it, although there are a few lone wolves. But . . ."

"You don't want to be one of them?"

"Even if I did, it would never be allowed."

"Because you're a female?"

"No." She took a deep breath and blew it out in a long, slow sigh. "Because my father is also my Alpha."

Chapter 13

Verah hurled the black bowl across the room. It hit the fireplace with a resounding thud, raining broken glass and water on the hearth stones. She had spent the last several days trying to locate Gideon, but to no avail. She had a few hairs from his head, she had vials of his blood, but no matter which spell she used to conjure his location, nothing happened. What was she doing wrong?

Seething with frustration, she pulled her favorite grimoire from the shelf and thumbed through the pages, her exasperation growing as spell after spell failed to provide the information she needed. Near the end of the book she found a page devoted to vampires and vampire lore. A notation, written in the margin in a spidery hand, declared there were no known spells whereby vampires could be tracked because they were, for all intents and purposes, dead, and one could only perform ritual magic on the living.

It took all her self-control to keep from sending the grimoire after the scrying bowl.

Eyes narrowing, Verah went upstairs and sank into the chair beside the hearth. Rama immediately jumped onto her lap. For a time, Verah stared into the flames, her hand absently stroking the cat's head. It was soothing, petting the cat, listening to its low purr. Gradually, her anger receded and her mind cleared.

"We've been going about this all wrong," Verah murmured. "We can't use magic to find the vampire, but it should be easy enough to locate the girl."

Yes, she thought, nodding. The girl might well be the answer to her dilemma.

"Come, Rama," Verah said, rising. "We have work to do, you and I. And if we work it just right, perhaps the werewolf will lead us to the vampire."

Chapter 14

Three nights later, Gideon was still mulling over the fact that Kay's father was an Alpha werewolf. Although she was the first of her kind Gideon had ever met, he had heard enough stories to know that messing with an Alpha werewolf was not to be considered lightly. They were strong. They were territorial. They were loyal. And they were vicious. And while a bite from your run-of-the mill werewolf was extremely painful, the bite of an Alpha male was usually fatal to humans and lesser wolves.

He looked up as Kay entered the living room. Tonight, she wore a pair of black leggings and a white sweater and, as always, she looked good enough to eat. Literally and figuratively. A pair of black sandals dangled from one hand.

"Are we going out?" she asked.

"If you like."

"I'd just as soon order a pizza and a salad and stay in."

"Whatever you want."

Dropping the sandals on the floor, she pulled out her cell phone and ordered a large pizza with all the trimmings, then curled up on the sofa next to Gideon. "It's raining."

He nodded.

"I love the rain. Maybe we could go for a walk later."

"Sure." He slid his arm around her shoulders and eased her closer. "Are you enjoying your stay in New York?"

"Oh, yes. I can see why you like it here."

"What's not to like?" Of course, the main thing he liked about the city was the constant influx of fresh prey. Hunting was always good here. From dusk till dawn, you could always find someone wandering the streets alone.

But he wasn't thinking about prey now.

He lifted one hand, his fingers trailing through the silky fall of her hair. "You smell like flowers."

She laughed softly. "That's hardly surprising, considering the apartment is filled with roses."

His knuckles caressed her cheek, then slid down her neck and along her collarbone. "You said you wanted to be romanced," he reminded her. "How am I doing?"

Kay met his gaze, and immediately forgot what she'd been going to say. His dark eyes smoldered with desire, causing her mouth to go dry and her heart to skip a beat. She swallowed hard as heat speared through her, threatening to turn her bones to liquid and her insides to mush.

His voice was little more than a groan when he said, "Kiya, I can't wait any longer."

She didn't have to ask what he meant. She remembered all too clearly the first night she had spent here with him. He had asked if she would like to try out his bed, and she had replied, rather primly, that she wanted to be romanced first. Hence the dinner dates, the nights at the opera, the tour of the city, the bouquets of flowers.

She let out a long shuddering sigh with the realization that it was time to pay the piper.

Not that she was complaining. Gideon was far and away the sexiest man she had ever met and there was no sense in pretending she didn't want him just as much as he wanted her. And since she had to go home in the spring and accept the betrothal of a man not of her choosing, it seemed only right that she be allowed to pick her first lover. Of course, she knew her father would not be pleased. And Victor would undoubtedly be outraged to discover that his bride was not a virgin, but she really didn't care whether he liked it or not.

And then, as a new thought occurred, she smiled inwardly. Perhaps, when Victor discovered she was no longer untouched, he wouldn't want her.

Problem solved!

Smiling, she drew Gideon's head down and kissed him. It was like touching a match to gunpowder. The resultant explosion rocked her to her core, setting every nerve ending and cell on fire as his tongue slid over hers in a silent duel. His mouth was hot, his arms strong around her as he kissed her back. There was nothing reserved in his kisses, no uncertainty in his touch as his hand boldly stroked her from shoulder to thigh.

She fell back on the sofa, moaned softly as his body covered hers. Desire stirred deep within her, growing hotter with every kiss and caress. She delved under his shirt, eager to explore the hard muscles in his back and shoulders. His skin was smooth and cool beneath her hands.

Impatient with the layers of clothing between them, she quickly divested him of his shirt and dropped it on the floor. Her sweater and bra quickly followed and then they were wrapped in each other's arms, her breasts crushed against his chest, their mouths fused together. She moved restlessly beneath him, her breath coming in ragged gasps between kisses as he caressed her ever more intimately.

She made a soft sound of protest when Gideon sat up, carrying her with him.

She looked at him askance. Surely he didn't mean to stop? Not now.

Muttering, "No way," he carried her into the bedroom.

Standing her on her feet, he stripped away her leggings and panties, then tossed her, gently, onto the bed. Quickly removing the rest of his clothing, he stretched out beside her and gathered her into his arms.

"Now, let's see," he drawled, "where were we?"

"Don't you remember?" she asked with mock disappointment.

"Here, perhaps," he said, dusting kisses along the length of her collarbone. "Or was I here?" His tongue laved her breast. "Or here." His fingertips made lazy circles on her belly.

"How about here?" she said, and pulling him down on top of her, she cupped his face in her hands and kissed him.

"Ah, yes," he said with a wicked grin. "I remember now."

The pleasure of his touch, the heat of his kisses, the welcome weight of his body pressing her onto the mattress made a heady combination.

Whispering, "Now, Gideon," she held him closer, her hips lifting to receive him. She cried out as his body melded with hers, cried again, in protest, when he withdrew.

He stared down at her. "What the hell!"

She looked up at him, her whole body throbbing with need. "What's wrong?"

"What's wrong?" Swinging his legs over the edge of the bed, he stood glaring down at her. "Why the hell didn't you tell me you were a virgin?"

She blinked at him, confused by his anger.

"I thought . . ." He shook his head. "When you told me you were 'engaged to be engaged' I figured you just wanted a last fling before you settled down. I didn't realize you were . . ." He made a vague gesture with his hand. "Shit."

"Oh." She felt a blush heat her cheeks as embarrassment overcame desire. "I . . . that is . . . since I don't have any choice in who I marry, I thought . . ."

"I guess I know what you thought." Gideon sat on the edge of the bed, his fingers idly stroking the back of her hand. "I guess I should be flattered."

Pulling the bedspread over her nakedness, she muttered, "Do we have to have this conversation now?"

"No." Why leave her unsatisfied when the damage was already done? It was, after all, her first time. He reached for her, determined to make her first time memorable in spite of what had just happened, then paused, nostrils flaring. "Someone's here."

No sooner had he said the words than the doorbell rang.

"Must be the pizza." Kay shook her head in exasperation. Talk about bad timing!

Gideon brushed a kiss across her cheek, then pulled on his pants when the doorbell rang again. "Stay here. I'll get it."

Kay stared after him. Who needed food at a time like this? For once, it wasn't food she was hungry for, but Gideon's strong arms and passionate kisses. She smiled, remembering how incredible he had made her feel.

She let out a startled cry when Gideon suddenly materialized beside the bed.

"What's wrong?" she asked, worried by the angry look in his eyes, the tension in his arms.

He said only one word. "Verah."

Before she could say anything else, he pulled her into his arms and held her close. She experienced a slightly queasy sensation in the pit of her stomach, a disorienting sense of spinning through time and space as everything went black.

When her vision returned, she was cradled in Gideon's arms. A quick glance showed they were in a large rectangular room made of cement painted light blue. Dark blue carpet covered the floor. A trio of candles in tall, wrought-iron stands provided pale, flickering light. A king-sized bed covered by a thick black quilt took up most of one end of the room. The only other furniture was an old-fashioned wardrobe made of rosewood and a good-sized, iron-bound chest that stood at the foot of the bed.

But it was the polished ebony casket on a raised wooden dais at the far side of the room that held Kay transfixed.

She had only one question, and it came out in a hushed whisper. "Where are we?"

"An underground lair near Gatlinburg, Tennessee." He owned the property. The building overhead was empty, but it was equipped with electricity and water, which had been rerouted to his lair. Anyone breaking into the building above would find what looked like an abandoned warehouse. A large sign nailed to the front door advised would-be vandals that the building was unsafe. Nevertheless, in times past, he'd had to chase kids who were high on drugs of one kind or another out of the place, not to mention the occasional transient.

His lair consisted of three large rooms—living room, bedroom, and bathroom—and one small alcove adjacent to the bathroom that contained an apartment-sized refrigerator where he kept a supply of bagged blood for emergencies when he was in town. Thankfully, he'd rarely had to resort to using it. He far preferred his nourishment to be hot and fresh.

"What are we doing here?" Kay asked. She couldn't draw her gaze away from the ebony casket, couldn't stop imagining Gideon lying inside, his eyes closed, his body as cold and still as death.

"Kiya? Kiya, look at me."

With a shudder, she dragged her gaze from the coffin.

"It's just an old box made of wood."

She nodded. "I know, but . . ."

"I don't sleep in it."

"Then why is it here?"

"Every vampire needs one."

"If you don't sleep in it, why do you need it?"

"It contains a little dirt from the town where I was born. If I get seriously injured, I heal faster if I sleep on the earth from my homeland. I've never had to use it."

"Why do you have one here, but not in Phoenix or New York?"

"There's one in Phoenix, behind the bookcase, and one in New York, behind the fireplace."

"And they all have dirt in them?"

He nodded.

"So, you have three." She digested that a moment, then asked, "How did Verah find us?"

"How do you think?"

"Oh, right. Magic."

"Right the first time. You're cold." He could feel her shivering in his arms. Not surprising, since she was stark naked.

"A little."

Carrying her to the bed, he drew back the covers and tucked her in.

She pulled the blankets up to her chin. "Will we be safe here, do you think?"

"I don't know." He raked a hand through his hair, wondering what spell Verah had used to track them down and if there was any way to shield their whereabouts if she tried again.

"How long are we going to stay here?"

"I don't know." Cussing under his breath, he paced the floor. He should have put a shield around his apartment in New York, but he had been so enamored of Kay, he just hadn't thought of it. Had he done so, it might have prevented Verah from entering his lair. As it was, he had barely managed to get himself and Kay out in time. Alone, he might have done battle face-to-face with the old witch, but not with Kay in the house.

This lair, heavily warded against intruders, had been built over a hundred years ago, when vampire hunters roamed the land, ready to take the head and heart of anyone they suspected might belong to the supernatural community. Many innocent people had been killed in those turbulent days. He could only hope his wards were strong enough to repel vindictive witches.

Gideon rubbed a hand across his jaw. Maybe what he needed was a witch of his own. But for now, he had some unfinished business with the sexy werewolf waiting in his bed.

Kay woke smiling, reluctant to abandon the dream she'd been having. Stretching her arms over her head, she glanced at the man sleeping beside her. Gideon had made slow, sweet love to her last night and she knew, without a doubt, that she would never be satisfied with any other man. He had been gentle and tender the first time, infinitely patient as she explored his body from head to foot, and all the interesting places in between. She had been surprised to learn he was ticklish on the bottom of his feet. It seemed incongruous, somehow, for a vampire to be ticklish. And then he had turned the tables on her, his hands and lips touching and tasting every inch of her, arousing her until she thought she would die if he didn't take her. There were no words to describe the sensations that had engulfed her. Ever considerate of her needs, he had made sure that her pleasure came before his own.

He had held her in his arms while her flesh cooled and her breathing returned to normal, and then he had made love to her again. He had been bolder this time, more inventive. And as their bodies melded together, she had felt his fangs at her throat. Her momentary panic had quickly faded as the pleasure of their joining had intensified a hundredfold. It had been a most incredible experience. She had imagined them as one being the first time he made love to her, but it paled in comparison to the second time. She had experienced everything he felt, everything he thought, unable to tell where her body ended and his began.

With a sigh, she sat up, her hand lightly stroking his cheek. How was she going to marry Victor after this? No matter how wonderful a lover her future husband might be, he would never be able to measure up to Gideon. Of course, Gideon had hundreds of years of experience behind him . . . and how had he gotten all that experience? The thought gave her pause. No doubt by making love to hundreds of women. She told herself it didn't matter. What was past was past. She knew she hadn't been his first, nor would she be his last.

The thought brought a rush of tears to her eyes and she blinked them back. She had never intended to fall head over heels for Gideon. Her only thought had been to defy her father. If she couldn't choose her own husband, she could at least decide for herself who her first lover would be. Too late, she realized she had been caught in her own trap. What had started as a casual fling had quickly become something far more serious, at least on her part.

Slipping out of bed, she went into the bathroom. The door was painted the same pale blue as the walls and had no handle, making it practically invisible. If Gideon hadn't pointed it out to her between bouts of lovemaking last night, she never would have known it was there. A touch opened it. Crossing the threshold, she closed the door behind her and turned on the shower. When the water was hot, she stepped inside and let the tears flow.

Gideon woke with the setting of the sun, his first thought for Kay. Sitting up, he opened his senses, relaxing only when he determined that she was nearby.

Grabbing his pants, he pulled them on, then padded barefooted into the living room. He found Kay curled up on the sofa, clutching a pillow to her chest. She looked cute as hell in one of his T-shirts and a pair of faded black sweatpants. He realized two things immediately—she had been crying, and she was hungry.

She looked up as he moved toward the sofa.

"What is it?" he asked, kneeling in front of her. "What's wrong?"

"Nothing," she said, sniffling.

He lifted a skeptical brow. "Nothing?"

"All right," she conceded. "Everything."

"Want to talk about it?"

She drew a deep, shuddering breath, then shook her head.

"Is this about last night?" It wouldn't be the first time a virgin woke up with regrets, he thought ruefully. But it would be the first time he had been involved.

"No." She took a deep, shuddering breath. "It's about the rest of my life."

"Come on, sweetheart, you're young and beautiful. It can't be all that bad."

"Can't it?" Her brows rushed together in an angry frown. "I have to go back home soon. I have to marry a man I can't stand and spend the rest of my life with him. Assuming that a vindictive witch doesn't hunt me down and kill me first."

Gideon clenched his hands at his sides, his jealousy springing to life as the word *marry* echoed in his mind. He had known going in that Kay was—how had she put it— "engaged to be engaged"? So why was he letting it bother him now? He knew why, and it had everything to do with what had happened between them last night.

"You're hungry," he said curtly. "I'll go get you something to eat."

Before she could respond, he was gone.

Gideon stalked the hills and valleys of the Blue Ridge Mountains until his anger subsided. When he was again in control of his temper, he returned to his lair in New York to pick up a few of his things.

His nose wrinkled with distaste when he caught Verah's scent. Damn the meddlesome witch. What spell had she used to track them, and how could he prevent her from using it again?

In the bedroom, he changed into a long-sleeved black T-shirt, jeans, and boots, pulled on a black leather jacket, slipped his wallet into his back pocket. It took only minutes to gather up his own things, several more to gather up the wardrobe he had bought Kay.

He grinned as he shoved everything into a large cardboard box. No matter how many times he bought her new clothes, she always seemed to end up in his sweats.

After closing the lid, he willed himself to his lair in Gatlinburg. He dropped the box off in the bedroom and left the house again without Kay being any the wiser.

And then he went hunting. The pickings weren't as easy here as in New York. Wandering down Parkway, he passed the Hollywood Star Cars Museum, home of more than forty cars that had been featured in movies and TV, including the Batmobile, the car driven by Tom Cruise in *Days of Thunder*, and the 1981 DeLorean driven by Michael J. Fox in *Back to the Future*.

He found his prey farther down the street in front of Ripley's Museum: a middle-aged man and a woman, both a little tipsy.

He mesmerized them both, took what he needed from the woman, and sent the two of them on their way.

After leaving the museum, he went to a fast-food joint and ordered two double cheeseburgers, a large order of fries, and a double thick chocolate malt. He made another stop at a drugstore where he bought a handful of candy bars before returning to his underground lair.

Kay was sitting on the sofa where he had left her, her expression morose. She perked up as soon as she caught the scent of food.

"Dinner and dessert," he said as he dropped the sack containing the burgers and fries in her lap, then set the malt and the bag with the candy bars on the end table.

Murmuring "Thank you," she tore into the sack.

Gideon watched in amazement as the first double cheeseburger disappeared in four bites. "You know," he remarked with a grin, "I've seen piranhas eat slower and leave more behind. I'm surprised you didn't gobble up the wrappings, too."

Kay stuck her tongue out at him as she inhaled a handful of fries, then unwrapped the second cheeseburger. She ate this one slower, savored the fries, sipped the malt, then sat back looking sated and content as she unwrapped a Midnight Milky Way. "My favorite," she murmured.

Gideon shook his head. From the look on her face, you'd think she was having great sex instead of eating a candy bar.

Kay blew out a sigh as she dropped the wrapper into the sack with her other trash.

"There's five more in the bag," Gideon remarked wryly.

"Maybe later. What's that look for?"

"I was wondering if I could put that same blissful expression on your face."

"Hmm. Maybe if you were covered in chocolate," she said, stifling a grin.

"Light or dark?"

"Oh, definitely dark." She rummaged in the bag, pulled out another Milky Way, and held it up. "We could melt a few of these and find out."

"I can't wait that long," he said with a growl. "I'm about three seconds from taking you to bed, unless you tell me no."

Refusing never crossed her mind.

Reading the answer in her eyes, Gideon swept her into his arms and carried her to bed. Stretching out beside her, he wondered what enchantment she had worked on him. In all his years as a vampire, he had never taken anyone—mortal or vampire—to any of his lairs, never confided what he was to any of the women he had seduced. He didn't stop to think what that might mean. Right now, all he wanted was Kay writhing beneath him.

He undressed her slowly, savoring each inch of honey-gold skin exposed to his gaze. She had the body of a goddess, firm, smooth, warm. He nuzzled her breasts, stroked her thighs, ran his tongue along the curve of her throat. Sweet, so sweet. His yearning kicked up a notch when she began to undress him.

She explored his body boldly, her beautiful golden brown eyes glowing with passion, her hands like living flames as they moved seductively over him, igniting his desire still more. She clung to him, restless hands measuring the width of his shoulders, admiring the way his muscles flexed at her touch. Her fingers tangled in his hair, slid over his chest and down his belly.

He pulled her body against his, his mouth claiming hers, his tongue dipping inside to mate with hers.

Tucking her beneath him, he kissed and caressed her, arousing her until she trembled with need, her voice sobbing his name, begging him to take her.

With a low growl, he buried himself deep within her, felt her body convulse as he carried her over the edge into paradise.

Kay stretched her arms over her head, then smiled languidly at Gideon. "That," she drawled with a smile, "was absolutely amazing. Can we do it again?"

"Maybe later," he said, one hand lightly stroking her bare belly. "Right now, we need to talk."

The smile faded from her face. "That doesn't sound good," she said, rolling onto her side. "If we were going steady, I'd think you were about to break up with me."

"Not quite. I made a stop at my place in New York while I was out."

"Do you think that was safe?"

"I didn't give it much thought. You needed something to wear. I can't be buying you a new wardrobe every day, you know."

She grimaced, annoyed by his attempt at humor. "Magic or no magic, I can't believe she found us so quickly."

"I've been thinking about that. The way I see it, she didn't find *us*. She found *you*."

"What makes you say that?"

"All she needed for a tracking spell was something that belonged to you," he explained, thinking out loud. "Clothing, hair. Blood."

"How do you know it was me she was following and not you?"

"I don't know a lot about witches, but I know they can't compel vampires, and they can't work their magic on the dead or the Undead. Only on the living."

"Then we're probably not safe here, are we?" Kay bolted upright, one hand clutching the sheet to her breasts, her eyes widening in alarm as she glanced around the room, her gaze searching every corner, as if she expected to find Verah lurking in one of them. "Are we?" she repeated when he didn't answer.

Gideon shook his head.

Kay stared at him a moment, and then her eyes widened. "You're not safe, either, are you, as long as you're with me?"

"I'm not worried about me." His existence wasn't in danger, only his freedom. He was the one Verah wanted. Kay was only the means to an end. If they split up, Verah would hunt for Kay until she found her. When that happened, the witch would try to use Kay as bait to trap him. If that didn't work, Verah would have no reason to keep Kay alive.

He knew by Kay's expression that the same realization had occurred to her. "How long do you think it will take her to concoct another spell?"

"I don't know. A few hours. Maybe a few days." Whatever the future held, he wasn't about to let Kay face Verah alone.

"We should leave, right now."

"Right now?" His gaze moved over her, lingering on the swell of her breasts.

Blushing, she pulled the sheet higher. "After we get dressed, of course."

It was a shame to cover that luscious body, he thought regretfully, but with Verah breathing down their necks, Kay was right. It was time to get the hell out of Dodge. They couldn't afford to stay in any one place too long.

Leaning forward, he pressed a kiss to the hollow of Kay's delectable throat. "I think you're right, dammit," he muttered. "We need to get out of here."

Chapter 15

Verah paced the floor in the windowless room where she performed her magic, her anger and frustration growing with every step. From time to time, she plucked a jar or a bottle from one of the floor-to-ceiling shelves that lined the east wall and hurled it into the small brick fireplace.

She had found the perfect location spell. Quick and easy to execute, it had worked flawlessly, yet when she had arrived in New York City at the place where the vampire and the werewolf were supposed to be, they were gone. She had found evidence that they had been there in the scattered clothing they had left behind, and the arrival of the pizza deliveryman who had shown up only moments after she did. Since the pizza had already been paid for, she had taken it home with her.

A swipe of her hand cleared the rough, wooden table in the center of the room. If the location spell had worked once, it would work again. But it would have to wait. She could feel her body aging, her steps becoming slow and uncertain, her joints aching. When she'd looked in the mirror last night, she had noticed several strands of gray in her hair, fine lines around her eyes, faint age spots on her hands.

It was galling to know that the vampire would never have

taken her to bed if he had seen her as she really was. The spell she had used to transform herself into a young, beautiful woman had been fleeting, lasting just long enough to get him into bed and bind him with silver.

She plucked a vial filled with dark red blood from a glass-fronted cabinet and poured it into a delicate crystal goblet.

She stared at the liquid with mixed anticipation and revulsion. After taking a deep breath, she lifted the goblet to her lips. Warm or cold, the taste was incredibly vile, but the results made the horrible taste worthwhile.

Shuddering, she drained the glass in a single swallow, then threw it into the fireplace.

Only one vial of the vampire's blood remained. She would have to use it soon, or it would lose its effectiveness.

Time was of the essence.

Chapter 16

Leaving Kay to get dressed and pack, Gideon made a quick trip to a car rental agency where he rented a late-model black Lexus. His next stop was a shopping mall where he bought two large suitcases for Kay and a smaller one for himself. He also picked up a case of bottled water, a family-sized bag of chips, and three dozen assorted granola bars.

Kay was still folding their clothes when he returned.

"Where are we going?" she asked as she began placing her clothes in one of the suitcases. It wasn't easy, cramming everything Gideon had bought her into two suitcases, but she couldn't bear to leave anything behind, and who knew when they might be here again?

"Beats the hell out of me." He threw several changes of clothes and underwear into the remaining suitcase and closed the lid. "You about done there?"

"Yes." She tossed in the last pair of jeans. "Are you sure we should stay together?"

Gideon picked up the three suitcases and headed for the door. "Would you rather be alone?" he called over his shoulder.

"No," she said, hurrying after him, "but . . ."

"Hush, then. She has no power over me, and you can be damn sure I won't fall for her tricks a second time."

Outside, he stowed their luggage in the trunk, then held the passenger door open for Kay. "Anyplace in particular you'd like to go?"

Kay shook her head. "Do you think it matters?"

"Probably not." Gideon slid into the driver's seat, his fingers tapping the steering wheel. As long as Verah was able to locate Kay, it didn't really matter where they went.

Pulling out of the driveway, he headed for the open road.

Kay stared out the window. She didn't know where Gideon was headed, but what was the point in running? Weren't they just prolonging the inevitable? She frowned. That kind of negative thinking wasn't going to get them anywhere. She was a werewolf, not a wimp. No way was she going to give up without a fight, or let Gideon fight her battles for her.

Gideon. She glanced at him, admiring his profile. Why was he putting his life in danger by staying with her?

He turned his head, his gaze meeting hers. "I think I'm falling in love with you, Kiya. That's why."

Kay looked at him in astonishment. "What?"

"You heard me."

"But . . . we've only known each other a few weeks."

He shrugged. "I'm just as surprised as you are. Maybe more so."

Unable to think of anything to say, she continued to stare at him. He was falling in love with her? She shook her head. Considering all they'd been through, when had he found the time?

"I think it started that first night," he said, returning his attention to the road. "I knew you were scared out of your mind and yet, even though you didn't have a chance in hell of stopping me, and there was nowhere to run, you tried to fight me off." He grinned with the memory. "Out of all the women the witch brought me, you were the only one who didn't give up without a fight. I had to admire that. Of course, the fact that you're a knockout didn't hurt."

"Thanks," she muttered dryly.

"Don't write us off yet," he said. "We might get out of this just fine. Nothing is impossible."

"Except keeping you out of my head."

He flashed her a shameless grin. "Except that."

Kay settled back in her seat, her mind replaying Gideon's words. *I think I'm falling in love with you.* His confession had surprised her. More than that, it pleased her, because even though she couldn't admit it—didn't want to admit it, even to herself—she was falling in love with him, too. And that was wrong on so many levels. He was a vampire. She was a werewolf. He slept days. She slept nights. He hunted people. She hunted animals. But the biggest impediment of all was her father, not to mention the fact that she was about to be engaged to another man.

She was staring out the window again when satellite radio filled the car with the latest love song.

"You're not playing fair," Kay muttered.

"Should I change the station?"

"No." Even though a lasting relationship between them was impossible, there was no reason not to enjoy what little time they had left.

The soft music and the darkness soon made Kay drowsy.

Gideon heard the change in her breathing, knew the exact moment she fell asleep. He shook his head, wondering what had possessed him to tell her that he was falling in love with her. He drummed his fist on the steering wheel. Who was he kidding? He was already in love with her.

He glanced at her again, noting her sweet feminine curves. He never should have made love to her, but what man past puberty, dead or Undead, could resist her? She was warm and vibrant, so easy to love with her gentle laughter and sparkling eyes.

Staring at the road ahead, his thoughts turned to Verah. The only way to stop the witch once and for all was to kill her. True, she had her magic, and that was formidable, but she was still human. He was confident that his preternatural powers were stronger than her witchcraft. All he had to do was get close to her.

But first he had to ensure Kay's safety. And try as he might, he could think of only one place where she would be safe. And that was in Wyoming, with her father's pack.

When Kay woke an hour later, he told her what he had decided. She was less than enthusiastic at the idea.

"I don't want to go home." She loved her mother and her father, but she wasn't ready to surrender her freedom, not yet. Once she returned to the compound, she would be absorbed into the pack again, no longer truly an individual but a part of the whole, subject to her father's will and the law of the pack.

She couldn't help but envy Gideon. His life was his own. He had no one telling him what he could or couldn't do, no one deciding who or when he would marry. He enjoyed the kind of freedom she would never have once she returned home.

On the other hand, he didn't have anyone to care for him, either. No one to share his life, or comfort him when he was down. Still, it would be nice to be her own woman, to make her own decisions.

"Be reasonable, Kiya. It's the only place I can think of where you'll be safe. You know, safety in numbers. Even Verah doesn't have the *cajones* to go up against a pack of werewolves."

"But . . ." She shook her head. "I'll never get the chance to be on my own again."

That wasn't the worst of it, he thought. Once she was back home, it was unlikely they would have many chances to be alone together. But it was just as well. She was practically engaged to another man. He had to remember that.

Kay stretched her back and shoulders. "How long will it take to get there?"

They had been driving for almost ten hours, stopping only to buy gas, or when she needed to get something to eat or drink. Gideon had left her alone in a truck stop restaurant for a few minutes while he preyed on one of the truckers.

He glanced her way. "Another ten hours or so. We'll have to stop at the next hotel. The sun will be rising in about thirty minutes."

Kay nodded, her thoughts turned inward. When she had convinced her father to let her leave the pack for a year, she hadn't stopped to consider how she would feel about going back home when that year was up. It had never occurred to her that she wouldn't be happy to go back. She hadn't expected to find such joy and satisfaction in making her own decisions, or such relief at being away from her father's constant demands. Knowing she was going home filled her with resentment.

There was a hierarchy in the pack that couldn't be broken. As alpha male, her father was the undisputed leader. His word was law and pack members disobeyed him at their own peril. Kay's mother was treated with the respect due the pack leader's mate, but, as a human female, she had no say in pack affairs. No other pack Alpha had a human woman for a wife. If any of the pack's members had objected to his choice, it was their right to protest, which would have involved challenging the Alpha, something that had never happened in Kay's lifetime.

Kay's aunt Greta was the Alpha female. Since Kay was only half werewolf, she had no more influence in the pack than did her mother. That had never bothered her until now, when she had lived on her own for almost a year and made all of her own decisions.

Among wild wolves, only the Alpha pair mated, but that wasn't true with werewolves.

There were eleven other pairs in her father's pack, thirteen children ranging in age from eighteen months to eighteen years, and three adult females who were in their early twenties.

Her aunt and uncle had one son, Isaac, who was sixteen. If he showed any Alpha tendencies when he reached adulthood, her father would send him away.

During the full moon, the dynamics of the pack changed, becoming more like that of feral wolves. As Alpha, her father stood more erect and carried his tail higher than the others. Lower-ranking wolves slouched toward the ground in his presence. The Alpha urinated by lifting his leg, the other males squatted. When a submissive wolf approached her father, it would lower its ears and put its tail between its legs, or show its throat to demonstrate subservience. Most of the pack did this without conscious thought.

Although Victor was the eldest son of the Green Mountain Pack's Alpha, he was still subservient to his father, something she knew didn't sit well with Victor. He had never said or done anything to indicate he coveted his father's position, and yet Kay knew he resented his placement in the pack. She had often wondered if the day would come when he would openly challenge his father for leadership.

Kay sighed. One thing she had missed about being home was running with the pack during the full moon. In her wolf form, the world was a remarkable place. Wolves detected scents ten times better than dogs and a hundred times better than humans. She could determine where a particular scent had come from, who or what had made it, and how long it had been there. The males scent-marked pack territory by urinating on targets above the ground, like tree trunks and bushes, which warned members of other packs to keep out.

A short time later, Gideon pulled up in front of a five-star hotel, putting an end to her random thoughts.

She was all too glad to get out of the car and stretch her legs, even though she could scarcely keep her eyes open.

Gideon pulled their suitcases out of the trunk, then locked the car. Inside the hotel, he registered them as Mr. and Mrs. Samuel Adams of Palm Beach, Florida. He waved off the bell-boy, picked up their suitcases, and headed for the elevator.

"Samuel Adams?" Kay lifted one brow as they stepped into the elevator.

Gideon shrugged. "You don't want to be Mrs. Adams?"

"Why not?" she replied, chuckling. "I hear he makes a great beer."

When they reached their room, Gideon inserted the key-card into the slot and opened the door. He took a quick glance around, grateful for the room-darkening drapes.

"Nice place." Kay stifled a yawn while she waited for Gideon to lock the door, then she followed him into the bedroom.

"I don't want you to leave the room," Gideon said, dropping the suitcases on the flat wooden bench at the foot of the bed. "Not for anything. Understand?"

Nodding, Kay quickly changed into her nightgown and crawled under the covers. Five minutes later, she was asleep.

Stripping off his clothes, Gideon slid into bed beside her. He watched her until the sun came up and then he tumbled headlong into oblivion.

Kay sat up, yawning. A glance to her right showed Gideon was, for all intents and purposes, dead to the world. Undead or alive, awake or asleep, he was still the most gorgeous hunk of man she had ever known. She traced his lips with her fingertips, then leaned forward and kissed him. His lips were cool beneath hers. She brushed a lock of hair from his brow. It must be nice, she thought, never growing old or sick or feeble. Gideon would always look just as he did now, exactly the way he had looked when he became a vampire. Her people aged, but at a much slower rate than humans.

Being half werewolf and half human, Kay wasn't sure if she would take after her mother, who was forty-three and looked it, or her father, who was in his mid-seventies and looked twenty-five. She was hoping the latter.

As a child, Kay hadn't stopped to wonder why her mother aged and her father didn't. She hadn't really given it any thought until she turned twenty and realized that her father didn't look much older than she did, which had made her wonder what it was like for her mother, being married to a man who looked so much younger.

Kay remembered asking her mother once if it bothered her that she looked older than her husband. Dorothy had shrugged, then said, "Of course it bothers me, but there's nothing I can do about it now."

The bitter edge in her mother's voice had squelched any further questions on Kay's part. At the time, Kay recalled wondering if one of the reasons her mother never left the compound was that people who saw the three of them together would likely assume that Kay and her father were siblings and that Dorothy was their mother, or perhaps assume that Kay's father was her husband.

Rising, Kay went into the bathroom and closed the door. Slipping out of her nightgown, she turned on the taps in the shower and stepped into the stall, her thoughts still on her mother. Maybe Gideon could change Dorothy into a vampire, she thought, pulling the door closed behind her. Not exactly the best solution in the world, but it would keep her mother from growing any older.

Kay shook her head, horrified by the turn of her thoughts.

Her gentle, soft-spoken mother, a vampire? She almost laughed out loud as she tried to visualize her mom with red eyes and fangs, stalking the night for prey. And then she did laugh. What on earth was she thinking? No doubt about it, hanging around with Gideon had definitely warped her mind. It was a moot point, anyway. Neither her mother nor her father would ever consider or consent to such a thing.

When she was clean from head to foot, Kay stepped out of the shower, dried off, and shrugged into the plush white robe the hotel had provided. A glance at her cell phone showed it was only eleven-thirty in the morning. What was she supposed to do all day while Gideon slept?

A rumble in her stomach made the decision for her. "Breakfast first." Calling room service, she ordered French toast, scrambled eggs, bacon, orange juice, coffee, and the morning paper.

With that done, she settled back on the sofa and turned on the TV. Switching through the channels, she was appalled by her choices—insipid game shows, silly soap operas, movies that were older than she was, and news, news, news, none of it good. Jobs were at an all-time low. The Dow was down five hundred points. The deficit was up another billion or trillion—who could keep track? The price of gas and groceries was rising every day. And Israel was at war again.

She had just settled on an old Clint Eastwood movie when her breakfast arrived. She thanked the young man who delivered it and signed Gideon's name to the bill. Resuming her seat on the sofa, she ate slowly to prolong the meal.

When she was finished, she set the tray aside, then sat there, impatiently tapping her foot. Did she dare go downstairs and browse the hotel gift shops? It would only take a few minutes. She could buy a candy bar and a book and come right back. But even as she considered it, she heard Gideon's voice in the back of her mind. *I don't want you to leave the room. Not for anything. Understand?*

He was right, of course. Even though Kay was fairly certain Verah wasn't anywhere in the vicinity, discretion was, after all, the better part of valor. Besides, there was always a chance, however slim, that she was wrong. For all she knew, the witch could be prowling around the lobby right now. Having been the witch's captive once, Kay wasn't willing to take the chance.

Bored, she forced herself to watch the movie until the end of the credits. When it was over, she called the front desk and asked if someone could please send up an assortment of snacks and a couple of the latest paperback novels.

She spent the rest of the afternoon indulging her love for chocolate, her nose buried in the latest *New York Times* bestseller.

She ordered lunch when she finished the first book.

She was halfway through the second novel when she dozed off.

Gideon came fully, instantly, awake with the setting of the sun. A quick check of his preternatural senses told him Kay was asleep in the other room. The lingering scents of bread, bacon, eggs, roast beef, French fries, orange juice, and coffee hung in the air. And chocolate, he noted with a grin. Lots of chocolate.

Rising, he took a quick shower, then pulled on a pair of well-worn blue jeans and a black T-shirt. Barefooted, he padded into the other room where he roused his sleeping beauty with a kiss.

"I was dreaming of you," Kay murmured. Twining her arms around his neck, she pulled him down on the sofa.

"Were you?" He stretched out beside her, one arm drawing her close. "What were you dreaming about?"

"We were making love on a deserted beach at midnight. It was so quiet and peaceful, with the man in the moon smiling down on us, and the sound of the waves lapping against the shore. It was like there was nothing and no one else in the whole world, just you and me on a white sandy beach that stretched away into infinity."

He chuckled softly. "No beaches around here, I'm afraid. But if you really want to make love in the sand . . ."

She cupped his cheek in her hand. "You don't have to whisk us away to the ocean. The sofa works just fine for me."

"I'm glad to hear it." Slipping his hand under her robe, he started at her ankle and caressed his way up her calf to her thigh. Her skin was warm with life, silky smooth beneath his fingertips.

"Oh, my." She breathed the word on a shuddering sigh as his hand moved higher.

"Something wrong?" he asked with a wicked grin.

"Yes." She gasped as his hand made lazy circles over her bare belly. "I'll give you an hour to stop that."

"Only an hour?" he asked, his voice growing husky.

"Maybe two or . . . oh!" she exclaimed as his hand slid seductively upward to cover her breast. "Better make it three."

Chapter 17

Holding Rama in her arms, Verah gazed, unblinking, into the ebony bowl on the table. The surface of the water, as smooth and black as midnight, should have revealed the wolf girl's whereabouts. Instead, there was only confusion, the marker shifting from one place to another.

Turning away from the bowl, Verah stroked her familiar's head.

"She knows we're after her," Verah mumured. "She's on the run, heading west."

Rama answered with a throaty "Meow."

Verah smiled. "Be patient, my sweet. She'll have to stop sooner or later. And then we'll have her. With luck, we'll have them both."

Still carrying the cat, Verah climbed the stairs to her bedroom. Before Gideon, she had covered every window in the house, every mirror, every reflective surface, to ensure that she couldn't see her reflection. She had refused to leave her house or to see anyone. But that had quickly grown old so that, whenever she left the house, she had invoked a spell that gave her the illusion of youth and beauty. But the illusion only worked on her outward appearance. Her body had still ached with the weight of her years, her steps remained unsteady, her voice creaky with age.

But Gideon's blood had changed all that, restoring her youth and her beauty.

Verah paced the bedroom floor, growing more desperate with each passing hour. What if she couldn't find the girl? What if she found the girl and the vampire wasn't with her?

She had gone out several times, hoping to find another vampire lurking somewhere in the shadows, but to no avail.

Taking a deep breath, she yanked the cloth away from the mirror over her dresser, her stomach churning at the sight of the hideous creature that stared back at her—the wrinkled papery skin, the ugly purple veins, the triple chin, the rheumy eyes, and the sunken cheeks.

"I have to find her," she said, hating the raspy croak in her voice. "It's the only hope we have of catching that damn vampire!"

Chapter 18

Kay stood at the hotel window, staring down at the street below. Another boring day loomed before her. True, this day wouldn't be as long as yesterday, since she had slept until almost two in the afternoon, due, no doubt, to the fact that Gideon was the most amazing lover in the world. Slow and gentle one minute, rough and intense the next, he had aroused her and brought her to fulfillment time after time. Thanks to her werewolf side, she had the stamina to keep up with him. Each time they made love had been better than the last.

They had shared the shower, taking turns washing each other, which had turned into another lusty bout of lovemaking that started in the shower and ended on the bathroom floor.

Had she been human, she thought with a grin, she probably wouldn't have been able to walk after all that incredibly acrobatic, soul-searing, breathtaking loving.

How was she ever going to let him go?

How was she going to marry Victor and bear his children when she loved someone else?

How was she going to endure another day in this blasted hotel? They should have left last night, but all that lovemaking got in the way, and then it was too close to sunrise to hit the road. Which meant another day in the hotel. But another boring day was a small price to pay for a night in Gideon's arms.

She ordered a big breakfast; then, not in the mood to read or watch TV, she went into the bedroom. She stood beside the bed a moment, watching Gideon sleep. She wished she could kiss him awake and they could spend the day making love. Just thinking about it made her cheeks grow warm with the memory of the night before.

Shrugging out of her robe, she slid under the covers. If she had to spend another day locked up in a hotel, what better way to spend it than with Gideon, even if he didn't know she was there?

Propping herself up on one elbow, she studied his face, her fingers lightly tracing his brow, his nose, the line of his mouth. She stroked his neck, ran her hand along his shoulder, down his arm. She rested her palm on his chest, then walked her fingers down his flat belly to his waist.

A startled gasp erupted from her throat when his hand closed over hers.

"Some of us are trying to sleep here," he muttered, gazing at her through narrowed eyes.

"I thought you only woke up when your life was in danger?"

"Your thoughts woke me." Heat flared in his eyes. "No man, living or dead, could ignore the siren song of your desire."

Kay felt herself blushing at his words, which were almost poetic, but it was the touch of his hand sliding up and down her thigh that made her cheeks grow hot and her toes curl with pleasure.

"After last night, I expected you to sleep the day away."

"I was bored."

"I'm sorry, love, but I don't have the energy to entertain you now."

"Too bad." She kissed his cheek. "I'm sorry I woke you. Go back to sleep."

When she tried to withdraw her hand, he tightened his grip. "Stay with me. I like having you here."

And she liked being there, with him.

Sighing, she snuggled against his side and closed her eyes. If they left tonight, they would be in Wyoming tomorrow before sunrise. They would find a place to spend the day, so Gideon could rest. By tomorrow night, she would be home.

What then? Would Gideon stay with her? Would her father allow him to stay? Would the pack accept him?

How was she to go on without him?

The question followed her to sleep.

They left the hotel as soon as the sun went down. Kay had awakened an hour before Gideon. She showered, pulled on a pair of jeans and her favorite aqua sweater, and brushed her hair. When that was done, she ordered a late lunch from room service, and was ready to go when Gideon awoke at sundown.

Now, she glanced at him curiously. To her knowledge, he hadn't eaten anything in the last day or so. But maybe he didn't need anything. He had told her he only needed to feed once a week, though he usually fed more often. "Are you . . . ?"

"Hungry? Not really," he said, sending her a sidelong glance. "But I can always use a snack."

Kay shook her head. It was exasperating, having him read her mind.

He shrugged. "Sorry."

"Yeah, right." She stared out the window, watching the scenery fly past, hating that each hour carried her closer to home, to a man she despised and a marriage she didn't want.

She looked over at Gideon when he covered her hand with

his. "It'll be okay, Kiya. I won't leave you unless you tell me to go."

"Thanks, I appreciate that. But it isn't up to you."

"I'm not afraid of your father."

"Then you're the only one who isn't." She loved her father. She knew he loved her, in his own way. But he wasn't just her father. He was her Alpha and like the rest of the pack, she had no choice but to do what he said, or suffer the consequences.

At eleven, Gideon pulled into a restaurant parking lot. He escorted Kay inside, waited until her food arrived, and then left to go in search of a meal of his own.

He found what he was looking for at a gas station—a stocky, jeans and T-shirt-clad middle-aged woman just emerging from the restroom behind the station. Reluctant to leave Kay alone too long, Gideon took a few quick swallows, wiped the incident from the woman's mind, and was back at the restaurant before Kay's dinner had arrived.

She lifted one brow when he slid into the booth across from her. "I guess you really weren't very hungry." She took a dinner roll from the basket in the center of the table and cut it in half.

"It was a meal, but not a banquet."

Kay stared at him. "A banquet? Of blood?" she asked, grimacing.

He shrugged. "A stranger on the street, taken quickly, is just a meal. A woman I care for, savored slowly, is a banquet." His gaze moved to the pulse throbbing in the hollow of her throat. "In spite of the slight bitterness in your blood, you, my furry friend, are a feast."

It was the oddest compliment she had ever received but, for all that, Kay felt a faint flush creep up her neck. Lowering her gaze, she buttered the roll and took a bite.

"You're blushing," Gideon said. "Why?"

"Why do you think?"

"If I knew, I wouldn't ask."

At least he wasn't reading her mind. She shook her head, and then she grinned. "No one's ever called me a feast before. It just took me by surprise, that's all."

His gaze moved over her, lingering on her lips, the pulse in her throat. "You are indeed a feast in every way, Kiya Marie Alissano."

Kay was searching for a reply when her dinner came.

Gideon sat back, leaving her to enjoy her meal in silence. She had ordered prime rib—rare and big enough for two— a baked potato, broccoli, and a Coke. He eyed the juice pooled beneath the meat. The color made his mouth water.

She ate with gusto. It was one of the things he liked best about her.

Kay heaved a sigh when she pushed the plate away.

"No seconds tonight?" he asked, grinning.

"Not tonight. I'm stuffed." And then, seeing the dessert cart, she said, "But I think I might have just enough room for a little chocolate mousse."

Noticing that Kay was growing increasingly more with-drawn as they neared their destination, Gideon pulled off the highway. "Are you all right?"

She nodded.

"Are you sure?"

"I just don't want to go home, that's all. I still have a few months of freedom left." It surprised her to find that it wasn't the compound she thought of when she spoke of home, but her apartment back in Custer. Would she ever see it again?

"I thought we agreed that staying with your father was the safest thing to do."

"I know," she said glumly.

"Maybe we could spend a few days somewhere close by," he suggested.

"I'd like that." A sudden smile lit her face. "Bondurant isn't far."

"What's there?"

"Not much. It's just a small community named for the man who established a ranch in Hoback Canyon early in the 1900s. Later, he built a store and a post office. It's a pretty place. Probably not more than a hundred people live there year-round."

"Okay, Bondurant it is."

Kay leaned back against the seat. She loved Bondurant. In years past, she had attended the annual barbeques held in June, and Heritage Days in August. Best of all, the Gros Ventre Wilderness area was close by; remote and relatively unknown, it was one of her favorite places to hunt, second only to the Black Hills.

They reached the town just after midnight. All the houses and businesses were dark save for a quaint bed-and-breakfast at the south end of town. A single light burned in one of the downstairs windows; a small neon sign indicated a vacancy.

Gideon parked the car in the driveway, pulled their suitcases from the trunk, and followed Kay up the steps. A handwritten sign on the front door invited them in.

Gideon hesitated, wondering if a welcome sign from the owners of the house would be invitation enough to allow him inside. He opened the door for Kay, felt a faint shimmer of subdued power when he stepped warily across the threshold.

Inside, he glanced around. A small office was located to the left of the stairway. It was empty. "Nobody here."

"Look." Kay pointed to a wooden sign sitting on a small table. "It says to take the key and check in tomorrow."

"Awfully trusting, aren't they?"

"Well, it's a small town. Not much to steal, I guess."

"Good thing I'm just a vampire and not a thief or a mass murderer," Gideon muttered.

With a shake of her head, Kay plucked the key from the table and started up the stairs.

Gideon trailed behind her, wondering if the owners would be as trusting if they knew a werewolf pack made its home a few miles away.

The room, decorated with antique oak furniture, was large and airy. A king-sized bed occupied a place between two windows that offered views of the distant mountains. Crisp white lace curtains hung at the windows, a wedding ring quilt covered the bed. A Bible and a Wyoming guidebook sat side by side on the four-drawer dresser.

"It's nice, isn't it?" Kay remarked.

Nodding, Gideon dropped their suitcases on the floor. "Are you tired?"

"No, why?"

"Well, we've got a few hours until dawn. I thought maybe we'd go for a walk."

"I know just the place," Kay said. "Just give me a minute to change my clothes and my shoes."

Gideon sat on the end of the bed, his desire quickening while he watched Kay undress. Suddenly, the thought of going for a walk wasn't as appealing as it had been. Scooting back against the headboard, he closed his eyes and took a deep breath, afraid that if he took her in his arms here and now, he would never be able to let her go.

"Are you ready?"

He opened his eyes to see Kay—clad in jeans, sweater, and tennis shoes—standing beside the bed.

She lifted an inquisitive brow. "I thought you wanted to go for a walk."

"Right."

"The river isn't far," Kay said. "And it's beautiful at night."

Hand in hand, they left the house and made their way toward the river. He heard the hushed sound of slowly moving water before he saw the river. As Kay had said, it was beautiful. By moonlight, the river looked almost otherworldly as it meandered between low hills covered with pine trees and the brush-covered riverbank.

"Is it true vampires don't change?" Kay asked after a time. "I mean, do they really stay the same as they were when they were turned?"

Gideon nodded. "Forever the same," he murmured, and couldn't hide the slight note of wistfulness in his voice.

"Hmm." She couldn't imagine what that would be like. Not growing old and sick would be nice, and yet change, whether good or bad, was a part of life. She studied him surreptitiously while they walked, admiring his broad shoulders, the way his jeans clung to his backside, the way the moon's light bathed his long black hair with silver. Lucky for Gideon, that he had been turned while he was still young and virile, a man in the prime of his life, she mused. And lucky for her, too.

"Hmm, what?" he asked.

She shook her head. "Nothing. I was just . . . nothing."

He slid a glance at her, then stooped and picked up a rock. He skipped it across the water, then burst out laughing.

"What's so funny?"

"You are."

Kay sucked in a deep breath, knowing, even before he said anything else, that he had been walking around in her head again.

"So," he drawled, "you think it's lucky that I was turned in my prime?"

"Gideon!"

"Because my—let me put this as delicately as I can—because my backside is so fine?"

"I hate you," she said, between clenched teeth. "I really hate you."

He laughed as he pulled her into his arms. "Doesn't sound

like it to me, not when you think I'm the sexiest man you've ever met."

"Please stay out of my head," she implored. "It's so unfair."

"I know." He cupped her face in his hands. "And I'd be happy to kiss you, right here, right now." No longer laughing, he lowered his head to hers and kissed her deeply, almost desperately. She leaned into him, the lush curves of her body warming his, chasing away every thought but the need to possess her.

It took all of his willpower to let her go, to remind himself that he had brought her here to keep her safe.

"Gideon," she murmured. "Maybe we should go . . ." Her head jerked up when a melancholy howl shattered the quiet of the night.

"You're not afraid of a wolf, are you?" Gideon asked with a teasing grin.

"It's not just any old wolf," Kay said. "It's my father."

Gideon glanced up. A crescent moon hung low in the night sky. "I thought your people only changed when the moon was full?"

"Alphas can change anytime."

"You neglected to mention that little fact," he muttered.

"Did I? A few of the other wolves can also change at will."

"I'm not worried about them," Gideon said with a dismissive wave of his hand. "Do you think your father knows we're here?"

"I don't know." Her gaze swept the hills. "I don't think so. He usually goes out every night about this time and runs the perimeter of our territory."

Another howl rumbled through the night. "So," Gideon said, his gaze sweeping the darkness, "tell me about your old man."

Kay wrapped her arms around her waist and stared into the distance. "What do you want to know?"

Gideon shrugged. "Anything. Everything."

"He's very strict. Very honest. Very Indian. His ties to the past, to the old ways, are strong. There are legends of shape-shifters among our people, tales told around camp-fires late at night."

"Only they aren't legends, are they?"

"Not entirely. It's believed that the first true werewolf was a distant ancestor who was cursed by a witch for killing her pet wolf. Angry and afraid of what he'd become, the young warrior went crazy, killing everything that crossed his path.

"That first werewolf was the son of a Lakota medicine man. The shaman trapped the werewolf, intending to kill it for the good of the tribe, but he couldn't do it. Instead, he tried to remove the witch's curse, and when that failed, the shaman met with the witch and begged her to remove the spell, but she refused. He went to her every day until, after six months, she took pity on the old shaman and altered the curse so that it was only in effect on the night of the full moon."

"Good thing the warrior didn't kill a grizzly bear," Gideon remarked.

"Anyway," Kay went on, "the curse was passed from father to son. Over the centuries, our people learned to control their feral side until, today, we are a relatively civilized race. The Alpha keeps the pack in control. The pack keeps the individual members in line. There's no room in the pack for rogue wolves. They're dangerous to others, and to our existence."

"And the compound is to help keep the pack in line?"

"More or less. We can hunt here, on our land, without fear. Our children are schooled here. They're taught the old ways, the old stories. There was a time when we were a proud people. My father is trying to instill that same sense of pride and honor in our youth. It isn't easy."

"I'm surprised he let you go off on your own."

"I think he was hoping that living on my own would scare me back here, that I wouldn't be able to cope with life in the real world and that I'd come running home. Instead, just the opposite happened. For the first time in my life, I felt like I was where I was supposed to be. I had friends, a job, responsibility. I had the freedom to make my own decisions, my own mistakes."

He mulled that over a moment or two before asking, "So, who are the other wolves that can change at will?"

"My aunt Greta. She's the pack's Alpha female. Victor and his father. Of course, they aren't members of our pack, but allies."

Gideon nodded. "Come on," he said, as another howl filled the air. "Let's get back to our room before we draw a crowd."

Kay didn't argue. Whether she liked it or not, her days of freedom were over.

Chapter 19

Kay sat in front of the TV, though she had no idea what she was watching. Her eyes felt gritty from lack of sleep. All night and into this morning, she had heard her father howling. Had she been able, she would have shifted and gone out to meet him. Her sudden desire to run through the night with him had come as a surprise. Since leaving the pack, she had rarely thought about changing except when the moon was full, but last night, she had wished for the ability to change at will and join her father. Almost, it had felt as though she had the power to call on her wolf if she could only concentrate hard enough, but it was just wishful thinking. Only full-blooded Alphas and those of their bloodline had the power to shift back and forth at will.

She glanced at the bed where Gideon lay sleeping. Gideon had made love to her when they'd returned to the bed-and-breakfast. Never had he caressed her so gently or kissed her so tenderly. He had held her close all night long, kissed her one last time before surrendering to the dawn.

It had felt like good-bye.

With each passing hour, Kay's uneasiness at the thought of returning to the pack grew stronger. What would her parents think when she brought a stranger home? To her knowledge, no one other than her father had ever brought an outsider into their compound—especially someone who was a vampire. Gideon was vulnerable during the day. Was she putting his life in danger by not sending him away?

Her thoughts returned to her father. She had spent a good part of the morning wondering if he had known she was nearby, but if he had known her whereabouts, she was pretty sure he would have been knocking at her door, demanding to know why she hadn't come straight home.

Curling up in a corner of the sofa, she hugged a pillow to her chest. Between her father and the witch, neither her future nor Gideon's seemed very secure.

Gideon woke with the setting of the sun. Sitting up, the first thing he saw was Kay, staring out the window. He didn't have to read her mind to know she was unhappy. He couldn't really blame her. It was hell, being forced to submit to another's will. Thanks to Verah, he knew that firsthand. His only real chance of avoiding the witch was to stay away from Kay. If they separated, Verah would never find him. His problem would be solved. But Kay would still be in danger. And if Kay couldn't or wouldn't tell Verah what she wanted to know, Verah was as likely to kill her as not. And that was a chance he couldn't take.

"Kiya."

She glanced over her shoulder at the sound of his voice.

"Come here, Wolfie."

Turning away from the window, she cocked her head to the side. "Wolfie?"

Shrugging, he held out his arms.

She crawled over the foot of the bed and snuggled up beside him. "Does this mean I can call you Vampy?"

"Honey, you can call me anything you want, as long as you call me."

Kay groaned. "I can't believe you used that old line."

"What can I say, I'm old." He stroked her hair, frowning when she remained silent. He knew what she was thinking because he was thinking the same thing. This was likely the last night they would be alone with each other for a while, perhaps forever.

Kay nibbled on her thumbnail a moment, then said, "Maybe she'll stop looking, after a month or so."

"Maybe."

But Kay would be married before that happened.

Neither of them spoke the words, but the knowledge hung in the air between them.

It didn't take long to pack, and as far as Kay was concerned, it didn't take nearly long enough to drive to the Shadow Pack's compound.

Hoping to delay her reunion with her father for a few more minutes, she said, "Go around to the back."

Gideon sent her a questioning glance but did as she asked. Pulling up alongside a ten-foot-high electrified fence, he switched off the engine, then rested his forearms on the steering wheel.

"Pretty country," he remarked, glancing around. Nothing but trees and hills as far as the eye could see. Tall pines grew close together near the compound, shielding the occupants from casual observers.

"We own several thousand acres of land, but only the compound is fenced," Kay explained. "Ostensibly, the barrier is to keep predators from attacking our stock. In reality, it's to alert the pack to intruders."

She had scarcely finished speaking when Gideon sensed they were no longer alone. Before he could react, he felt the sharp edge of a silver-bladed knife at his throat.

Glancing out of the corner of his eye, Gideon saw a

stocky man standing beside the car door, a man with dark brown hair and yellow eyes that gleamed like molten gold in the moonlight.

"Father!" Kay exclaimed. "What are you doing?"

Gideon went still, his body tense and poised to strike as the blade nicked his flesh. "Maybe we should have called first."

"Shut up, vampire." The Alpha glared at his daughter. "Kiya Marie, why have you brought this bloodsucker to our land?"

"Maybe because his life is in danger for saving mine," Kay snapped.

"Explain," her father said, his voice equally sharp.

"It's a long story," Kay said. "Perhaps we could make our guest comfortable while I tell you."

A muscle throbbed in the Alpha's jaw as he slowly withdrew the blade. "What's your name, vampire?"

"Gideon Marquet."

"I am Russell Alissano, leader of the Shadow Wolf Pack."

"I know who you are." Gideon clenched his hands on the wheel, resisting the urge to wipe away the blood trickling down the side of his neck.

Alissano slid the knife into the sheath on his belt. "Bring your car into the compound, Marquet. Kiya, we'll be waiting for the two of you in the den." His gaze moved from his daughter to Gideon and back again. Then, in a move so quick it would have been little more than a blur of motion to mortal eyes, Alissano sprang over the fence and disappeared into the shadows.

"Well," Gideon drawled, "that went better than I expected."

At Kay's direction, Gideon drove to the front entrance and through the wrought-iron gate that opened onto the compound. He whistled softly as he parked the car. He didn't know what he had expected a werewolf's home to look like, but this wasn't it.

Exiting the vehicle, he looked out over the pack's domain. A large white house—a mansion, actually—dominated a slight rise surrounded by ancient oaks, affording an excellent view of the surrounding area. Below the rise, laid out in a large circle around the mansion, stood a dozen smaller houses painted in a variety of earth tones.

Spread out behind the smaller houses were courts for basketball, volleyball, and shuffleboard, a couple of horseshoe pits, a number of swings, monkey bars, and a sandbox. There was also a baseball diamond, a swimming pool, and a wading pool. Tables, chairs, and chaise lounges were scattered on the deck between the two pools; a built-in brick barbeque was anchored to one side.

A number of old-fashioned Lakota lodges made of buffalo hides, their tops blackened by countless fires, lined one side of the property, along with what he guessed was a sweat lodge.

A large barn painted a traditional red and white stood near the far corner of the property, along with several peeled-pole corrals, three wooden sheds, and what looked like a chicken coop. A faint breeze carried the scent of cows, goats, sheep, horses, pigs, and chickens.

"Home, sweet home," Kay murmured, moving to stand beside him.

"Beats the hell out of Verah's basement," Gideon remarked as he opened the trunk and removed her luggage.

Kay couldn't argue with that. But no matter how lavish the rooms or how kind the guards, a prison was still a prison. And after spending nine months on her own, the compound seemed more like a jail than ever.

Gathering her self-control, she climbed the porch steps, hesitated a moment, then opened the door.

Gideon trailed at her heels, his senses on high alert. He paused outside the front door, repelled by the power of the threshold.

Kay glanced over her shoulder when he didn't follow her inside.

Gideon arched one brow. "Vampire, remember?"

"You really can't come in? I always thought that was just some sort of myth."

"I wish it was."

"What happens when you try?"

"It's like butting my head against a brick wall."

"What happens if someone invites you in and then changes their mind?"

"They can revoke the invitation."

She considered that a moment, then smiled and said, "Gideon Marquet, come in, and welcome."

With a wry grin, he followed her into the house, across a tiled entryway, through a living room decorated in earth tones, and down a wide hallway lined on both sides with family portraits. They passed several closed doors before coming to a den paneled in rich, dark mahogany.

Gideon dropped her suitcase beside the door, then stood there, his arms crossed over his chest as he perused the room.

An antique rolltop desk stood against one wall; a floor-to-ceiling bookcase took up most of another. Four comfortable-looking chairs and a pair of love seats, all covered in a deep red fabric, were clustered together in one corner.

Kay's father sat on one of the love seats, his back erect, his expression shuttered. A pretty woman with light brown hair and vivid blue eyes sat beside him, her hands tightly folded in her lap. Kay's mother, Gideon supposed. A younger woman with the same stocky build and coloring as Kay's father occupied the second love seat; a dark-haired man sat beside her. A tall man with short white-blond hair and pale, close-set brown eyes slouched in one of the chairs, his long legs stretched negligently in front of him.

As soon as Kay entered the room, the brown-haired woman

leaped to her feet and threw her arms around Kay. "Welcome home, Kiya."

"Hello, Mother."

"I've missed you." Kay's mother stood back, her gaze moving over her daughter in a long, assessing glance. "You look well."

"More than well," the young blond male said, rising. "You're even prettier than when you left us."

"Hello, Victor," Kay said, her voice cool.

He stepped toward her, smiling.

When he bent to kiss her, she turned her head to the side so that his lips grazed her cheek.

"Who is this with you?" the stocky woman asked.

"His name is Gideon Marquet, but I'm sure my father has already told you that. What you may not know is that Gideon saved my life, and I saved his. Gideon, this is my aunt Greta, and my uncle Brett. My mother, Dorothy. And Victor Rinaldi."

"Her betrothed." The hostility in Victor's eyes held a silent warning for Gideon to keep his distance.

Dorothy and Victor returned to their seats.

Kay sat on the chair farthest from Victor's.

After a moment, Gideon took the chair beside her, putting himself between Kay and Rinaldi. He grinned inwardly when Rinaldi scowled at him.

"How long do you plan to stay with us, Mr. Marquet?" Kay's mother asked politely.

"I'm not sure."

"My daughter said you saved her life, and she saved yours," Alissano remarked. "I should like to hear that story in more detail, Kiya, if you don't mind."

It wasn't really a request. She took a deep breath and then, never taking her gaze from Gideon, she related the story of how she and Wanda had gone clubbing, how she had been drugged and how, when she came to, she was in Verah's basement. She told her father everything that had happened from that night on, leaving out only the intimate details of the time she had spent with Gideon, the times he had tasted her blood, and she had tasted his.

The room was silent when she finished.

After several moments, the Alpha rose. "You have my thanks, Marquet, for saving my daughter's life and for bringing her safely home, where she belongs. As leader of the Shadow Pack, I grant you leave to stay with us for as long as you wish, with the understanding that you will not try to feed on any of my people. And that, if you hunt in the town, you leave no visible evidence of it."

Gideon inclined his head to show he understood what the Alpha was saying. Or not saying. It was okay to hunt, it was okay to kill, as long as he didn't leave any bodies drained of blood in the gutter.

"Kiya will show you to your room. You have my word that no one here will intrude on you while you are at rest."

"Thank you." Gideon was sure the Alpha meant well, but he had no intention of spending the day inside the compound. He hadn't survived this long by taking his rest among strangers, and he sure as hell didn't intend to start in a den of werewolves.

The Alpha's gaze rested on each one present. "Please let everyone know we have a guest and that he is here with my consent."

Greta, Brett, and Dorothy each bid Gideon good night and left the room. Victor Rinaldi nodded curtly in Gideon's direction, his expression virulent, before following Dorothy out the door.

When the others were gone, Kay's father embraced her. "Rest well, daughter."

"Thank you, Father. Good night."

With a last cautionary glance at Gideon, Alissano quit the room.

Gideon stared after Kay's father. Though no words had been said, the Alpha's message had been clear—leave my daughter alone. Which was pretty much the same message that pompous ass, Rinaldi, had sent him.

Gideon shoved his hands in his pockets. Too bad, fellas, he thought as he followed Kay up the winding staircase, because he had no intention of leaving Kay alone, now or ever.

Kay didn't say anything as she climbed the stairs to the third floor. While she wouldn't call her father's invitation either warm or cordial, at least Gideon had been invited to stay as long as he liked. How long would that be? A day? A week?

She stopped in front of the last door on the left at the end of the corridor. "Here we are."

He gestured at the closed doors up and down the length of the hall. "Are these all bedrooms?"

"Originally, yes, but now my father uses one at the other end of the hall for his workout room. The one across from that is my mother's sewing room. The one next to yours is filled with old furniture and other odds and ends, and the one across the way is another guest room."

"Where do you sleep?"

"Why? Are you going to come visit me in the middle of the night?"

"Probably not a good idea. I don't think your dad misses much."

"Well, if you change your mind, my room's on the second floor, below yours."

"I guess your parents sleep on the second floor, too, don't they?"

"Yes, but at the other end of the hallway. My brother's old room is between theirs and mine."

"Good to know." He brushed a lock of hair behind her ear. "I don't think your father likes me."

"That's okay," she said, opening the bedroom door. "I like you."

Smiling, Gideon wrapped his arm around her waist, drew her into the room, and closed the door. "I'm glad to hear it, because I'm rather fond of you, too."

"Are you?"

He didn't answer. Instead, he lowered his head to hers and kissed her.

Rising on her tiptoes, Kay slid her arms around his neck and kissed him back, her tongue mating with his as he drew her body closer.

Time stopped and nothing seemed to matter but his mouth on hers, his hands moving restlessly over her back. She moaned when he lifted his head, sighed as he rained soft kisses along the length of her neck. Pleasure coursed through her when she felt the brush of his fangs against her skin.

"Gideon . . ."

There was no need to ask what she wanted. Swinging her into his arms he carried her swiftly to the queen-sized bed and lowered her onto the mattress. He was about to stretch out beside her when he heard footsteps in the hallway.

Grabbing Kay by the hand, he pulled her to her feet and straightened her clothes.

A knock at the door was followed by her mother's voice. "Kiya? Are you in there?"

"Yes, Mother. Was there something you wanted?"

"A few minutes of your time, if you don't mind."

Kay glanced at Gideon. "Sorry." She mouthed the word.

"No problem." Bringing her into his room, with her parents in the house, wasn't the smartest thing he had ever done. He had no excuse, except that it was getting harder and harder to keep his hands off of her, to remember that she was "engaged to be engaged" to another man.

He was standing well away from the bed when Kay opened the door. "Thanks for showing me to my room, Kiya. Good night, Mrs. Alissano."

Kay's mother forced a smile. "Good night, Mr. Marquet."

Gideon nodded. First the boyfriend. Then the father. And now the mother, all with the same, unspoken warning in their eyes. *Leave Kiya alone*.

He chuckled softly as he closed the door. Ain't gonna happen, he thought, not in this lifetime, so they'd better get used to it.

Gideon paced the floor while waiting for the people in the house to turn in. It was a nice room. Off-white walls. Good quality beige carpet. A small maple desk and matching chair. Flowered drapes at the single window. A private bathroom with an enclosed tub and shower, a walk-in closet.

Opening his preternatural senses, he listened to the sounds of the house—Kay and her mother getting ready for bed in their rooms downstairs. Kay's father pacing the floor in the den, his footsteps quick and angry.

It was a big house for only three people. Of course, it was more than just a house, it was a symbol of the Alpha's rank.

Moving to the window, Gideon stared into the darkness, his eyes narrowing when he spied a man walking the perimeter of the backyard. Gideon frowned. Was it normal for someone to keep watch at night, or was it because there was an unwanted guest in the house? A closer look told Gideon it was Victor Rinaldi.

Curious, Gideon left the house and made his way into the backyard.

Rinaldi detected his presence almost immediately. "What are you doing out here?" he demanded.

"Just getting some air," Gideon replied mildly. "What are you doing out here?"

"Keeping watch, what else?"

Gideon thought it odd that it was Victor, and not a member of the pack, doing sentry duty. "I'd think that electrified fence would be deterrent enough."

Rinaldi shrugged. "It doesn't pay to let your guard down. I'd think a vampire would know that."

Gideon clenched his hands, annoyed by the man's derogatory tone.

"I don't like the way you look at Kiya," Rinaldi said flatly. "I know the Alpha said you were welcome here, but I think it would be better for everyone if you took off."

"Maybe, but I'm not ready to leave."

"Stay or go, it makes no difference. Just remember that Kiya is mine." There was no mistaking Rinaldi's defensive posture, or the unspoken challenge in his eyes.

"Is that right?" Gideon cocked his head to the side. He had never been able to resist a challenge, and he saw no reason to start now. "What if she changes her mind?"

"That's not going to happen," Rinaldi retorted, bristling.

"Yeah?" Gideon grinned, just to further piss off Rinaldi. "Well, I wouldn't bet on it if I were you."

Chapter 20

Kay woke late after a restless night. Sometime around two in the morning a bad dream had awakened her. Though the details of the nightmare had eluded her on waking, she hadn't wanted to go back to sleep. What she wanted was Gideon, lying beside her, assuring her that everything would be all right.

Slipping out of bed, she had tiptoed up the stairs to his room, only to find his bed empty. Wondering where he had gone had kept her awake until sunrise. She had told herself he had gone hunting, or for a walk, but a nagging voice in the back of her mind kept whispering that he had decided to leave and hadn't wanted to tell her good-bye.

Yawning, she sat up. In the clear light of day, she knew her fears of the night before were groundless. He wouldn't leave without saying good-bye. So, where had he been last night?

Pulling on her bathrobe, she hurried up the stairs and peeked into his room again, unable to stave off a wave of fresh doubts when he wasn't there.

After a long, hot shower, she dressed and went downstairs. To her surprise, she found her mother and father in the kitchen, still at breakfast. Apparently they had also had a late night. She took a moment to study her parents. As usual, her mother was dressed for the day. She wore a neatly pressed blue print shirt, white skirt, and low-heeled shoes. A lacy white apron was tied around her waist. Her father wore a crisp white shirt and gray trousers with a razor-sharp crease. She could never remember her parents taking their breakfast in robes and slippers, not even when she was a little girl on Christmas mornings.

"Good morning," her mother said, smiling. "I was about to make your father another stack of pancakes. Would you like some?"

"Thanks, Mom. Anything I can do to help?"

"No, everything's ready."

"Where's Greta?" Her aunt and uncle often dined with them.

"She's gone into town. Brett went with her."

Nodding, Kay sat down across from her father and reached for the coffeepot. As usual, he had his nose buried in the newspaper, which suited her just fine. She really wasn't in the mood for idle chitchat, not when she was worrying about Gideon's whereabouts.

She sipped at her coffee, which was hot and strong and black, just what she needed to kick-start the day and clear her head.

Her father turned the page. "You were prowling around early this morning," he remarked, glancing at her over the top of the paper. "Is everything all right?"

"Of course. I've been keeping company with a vampire, you know. It'll probably take me a while to adjust my sleeping schedule back to normal."

He regarded her a moment; then, grunting softly, went back to the news.

"Here you go," Dorothy said, placing a plate in front of Kay. "Light brown, covered with butter and powdered sugar, just the way you like them."

"Thanks, Mom." Kay helped herself to several sausage

links and two strips of bacon from the platter in the center of the table.

Laying the paper aside, her father poured syrup over his pancakes. "Dorothy, stop hovering like a bird of prey and sit down. If Kiya wants anything else, she knows where it is."

"Russell, it's her first day back home."

"It's okay, Mom. Dad's right. I'm a big girl now. You shouldn't be waiting on me." Kay turned her attention to her breakfast. Nothing had changed at home, she mused. Her father was still a dictator. She had often wondered why her mother had married him. They had never seemed happy together. There was always a fine edge of tension between the two of them.

Kay ate quickly, then excused herself from the table and left the house by the back door.

Outside, she stood on the patio, one foot tapping impatiently. Her father had been right. She never should have left here. Having enjoyed the freedom to come and go as she pleased, to do what she wished when she wished, she was never going to be happy being under her father's thumb again. And being married to Victor Rinaldi would be even worse. Bad enough to be the Alpha's daughter. Being the wife of a man she couldn't stand would be a million times more terrible. Not to mention the unpleasant prospect of living with Victor's parents, two of the most unlikable people she had ever known, neither of whom was particularly fond of her. But then, she wasn't particularly fond of them, either.

Feeling thoroughly depressed, she made her way to the barn. Twenty minutes later, she was astride her favorite Arab mare, Barika, galloping along the southern fence line that paralleled the grassy banks of a shallow, slow-moving stream.

She loved riding, loved the sense of speed and freedom that it gave her. Loved the feel of the wind in her face. She let Barika run until the mare slowed of her own accord. Pulling up in the shade of an ancient oak, Kay dropped down on her belly and drank from the stream. The water was cold and sweet.

She ground-tied the mare, then stretched out on her back and gazed up at the sky. Puffs of snowy white clouds drifted across the bright blue expanse. A red-tailed hawk floated lazily overhead, its keen eyes scanning the ground for prey.

It was peaceful here, with the stream bubbling happily over the rocks, and the bees buzzing as they flitted among the wildflowers. A warm breeze whispered through the trees and teased the tall grass.

Kay rolled onto her stomach. The only things she had truly missed about this place were her mare, this patch of land, and the serenity it brought her.

She plucked a dandelion and twirled it between her thumb and forefinger, thinking it was kind of sad that she had missed her horse more than her mother and father. She loved her parents, knew they loved her in return, but she hadn't missed their company the way she imagined mortal daughters missed their folks. There had been no chatty letters from home, no weekly phone calls exchanging gossip, no e-mails or text messages. But then, her family wasn't like other families. There were pack rules to follow, secrets that must be kept, and always the awareness of the phases of the lunar cycle, the increasing tension that colored everything as the night of the full moon grew closer.

Her feelings about running wild through the night had always been ambivalent. Chasing through the timbered hills with the pack could be exciting, but it could also be dangerous. From time to time they had encountered others of their kind who were more feral—renegade males who had been cast out of their own packs and wanted to fight for territory. Single males in search of a female. An occasional Alpha who had completely forsaken his humanity and ran with the wild wolves.

Sitting up, Kay stared at the water and wondered yet again

where Gideon was spending the day, and if he dreamed while trapped in the dark sleep of his kind, and how long he would stay here before he grew bored or restless and moved on. And what she would do without him.

There was so much about him she didn't know, yearned to know. He was nothing like she had expected a vampire to be. The werewolves claimed vampires were soulless, bloodsucking monsters with no shred of humanity or decency. But Gideon wasn't like that. Being with him filled her with a sense of belonging that she had never felt here, among her own kind. She had known him only a few short weeks, and yet she not only loved him, she trusted him more than anyone else she knew.

She looked up in surprise when her mother rode into view.

"I thought I'd find you here," Dorothy said. Dismounting, she sat beside Kay. "This was always your favorite place to come when you were unhappy or troubled. Or pouting." She smiled faintly. "Which is it today?"

"None of them. All of them."

"Does it have anything to do with Mr. Marquet?"

Kay glanced away. There were times when her mother was far too perceptive.

"Kiya?"

"It has everything to do with him," Kay admitted. Though it was more than just her feelings for Gideon. She missed her job, missed having her own place. She missed Wanda. Her friend must be wondering what had become of her.

Dorothy rested her forearms on her bent knees, her expression pensive. "It would be better for everyone if he left. You know that, don't you? Vampires and werewolves are natural enemies. His being here puts an emotional strain on all of us."

"If it wasn't for him, I wouldn't be here at all."

"Be that as it may, you must know the two of you have no future together. Your path has already been decided."

Kay crushed the petals of the dandelion, then tossed it away. "What if I don't want to follow that path? What if I don't want to marry Victor and live with his family? What if I want to live my own life, make my own decisions?"

"I'm afraid those choices aren't yours."

"Were they yours? I know you're not happy here." Kay took a deep breath, and then asked the question that had plagued her for years. "Why did you marry my father?"

"We never should have met. Maybe it was fate. Maybe it was just bad luck. What difference does it make now?"

"I'd like to know."

Dorothy gazed into the distance, her expression pensive as she related the story of how she had met Russell.

Kay listened intently, her gaze never leaving her mother's face.

Dorothy paused a moment, her thoughts obviously turned inward as she ran her thumb back and forth over her wedding ring. "It wasn't until a few days after you were born that I found out your father was a werewolf. I'm amazed now that I didn't realize it sooner. Maybe I didn't want to admit it. I don't know if he ever intended to tell me, but one night I went outside for something, I can't remember what, and I saw him change from wolf to human. It terrified me and I ran into the house. I grabbed you and Mark, then ran into the nursery, and locked the door. My fear enraged your father. When he broke down the door, I told him I wanted a divorce, but he just laughed and told me that werewolves mated for life.

"I ran away a few times, but"—she shrugged—"he always came after us. He became even more possessive after Mark died. Then, when he found out you had inherited the wolf gene even though you were part human, I knew there was no chance he would ever let you go. And I couldn't leave without you. You were all I had left."

"So, you just, what? Gave up?"

"You have to understand. I didn't know how being half

werewolf would affect you. It just seemed like you'd be better off here, with those who would understand you, who would be able to help you handle the change when the time came." She sighed again. "Once I resigned myself to staying here, it wasn't so bad." She took Kay's hand and gave it a squeeze. "I had my little girl. I had a lovely home and every luxury imaginable."

"Mom . . ." Kay shook her head. "I don't know what to say, except that I don't want to live your life. Ever."

"I know," Dorothy said sadly. "But I'm afraid you don't have any other choice."

It was near dusk when Kay returned to the house. As soon as she stepped inside the back door, she knew something was up. The house was ablaze with lights. Peeking into the dining room, she saw a number of buffet tables groaning under the weight of numerous large platters of meat and cheese, roast hens, hams and spareribs, and a variety of side dishes. A square table held bottles of wine and champagne, as well as a crystal punch bowl filled with sparkling cider for the kids. A quartet of smaller tables held an assortment of cookies, cakes, pies, muffins, and scones.

Her father met her in the hall. "There you are!" he exclaimed, his voice sharp with impatience. "Hurry and get dressed. We're having a party."

Kay's heart skipped a beat. "What kind of party?" she asked, though she was certain she already knew the answer.

"We're announcing your engagement tonight."

"Don't you think you might have mentioned it to me?"

"I thought it would be a nice surprise," he replied, his voice cool. "Hurry and change. Most of our guests are already here."

"I'm begging you, please don't make me do this."

Her father's eyes narrowed ominously. A muscle throbbed

in his jaw. "I am not going to discuss this with you again, Kiya. My decision stands and will be obeyed. Now go upstairs and make yourself presentable."

She wanted to argue with him, to beg him to reconsider, but there was no changing his mind once it was made up. As Alpha, he held the power of life and death over her and everyone else in the pack. His word was law. Knowing that, she lowered her gaze in surrender. "Yes, sir."

Blinking back hot tears of resentment and frustration, she ran up the back stairs to her room. Mindful of the guests gathered in the dining room, she fought off the urge to slam the door.

A new dress of dark blue silk was laid out on the bed. She stared at it, thinking it should have been black, to match her mood.

Her father had never been one to express his affections openly, yet Kay had always been sure he loved her in his own way, but now . . . she shook her head. If he truly loved her, he wouldn't force her to marry a man she despised. How could he condemn his only daughter to a life without love? It wasn't fair. Worse than that, it just wasn't right. But there was nothing she could do about it.

Forcing everything from her mind, Kay brushed her hair, carefully applied her makeup, put on the blue silk dress, and stepped into the matching heels.

When her father knocked on the door twenty minutes later, she was ready.

"Smile, daughter," he said. "This is a happy occasion."

She didn't reply. And she didn't smile as she followed him down the stairs.

A number of people milled around in the large family room that served as the pack meeting place. Men, women, and children smiled and nodded as she entered the room on her father's arm. Her mother stood between Victor and his parents. There was a smile on her mother's face, but her eyes were sad.

"Welcome!" Alissano said jovially. "As you all know, we're gathered here tonight to celebrate my daughter's betrothal to Victor Rinaldi."

Cheers and applause greeted his announcement.

"Victor, join me, please," Alissano said.

Looking like the cat that ate the canary, feathers and all, Victor strutted forward.

Alissano pulled a diamond-and-ruby ring from his coat pocket. "This ring has been handed down from father to son in my family for generations. Since I have no blood son, I would be honored if you would use it to plight your troth to my only daughter."

"It is I who am honored," Victor said. "I will be proud to call you Father."

Beaming, Alissano handed the ring to Victor.

"Kiya Marie Alissano," Victor said, slipping the ring on her finger, "with this outward symbol of my love, I plight thee my troth."

Kay stared at the ring. It felt like a lead weight on her finger. She flinched when Victor put his arms around her, closed her eyes tightly when he kissed her.

There was more cheering. More applause.

When Kay opened her eyes, the first thing she saw was Gideon standing in the doorway.

Chapter 21

Gideon's first thought was that Kay was the unhappiest looking bride-to-be that he had ever seen. Of course, he hadn't seen that many, but even vampires knew that brides were supposed to have some kind of inner glow. Whatever fire had once burned inside Kay, it had gone out. No surprise, he thought, glancing at the prospective groom. Victor Rinaldi was strutting around the room like the pompous ass he was, grinning as if he had just won the lottery which, in a way, he had. Being married to the daughter of the Shadow Pack's Alpha probably carried a lot of weight within the werewolf community.

Gideon remained where he was as the guests moved into the dining room.

Smiling and nodding at those she passed, Kay made her way toward him.

"Looks like congratulations are in order," Gideon remarked sourly. "Although I must say, I've seen brighter smiles on condemned prisoners."

"They were probably a lot happier than I am," she muttered glumly.

"I might have an answer to your problem."

"Really? I'd love to hear it."

Gideon took a deep breath. "You could marry me instead."

Kay blinked up at him, wondering if she had heard him right.

Gideon rocked back on his heels. "Not such a good idea, I guess."

"No. I mean, I don't know what to say." She shook her head. "Are you serious?"

"Yeah, I'm afraid I am." Looking over Kay's shoulder, he said, "We've got company."

"Kiya," Russell Alissano said, "you can talk to Mr. Marquet later. Your guests are waiting."

"Yes, Father."

"You're welcome to join us for dinner, Mr. Marquet," Alissano said, taking a possessive grip on his daughter's arm.

Kay sent Gideon a pleading glance, then obediently accompanied her father into the dining room.

Gideon waited a moment; then, muttering, "What the hell," he followed Kay and her father.

The dining room was papered in a rich dark red stripe. Long white tapers set in elegant gold wall sconces cast a warm golden glow over the room. A glance through the archway revealed four antique trestle tables laid with crisp damask cloths, delicate china and crystal flutes. These were arranged in a square in the center of the room. The buffet tables against the back wall held enough food to feed a small army. Or maybe just a pack of hungry werewolves, he thought, remembering Kay's prodigious appetite.

A round table covered with crisp white linen stood in the center of the square formed by the other tables. Kay's mother, Greta and Brett, and Victor were seated at this table. A tall austere man and a fair-haired woman sat at Rinaldi's left. Victor's parents, Gideon surmised, noting the resemblance between Victor and the couple.

The invited guests had already been seated. Assuming the entire pack had been invited to the party, Gideon counted twelve couples, three girls who were in their early twenties, and thirteen kids under the age of eighteen. The youngest was perhaps slightly more than a year old. Everyone applauded when Kay and her father entered the room. Bringing up the rear, Gideon took a seat at the far end of one of the long tables. Several of the men cast suspicious looks in his direction.

The Alpha raised his hands for silence. When the applause died down, he smiled expansively. "Once again, I wish to welcome you all here tonight on this joyous occasion. There will be dancing for the adults after dinner, and movies and games for our younger guests. But first, a toast." Lifting his champagne glass, he said, "To my daughter, Kiya Marie, and my future son-in-law, Victor. I wish you both long life and happiness."

Scattered shouts of "Hear, hear" rang out as men, women, and children raised their glasses.

When Victor leaned toward Kay and kissed her, it was all Gideon could do to keep from grabbing the man by the neck and ripping his heart out. The fact that Gideon could sense Kay's revulsion at Victor's touch only made it worse.

He had to get out of there before he did something stupid. Cussing under his breath, Gideon eased away from the table and left the house.

Outside, he stared up at the sky. Here, away from the lights of the city, the star-studded heavens stretched away into infinity. He rarely thought of the past, or dwelled on how many years he had lived as a vampire, or what he had lost when his mortality had been stolen from him.

Until now, mundane things like home and family had seemed insignificant when compared to what he had gained. He liked being a vampire. Living forever, never growing old and feeble, never getting sick, more than made up for whatever he had lost. He reveled in the incredible speed and power of his kind, the ability to read minds, change shape, dissolve into mist, will himself from one place to another. Who would give all that up for a few paltry years of humanity?

Gideon glanced back at the house, which was lit up like a Christmas tree. He could hear the musicians tuning up, the clink of silverware against china, the mingled sounds of conversation and laughter, the aromas of roast beef and fried chicken. With a shake of his head, he admitted he would happily give up the next five hundred years of immortality to spend one human lifetime with Kay.

And even as her name crossed his mind, she was hurrying toward him, throwing her arms around his neck.

He gathered her close, inhaling the fragrance of her hair and skin. The underlying scent of her blood called to him, clouding his senses. "How'd you get away from your guests?"

She shrugged one shoulder. "I said I had to make a trip to the ladies' room." She looked up at him. "Gideon . . . ?"

"I know." Lowering his head, he claimed her mouth with his.

She held nothing back as she returned his kisses, her arms tightening around him as if she would never let go.

"You never gave me an answer to my proposal," he murmured between kisses. "Although I'm guessing it might be yes."

"Yes," she whispered, then shrieked as someone jerked her out of Gideon's arms.

Before Gideon could react, two men wrestled him to the ground, holding him immobile while a third dropped a heavy silver chain across his chest.

Rendered physically powerless, Gideon glared at the man holding tight to Kay's forearm. "Rinaldi." He hissed the word between clenched teeth.

"I told you before, bloodsucker. She's mine."

Kay struggled in Victor's grasp and when he failed to release her, she sank her teeth into his arm.

Grimacing in pain, he slapped her, hard.

A low growl rose in Gideon's throat, but he was helpless to do anything.

"Lock him up," Victor said.

"And then what?" one of the men asked.

Victor shrugged. "Kill him or let him go. I don't care."

"Rinaldi! Damn you!" Gideon stared after the man as he dragged Kay into the darkness. A moment later, he heard the throaty purr of a car's engine, felt his anger and frustration mount as Kay's panicked voice rang out in his mind. *Gideon!*

I'll find you, he promised.

Looking at the trio of burly men staring down at him, he hoped it was a promise he could keep.

"Let me out of here!" Kay shrieked as Victor stuffed her into the trunk of his Lexus and slammed the lid. "Let me out!" She couldn't believe what was happening. She had resisted with all her might, but her struggles had been in vain. Now, with her hands tied behind her back and her ankles lashed together, there was little she could do except scream her outrage. Sadly, there was no one to hear her.

And what of Gideon? Once again, his life was in danger because of her.

Victor drove for what seemed like an eternity. Where was he taking her? What would her father do when he found out Victor had kidnapped her? She frowned as a new thought wormed its way into her mind. What if her father knew that it was Gideon she wanted? Her father's hearing was exceptionally keen. Had he overheard Gideon's proposal? What if it had been her father's idea for Victor to abduct her?

The more she thought about it, the more likely it seemed. Victor didn't have the guts to do something as outrageous as this on his own.

Anger replaced fear as certainty overcame doubt. She knew her father loved Victor like a son, knew that Victor had taken Mark's place in her father's heart. If her father had any weakness, it was his inability to see Victor for what he really was.

She would never forgive her father if he had had any part in this, whether he had planned it, or had merely given Victor his blessing. Never! But what hurt worst of all was realizing that her father cared more for Victor than he did for his own daughter.

That knowledge unleashed the tears she had been holding back. Closing her eyes, she cried herself to sleep.

Gideon glared at his captors as they debated what to do with him. The oldest of the three was in favor of killing him then and there. The other two—younger and less bloodthirsty— opted for letting him go.

Gideon's physical power might be negated by the silver, but he retained enough power to mesmerize those around him. Focusing on the youngest of the bunch, he willed the man to remove the thick chain that held him immobile.

"What the hell are you doing?" the other two men exclaimed in unison.

But the question came too late. As soon as the young man lifted the chain, Gideon dissolved into mist and disappeared from their sight. Had he been in corporeal form, he would have laughed at their startled expressions.

But there was no time for that. It was almost dawn. Leaving his car behind, he sought shelter from the rising sun.

The sudden absence of noise and motion roused Kay from a horrible dream. Forgetting where she was, she sat up. A harsh gasp escaped her lips when she hit the back of her head.

Reality returned with the pain.

She blinked against the early-morning light when Victor opened the trunk. "My father will kill you for this." There was little conviction behind her words; the smug look on Victor's face only served to reinforce her earlier suspicions that her father was behind the whole thing.

Smirking, Victor untied her ankles, then grabbed her around the waist and lifted her, none too gently, out of the trunk and set her on her feet.

Kay glanced around, a groan rising in her throat when she recognized her surroundings. Victor had brought her to his pack's home.

"How long do you intend to keep me here?" she demanded.

"Until we're married and you give me an heir. After that, I don't care what you do, or where you go."

Kay stared at him. Victor had always been concerned with pack politics. As the eldest son of the Green Mountain Pack's Alpha, he was next in line to be pack leader. With Kay as his wife, the bond between the Green Mountain Pack and the Shadow Pack would be solidified. Add a son or daughter who was the grandchild of the two pack Alphas, and Victor's rank would be secure.

"Are you going to keep me tied up until then?" she asked, her voice laced with venom as he dragged her toward the house.

"Maybe. I haven't decided yet."

"I'll never marry you."

"I think you will," he said smugly.

"You can't force me to marry you."

"True enough. But your Alpha can. And will."

Kay's shoulders sagged. Victor was right. As much as she might wish to resist her Alpha's wishes in the matter, she wasn't sure she had either the strength or the courage to do so.

Victor's father was waiting for them when they reached the house. Diego Rinaldi was tall and slim. He wore his brown hair cut short. His eyes, as hard and gray as stone, were cold when he looked at her. His wife stood behind him, her blue eyes worried. Vivian Rinaldi was almost as tall as her husband. She smiled uncertainly as Victor pushed Kay across the threshold.

"The room downstairs has been prepared for her," Diego said. "I'll call Russell and tell him you've arrived safely."

Kay's insides went cold at his words. So, they were all in this together. Knowing it was useless, she sent a mute plea for help in Vivian's direction. The woman managed to look ashamed, but Kay knew she couldn't expect any aid from that direction.

Nodding, Victor tugged on Kay's arm, forcing her to follow him down two flights of stairs and into the cellar. He flicked on the light, revealing a dozen or so wine racks. At the far end of the room, a door stood ajar, revealing another, smaller room.

Victor stopped at the threshold. Jerking her around so that her back was toward him, he untied her hands. "Welcome to your new home," he said, and shoved her inside.

"Wait!" She whirled around, but he had already closed the door. She heard a sharp click as he turned the lock. "Victor!" She pounded on the door. "Victor! Let me out of here!"

Blowing out a breath, she turned around, her gaze moving quickly over the room. Until recently, she guessed it had been used for storage. Now, there was a twin bed covered by a patchwork quilt, a small round table and a ladder-back chair in one corner, a sink and a porta-potty in the other.

Filled with restless energy, she removed her shoes and paced the floor. She had to get out of here before her father showed up with a priest, before she was forced into a marriage she didn't want to a man she loathed. She had no doubt Victor would let her go once she gave him a child; she was just as certain that he would not let the child go with her, thereby keeping her under his thumb, at least until the child was grown.

It sounded all too horribly familiar. Only a short time ago

she had declared that she never wanted to live the way her mother had.

I know, her mother had replied. *But I'm afraid you don't have any other choice.*

Kay shook her head. She refused to believe that. There was always a choice.

Right now, her biggest concern was Gideon. Was he all right? Had her father killed him?

She closed her eyes, searching for him with her mind, but all she found was a dark abyss. "Calm down," she murmured. Pressing one hand to her heart, she fought down her rising panic. The sun was up. He was probably asleep. *Please, Lord, let him be resting.*

Sinking down on the bed, she stared at the ceiling. He had to be all right. The worst times of her life, the best times, had been spent with Gideon. She couldn't lose him now. It didn't matter that he was a vampire and she was a werewolf, or that they were supposed to be enemies, or that she would have to change her lifestyle to be with him. Without Gideon, nothing would ever matter again.

Tears stung her eyes and she blinked them back. She had endured worse than this at Verah's hands and survived. She wouldn't cry, wouldn't give Victor or her father the satisfaction of hearing her beg or seeing her tears. She was the daughter of an Alpha and she would act the part, even if her heart was breaking.

Chapter 22

Gideon woke with the setting of the sun. It was an odd feeling, rising up out of the ground like some resurrected being, but when he was among strangers, there was no safer place to hide from his enemies or from the light of a new day than in the welcoming arms of Mother Earth. Miraculously, the creatures who spent their lives underground avoided him; dirt did not cling to his body or his clothing. When he had first been made, he had spent months trying to figure out why; now, he simply took it for granted, as he did so many of the other supernatural perks that came with being one of the Undead.

Running a hand through his hair, he opened his preternatural senses, searching for his link to Kay.

Gideon?

Her voice rang out in his mind. The relief he felt at hearing it was a palpable thing. *I'm here.*

Thank goodness! I was afraid they'd killed you.

I'm all right, Kiya. Are you?

Yes.

Where are you?

Victor took me home to his pack. I'm his prisoner.

Does your father know?

He was in on it. For all I know, kidnapping me was his

idea. Her father was a smart man. Little escaped his notice. She supposed she shouldn't have been surprised that he knew her well enough to suspect she might try to run away and that he would take measures to ensure that she didn't succeed. One way or another, he always had the last word.

Gideon heard the bitterness in her voice. Well, he couldn't blame her for that. Fathers were supposed to protect their daughters. *What makes you think he was behind it?*

I think he overheard you propose to me. That's the only thing that makes any sense.

Gideon mulled that over for several moments. She was probably right. Like vampires, werewolves were supernatural creatures. No doubt the Alpha's hearing was as acute as his own.

Gideon?

Just sit tight, sweetheart. I'll find you. Finding her would be the easy part. Getting into the home of the Alpha werewolf unobserved and uninvited might prove a little more challenging. It was unlikely that the Green Mountain Alpha would welcome him inside.

Be careful, Gideon. Don't take any . . . oh! Someone's here!

He sensed her trepidation, swore as her voice ended abruptly, breaking their connection. But the blood link remained, as clear and easy to follow as a lighthouse beacon on a cloudy night.

Victor's home place was set in a shallow valley thick with ancient oaks and evergreens. Like the Alissano compound, it was surrounded by an electrified fence.

Instead of a large house set amidst a number of smaller, individual dwellings, there was one main residence flanked by a pair of apartment complexes, each with its own covered patio. This compound also provided outdoor games and a swimming pool.

There were two sentries patrolling the perimeter.

Standing out of sight in the shadows, Gideon timed them as they passed by. The fence wouldn't slow him down. He could take the sentries out before they knew what hit them. Locating Kay would be a snap. It was getting into the house that presented the problem. One way or another, he had to convince someone who lived in the house to invite him inside.

But first, he needed to hunt.

Leaving the compound behind, he sniffed the air. The smell of burning wood and cooked meat drew him into the hills where he found three families—six adults and seven kids— roasting hot dogs over a campfire near a narrow stream.

Smorgasbord, he thought, and settled down to wait for the campers to turn in for the night.

It was well after midnight when Gideon made his way back to the Green Mountain compound. Most of the lights in the house and the apartments were off. Two new sentries patrolled the fence line.

Gideon went suddenly still as a light went on in the main house. A moment later, the back door opened and Victor and his father stepped outside. The two men spoke for a short time, then shed their clothing. The air shimmered around them, followed by a palpable surge of preternatural power.

When it was over, a large black wolf and a pale brown wolf touched noses, then turned and loped across the yard toward the back fence. In unison, they leaped the barrier with effortless grace and disappeared into the night. Moments later, a wolf's howl rang out, and was quickly answered by another wolf, and then another.

Gideon blew out a breath. From the sound of it, the Alphas were running the hills together. For a moment, he was tempted to shift into wolf form and join them, just for the hell of it, but he quickly discarded the idea. With the Green

Mountain Alpha gone, this might be his best chance to get into the house.

Vaulting over the fence, he moved silently through the night, every sense alert. He paused outside the patio door, listening to the hearts beating inside the house. There were three people inside—two females and a male. He recognized the beat of Kay's heart, knew she was asleep. The male was also asleep. The other female—Victor's mother—was awake.

Compelling mortals was generally easy. Members of the supernatural community were more difficult; some, like Alpha werewolves and master vampires, were impossible to influence. Focusing on the female werewolf, he probed her mind, implanting the idea that she wanted to go out into the backyard.

Moments later, he heard the sound of her footsteps coming toward him. The handle was turning when he caught the pungent scent of werewolf on the wind, followed by a howl that was too close for comfort.

Hissing softly, Gideon dissolved into mist. Mere seconds later, three wolves bounded onto the patio and quickly shifted into human form. One of the men was Kay's father. The other was Victor. The third man was Victor's father. Victor and Russell grabbed towels from a nearby shelf to cover their nakedness as the patio door swung open.

"Vivian, is something wrong?" Victor's father asked.

"No, Diego," she answered, sounding confused. "I . . ." She shook her head. "I just had the strangest urge to go outside." She laughed self-consciously. "I don't know what came over me."

"What kind of urge?" Alissano asked sharply.

"I don't know." Vivian shook her head. "I can't explain it. I didn't really want to go outside, but I couldn't seem to stop myself."

Alissano and Diego exchanged glances.

Diego frowned. "You don't think . . . ?"

Alissano nodded, his nostrils flaring as his gaze swept the shadows. "The vampire's been here. Inside, quickly."

Drifting away from the main house, Gideon resumed his own form. Odd, he thought absently, that his clothing changed with him, but the werewolves shed theirs when they shifted.

Cursing the untimely return of the Alphas, Gideon left the compound.

On the other side of the fence, he hunkered down on his heels, brow furrowing as he stared at the main house. He had little doubt about what was going on in there. He could think of only one thing that would bring Alissano to the Green Mountain compound.

Kay's upcoming marriage to the Rinaldi heir.

All he had to do now was figure a way to get her out of there before she became Victor's bride.

Chapter 23

Verah studied the three dwellings clustered inside a high, electrified fence. After much trial and error, she had finally tracked the werewolf girl to this place hidden in the hills of Wyoming. Now, standing in the drifting shadows near the front entrance, she pondered how best to get inside—and out again—without being caught. Vampires could not be compelled; she had no idea if compulsion would be effective on the fanged and furry members of the supernatural community.

Perhaps the best approach would be to wait for everyone to go to bed, then cast an invisibility spell that would allow her to enter the house undetected. Once she found the werewolf, she could try to compel her. If that didn't work . . .

Verah smiled as she patted the hypodermic needle resting inside the left pocket of her traveling cloak. Drugs were an effective backup plan when magic wasn't quite enough.

She glanced down at the black cat circling her ankles. "All we have to do now is wait."

With a throaty purr, Rama stretched out at her feet, tail swishing back and forth.

Gradually, the house's interior lights winked out one by one.

"Now," Verah said. Lifting the cat into her arms, she stroked its head as she chanted softly, invoking an invisibility spell.

When it was complete, she moved toward the front gate, still stroking the cat's head. A second spell disabled the electrical current and unlocked the gate.

Pulling her wand from her pocket, she made her way to the front door. Another quick incantation and the front door opened.

Whispering, "Wait here," she put the cat down. She glanced left and right, then stepped lightly across the threshold.

Her tracking spell had indicated that the werewolf she sought was being held in a cellar or a basement in the nether regions of the house. Following the path the spell revealed, Verah moved unerringly down two flights of stairs. A flick of her wand unlocked the door at the bottom of the steps.

Moving inside, she willed a little power into her wand, which caused the tip to glow, illuminating the room. Frowning, she glanced around. There was no sign of the werewolf, just racks of wine bottles.

Lifting the wand higher, she noticed the door at the far end of the cellar. Another flick of her wand, and the door opened on well-oiled hinges.

The werewolf was on a narrow cot, asleep, her cheeks damp with tears.

All too easy, Verah mused. Moving closer to the bed, she plucked a hair from the werewolf's head and wound it around the end of her wand. Lamenting the fact that it was necessary to shed the invisibility spell to invoke a new one, she murmured softly into the werewolf's ear, planting her compulsion.

For a moment, she thought the spell had failed. But then, moving zombielike, the werewolf girl stood, her eyes open and unfocused.

Smiling, Verah whispered, "Follow me," and led the way out of the house and into the night.

* * *

Gideon leaned forward, his eyes narrowing as the wind shifted, carrying with it a scent he would never forget. Verah. Damn! He had told Kay the witch didn't have the nerve to beard the lion in his den. Just proved how wrong he could be. The witch had to be desperate to risk coming here, and that meant Kay's life was in danger.

With preternatural speed, he was on his feet. He rounded the front corner of the house in time to see Verah step out onto the porch. Kay followed close behind, her movements wooden and unnatural.

Gideon stared at her, his hands clenching when he noticed the glazed look in her eyes. Damn the witch! She had put Kay under some kind of spell.

Muttering, "You can't have her," Gideon flew across the yard. The black cat hissed.

Verah raised her wand and screeched an incantation, but by the time the words had passed her lips, Gideon had wrapped Kay in his arms and vanished from sight.

Verah stood momentarily frozen, like a deer caught in the lights of an oncoming truck. While she was trying to decide what to do next, the porch light came on.

Verah scooped Rama into her arms, intent on hastening away, when she suddenly found herself surrounded by three men with glowing yellow eyes.

Before she could invoke her invisibility spell again, one of the men snatched the wand from her hand, another grabbed Rama by the scruff of the neck, careful to hold the snarling cat at arm's length. The third man sank his teeth into Verah's neck.

Standing in the shadows a safe distance from the house, with Kay cradled tightly against his chest, Gideon watched it all happen.

At the werewolf's bite, the witch went limp as a rag doll, offering no resistance as the werewolf dragged her into the house. The other two men followed. The last one inside slammed the door.

Gideon glanced at the sky. Dawn was only minutes away. With that in mind, he summoned his power and willed himself and Kay to his lair in Arizona. He figured they would be safe there, at least for now, what with Verah being held by Victor's family. He would have much preferred his lair in New York, but the sun was already shining there.

Moments later, Gideon sat on the sofa in the living room of his Phoenix lair with Kay still cradled in his arms. Kissing the top of her head, he whispered her name.

She didn't stir, simply stared blankly into the distance.

"Kiya!" He shook her shoulder. "Dammit, Kiya, snap out of it!"

Still nothing.

He tried speaking to her mind, but it was closed to him.

Gideon cursed softly. The sun was rising. There was nothing he could do until nightfall.

Carrying Kay into the bedroom, he tucked her under the covers, removed his shoes, socks, pants, and shirt, and crawled into bed beside her.

His eyelids grew heavy as the sun rose over the horizon. He hated to leave her lying there, staring up at the ceiling, but there was no help for it. The darkness was wrapping him in its snare, dragging him down into oblivion.

Gideon woke with the setting of the sun. Jackknifing into a sitting position, he looked at Kay, hoping to find her sleeping peacefully. Instead, she was lying rigid beside him, still staring blankly at the ceiling. If not for the faint rise and fall of her chest and the slow, steady beat of her heart, he would have thought her dead.

Pressing a kiss to her cheek, he went into the bathroom. He took a quick shower, dressed, and left the apartment.

What he needed now was a witch. Easier said than done, he mused. Where the hell was he going to find a witch? A good witch, he amended.

He mesmerized the first man he saw, borrowed the man's cell phone, and did a quick search for practicing witches. He hadn't actually expected to find one, but, to his surprise, he found one listed in Apache Junction, Arizona, by the name of Kusuma Ila. Of course, there was no guarantee that she was a genuine witch and not just some deluded old woman who read tea leaves. But it was the only lead he had.

After returning the man's phone and wiping the incident from his mind, Gideon transported himself to Apache Junction.

He hadn't been there in decades. It was an old town bordered by the Superstition Mountains on the east, the Goldfield Mountains on the north, and the town of Mesa on the right.

Even at night, the Superstition Mountains, well-known as the home of the fabled Lost Dutchman Gold Mine, were an impressive sight. Goldfield Ghost Town nestled near the western face of the mountains. On more than one occasion, Gideon had seen the ghosts of an old prospector and his mule walking through the town.

Kusuma Ila's small, square house was located on a quiet residential street, literally the last place he would have expected to find an Apache witch. Dozens of rosebushes grew in wild profusion along a white picket fence. An ancient cottonwood tree shaded the front porch.

She answered the door before he knocked. As soon as she saw him, she made some kind of intricate sign with the fingers of her right hand, no doubt meant to ward off evil.

"Kusuma Ila?" She was a hundred if she was a day, Gideon thought, with skin as brown and wrinkled as old saddle leather. Her hair, worn in a long braid over her shoulder, was snow white; her eyes were deep-set, as black and sharp as those of a raven. She sure as hell looked like a witch.

She tilted her head to one side. "Have you come to drink my blood?"

"Do I look hungry?"

She grinned. "My blood is so old, one taste and you would spit it out."

"Keep your blood, old woman. It's your professional help I need."

She studied him for several moments, then stepped back. "Come in, nightwalker."

In spite of the old woman's invitation, Gideon felt the threshold's resistance as he stepped across it. It was, he thought, a sign of the witch's power.

The handkerchief-sized living room was crowded with a curved sofa, a round coffee table, an end table with a wrought-iron lamp, and a well-used rocking chair. A crooked shelf held a turtle rattle, a length of braided rope, a turquoise rock, and what looked like the bleached skull of a cat. Every surface was piled high with old newspapers and magazines. A battered bookshelf was stuffed with paperback books, mostly mysteries. A deer head was mounted over the sofa. A pretty yellow canary occupied a white wicker cage in one corner. Two black cats were curled up beside the rocker.

The witch cleared off a section of the sofa and gestured for Gideon to sit down. When he was seated, she lowered herself into the rocking chair. "What brings you here?"

"My woman is under some sort of enchantment cast by another witch. I want to know if you can break it."

"What kind of enchantment?"

"She doesn't respond to anything. It's like she's asleep with her eyes open."

Kusuma Ila nodded as she rocked back and forth. "It is a simple spell, easily undone."

"That's great. Can you come now?"

"No. You must bring her here. I did not live to be an old woman by taking foolish chances, or visiting the lairs of nightwalkers after dark."

Gideon chuckled. "Right," he said, liking her humor and her forthright attitude. "Is now a good time?"

She nodded. "I will be here."

"I'll be back in a few minutes." Since the witch knew what he was, Gideon didn't see any reason to hide his powers from her.

A thought took him back to his place. Kay was as he had left her.

He lifted her gently into his arms, then willed himself back to Kusuma Ila's crowded house.

If the old woman was startled by his abrupt reappearance in her living room, it didn't show on her weathered countenance. "Put her on the sofa."

Gideon did as she instructed.

Rising, the witch hobbled toward the sofa. "Who did this to her?"

"A witch named Verah."

"Ah."

"You know her?"

Kusuma Ila nodded. "I know of her. Nothing good."

"I can believe that," he muttered darkly.

Kusuma Ila nodded to herself, then left the room. She returned a moment later bearing a wooden bowl, an eagle feather, a book of matches, and a small bag. She set the bowl on the coffee table, opened the bag, and poured the contents into the bowl. After striking a match, she set the bowl's contents on fire. Blue smoke rose in the air, and with it the scents of sage and sweetgrass.

Murmuring softly in what Gideon assumed was Apache, Kusuma Ila waved the eagle feather over the bowl, drawing the smoke toward Kay. Gradually, the old woman's chanting grew louder, stronger. This went on for several minutes.

Gideon stood near Kay's head. His hands clenched into fists as the old witch's power filled the room. He could feel it pushing against him, moving over his skin like an invisible hand. It didn't hurt, but it made the hair on his arms stand at attention.

With a sharp cry, Kusuma Ila dropped the feather on the table, then clapped her hands together three times.

Gideon swore in amazement when Kay blinked, gasped, and then sat up, her expression bemused as she glanced around. "What happened?" She looked up at Gideon. "Where are we?"

Taking her hand in his, he gave it a squeeze. "I'll tell you all about it later. Kusuma Ila, thank you. What can I give you in return?"

"The wand of the witch who enchanted your woman."

"That might not be so easy to obtain. If I can't get her wand, would you settle for a broom?"

Kusuma Ila lifted one brow, apparently not amused by his reference to witches and their ubiquitous brooms. "It is the wand or nothing."

"And if I can't get it?"

"Do not worry," Kusuma Ila said with a wave of her hand. "If you cannot, you cannot. No harm will befall you, or your woman."

"I'll do my best to get it," Gideon promised.

"That is all I ask. *Yadalanh,* nightwalker."

"Until we meet again, old one," Gideon replied.

He took Kay to his lair in New York.

"So," she said when they were safely curled up on the sofa in his apartment. "What happened? Who was that old woman? How did I get there? And why can't I remember?"

"Slow down, darlin'. One question at a time. Verah managed to get inside Victor's house. I saw her coming out.

Apparently she put some sort of spell on you. It left you like a . . . I don't know, like a zombie, I guess. You didn't talk. You didn't blink. I took you to my lair in Phoenix, then went looking for a witch to see if she could break the spell. And she did."

Kay digested what he had told her, her brow furrowed thoughtfully. "All I remember is going to sleep at Victor's, and then waking up in that old woman's house."

She frowned. All hell must be breaking loose back home. Victor was probably furious. Her father, too. They were no doubt scouring the countryside looking for her. She didn't want to think about what would happen if they found her. For a moment, the thought frightened her, and then anger took over. If anyone should be furious, it was her! She had been kidnapped, thrown in a trunk, and locked in a cellar. Enough was enough.

"Kiya? Are you all right?"

"What? Oh, of course. How on earth did you find a witch?"

"The Yellow Pages," Gideon said, laughing.

"You're kidding!"

"Nope. Just looked under 'Witches,' and there she was. The only one in the book."

"That's amazing. I never knew witches advertised." Kay shook her head. "After our experience with Verah, I'm surprised you went looking for another one."

"You were under a witch's spell. I didn't know any other way to break it."

"So," she asked after a moment, "where's Verah now?"

"Your future father-in-law has her."

"I feel sorry for her, then. Victor's father hates witches even more than he hates vampires."

"How the devil can you feel sorry for her?" Gideon shook his head in disbelief. "Verah would have killed you in a heartbeat and dragged me back to her torture chamber if she'd had the chance. I hope to hell he kills her. That's the only way you'll ever be safe."

"Hey!" she admonished as his eyes went red, "don't go all vampire on me, okay?"

He took several deep breaths. "Sorry." Gathering her into his arms, Gideon kissed her cheek. "I proposed to you a while back. And if I remember correctly, you said yes. You haven't changed your mind, have you?"

With a sigh, she snuggled against him. "No way."

"So, what do you say, Wolfie? Should we go find a justice of the peace and tie the knot?"

"I say the sooner, the better, Vampy." She refused to think about her parents. No doubt they would be angry and upset. Well, turnabout was fair play. Besides, she was too excited at the prospect of marrying Gideon to worry about the consequences now.

"Tomorrow night?" he asked.

"Tomorrow night sounds perfect." She glanced at her wrinkled blue dress, noting the grease spot on the hem, then burst out laughing. "But first I need something to wear."

Chapter 24

Kay wandered through Gideon's apartment, too restless to sit still, too excited at the thought of becoming his wife to think about anything else. Mrs. Gideon Marquet. Kiya Marie Marquet. She giggled, thinking that if she was still in high school, she would be drawing red hearts around her name and Gideon's on her notebook.

Around noon, hunger drove her into the den. Earlier, she had found a note advising her that he had gone shopping while she slept, and that she would find bread and doughnuts in the den, milk and sandwich makings in the refrigerator.

Now, she stood in front of the small refrigerator, reluctant to open the door. What if it was also filled with bags of fresh blood? She wasn't really squeamish; she killed rabbits and deer on a regular basis, but dining on blood in bags? It was just too creepy. Taking a deep breath, she opened the door, relieved that the only items in the fridge were a quart of milk, a package of cheese, and three kinds of deli meat.

She ate three doughnuts—two chocolate, and one chocolate buttermilk—as well as a ham and cheese sandwich, then washed it all down with milk straight from the carton, since Gideon didn't keep any dishes or glassware in the apartment.

Time and again, she tiptoed into the bedroom just to look at him. He was gorgeous, like an enchanted prince condemned to live only by night. She grinned as her imagination took flight. He was the prince and she was the princess; only, in her fairy tale, it was the kiss of the princess that brought the prince to life.

The day dragged on. And on. She switched on the TV, flipped through the channels, and turned it off.

Finally, about four o'clock, she went into the bedroom and crawled into bed beside Gideon. Resting her head on his shoulder, she closed her eyes. And fell asleep, content at last.

Gideon woke with the soft, round curves of Kay's body pressed close to his side, one of her legs lying across his, her breath warm on his neck, her hair like silk against his shoulder. He lay there, unmoving, basking in her nearness. Until Kay entered his life, he had never fallen asleep with a woman in his bed, nor wakened to find one beside him. It was a rare pleasure, and a sign of his complete trust in her that he allowed her to know where he took his rest.

Tonight, she would be his bride. The thought made him smile. He had never expected to marry anyone, let alone a werewolf. He chuckled softly. A strange union, that, vampire wed to werewolf, monster to monster.

"What's so funny?" she asked, nudging him in the side.

"We are."

Kay raised up on her elbow and stared down at him. "Why do you say that?" she asked, looking offended.

"You don't find it amusing, a marriage between a vampire and a werewolf?"

"No. I find it . . . strangely romantic."

"*Strange* is the word, all right."

"Well, I'm sorry you feel that way." Scooting to the far side of the bed, she sat up, her arms folded over her breasts. "Maybe you'd like to call the wedding off."

"Hey, Wolfie, I didn't mean to hurt your feelings. But, come on, have you ever heard of a vampire and a werewolf getting hitched? It's like a cat marrying a mouse, or a lion falling in love with a lamb."

"Well, when you put it that way, I guess it is unusual."

In a blur of movement, he was beside her, his arm stealing around her waist, drawing her back down on the mattress beside him. "You don't want to fight on our wedding night, do you?"

His hand slid under the slip she had worn to bed, caressing her thigh, sliding up and down in long, sensual strokes that made her toes curl and her stomach clench with pleasure.

"Kiya?"

"No." She gasped as his hand moved to her belly. "I don't want to fight. But I still need something to wear."

"Women," he muttered good-naturedly. "All they think about are clothes."

"And chocolate," she said. "And right now, I need both."

"Here." Quitting the bed, Gideon pulled a pair of sweats and a T-shirt from his closet and tossed them to her.

Kay looked at him, one brow raised. "This is getting to be a habit," she muttered darkly.

He shrugged one shoulder. "Well, you could go out as you are. You look mighty fetching in that slip. Of course, people are likely to stare."

With an incredulous shake of her head, Kay turned her back to him, yanked the slip over her head, and pulled on the sweatpants and T-shirt. Both were miles too big. Sometime in the near future, she was going to buy a few outfits and leave changes of clothes in each of his lairs.

"I just hope you don't expect me to wear your shoes," she muttered irritably.

"Don't worry, Wolfie," he said, stifling a grin. "Your feet won't touch the ground."

He was as good as his word. Sweeping her into his arms, he transported them to the sidewalk in front of Bloomingdale's.

Kay didn't know whether to blush or laugh when he carried her up to the third floor. One of the salesclerks— ever polite no matter the circumstances—came forward. She tsked softly as she noted Kay's outfit. "My dear, I can see that you need help immediately."

"You have no idea," Kay said, squirming in Gideon's arms. "Gideon, put me down."

He lowered her to her feet—her bare feet—and bowed from the waist. "I'm going downstairs. I'll meet you back up here in, what? An hour?"

"At least," the saleswoman said emphatically.

Gideon had been waiting about ten minutes past the agreed upon hour when Kay finally emerged from the dressing room wearing a clingy pink sweater and a pair of slinky black pants. Sometime during her shopping spree, she had bought a pair of shoes. He paid the bill, then picked up two large brown bags. "Ready?"

A smile twitched the corners of her mouth. "Aren't you going to carry me home?"

Gideon glanced at the numerous shoppers milling around, several of whom were glancing surreptitiously in their direction. "Not right now."

Their next stop was the wedding salon on the eighth floor of Macy's, where Kay bought the first gown she tried on. White heels and a shoulder-length veil came next and she was ready to go in less than twenty minutes.

Gideon shook his head as they left the store. "It took you over an hour to pick out some jeans and sweaters, and less than thirty minutes to buy a wedding dress?"

"I loved the first one I tried on. What was the point in going through a dozen more?"

"None, I guess. Next stop, Las Vegas."

Kay knew she looked like a tourist, but she couldn't help staring as Gideon led the way toward one of the casinos. She had heard about Vegas; she had seen pictures online and on TV and in movies, but the real thing was amazing. Cars, taxis, campers, and RVs crowded the streets; the sidewalks were thronged with people, many of them tipsy, and all of them apparently having the time of their lives. She saw men and women in shorts and flip-flops, men in suits and ties, women in dresses and heels, and everything in between.

The hotel lobby was lavishly appointed. Imported carpets muted her footsteps. Sofas and chairs covered in plush velvet vied for space with low tables, potted palm trees, and exotic statues. The whole place reeked of opulent decadence.

The clerk at the desk informed Gideon that there were no vacancies; nevertheless, five minutes later they were checking into a luxury suite on the top floor.

"How did you do that?" Kay asked. "He said every room was either booked or reserved."

"A little mind control, that's all."

"That's all," she muttered under her breath. "Just a little mind control." With a shake of her head, she draped her wedding gown over the back of a chair. "Now what?"

"We need to get to the marriage license bureau over on Clark."

"I didn't even think about a license," Kay said, glancing at her watch. "Isn't the office closed by now? It's after nine."

"Honey, everything is open late in Vegas, including the license bureau. They call New York the city that never sleeps, but the title really belongs to Vegas. Are you ready? Then let's go."

Getting a license was remarkably easy. No blood tests were required. Since Kay didn't have any identification with her, Gideon performed another bit of mind magic to convince the clerk that he had seen her ID. Gideon showed the man his driver's license, handed over sixty dollars cash, and the clerk handed them a marriage license good for one year from the date of issue.

"I wish I had that mind control thing," Kay remarked when they returned to their room.

"Comes in handy, that's for sure."

Kay kicked off her shoes. "Since there's no hurry, I'm going to take a shower."

"Okay."

"Did you buy something to wear to the wedding?"

"Of course," he said with a wink. "What do you think's in that garment bag hanging on the door?"

She smiled at him as she picked up her wedding gown and headed for the bedroom. "I won't be long."

Gideon dropped into an overstuffed chair and stretched his legs out in front of him. In his mind's eye, he pictured Kay in the bedroom, getting undressed, stepping into the shower. If it hadn't been so late, he would have joined her, but there wasn't time, not if they were going to be married tonight. It was already after eleven. And he wanted to spend as much time as possible with his new bride before the sun came up.

Just when he was about to go in and tell her to get a move on, she stepped out of the bedroom. Gideon whistled softly. If she had tried on a hundred dresses, she couldn't have chosen a better one. The neckline was square, the skirt long and full and sprinkled with rhinestones that reflected the light when she moved. In all his life, he had never seen anything more beautiful than Kay in her wedding gown. She wore her hair down; it fell over her shoulders like a river of ebony silk beneath the shoulder-length veil.

"Thank you," she murmured, pleased by the open admiration in his eyes.

"Thank *you*." Grabbing the garment bag that held his tux, he went into the bedroom and closed the door.

Kay paced the floor, thoughts sifting through her mind like sand in an hourglass. She was going to marry Gideon. Sooner or later, her father would find out. What would he say? Worse, what would he do? Was she making a mistake? Or would this act of defiance convince her father once and for all that she had a mind and will of her own?

Her troublesome thoughts came to an abrupt halt when Gideon stepped out of the bedroom. The well-cut black jacket and trousers emphasized his broad shoulders and long legs. The coat and pants fit him as though they had been hand-tailored. No doubt about it, he had been born to wear a tux. She grinned inwardly. She could hardly wait to get him out of it!

After a quick check on Gideon's cell phone, they decided to get married in the Victorian Chapel at the Chapel of the Flowers. The room was adorned with bronze-colored velvet draperies, crystal chandeliers, beige marble floors, and mahogany pews.

The ceremony was traditional, yet Kay was sure she had never heard more beautiful words in her life as she promised to be Gideon's lawfully wedded wife, to love him for richer, for poorer, in sickness and in health, for as long as she lived.

She felt a moment of regret when it came time to exchange rings, because they didn't have any. But, to her surprise, Gideon pulled a thick gold band from his pants' pocket and slipped it on her finger.

A moment later, she was his lawfully wedded wife, for better or worse.

Murmuring, "I'll love you forever," he drew her into his embrace and kissed her, a long, lingering kiss filled with the promise of eternity.

Swinging Kay into his arms, Gideon unlocked the door to their hotel suite and carried her over the threshold.

"Alone at last," he murmured as he slowly lowered her feet to the floor. His body reacted as expected at her nearness. "So, Mrs. Marquet," he drawled. "What would you like to do now?"

"Gosh, I don't know," she said, trying not to laugh. "Maybe paint my nails or wash my hair?"

He lifted one brow, his hands sliding up and down her sides, his palms skimming her breasts. "Now, tell me what you really want, wife."

"You," she said, all humor gone. "Here, now. Inside me."

"No sooner said than done," he replied, and in an instant, she was lying in bed beside him, with nothing between them but desire as he kissed and caressed every inch of her, from the top of her head to the soles of her feet.

She moaned in an agony of wanting, sighed as he rose over her, his dark eyes alight with an inner fire as his body blended into hers, two incomplete halves now and forever one.

Just when she thought it couldn't get any better, she felt his fangs at her throat. A mere taste was all he took and yet it amplified her pleasure a hundredfold. Each touch was like silken fire on her skin, each caress unlike any that had come before. She knew what he wanted, what he needed, even as he knew how to please her. Each kiss, each bold stroke carried her past pleasure, past bliss, to nirvana. She held him close, closer, her nails raking his back.

She cried his name as ripples of ecstasy shuddered through her, leaving her sated and spent and complete as never before.

Holding Kay against him, Gideon rolled onto his side, carrying her with him, holding her close while their breathing returned to normal and their bodies cooled. He had been alone for centuries but now, seeing the love in Kay's eyes, he knew that whatever the future held for the two of them, he would never be alone again.

Chapter 25

Jaw clenched, his thoughts churning with malice, Victor Rinaldi paced up and down the length of the driveway. Try as they might, threaten as they would, the witch refused to tell him or his father why she had been in the compound, who had taken Kiya, or where they might have gone.

Kiya. Damn the girl. She was more trouble than she was worth. Almost. If she wasn't an integral part of his plans, he would consider himself well rid of her. But marrying the Shadow Pack heir was the only way to assure a lasting bond between the two packs. The only way he could one day take over leadership of Alissano's pack, and his own, as well.

He slammed his fist against a tree. He was tired of being a civilized werewolf, tired of hiding his true nature, tired of pretending he was content to hunt rabbits and deer when he hungered for human flesh, thirsted for human blood.

The Alpha of the Shadow Pack and his own Alpha had grown soft, almost as if they had forgotten that werewolves were superior to all other forms of life. In the old days, were-wolves had been feared, and rightly so. The ancients had sacrificed their young to his kind—the loss of a few to save the many. But in this time and place, humankind no longer believed in the supernatural. Of course, the fault didn't just lie with the werewolves. Vampires and witches had also disguised their true natures, walking undetected among mortals, lulling humankind into a false sense of security.

He had never understood why. There wasn't a werewolf, vampire, or a witch alive who wasn't smarter, faster, or more powerful than any human who had ever walked the earth, and yet the whole supernatural community pretended to be what they weren't.

But he intended to change all that. It would take a little time, a little patience, and a good deal of planning, but he would do it, or die trying. Once Kiya was his wife and her pack had accepted him as one of their own, he would arrange for her and her father to meet with an unfortunate, fatal accident, at which time he would step in and assume the role of Alpha. And then, after a suitable amount of time, he would dispatch his own father and in so doing, become Alpha of both packs. United under one leader, they would be invincible. Other packs would follow his lead and his kind would take their rightful place in the world.

He smiled as he envisioned the kind of life he yearned for. When he was Alpha, he would claim the woman he truly desired. Selene was a full-blooded werewolf, far more suited to be his mate than Alissano's half-breed daughter. With Selene at his side, he and his kind would be able to live the life they were meant to live. Humans would quickly learn they were no longer at the top of the food chain.

But first, he had to find a way to make that damn witch tell him what she knew.

Verah stood against the wall, her hands bound behind her back, her expression impassive as the Alpha's son strutted back and forth in front of her.

She had been stunned by their ability to render her powerless. How had they known that binding her hands with rope braided with sprigs of rowan would negate her powers? She had spent hours turning it over in her mind, finally concluding that being supernatural creatures with weaknesses of their own, they had most likely studied the strengths and weaknesses of vampires and witches, searching for ways to subdue their enemies for just such an occasion as this.

Few people these days were aware that rowan wood had often been used by druids for staves. Its branches had been used by people of old for dowsing rods and magic wands. Some believed rowan protected homes from lightning; others held to the belief that it could keep the dead from rising. An ancient legend claimed the Devil had hanged his mother from a rowan tree.

Verah yawned in the boy's face when he threatened her life again. Insolent pup, she thought scornfully, so full of himself, so certain he had the upper hand.

Which, at the moment, he did. But she was counting on the fact that he needed her alive to obtain what he desired.

Face mottled with rage, he slapped her, once, twice, three times. The sound of his hand striking her echoed like gunshots off the stone walls.

"There will be no food for you, no water, no rest, until you answer my questions!"

Cheeks burning from the force of his blows, she shook her head and repeated the answer that had made him so angry. "I cannot help you."

He could threaten her until he was blue in the face, beat her until she was too weak to stand, but she would never tell him what he wanted to know. She needed the werewolf girl for her own ends. As for the son of the Green Mountain Pack's Alpha, he could go straight to hell. And when she escaped from this place, as she surely would, she intended to send him there.

He stared at her for several minutes, his frustration a

palpable presence in the room, and then he spun on his heel and stormed out the door.

Verah exhaled a sigh of relief. Yesterday, he had quizzed and questioned her for hours.

Grateful for a reprieve, she was about to sink down on the floor when the door flew open and her tormentor stepped inside carrying a covered box.

Verah gasped when Victor removed the cover, revealing a cat carrier.

Rama meowed loudly when he saw his mistress.

"You will tell me what I want to know, now," Victor said, "or I will slit the cat's throat and drink its blood."

Chapter 26

It was midafternoon when Kay woke. Happiness welled inside her when she saw Gideon sleeping beside her. So, it hadn't been a dream, after all. She was really Gideon's wife and nothing would ever be the same again.

Last night had been beyond wonderful, beyond anything she had ever imagined. She glanced at her watch, willing the hours and minutes until nightfall to pass quickly so she could be in her husband's arms again, taste his kisses, feel the hard masculine length of his amazing body pressed intimately against her own. Who would have thought that a chance meeting in the most unlikely of places would turn out so well? Or that a half-breed werewolf would fall hopelessly, helplessly, in love with a centuries-old vampire? Or that she could be this happy?

Or this hungry.

She kissed Gideon on the cheek, then slid out of bed. Closing the door behind her, she padded naked and barefooted into the living room and called room service. Certain that she would need all her strength for another bout of lovemaking with Gideon when he awoke, she ordered the biggest breakfast the hotel had to offer, then sat back, wriggling her feet in the thick carpet and smiling as she anticipated the night to come.

After breakfast, she dressed and went downstairs to try her hand at the slot machines. Vegas in the daytime wasn't nearly as bright, loud, crowded, or exciting as it was after dark.

She exchanged a fifty-dollar bill for fifty-dollar tokens, then found a vacant seat in front of one of the slot machines.

It was fun at first, but after half an hour or so, she found herself constantly checking the time. Even winning a small jackpot didn't really take her mind off Gideon. She wished he was there beside her. It would be much more fun to win if Gideon was there to share the moment with her.

After scooping her change into a handy cup, she tried her hand at blackjack but quickly grew bored with that, as well.

Leaving the casino floor, she strolled through the gift shops. Lots of salt-and-pepper shakers, shot glasses, and T-shirts with Vegas logos.

She ate a quick dinner, then returned to the room, thinking that spending the day with a sleeping husband was better than anything Vegas had to offer.

Gideon woke to the feel of a warm, deliciously naked, feminine form pressed close to his side. Eyes still closed, he slid his arm around her waist, felt his body come alive as Kay leaned up on one elbow and kissed him, lightly at first, and then with growing intensity.

With a low growl, he flipped her onto her back and straddled her hips, his body holding hers in place, one of his hands trapping both of hers above her head.

She fluttered her eyelashes at him, a seductive smile curving her lips.

"Didn't your father ever tell you that it isn't safe to wake a sleeping vampire?"

"Actually, the subject never came up," she replied with a saucy grin. "Although I see something else has sprung to life."

Gideon grinned back at her. "Nice of you to notice." He lifted a lock of her hair and let it slide through his fingers. And then he frowned. "What did you do today?"

"Nothing much. I went down to the casino for a little while, but it wasn't any fun without you."

"Do you think that was wise?"

She shrugged. "No one knows we're here. And I can't just sit around and watch TV all day, you know. I had to do something to pass the time waiting for you to wake up."

"Impatient are you, Wolfie?"

"Of course not!" she replied, as if that were the most ridiculous thing she had ever heard. "I was just bored."

"Oh, well, if that's all it is, I'm sure I can think of something to arouse your interest for the next ten or twelve hours."

"Really?" She slipped one hand from his and trailed her fingertips over his chest. "What did you have in mind?"

"Oh, a little of this . . ." Leaning down, he kissed her, his tongue teasing hers. "A little of that." He nuzzled the valley between her breasts, then moved to the soft sweet spot beneath her ear.

Writhing beneath him, she murmured, "I'd like a little more of that."

Chuckling, he ran his tongue along the side of her neck, then grazed her skin with his fangs.

"More." She cupped the back of his head in her hands, holding him in place as she turned her head to the side. "Do it," she urged. "Bite me."

There was no way to resist, not when he could hear the way her heartbeat accelerated, the whisper of her life's blood flowing hot and sweet through her veins.

She moaned softly as his bite coincided with the joining

of his body to hers. Her hands moved restlessly up and down his back as pleasure upon pleasure swept through her.

There was a dull roaring in her ears that gradually morphed into the sound of someone pounding on the door. Confused, she looked at Gideon.

His expression brought her quickly back to reality. Springing from the bed, he hissed, "Your father is here. And he's not alone. Victor and his father are with him."

Jackknifing into a sitting position, Kay grabbed the bed-spread and wrapped it around her, toga-style. "How did they find us?"

"Verah." He swore under his breath.

"Why would she tell them . . . ? Oh."

Gideon nodded. Verah wanted his blood. Victor wanted Kay.

There was another knock on the door, louder this time. "What'll we do?" Kay asked, her gaze darting around the room.

"Get the hell out here."

He reached for her hand as the door burst open. Russell, and Victor and Diego Rinaldi, rushed into the room.

With a savage howl, Russell grabbed hold of Kay's arm and wrenched her away from Gideon.

Victor brandished a stake, his lips pulled back in a feral grin. His father, looking wary, held a bottle of what Gideon assumed was holy water.

Gideon glared at the three men. He had never run from a fight. He could have killed them all, but how could he de-stroy Kay's father with her standing there, watching?

"Gideon, get out of here!" Kay hollered, tugging against her father's hold. "Go! Now."

He stared at her for stretched seconds; then, muttering a sharp oath, he dissolved into mist and vanished from sight.

Victor took a step toward her, his face mottled with rage. "You little whore. . . ."

"Shut up, Victor! That's my daughter you're talking to."

Victor closed his mouth with an audible snap, but he continued to glare at Kay, his eyes filled with contempt.

Russell glanced around the room, noting Gideon's clothes folded over the chair, his daughter's clothing scattered on the floor, the bed rumpled, the sheets smelling of sex. "What have you done?"

Kay lifted one shoulder and let it fall. "I'd think the answer should be obvious."

Without warning, her father slapped her, a single, stinging blow.

She reeled backward, her hand flying to her cheek, her eyes watering from the pain. But it was the disdain in her father's eyes, the fact that he had actually struck her, that hurt the most.

"Victor, Diego, wait in the other room. Kiya, get dressed."

She held her ground, waiting for her father to leave.

Russell shook his head, then moved to stand in front of the window, his back toward her. "You've defied me for the last time, daughter," he said, his voice cold and without affection. "Get dressed."

Kay's hands were shaking as she pulled on a pair of jeans and a sweater. Never in all her life had she been so humiliated, or seen her father so angry. Sitting on the bed to put on her shoes, she wondered how far Gideon had gone. And when, if ever, she would see him again.

Gideon hovered outside the Shadow Pack's compound, invisible to human—and werewolf—eyes. He had dissolved into mist on leaving Kay, had followed her and the werewolves when they left the hotel. A taxi had awaited the four of them at the curb. It had been easy to stow away in the trunk.

The cab had stopped a short time later at a local airport, where Kay's father had ushered her and the others into a private plane. Victor and his father, both silent on the ride to the airport, remained subdued as Kay's father took the controls and taxied down the runway.

It had been an odd experience, taking to the air in a plane when he wasn't in corporeal form. The flight from Vegas to a small landing strip outside the Pack's compound had taken little more than an hour. He had stowed away in the trunk of the waiting car, only to be jerked out of it when the car passed through the gate in the fence. Someone—Kay's father, no doubt—had rescinded Gideon's invitation, rendering it impossible for him to cross the fence line.

A minor setback. He had more pressing needs at the moment; namely, to obtain something to wear. And something to eat. Not necessarily in that order.

When he returned, he would open the mind link between himself and Kay and let her know he was nearby.

And God help Russell Alissano if the man laid so much as a finger on Kay again.

Kay felt like a condemned felon as her father escorted her to one of the tiny rooms in the basement. They were little more than cells, really, a place where he confined new wolves who were having difficulty making the transition, or wolves who wantonly disobeyed pack rules. She supposed she fit the latter category.

Sitting on the narrow cot, with her knees drawn up to her chin, she stared at the wall. She had been locked up three times in a remarkably short period—first by Verah, then by Victor, and now by her father—and she was getting mighty damn sick of it. She was on her honeymoon, for crying out loud. She should be with Gideon, not locked up like a common criminal.

She growled low in her throat when she recalled the way Victor had looked at her, as if she was some kind of whore.

Where did he get off judging her when he had kidnapped her? She frowned, certain he wouldn't have dared such a thing without her father's approval. And just as certain that her father had given it.

As if conjured by the thought, the door opened and her father stepped into the room.

One look at his face, and she went cold all over. She had only seen that expression once before, when he had sentenced a rogue werewolf to death.

He closed the door behind him. "We need to talk."

Those four words always meant bad news. Unable to help herself, she began to tremble.

"You have defied me at every turn. You have humiliated me in front of our people, and what's worse, in front of the Green Mountain Pack."

She stared at him, her mouth dry, her palms damp. She would have been less frightened if he had slapped her or yelled at her. Anything would be better than his soft words, the quiet menace in his eyes.

"You ran away with that bloodsucker, and then you shamed yourself, and me, by sleeping with him."

"We . . . we're . . ." She took a deep breath; then, hoping the truth would make him think better of her, she said, "We're married."

"I guess you've forgotten that marriages performed outside the pack aren't valid. In nine days, the moon will be full. You will wed Victor at that time."

Gathering her courage, she said, "Father, I'm begging you, please don't make me do this."

He squared his shoulders, his hands clenching at his sides, his expression implacable. He wasn't her father now, but her Alpha. "If you openly defy me again, Kiya Marie, I will have no choice but to sentence you to death. Do you understand?"

She nodded, unable to speak past the thick lump in her throat.

"I have rescinded the vampire's invitation. He will no longer be able to enter the compound or any of the houses inside the fence. Nor will anyone else be able to invite him in. If I see him again, I will destroy him." He fixed her with a hard stare. "I am aware of his ability to communicate with you telepathically. If he contacts you, you will tell me immediately. Is that clear?"

Kay bit down on her lower lip.

"Is that clear?" the Alpha repeated, his warning as sharp and clear as glass.

She nodded. It was hard to lie while meeting her Alpha's gaze, but Kay knew she would die before she betrayed Gideon into her father's hands.

Chapter 27

Verah glared at the Alpha's son. "I gave you the information you desired. Alissano has the girl. Now, let me go."

Victor shook his head. "Not yet."

"What more do you want from me?" she asked impatiently.

"I find I rather like having a witch at my disposal. I have plans for the future and it occurs to me that, with your help, I'll be able to achieve them much faster."

"And if I refuse, will you threaten my familiar again?" She shook her head. "You can only play that card so many times."

He scowled. She was smarter than he gave her credit for. "Perhaps we can strike a deal."

"What do you have to offer?"

"What do you want?"

She held out her bound hands. "My freedom."

Victor made a dismissive gesture with his hand. "What else?"

"I need the vampire that accompanies the girl." She was addicted to his blood, not only the vile taste of it, but its effect on her health and outward appearance. Vanity might be a sin, but she didn't care. She had always been proud of her fine, clear skin, her thick pale blond hair, the slender figure that growing old had stolen from her.

Victor frowned. "What possible use can you have for a bloodsucker?"

"My reasons are my own." And they grew more urgent with every passing day. "I need the girl for bait."

"That's why you broke into the house?" Victor exclaimed. "You were looking for Kiya?"

Verah nodded. "If I have the girl, I'll have the vampire, as well." And she needed him desperately. She didn't have to see her reflection in a mirror to know that she was growing older, more feeble, more hideous, with every passing day. Her ugliness was evident in the revulsion in the boy's eyes every time he looked at her.

Victor frowned thoughtfully, then nodded. "Agreed, but with one condition."

"I'm listening."

"Once you have the vampire, I want you to kill the girl."

"My pleasure."

Victor grinned. "There's just one other condition. The girl must live long enough to give me an heir. Until then, you'll remain here."

"No!" she shrieked. "I need the bloodsucker now!"

"That's my deal, witch. Take it or leave it."

She hissed at him, but in the end, she knew she had no other choice. Forcing a smile, she said, "I'll take it."

"Make that two conditions," Victor decided.

"What else do you want?" She hissed the words at him.

"Tell me why you need the vampire."

"I need his blood."

"Very funny," he muttered, then frowned thoughtfully. "You're serious, aren't you?"

She didn't answer, just glared at him.

With a shake of his head, the Alpha's son left the basement.

"You'll rue the day you were born," Verah murmured. "When I am free, you will curse the man who spawned you and the woman who gave you life."

Chapter 28

Kay sat on the edge of her bed, staring at nothing. She was, for all intents and purposes, a prisoner in her own home. She wasn't allowed to leave the house. There was a guard outside her bedroom window, and another at her door. She was never alone, except in her room. She supposed she should be grateful her father hadn't left her in the dungeon, but at a time like this, it was hard to summon any feelings of gratitude.

At her father's request, Victor had moved into the house. If her father hoped that spending more time in Victor's company would make her care for him, he had been badly mistaken. The more she saw him, the more she despised him. He was a vain and selfish man. And he was hiding something; she was sure of it. Why couldn't her father see that?

Not only was she forced to endure Victor's company at mealtimes, but her father insisted she remain downstairs on those nights when he called the pack together, whether it was for a movie night or to discuss pack business.

Victor, who had always been arrogant, grew more so with every passing day. And the days leading up to her wedding were passing far too quickly.

She had never been more miserable in her whole life, not even when she'd been locked up in Verah's basement.

She spoke only when spoken to. On the few occasions when she was given a choice, she opted to stay in her bedroom, preferring her own company to that of her parents, members of the pack, and most especially Victor Rinaldi. The thought of being his wife, of having to bear him a child, made her physically ill. She longed for someone to talk to, a girlfriend she could confide in. For the first time, she realized she had no close friends within the pack. And even as she wondered why, she knew it was because she was the Alpha's daughter and that her standing placed an invisible gulf between her and everyone else.

The only bright spot in her life came late at night, when Gideon opened the blood bond between them and spoke to her mind, promising her that, somehow, he would get her safely away, assuring her that he loved her, would always love her.

But the days hurried by, one after another, and all too soon, eight days had passed. She was in tears when Gideon opened the link between them the night before she was to marry Victor.

He didn't have to ask what was wrong. *We still have time,* he said.

She shook her head. *I'm to be married tomorrow afternoon.*

Gideon swore a vile oath. He should have expected that her father would arrange for the wedding to take place during the day, thereby assuring that Gideon couldn't crash the wedding and steal the bride. Hardly necessary, since Alissano had revoked his invitation. Damn the man.

Tomorrow night, the pack will run, and I'll have no choice but to run with them. And then . . . she couldn't say the words, not even in her mind.

Jealousy sprouted like a noxious weed in Gideon's soul as

he imagined Victor and Kay running side by side through the night, mating under the light of the full moon. The sound of her tears was like a stake through his heart.

I'll think of something, he promised, and hoped to hell he could keep his word.

Filled with impotent rage and a bitter sense of helplessness, Gideon stalked the dark streets of Jackson. Anger and frustration fired his hunger and he attacked the first man he saw. He felt a rush of guilt for the brutal way he assaulted his prey. Usually, he spoke to their minds, telling them not to be afraid, assuring his prey that he meant them no harm. But not tonight. Tonight, he was the monster of myth and legend, a predator without equal, without mercy, who took what he wanted, what he needed, with no regard for the mortal he preyed upon.

It was only when the man's heartbeat grew slow and erratic, when his eyes rolled back in his head, that Gideon came to himself.

Tamping down his anger, Gideon ripped into his own flesh and let a few drops of his blood drip into the man's mouth. Dammit, he had almost killed the guy.

As color returned to the man's cheeks, Gideon spoke to his mind, erasing the horror of what had happened before sending the dazed mortal on his way.

Gideon stared at his wrist, watched the edges of the ragged wound knit together, leaving no trace of injury. He shook his head. He couldn't remember the last time he had given in to the lust for blood. He didn't count the years he had spent locked up in Verah's basement. The women and occasional men he had preyed on back then had been a matter of survival. The people the witch had brought to him were fated to die, either at his hands or by slowly starving to death, since the witch had never seen fit to feed any of them.

Gideon shoved his hands into his pants pockets. He regretted taking those lives, but like every other creature on the planet, he had a strong sense of self-preservation. Given the same choice, he knew he would do it all again.

Moving silently through the drifting shadows of the night, he thought about the lives he had taken in the last 360 years.

In the beginning, he had kept track of every kill. He had hated himself for what he was, for the lives he had taken to sustain his own. But, as he'd told Kay, as time went on, he had learned to control his hunger. He had discovered that he could enjoy the thrill of the hunt and satisfy his thirst without sacrificing a life.

Gideon glanced around. Without noticing it, he had made his way back to the Alissano compound. He opened his senses, searching for Kay. She was in her room, asleep. A young male werewolf stood guard outside her door. Another paced restlessly below her window.

Gideon raked a hand through his hair. He couldn't get into the main house, or even inside the perimeter fence. Alissano had made sure of that. Of course, he could try a little mind control on the werewolf standing guard below Kay's window, but even if he managed to get inside the fence, the odds of compelling one of the werewolves inside the house were slim, since Gideon was certain that Alissano would have chosen men with strong powers of resistance to guard his daughter.

So, getting inside the Alissano house was not an option, at least not for him. But what if someone else could get inside the Alissano residence, stop the wedding, and steal the bride away? Even if Gideon couldn't have her for himself, he might be able to arrange it so she didn't have to marry that ass, Victor Rinaldi, or spend the rest of her life in servitude to a man she hated, forced to submit her will to that of another.

Gideon scrubbed a hand across his jaw. He knew just the person he needed. Someone who would be willing to spirit Kay away if the price was right.

Gideon stared at the single drop of dried crimson on his wrist. His blood, he mused. It was a small price to pay for Kay's safety.

All he had to do now was figure out how to free Verah and then persuade her to do what he wanted before it was too late.

Shit. Who was he kidding? His odds of getting inside the Rinaldi compound weren't any better than his odds of getting into Alissano's.

Her wedding day. Kay stared at her reflection in the mirror. She recalled Gideon remarking that she was the most unhappy-looking bride he had ever seen. He should see her now, she thought glumly. She looked even worse, if that was possible. There were dark shadows under her eyes, caused by a week of restless days and sleepless nights.

Her stomach growled loudly, a reminder that she had refused breakfast and lunch; but how could she be expected to have a hearty appetite on this, the worst day of her life?

There was a knock at the door, and then her mother peeked inside. "Kiya, you're not even dressed yet!" Dorothy entered the room, a frown creasing her brow. "You need to hurry. The ceremony starts in thirty minutes."

"Mom, can't you get me out of this?"

"I'm afraid not." Dorothy removed Kay's gown from the hanger. It was long and white, simple in cut and design, with a floor-length veil. "Keeping your father waiting will only make things worse."

"How could they possibly be worse?" Kay muttered. She pulled the gown over her head, then turned her back so her mother could fasten the long row of cloth-covered buttons.

She didn't know who had chosen the dress. She didn't care. "My father is forcing me to marry a man I despise with no regard for the fact that I'm already married to someone else. Someone I love. Someone I will always love."

"You may come to love Victor."

Kay snorted. "That will never happen! He's nothing but an arrogant ass."

Dorothy released an aggrieved sigh, then squared her shoulders. "Kiya, we don't have time for this. I knew it was a mistake for Russell to let you leave the pack. Now, brush your hair and put on your shoes and your veil. Your father will be here in a few minutes."

Kay stared at her mother, shocked as much by her words as the tone of her voice. Blinking back her tears, she ran a brush through her hair, set the veil in place, stepped into her satin pumps, then sat on the edge of the bed, her hands folded tightly in her lap.

Dorothy moved toward the door. Pausing, she glanced over her shoulder. "And try to smile."

Kay shook her head after her mother left the room. Smile, ha. What did she have to smile about?

All too soon, her father knocked on the door. "Kiya?"

"Come in."

His gaze swept over her. No doubt to make sure she was presentable. It didn't matter that he was forcing her to marry a man she despised. No, what mattered was that she make a good impression on the pack.

Stubbornly refusing to take his hand, she swept out of the room, her head held high.

She stopped outside the dining room, where the wedding was to take place. Fresh flowers, candles, and a long white runner made the room look more like a chapel than a place to eat. The tables, laid with a variety of cold cuts and cheese, had been pushed against the walls to make room for a piano. A woman Kay didn't recognize played softly. The invited guests were seated, chatting quietly. A white arch stood at the far end of the room. Victor waited beneath it. Her mother and Victor's parents occupied the front row, along with Aunt Greta and Uncle Brett.

Kay flinched when her father came up behind her. "Ready, daughter?"

"I will never be ready."

Taking her hand firmly in his, he said, "We will proceed, nevertheless." At his nod, the piano player began to play the wedding march. The guests rose and faced the aisle. All of them smiled at Kay as she passed by, except for Selene Thomas, who glowered at her.

Before Kay could wonder at the woman's sour look, they reached the arch. Her father placed her hand in Victor's, then took a step forward and turned to face them.

"As Alpha of the Shadow Pack, I hereby dissolve my daughter's previous union to one not of our blood or our faith. With that matter no longer an issue, and with the authority that is mine by right of blood, I now give my daughter, Kiya Marie Alissano, to Victor Rinaldi, to be his life mate according to the laws and dictates of our pack. Victor, do you swear to honor and protect this woman and no other all the days of your life?"

"I do."

"Kiya Marie, do you promise to honor and obey this man and no other all the days of your life?"

She stared at her father, silently begging him to end this before it was too late. He stared back at her, a silent warning in his eyes, a muscle twitching in his jaw.

Kay yearned to say no, would have said no but for the sure knowledge that defying her Alpha now would be the last thing she ever did.

His eyes narrowed ominously at her silence. "Daughter?"

His power rolled over her. When she spoke, the words that passed her lips were a barely audible "I do."

Her father smiled faintly. "By my authority, I now pronounce you, Kiya Marie Alissano and Victor Rinaldi, lifemated." His smile widened. "Victor, you may kiss your bride."

With a triumphant grin, Victor pulled her into his arms and kissed her, his lips grinding into hers.

"As is our custom," Russell said, "the pack will celebrate this union with a hunt as soon as the moon rises. Until then, help yourselves to food and drink."

As a dutiful husband, Victor brought Kay a plate and a glass of wine even though she had no appetite for either.

For the next three hours, Kay pasted a smile on her face and pretended she was having a good time. She endured the hugs of her pack mates. She accepted gifts and good wishes and bawdy advice. She dutifully danced with her father, then with Victor, then with Victor's father, and Greta's husband.

She listened to one story after another about the joys of wedded life and what to expect on her wedding night. Considering that she had already been married, she thought giving her marital advice was beyond peculiar, but no one mentioned her former marriage.

When the sun began to set, the guests departed to their own homes to get ready for the coming hunt.

Kay glared at Victor when he followed her to her room. "Where do you think you're going?"

"You're my wife now," he said smugly. "Where you go, I go."

"Not until our marriage is consummated," she reminded him, and shut the door in his face.

No sooner had she done so than she heard Gideon's voice in her mind.

Are you all right?

Yes, for now.

A pause. *Has he . . . have the two of you . . . ?*

Not yet. It's customary for newlyweds to break off from the others during the hunt, and . . . and . . . you know.

In wolf form?

Yes, the first time. She frowned when Gideon withdrew from her.

He returned a moment later. *If you can get away from him, I'll meet you in the woods.*

I'll try, but I don't think they'll leave me alone. I've got to go. My mother's calling.

Look for me.

"Kiya?"

"Come in."

Dorothy entered the room. "Your father sent me to look for you. Everyone is ready to go. I thought maybe . . ." She glanced around the room. "Where's Victor?"

"I sent him away so I could get changed."

"You sent him away?" Dorothy frowned.

"Yes." Kay turned her back to her mother. "Could you help me out of this dress?"

"Of course, but . . . Kiya, you're married now. Victor should be doing this."

"I'm not comfortable with him."

With a sigh of exasperation, Dorothy unfastened the long row of buttons.

Kay let the gown fall to the floor, then stepped out of it. She quickly removed her shoes and underwear and then, before her mother could ask any more questions she didn't want to answer, she shifted into her wolf form and padded out of the room.

The pack was gathered on the patio. In spite of the fact that her father had forced her into a marriage she didn't want, Kay couldn't deny the heady rush of excitement at the thought of running through the woods with the pack.

Her exhilaration faded when Victor trotted up to stand beside her.

Kay glanced at her mother, who was standing in the patio doorway. What did her mother think when the pack went hunting and she was left home alone? Was she happy to have a few hours to herself? Or envious because she couldn't join them?

The pack waited restlessly for her father to give the signal. Sensing their eagerness to run, he lifted his head and let out a howl, then loped across the yard and jumped effortlessly over the fence.

The pack followed hard on his heels, their yips and barks of excitement filling the air as they followed their Alpha.

Kay hung back, hoping Victor would go on without her. She should have known better. He stuck to her side like a dark shadow, while her aunt brought up the rear.

Sailing over the fence, Kay forgot, momentarily, how unhappy she was, forgot everything but the damp feel of the earth beneath her feet, the touch of the wind in her face, the myriad scents that assailed her nostrils as she ran. It was always a bit of a surprise, how much she loved being in her wolf form, how different the world looked through her wolf eyes. Everything was magnified. She tasted the wind on her tongue, smelled a rabbit cowering in its hole, heard a deer bounding through the underbrush, the fluttering of an owl's wings as it hunted prey of its own. Was it this way for Gideon, too? Did he revel in his power?

In her wolf form, it was sometimes easy to forget her human half. Sometimes she wished she could remain a wolf forever. Life was so much simpler for wolves. They didn't have to worry about the mundane things that occupied human minds.

Flushed from its hiding place, a jackrabbit darted in front of her. With an excited bark, Kay gave chase, quickly leaving her aunt and Victor behind.

There was a crunch of bones as Kay's jaws closed around the rabbit's neck, a warm rush of blood down her throat. She growled when Victor nosed her kill, snapped at him when he didn't back away quickly enough.

The rabbit was hers, and she wasn't sharing.

He wisely took the hint and backed off.

Minutes later, she was running again.

The pack was scattered now. She heard their barks and howls as they brought down prey.

She ran toward them, her instincts telling her to seek out the pack. There was safety there. Victor trailed behind her, and Greta behind him. Kay ran faster, faster, darting right and left, her need to lose him stronger than her need to reach the rest of the pack.

She paused when she came to a stream. Lowering her head, she drank deeply, then shook her head, washing the rabbit's blood from her muzzle.

When she looked up, a large, muscular, black wolf stood on the other side of the stream, staring at her.

She recognized him immediately. Gideon. Would their blood link work now, when neither of them was in human form? Only one way to find out. *Gideon?*

Yep. He turned in a slow circle. *How do I look, Wolfie?*

Very handsome.

He grinned a wolfish grin. *So, what do you say we lose those two?*

How?

Follow me.

Without a backward glance, Kay bounded after Gideon, splashing through the water, leaping over a low bush, ducking through a hole in a tangle of berry vines, racing up a low hill and over the other side.

When she reached the bottom of the slope, Gideon was standing there in human form, naked. She had scarcely come to a stop when he scooped her into his arms. Holding her close, he transported the two of them to the room he had secured for them in the bed-and-breakfast in Bondurant.

As soon as he put her down, she shifted to human form. And smiled at him. "That was brilliant."

"I thought so." His gaze moved over her, lingering on the swell of her breasts, her flat belly and long, shapely legs. She was slim without being skinny, curvy in all the right places.

And married to another man. He wasn't sure how he felt about that. But she had been his wife first.

"Gideon?"

He shook his head as he reached for her. "I'm not sure where we stand, so you'll have to tell me."

"In my heart and soul, you're still my husband, and always will be."

"That's good enough for me," he said, and kissed her.

Kay wrapped her arms around him and held him close. She didn't care what the consequences would be, so long as she could spend a few minutes with Gideon. No matter how long she lived, no matter if she was forced to live with Victor for the rest of her life, she could endure it as long as Gideon loved her.

Lifting her into his arms, he carried her to the bed and laid her gently on it. Stretching out beside her, he kissed and caressed his way from the hollow of her throat to the tip of her toes. Drowning in pleasure, she writhed beneath him and when she couldn't wait a moment longer, she straddled his hips, sighing with pleasure as his body became one with hers. She threw her head back, basking in the wonder of their love, the sense of belonging she had found in this man's arms and nowhere else.

Gideon stroked Kay's hair. He would have to take her back soon. Now that he was thinking more clearly, he wondered if whisking her away had been a good idea.

"How much trouble have I just caused you by luring you away from the pack?" he asked.

"I don't know," she said. "I don't care."

But he heard the worry beneath the bravado. He should never have brought her here. As long as Victor held Verah prisoner, the werewolves would always be able to find Kay. It was only a matter of time. He swore under his breath. The witch could be tracking them even now. And when Victor found Kay, there were sure to be repercussions.

He brushed a kiss across her cheek. "I'd better take you back."

"Not yet."

"I've been thinking. Sooner or later, Victor is bound to release Verah. When he does, I'll talk to her, maybe strike a deal with her."

"What kind of deal?" Kay asked, although she was sure she already knew what he was thinking.

He shrugged. "What difference does it make if I can convince her to stop following you?"

Kay sat up, one brow raised in disbelief. "Tell me you're kidding."

He shook his head.

"There's only one thing she wants from you. . . . No! I won't have it. You're not putting yourself in that creature's power for my sake."

"It seems a better alternative than knowing you're married to someone else."

"Oh, Gideon." Blinking back her tears, she flung her arms around him. "How could you even consider such a thing after what she put you through?"

He shrugged. "Three years isn't much when you've got eternity. I'd give her thirty years rather than see you unhappy, or married to a man you don't love."

She rained butterfly kisses on his cheeks, his nose, his brow. "I love you, Gideon, only you, and no one else, ever. Please don't ever surrender yourself to that witch for my sake. Promise me! I couldn't live with myself if that happened."

"I promise, darlin', unless the choice is you or me." If he was lucky, Verah would accept his promise that he would supply her with blood as long as she didn't reveal Kay's whereabouts to her family or Victor.

Kay hugged him tighter. He was, she thought, the bravest, most gallant man she had ever known. It was beyond comprehension that he would even think of contacting Verah . . . and even as the witch's name crossed her mind, the bedroom door slammed open and Victor, his father, and Aaron, one of Victor's pack mates, burst into the room. Looking past them, Kay saw Verah standing in the doorway. The witch was shrouded in a long black cloak, the hood pulled forward, her hands bound behind her back. Damn the woman. This was the second time in a matter of days that the witch had led Victor to her.

Before Kay could move or speak, Diego Rinaldi flung a pail of water at Gideon, then tossed the bucket aside. Victor and Aaron grabbed his ankles while Diego bound his feet together with a length of silver chain.

Kay gasped as the stench of burning flesh reached her nostrils. It took her a moment to realize the bucket had contained holy water. She stared in horror as the skin on Gideon's face, chest, and belly reddened and began to blister.

Diego pulled the spread from the foot of the bed and thrust it into her hands. "Cover yourself!"

She did so without thinking, her gaze focused on Gideon. He lay on his back on the mattress, unable to move, while Victor and Aaron sliced into his flesh. The knives left no lasting wounds, though she knew the cuts were painful. But it was the blood loss that concerned her more. Every drop they spilled made him weaker.

Screaming, "Stop it!" she hurled herself at Victor, driving him away from the bed.

He threw her off with ease, and when she would have attacked him again, Diego Rinaldi grabbed her arm, holding her in place, so that she could only watch in horror as the sheets on the bed ran red with Gideon's blood.

"All right," Diego said, "that's enough. Get her out of here while we clean up the mess."

"Don't kill him!" Kay cried. "Please, Victor, don't kill him. I'll do anything you want."

"Anything?" he asked.

"Yes, I swear it."

"Kiya, no!"

Victor backhanded Gideon across the face. "Shut up, bloodsucker!"

"Kill him," Diego said. "He is going to be nothing but trouble otherwise."

"No!" Kay dropped to her knees in front of Victor. "Please spare him."

Victor glanced briefly at Verah, and then at his father. "It might be wise to keep him alive for a little while."

Diego looked thoughtful, then nodded. As long as they had the vampire, the girl would do as she was told.

"We'll take the vampire to Alissano's. I don't think it's a good idea to have the bloodsucker under our roof," Diego said. "Take your bride and go home. I'll let Russell know she's all right."

With a nod, Victor grasped Kay's arm and yanked her to her feet. She glanced over her shoulder for one last look at Gideon before Victor dragged her out of the room.

Smiling, the witch followed them out the door.

Chapter 29

Kay stood in the middle of Victor's bedroom, holding tight to the bedspread while she tried not to gag as he ran his hands up and down her arms.

"It's time to fulfill your wifely duties," he said with a leer.

"Couldn't we wait until tomorrow night?"

"Oh, we'll do it tomorrow night, too, never fear. But tonight I intend to wipe the memory of that bloodsucker from your mind."

"That will never happen."

"No?" His eyes narrowed angrily. "You promised you'd do anything, remember?" He held out his hand. "Have you forgotten I hold the vampire's life in the palm of my hand? Give me a child, and the bloodsucker lives. Refuse me"—he made a tight fist—"and he dies. The sun is lethal to vampires. I wonder, do they burst into flames immediately, or do they die slowly, the flesh melting from their bones, the bones turning to ash? Either way, I'm sure the pain is excruciating."

"Stop it!" Still clutching the bedspread, she pressed her hands over her ears in an effort to block Victor's words and the horrific images they had conjured in her mind.

"You promised to do anything to save him," Victor reminded her again. "Did you mean it or not?"

"I meant it," she said, and squeezed her eyes shut as he ripped the bedspread from her grasp.

Later that night, after forcing Kay to fulfill her wifely duties, Victor went down to the basement.

The witch stood in her usual place in the corner of the room, the hood of her long black cloak pulled forward, her face shadowed in its folds.

Victor was grateful he couldn't see the witch clearly. In the days since they had captured her, she had grown increasingly hideous to look at, her skin wrinkling and shrinking, her back hunching over, her arms and hands looking more skeletal than human. He wondered, without really caring, how much longer she could cling to life.

"You did well, tonight," he said, "so I've brought you something. A reward for services rendered." Reaching into his pants pocket, he withdrew a clear bottle filled with dark red fluid. He hadn't brought it as recompense for her help, but simply out of curiosity. Why would anybody want vampire blood?

The witch's eyes glowed as she hobbled toward him, her bound hands outstretched. "Give it to me!"

Victor watched as she quickly uncapped the bottle and drained half the contents.

He stared at her in astonishment. He had never known anyone to drink vampire blood.

He was about to turn away when something remarkable happened. In moments, the ugly old hag was gone and a beautiful young woman stood in her place.

Victor shook his head, amazed by the transformation. Her skin was clear and unblemished, her eyes bright, her lips full and tempting, her hair a fall of gleaming pale gold silk. Shrugging out of her heavy black cloak, she let it fall to the floor, revealing a lush figure that was every man's dream. He fought down the urge to strip her of her clothing and take her, there, on the floor.

Damn. He shook his head, unable to believe the transformation wrought by a few drops of blood. No wonder she wanted the vampire alive.

A seductive smile played over those beguiling lips, almost as if she knew exactly what he was thinking.

And perhaps she did.

Hips swaying provocatively, she closed the distance between them. She gazed up at him, the tip of her moist pink tongue teasing her lips.

"You've given me a wondrous gift," she said, her voice becoming a seductive purr as she moved closer still. "I should like to give you something in return."

Victor shook his head. He wasn't a fool, to be suckered in by a pretty face, especially when he'd seen what lay beneath the surface. But he didn't back away when she lifted her bound hands and stroked his cheek with her knuckles.

He tried to remind himself of how she really looked, but his body was already reacting to her nearness, urging him to take her, here, now. No one would ever know.

Again, he told himself it would be a mistake, but she was humming softly, pressing her body against his, her hands stroking him, arousing him.

With a low growl, he wrapped his arms around her and lowered her to the floor.

She was bound and in his power. What harm could she do?

Verah slid out from under the boy's body, grimacing as her bare skin brushed against his. He had been insatiable, which made him easy to manipulate. There were some kinds of magic for which she didn't need her wand or Rama, and sex magic was one of them. While in the throes of passion, enchanted by her song, the boy had untied her hands and in the midst of venting his lust, he had told her where to find Rama.

Rising, she dressed quickly, drew on her cloak, and left the room. She paused in the hallway, listening to the sounds of the house. All was quiet.

It took only moments to find Rama and free him from his cage. Her wand waited for her on a table. Slipping it into the pocket of her cloak, she lifted Rama into her arms and hurried through the silent house toward the front door. After invoking her favorite invisibility spell, she left the house.

She hadn't forgotten her promise to make Victor suffer for keeping her imprisoned, but her vengeance would have to wait for a more opportune time. There were more important things to be done first.

Like getting that elusive vampire away from the Shadow Pack werewolves and back in her cellar, where he belonged.

Gideon lay on his back, staring blankly at the ceiling, his thoughts as dark as the prison he now inhabited. He had lived for over 360 years, bound to no one, free to come and go as he pleased. And then he met Verah. There followed three years of living in a cage, like a wild animal. Three years of misery. And then he met Kay, who transformed his life and showed him what true happiness was. Unfortunately, however much he hated Verah and loved Kay, associating with the two of them had led to captivity on more than one occasion, a state he was heartily sick of.

Knowing it was useless, he tugged against the heavy silver shackle that chained his right ankle to a thick bolt in the floor. The only thing it accomplished was a searing pain in the palm of his hand.

He sat up, eyes narrowing against the light, when the door to his prison opened. An oath escaped his lips when he recognized his visitor.

She held a candle in one hand. After closing the door, she stood with her back against it, obviously afraid to approach him.

He stood slowly so as not to scare her away. "What the devil are you doing here?"

"I don't know. If Russell finds out, he'll be very angry."

"So why did you come?"

"My daughter loves you," Dorothy said.

Gideon nodded. "That surprises you, doesn't it?"

"Frankly, yes. And no." She smiled faintly. "How can I condemn her for falling in love with a vampire when I married a werewolf?" She studied him a moment, then sighed heavily. "I've never been a very good mother, partly because I couldn't fully understand Kiya, but mostly because, as much as I love my husband, I've always been afraid of him."

"But you married him anyway."

"Yes, but that was before I knew what he was. I tried to leave him when I found out, but he wouldn't let me take my children with me, and I couldn't leave them behind."

"And now your daughter's trapped in a marriage she doesn't want," Gideon said.

Tears shimmered in Dorothy's eyes. "There was nothing I could have done to stop it."

He didn't have to read her mind to know that guilt was eating her up inside. "So, what do you want from me?"

"I want your word that you'll make Kiya happy for as long as you live."

Gideon snorted. "I doubt if that'll be very long, all things considered."

"Promise me!"

"I love Kiya," Gideon said quietly. "I'd never do anything to hurt her. Or you. You have my word that I'll take care of her and do my best to make her happy all the days of her life."

Dorothy stared at him for several moments, then reached

into her pocket and withdrew a large silver key. She moved
warily toward him, then bent down and unlocked the chain
that held him bound. "Go, quickly!"

"Come with me."

"I can't." She shook her head. "I wouldn't know how to
survive out there."

"He'll kill you for this."

"Maybe. It doesn't matter as long as Kiya is happy. She's
had a taste of freedom." Dorothy smiled sadly. "She told me
once that she never wanted to live my life. With your help, I
intend to see that she doesn't have to."

"If there's ever anything I can do for you . . ."

"Just tell her I love her."

Gideon nodded; then, with a last sympathetic look at a
courageous woman, he dissolved into mist and left the
house.

Dorothy stared at the place where Gideon had been standing only seconds ago. She had seen many amazing things
since coming to live here, but she didn't know which was
more astonishing, watching her husband and daughter transform themselves into wolves, or seeing Gideon dissolve into
a shimmering gray mist and simply disappear.

With a shake of her head, she started toward the door, only
to come to an abrupt halt when Russell filled the doorway.
His gaze swept the room, then came to rest on her.

"Where is he?" Russell asked.

His voice rang like thunder, echoing off the walls, filling
her heart with terror. "He's . . ." She took a deep breath. "I
let him go."

He glared at her, his eyes narrowed to angry slits.

"Kiya loves him." It was a weak excuse at best.

"What the hell does that have to do with anything?"

"She deserves to be happy."

"As her Alpha, Kiya deserves whatever I say." He took a step toward her, fists clenched at his sides. "She belongs to me. She will do as I say, when I say, the same as any other member of the pack. I thought you understood that." He took another step forward, towering over her, his rage a palpable thing. "Do you understand?"

She nodded, unable to speak past the lump of fear in her throat. She had never experienced his anger before, never truly understood how dangerous he could be.

Until this moment, she had never considered herself to be part of the pack, or thought of her husband as being her Alpha. It occurred to her that she was at his mercy. As Alpha, he held the power of life and death over the werewolves in the compound. None of them would condemn him, regardless of the punishment he imposed upon her.

It was a frightening thought. She wrapped her arms around her waist, chilled to her very core by the merciless expression in his eyes, the cruel twist of his lips.

This, she thought, taking a wary step backward, this is what death looks like.

Chapter 30

The night after Dorothy freed him, Gideon stood in the midnight shadows outside the Rinaldi compound. Earlier, he had tried to get inside the fence, but to no avail. It was obvious that Alissano had alerted Victor to the fact that Gideon was no longer a prisoner. And just as obvious that Diego and his family had been warned to take the necessary precautions to keep Gideon out of the compound and out of the house.

He ignored the temptation to contact Kay. Until he could come up with a plan to get her safely away from Victor, it seemed best to keep silent. No point in getting her hopes up.

Dammit! Unless he could find someone to invite him into the house—and the chances of that seemed pretty slim now that the werewolves knew he was on the loose—he would never get her out of there.

It seemed hopeless. Or was it?

A thought took him to Apache Junction and a small white house located on a quiet street.

Clad in a long white nightgown, Kusuma Ila opened the door, a rifle held rock steady in her hands, a black cat on either side of her.

Gideon blinked at her. "Who were you expecting?"

With a shrug, she took a step back, allowing him entrance.

"It is late." She closed the door behind him, then propped the rifle in the corner. "What brings you here at this hour?" she asked, and then chuckled softly. "I guess it is not late, for night-walkers."

She cleared a space on the sofa for him, then sat down in her rocker. "Why have you come?"

Gideon shook his head. "I didn't have anywhere else to turn."

"Are you still running from Verah?"

"You know about that?" He leaned back on the couch, his legs stretched out in front of him.

Kusuma Ila made a vague gesture with one hand. "I hear things." Leaning down, she stroked the cats.

Gideon cocked his head to one side. "What things?"

"Verah is no longer a prisoner in the Rinaldi house."

"Who told you that?"

Kusuma Ila picked up one of the cats and scratched its ears. "Does it matter?"

Gideon glanced from the cat to the witch. "The cat told you?"

"In a way."

"What else do you know?"

"Before Verah made her escape from the werewolf's compound, the boy gave her a vial of your blood."

Damn! That swine, Victor, must have helped himself to a few cc's of his blood while Gideon was at rest.

"Why would that old crone want your blood?" Kusuma Ila asked.

"Don't you know? You seem to know everything else."

"I have heard rumors," the witch replied. "Macabre rumors."

"Yeah? Like what?"

"Are they true, those rumors?"

"I don't know. It depends on what you've heard." He blew out a sigh of exasperation. All he needed was another witch who wanted to bleed him dry.

Kusuma Ila snorted. "You think I am like her?" she asked indignantly.

"I sure as hell hope not," Gideon muttered dryly. "Do you know where she is?"

Kusuma Ila put the first cat down and picked up the other one. Humming tunelessly, the witch gazed into the cat's eyes for several minutes.

Gideon felt the old woman's power rise, felt it coalesce around the witch and the cat. It skittered over his skin like tiny electrical sparks.

And then, abruptly, it was gone.

Kusuma Ila shook her head as if to clear it.

The cat curled up in Kusuma Ila's lap, purring loudly.

Gideon stared at the cat.

It stared back at him, slanted yellow eyes unblinking.

Gideon leaned forward. What the hell? He raked a hand through his hair. For a moment there, while staring into the cat's eyes, he could have sworn he saw Verah standing in a dark room, chanting softly while gazing into a bowl of dark water.

"She's gone home, hasn't she?" he asked.

Kusuma Ila nodded.

"And she's still hunting me?"

The witch's silence was all the affirmation he needed.

"She can't track me," Gideon muttered, thinking aloud. "So she'll go after Kiya again." But hell, he had known that all along, just as he knew there was only one way to protect the woman he loved, and that was to give the wicked witch of the west what she wanted.

"There is another way," Kusuma Ila said matter-of-factly. "Kill her."

Gideon glanced at Kusuma Ila. Sitting there, her long white hair in braids, one cat asleep in her lap and the other curled at her feet, she looked like someone's kindly grandmother, not someone who had just suggested cold-blooded murder.

"I'd love to kill her," he said, "but don't you think she knows that? She's not going to let me get close to her unless she knows I'm not a threat."

Kusuma Ila stroked the cat's head, her brow furrowed thoughtfully. "Give me a few days," she suggested. "And I might be able to help you."

Chapter 31

Kay was dreaming of Gideon when someone shook her shoulder. Murmuring, "Go away," she tried to find her way back into her dream, back into the warmth and safety of Gideon's arms.

"Wake up, Kiya!"

At the sound of Victor's voice, she came fully awake, all her senses alert as the horror of the previous week returned full force. If he dared laid a hand on her again, he'd lose it!

Victor yanked the covers from the bed. "Get up."

"What time is it?"

"What difference does that make? Your father is here."

"My father's here?" She blinked up at Victor as he switched on the light.

"Didn't I just say that?" Victor stood over her. For once, he didn't glare at her. Instead, he looked uncharacteristically subdued. "I wouldn't keep him waiting, if I were you."

Kay sat up, reaching for the robe at the foot of her bed. "What's going on?"

Victor didn't answer, merely turned on his heel and left the room.

Something was wrong.

She stared after him a moment; then, drawing her robe

tightly around her, she followed Victor downstairs. When she entered the living room, her father turned away from the window. Kay felt her stomach turn over at the somber expression on his face.

Something was definitely wrong.

"What is it?" she asked, unable to keep the worry from her voice. "What's happened?"

"I've come to take you home."

Arms wrapped around her waist, she stared at him. What wasn't he telling her?

"Get whatever you need for overnight. Victor can bring the rest of your things tomorrow."

She didn't argue. She was all too happy to leave Victor and his taciturn parents behind. All too happy to go home because Gideon was there. Somehow, she would find a way to see him. The thought made her smile inside; had she been alone, she would have laughed with the joy of anticipation, but that would never do, not with her father watching her.

Hurrying back upstairs, she grabbed a change of clothes and a pair of shoes. She was going home!

Returning to the living room, she glanced at Victor. He stood next to the fireplace, his arms folded over his chest, his expression sullen. He remained mute when she followed her father out to the car.

Once she was settled, her father put the car in gear and drove out of the compound. He refused to tell her why he was spiriting her away from the Rinaldi home place in the middle of the night, leaving her to imagine the worst. Her first thought was that something had happened to Gideon, but her father wouldn't come after her in the middle of the night because of that. The only other thing she could think of was that her mother was sick, dead, dying. . . .

Kay felt an immense sense of relief when her mother, clad in nightgown and robe, met her at the front door. But one look at her mother's face and Kay knew something was terribly wrong at home.

"Your old room is ready," Dorothy said, not quite meeting Kay's eyes.

"Mom, are you all right?"

"Yes, of course."

"Dorothy, go to bed," Russell said curtly. "I need to speak with Kiya."

Kay frowned when her mother lowered her head and hurried out of the room, shutting the door behind her.

Kay sank down on the sofa, the clothing she had brought with her clutched in her hands. "What's going on?" She was suddenly certain that something awful had happened to Gideon. It would explain why he hadn't opened the link between them, why she couldn't feel him. She bit down on her lower lip to keep from asking about him, knowing it would only make her father even angrier than he was already.

"You'll be staying here for a while," her father said.

Kay nodded. She wished he would just say whatever he had to say and get it over with.

Taking the chair opposite the sofa, he regarded her with hooded eyes.

It made her nervous when he looked at her like that, as if he was trying to see into her very soul.

"The witch managed to escape from Rinaldi's," her father said at last.

Kay stared at him. Verah was free? Of all the things he might have said, that came as the biggest surprise. Why had no one told her?

"That's not all. Tonight, your mother took it upon herself to free that damn vampire."

Gideon wasn't here? Kay shook her head in disbelief. "What happened? Did he hypnotize her or something?"

"No."

She couldn't imagine her mother doing anything so daring

on her own. And if it was true, and Gideon was no longer a prisoner, then why hadn't he contacted her?

"If she wasn't compelled, why would she do something like that?" Kay asked. She had to know, although she didn't really care. The only thing that mattered was that Gideon was free. If her mother had been in the room, Kay would have kissed her.

Russell cracked his knuckles. "Until we find him again, you'll be staying here, where I can keep an eye on you." He stood, his gaze capturing hers. "You will not contact him," he said, and it was no longer her father speaking, but her Alpha. "If he gets in touch with you, you will let me know. Are we clear?"

"Yes, Father."

"Go to bed."

Kay stood as well. "What have you done to my mother?"

His eyes narrowed. "Are you questioning my authority?"

She refused to be cowed by the tone of his voice or by the way he stood there, bristling. "I want to know what you've done to her."

"I taught her a lesson she should have learned a long time ago."

"You broke her spirit!" Kay exclaimed, remembering the vacant expression on her mother's face, the way she had bowed her head, as if she were a servant instead of a member of the family. "How could you do such a despicable thing? She's as good as dead inside!"

"I will not have anyone who resides under my rule defy me."

Kay felt her anger rise up, as bitter as gall. "You're her husband, not her master. You're supposed to love her, protect her. . . ."

"I am Alpha here," he said, his voice a low growl. "As such, I will be obeyed. By *my* pack. By *my* daughter. By *my* wife. I do not need your approval, Kiya, only your obedience.

I will not be judged by you or anyone else. Do you understand?"

"No, I'll never understand. Good night, Father."

"Remember what I said."

She nodded curtly. As if she could ever forget.

Kay paused on her way up the stairs when she heard footsteps behind her. Thinking it might be her mother, she glanced over her shoulder. It wasn't Dorothy, but Jerry Mule Deer, one of her pack mates. His gaze slid away from hers, as if he was ashamed to look at her.

With a sigh of resignation, she continued on to her room. Once again, she was to be under guard.

Jerry bid her a quiet good night when she closed her bedroom door.

Alone in her room, Kay sank down on the foot of the bed. Gideon was free. She shook her head, unable to wrap her mind around the fact that her mother had done something in blatant violation of her father's will. Kay didn't know what her father had done in retaliation, but whatever it was, it had drained the life out of her mother. Looking at her was like looking at a zombie.

Blinking the tears from her eyes, Kay fell back on the bed and stared up at the ceiling, her thoughts again turning to Gideon. He loved her. She knew he did. Where was he? And why hadn't he let her know what her mother had done?

Kay rolled onto her side, her head pillowed on her hand. It seemed like years since she'd seen Gideon. What if he had gone back to New York? Maybe he'd decided that butting heads with her family was just too much darn trouble. Not that she could blame him.

She gasped, remembering what else her father had said. Verah was free. Was that why Gideon hadn't contacted her? Merciful heavens, surely the witch didn't have him in her power again!

It was a thought that kept her tossing and turning until dawn.

Victor arrived with Kay's clothing and other belongings while she and her parents were at breakfast, a strained, silent meal. Kay was surprised that Victor hadn't brought any of his own things, since she had assumed he would be moving into the compound with her.

She was even more astonished when her father didn't invite Victor to stay for breakfast, or even offer him a cup of coffee.

Kay glanced at her mother, but Dorothy refused to meet her gaze. As soon as the meal was over, her mother began to clear the table.

Too nervous to sit still any longer, Kay said, "Have another cup of coffee, Mom, I'll do the dishes."

"It's your mother's job," Russell said sharply. "Let her do it."

Kay dropped back down in her chair. She knew better than to argue with that tone.

When Dorothy finished clearing the table and loading the dishwasher, she left the kitchen.

Russell laid his paper aside.

It took all of Kay's courage to meet his gaze across the table.

"You're probably wondering why Victor isn't staying here," her father said.

"It crossed my mind."

"I don't know how to tell you this except to say it straight out. He was apparently beguiled by the witch. I should have told you last night."

"Beguiled?"

Russell cleared his throat. "He slept with her and when he was . . . exhausted, she escaped."

Kay stared at her father, not knowing whether to laugh or

cry. Victor had slept with the witch. As far as she was concerned, it was a match made in heaven. Or, more likely, hell.

Russell sat back, his arms folded over his chest. "Have you nothing to say?"

"Yes. I want a divorce."

Russell scowled at her.

"He cheated on me."

"That's hardly an argument in your favor, considering I found you in another man's bed."

"I don't love Victor. I never have. I never will."

"Until I decide what to do about your marriage, I think it's best for the two of you to live apart."

She couldn't argue with that.

"He tells me the witch came after you because of the vampire. Is that true?"

"Yes. She wants to use me for bait so she can catch Gideon again. His blood keeps her young."

Russell grunted softly. "Victor told me that and I called him a liar. Seems I owe the boy an apology."

"I won't be safe anywhere as long as she's alive."

"Or as long as the vampire lives."

Kay felt her heart go cold. "If you destroy Gideon, I'll hate you forever."

"Forever is a long time," her father said, rising. "The only way to protect you is to kill them both."

Filled with impotent anger, Victor lingered outside the fence of the Shadow Pack's compound. Alissano had taken Kiya home without so much as a by-your-leave and then, after Victor had delivered Kay's clothing this morning, the old man had sent him packing as if he was some wet-behind-the-ears pup. Alpha or not, Alissano had no right to take Kiya home. She was his wife now, dammit, and he needed her. At least until she had given him a son. Without the Alissano heir, his plan for becoming Alpha of both packs was in jeopardy.

Damn the witch! If he ever got his hands on her again, she'd rue the day. He didn't know what kind of magic she had worked on him, but it must have been some powerful spell to make him forget the ugly old crone that lay beneath her outward beauty.

Dammit! Even now, he was hot for the old hag.

Verah reclined on the sofa in her living room, staring at her reflection in the window. She was young again, inside and out, filled with the vigor and beauty of youth. Rama lay curled up on the top of the couch's curved back, purring softly.

Verah glanced around the room, admiring the paintings on the walls, and the figurines of Morrigan, goddess of war and magic; Hathor, the goddess of cunning; and Vesta, the goddess of fire, that adorned the mantel. Her favorite was the life-size statue of Hecate, the Greek goddess of magic, that stood in the corner beside the fireplace.

It was good to be home again. She had showered for half an hour, scrubbing away the stink of the Rinaldis' cellar, and the touch of the boy who had vented his lust on her.

She grinned inwardly. Not only had she seduced him with her siren song, but she had bespelled him so that he would never be able to satisfy another woman. If there was one thing the world didn't need, she thought, it was the likes of Victor Rinaldi siring whelps that would grow up to be just like him.

Tomorrow, she would decide how best to recapture the wolf girl, but for tonight, she was content to be safely ensconced in her own home, rested, clean, and well fed, with Rama to keep her company, and thoughts of vengeance to keep her warm.

Chapter 32

It was near midnight a week later when Gideon left Kusuma Ila's untidy but cozy home, a small brown bottle tucked into his pants pocket. He made a brief stop at his lair in Phoenix where he took a long hot shower, then slipped into a comfortable pair of old jeans, a long-sleeved black T-shirt, and a pair of supple, knee-high leather boots.

He considered contacting Kay, but decided against it, knowing she would worry if he told her what he was about to do. If things worked out as planned, he would get in touch with her in a few days and together they would figure out how to get her away from Victor and her father. If this didn't work, well, it might be a good long while before he was able to contact her. Hell, if it didn't work, there was a chance Verah would kill him. But one thing he knew for certain: If he survived, Kay would be waiting for him when it was over, no matter how long it took.

Leaving his lair, he went in search of prey. He needed to feed, and feed well. Knowing Verah, it might be a long time between meals.

It was an hour past midnight when he transported himself to Verah's home in New Mexico. Standing on the doorstep, he took a deep breath, then rang the bell.

Moments later, the witch answered the door. Her startled expression when she recognized him was priceless.

Fear and surprise chased themselves across her face. Fear won out. "You can't come in!" she exclaimed. Taking a step backward, she called for her familiar. The cat came running and made a flying leap into her arms.

"I've come to surrender," Gideon said. "But first I'll have your word that you'll leave Kiya alone."

Verah stared at him, stunned into silence.

"Do we have a deal?"

When she found her voice, Verah said, "I don't believe you." She shook her head. "Why would you come here willingly?"

"Kiya is married to someone else. I want her to be happy."

Verah snorted. "You love the wolf that much?"

"I love the girl that much. I don't want her to keep looking over her shoulder, waiting for you to strike. So get your silver chains. I won't fight you. Just promise me you'll leave Kiya alone, and I'm yours for as long as you need me."

Eyes narrowed, the witch regarded him for several long moments; then, muttering to the cat, she pivoted on her heel and walked away.

Gideon waited, wondering if she intended to return.

He heard the rattle of chains first, then Verah approached the door. "Undress."

"What?"

"You heard me. Take off your boots and shirt."

Grimacing, he did as instructed. He had worn the heavy, long-sleeved shirt and boots so he'd have a layer of protection between his skin and the silver. He should have known Verah wouldn't allow such a thing.

And still the witch stood there, her eyes filled with suspicion.

She regarded Gideon for another few moments before tossing the shackles, and then a large silver key, onto the porch. "Put those on and I'll believe you."

She meant business this time. The heavy silver links blistered his skin as he locked the shackles in place around his neck, his ankles and wrists, then tossed her the key.

And still she hesitated.

He hissed as the silver burned deeper, scorching his flesh.

And then she smiled. "Come in."

Jaw clenched, Gideon crossed the threshold and followed the witch down to the basement. He hesitated at the cell door as vivid images of the years he had spent in that cramped cage flashed through his mind.

Ever the thoughtful hostess, the witch gave him a shove and he stumbled through the doorway.

The sound of the key turning in the lock echoed like the crack of doom in his ears.

Alone in her room, Kay stood at the window, gazing into the distance. As always, her thoughts were for Gideon. Where was he? Had he returned to his lair in New York? Or maybe the one in Gatlinburg? Wherever he was, she hoped he was safe.

A movement in the yard below caught her eye and she couldn't stifle a brief flare of hope that Gideon had come for her. But, of course, that was impossible. It was only Joe Yellow Bear, standing guard below her window to make sure she didn't try to escape. Her father claimed the guards were posted to keep her safe from the witch, but she knew better. They had been instructed to keep her in the house, and Gideon out.

But she hadn't given up hope. Sooner or later, one of the guards would make a mistake. They would fall asleep or get distracted and when that happened, she would be gone.

Knowing it was useless, she tried to open the link between herself and Gideon. She had tried and failed every night for the last week and a half. Tonight would probably be no different, but she couldn't give up.

As usual, her efforts were in vain. There was nothing there, just an aching emptiness. Maybe if she concentrated harder? Closing her eyes, she pictured him in her mind—tall and dark and dangerous, with inky black hair and enigmatic gray eyes. A man more handsome than any other she had ever known. Gideon. She recalled what it was like to be in his embrace—the strength of his arms around her, his mouth covering her own, his body arousing her until the rest of the world faded away and there was just the two of them.

She moaned softly, wishing he was with her now. Heat suffused her skin as she imagined him holding her, touching her. Imagined touching him in return, her hands exploring the hard length of his body, her fingers tangling in his hair while their tongues mated. . . .

Damn, woman, what are you trying to do to me!

Her eyes flew open at the sound of his voice, so real, so close, she glanced over her shoulder, expecting to find him there.

Gideon?

I'm here.

Relief poured out of her in a long, shuddering sigh. *I've been so worried about you.*

I'm fine, Kiya. Stop worrying. How are you?

I'm good. I'm at home.

Home? With your pack?

Yes. My father brought me here. Verah escaped from Victor's place.

Yeah, I heard that.

Where are you?

Where I need to be.

You need to be here, with me.

The sound of his laughter filled her mind and warmed

her heart. *I'll be there soon. In the meantime, take care of yourself.*

Don't go!

I'll be in touch. I love you, Wolfie. Stay safe.

You, too.

Before she could say anything else, he was gone.

Kay frowned. What had Gideon meant when he'd said he was where he needed to be?

Gideon rested his head against the wall and closed his eyes. Whatever happened, however this turned out, he wouldn't regret it as long as it ensured Kay's well-being. In 360 years, he had never loved a woman the way he loved her. Nothing had even come close. He had seduced women, made love to them, even courted a few, but it had always been a game, a way to pass the time, to satisfy a lust even more primal than the hunger that plagued him. But Kay was different. He had known it the moment he woke and saw her huddling in a corner of the cage. She had been afraid, he had smelled the fear on her, yet she'd never let it show. She had even made a joke about vampires and how he was just "doing what comes naturally," when he preyed upon those Verah had brought him.

He sat up straighter when he heard the witch's footsteps coming down the stairs. Moments later, she was standing outside his cell, a familiar goblet in one hand, her favorite dagger in the other.

"So soon?" he asked. "You're still looking good."

"How nice of you to say so," she said dryly. "But I can feel it wearing off, and I'd prefer to have some on hand as soon as I need it. Besides, orders were piling up while I was away." She moved to the left side of the cage and knelt down. "Hold out your arm."

Chains rattling, he did as bidden, then watched impassively as she jabbed the silver-bladed dagger into the large vein in his wrist. Blood flowed freely from the wound, quickly filling the jewel-encrusted cup.

When she withdrew the blade, the wound closed. "There," she said, "that should last a while."

Gideon met her satisfied gaze. The silver and the blood-letting weakened him physically, but he still had enough power to compel mortals. And, witch or not, Verah was mortal. It took only moments to implant a suggestion in her mind, and then he looked away.

Brow furrowed, the witch stared into the cup. She dipped her finger into the dark red fluid, then licked it off. "You know," she said, "the next time I need to drink your blood, I think I'll take it right from the source."

Gideon slid his arm between the bars, palm up. "Why wait? If you drink it while it's warm and fresh, it'll taste better and the effects will last longer."

She tilted her head to one side, as if considering his words, then reached for his arm. As if moving in slow motion, she dragged the dagger across his wrist. She leaned forward, her long blond hair falling over her shoulders, trailing in his blood as she ran her tongue over the shallow gash in his flesh.

Gideon held his breath as she drank deeply. Her hands gripped his forearm, her nails gouged furrows into his skin.

Abruptly, she lifted her head and pushed his arm away. When she tried to stand, he grasped the hem of her skirt.

"Let me go!" She clutched her stomach, a low moan rising in her throat. "What have you done?"

He reached into the pocket of his jeans and withdrew a small brown bottle. "I drank a little poison when the sun went down."

She stared at him, her eyes wild. "What's the antidote? Where is it? Give it to me!"

"There isn't any."

She sank to her knees, her breathing labored, her skin turning gray. "Help me. . . ."

Gideon shook his head, his eyes narrowing with revulsion as her years quickly caught up with her. Wrinkles spread across her face, the color faded from her hair, her hands turned skeletal, the skin liberally sprinkled with age spots.

She uttered an anguished cry and then toppled onto her side. Tremors wracked her from head to foot for several minutes, and then she went still.

Still clutching a handful of her skirt, Gideon leaned forward. Was she dead? But no, he could still hear the faint beat of her heart.

She let out an unholy shriek as her body began shriveling, shrinking, until she was as ugly on the outside as she had been on the inside. A last, desperate cry, and the life drained out of her.

Gideon stared at her a moment longer, his brow furrowing as her body disintegrated into dust.

Damn. He had never seen anything like that before. She really was old. Well, there was one good thing about it, he mused. He wouldn't have to worry about disposing of the body. Dragging her skirt into the cell, he withdrew the silver key from the pocket, cursing as it scorched his palm, but it was a small price to pay for his freedom.

Moments later, the shackles lay on the floor.

Dissolving into mist, he left the basement. Resuming his own form, he went in search of Verah's wand. He found it on a table in what he surmised was the room where she worked her magic. Her familiar was curled up on a high stool beside the table. The black cat sprang to its feet, back arched, teeth bared, when Gideon reached for the wand.

"You're out of a job." Gideon jerked his thumb toward the door. "Get lost."

The cat stared at him, unblinking, then jumped off the stool and ran out of the room.

Gideon stared at the wand. It was just a piece of wood,

perhaps sixteen inches long, yet he was reluctant to touch it. Still, a promise was a promise, and he had promised this wand to another witch.

He glanced around, looking for something to wrap it in. He settled on a scrap of toweling, felt a ripple of supernatural power when he picked up the wand. He quickly wrapped it in the towel and left the house.

A thought took him to his lair in New York. A tingling on his skin told him it was only minutes until sunrise.

Going into the bathroom, he stripped off his jeans. One good thing about being a vampire, his wounds healed quickly, even those made by silver. He took a hot shower, wishing all the while that Kay was with him. Closing his eyes, he imagined her hands moving over his shoulders and back, sliding lower, lower . . .

Shaking off his lustful thoughts, he stepped out of the shower, dried off, and stretched out on the bed. Lying there, his arms folded behind his head, he made a mental list of things to do when he rose on the morrow. First, he would call a florist and order five dozen roses for Kusuma Ila. Second, he would box up Verah's wand and arrange to have it delivered to her, payment in full for services rendered. And third, he would get in touch with Kay.

Closing his eyes, he summoned her image to mind, focused on it while the darkness wrapped its arms around him and dragged him down into oblivion.

Kiya?

At the sound of Gideon's voice, Kay glanced up from the book she was reading.

Gideon! How are you? Where are you? I haven't heard from you in days. I've been so worried.

I'm fine. I'm in New York. Are you still at your father's?

Yes. Kay looked over at her mother, who was asleep on the sofa.

Can you get out of the house?

I don't know. I'll try, but there's always someone watching me. Where did you go?

I went to Verah's. You can stop worrying about her. She won't be coming after you again.

She's dead?

Definitely dead.

You killed her. It wasn't a question.

I had a little help. Remember that witch in Apache Junction? She concocted a poison cocktail.

How did you get Verah to drink it?

Gideon chuckled. *I drank it, and when she drank from me . . .*

It killed her. Kay shook her head. It was brilliant.

As soon as you get away, let me know, and I'll be there.

I will. Gideon? I love you. If only she could invite Gideon into the compound, getting away would be so much easier. But her father had rescinded Gideon's invitation, which superseded any invite Kay or anyone else might issue.

I love you, too, Wolfie.

Tears stung her eyes when he closed the connection between them. He was alive. Verah was dead. If she could get away, no one would be able to find her.

"Kiya, what is it?"

Kay glanced at her mother, hoping she hadn't seen the tears in her eyes.

"You're crying. Why?"

Kay shook her head, but the harder she tried to hold back her tears, the swifter they fell.

Rising, Dorothy went to sit on the footstool in front of Kay's chair. "Whatever it is, you can tell me."

"No, I can't."

"It has something to do with Gideon, doesn't it?"

"Mom . . ."

"I know you love him. And he loves you."

Kay blinked back her tears. It was so tempting to pour out her heart to her mother, but she didn't dare. How could she trust her to keep her secret now, when her father had broken her mother's spirit?

Dorothy took Kay's hand in hers. "You can trust me, Kiya. I won't say anything to your father. I promise."

"Gideon's waiting for me, Mama. If I can get away from here, he'll come for me and take me away."

"Are you sure you want to go with him? He's a vampire, Kiya."

"It doesn't matter." Kay sighed. "My father will never let me go. Even if I can convince him to end my marriage to Victor, he'll just find someone else for me to marry. And Mama, I'm already married to Gideon. It doesn't matter if my father says the marriage is no longer valid. I'm married to Gideon in my heart, in my soul. I always will be."

"I see."

"When Victor . . ." Kay shook her head. "Even though he forced me, I felt like I was being unfaithful to Gideon, like I was breaking my marriage vows."

"Oh, Kiya, what have we done to you?"

"You didn't do it, Mom," Kay said, and in that moment, as tears spilled down her mother's cheeks, Kay hated her father, not only for what he had done to her, but for what he had done to her mother.

"Your father's gone to see Diego," Dorothy said, squeezing Kay's hand. "I don't know why, but if you want to leave, you should go now."

"How am I going to get past Tyler?" Tyler Red Elk was the werewolf who stood guard at her bedroom door. At the moment, he was standing in the hallway outside the living room.

"Leave that to me. When you hear me scream, leave the house as fast as you can."

"Mom . . ."

"You'll need a distraction to get out of the house," Dorothy said. "Who knows when you'll get another chance?"

"I love you, Mom."

"I love you, too." Leaning forward, Dorothy hugged Kay, then kissed her cheek.

"When you hear my signal, run as fast as you can. You'll only have a few minutes."

"I don't know. . . ."

"It'll be fine. Go to your room and wait." Rising, Dorothy moved toward the door. She paused to look over her shoulder. "Be happy, Kiya, and always remember that I love you."

Before Kay could say anything, her mother left the room.

Too keyed up to sit still, Kay paced her bedroom floor. What kind of distraction did her mother have in mind?

She glanced at her watch. It had been almost thirty minutes since her mother had left the living room.

Had her mother changed her mind? Or worse, had her father come home unexpectedly? She hated to think what would happen if her father learned of her mother's plan to help Kay escape.

Going to the window, Kay stared into the darkness. She could see Joe, standing in the shadows beneath her window. Poor guy. She could almost feel sorry for him.

She was about to turn away from the window when she heard it, a scream of such agony, she almost thought it was real.

Hurrying to the door, she opened it a crack. Tyler was gone. Murmuring, "Thank you, Mom," Kay hurried down the stairs. Opening the front door, she glanced left, then right. There was no sign of anyone guarding the front entrance.

It took only moments to punch in the gate code and then she was running down the driveway. Veering left, she ran for the hills. Only when the house was out of sight did she slow down.

Breathless, she closed her eyes and concentrated on Gideon and connecting to the blood bond that bound them together.

Gideon! Gideon, come for me! Hurry!

Chapter 33

Gideon had just bent over his prey's neck when Kay's voice, loud and urgent, sounded in his mind.

In an instant, he released the girl in his arms from his power and willed himself to the Shadow Pack's compound.

He found Kay in the Gros Ventre Wilderness area. Coming up behind her, he murmured her name as he swept her into his embrace.

"Gideon!" Wrapping her arms around his neck, she buried her face against his shoulder.

"What's happened? Are you all right?"

"I'm fine. We need to get away from here, now."

"Just tell me where you want to go, and we're there."

"I really liked New York."

She had barely spoken the words when she felt a rush of wind, followed by a familiar queasiness in the pit of her stomach. The next thing she knew, they were in Gideon's apartment.

"So," he said, still holding her in his arms, "how'd you manage to get away?"

"My mom helped me. She provided a distraction; I'm not exactly sure what she did, but it drew the guard away from my door and I ran like the devil was after me."

"Where's your old man?"

"He's at the Rinaldi place." Kay drew back a little so she could see his face. "Verah's really dead?"

"Oh, yeah, she's dead. Hell, she's dust."

Kay blinked at him. "Dust?"

"She was a lot older than I thought."

"So, there's no way for anyone to find us now, right?"

Gideon shrugged. "There's always a way, if someone wants you badly enough. Your father could hire another witch to find you."

Kay's shoulders slumped. "So, we're no better off than we were before."

"I wouldn't say that. Witches are pretty hard to find."

"Yeah? You found one in the phone book."

He chuckled softly as he set her on her feet. "She won't betray us. The best tracking spells need blood to work. Clothing is ineffective. Hair is kind of iffy. So, unless your old man has some of your blood, I think we're safe enough for now."

"Until the full moon," Kay said, frowning.

"What do you mean?"

"My father will be able to track me when I change."

"You might have mentioned that before."

"I know. I guess with everything else that was going on, I just didn't think of it."

"So, he can find you, even when he's in Jackson and you're here?"

"I'm not sure."

Gideon exhaled sharply, then pulled her into his arms and kissed the tip of her nose. "What do you say we worry about that tomorrow night?"

"I think that's a great idea." She smiled at him as he carried her down the hall.

In the bedroom, his clever hands quickly undressed her, then he tossed her, gently, onto the bed. He stretched out beside her moments later, those clever hands playing over her body, his fingers stroking along her skin like a master violinist tuning his instrument until she was humming with need. She buried her fingers in his hair, drawing him closer, her tongue sweeping across his lips, delving inside to duel with his own. Desire unfurled deep within her, making her forget everything but her yearning for this man and no other.

She moaned with pleasure as his fangs grazed her throat, lifted her hips to meet him as his body became a part of hers. Crying his name, she reached for the stars, felt them rain down around her as he carried her away to a secret place no one else could find.

With a contented sigh, Kay snuggled against Gideon's side, her head resting on his shoulder, her fingertips tracing lazy circles over his chest and hard, flat belly. He had an amazing physique. Had he had it before he became a vampire? Or was it just an added perk, like being able to zap himself from one end of the country to the other? If it was just part of being Nosferatu, she was certain men from all over the world would be lining up to become vampires. Of course, none of them would ever be as incredibly sexy as the raven-haired Adonis lying beside her.

"Adonis? Really?"

Jabbing him in the side with her elbow, she said, "Stop that!"

"Sorry."

"No, you're not, or you wouldn't do it."

"Sometimes I just can't help myself." He rolled onto his side and drew her body against his. "How else am I going to know what you like?" he asked, his voice whiskey smooth.

"I'll tell you."

"Will you?"

She sucked in a breath as his hand began to slide up and down the inside of her thigh.

Gideon laughed softly as he rose over her. "I guess I don't need to read your mind, after all."

Propped up on one elbow, Kay reviewed their situation while she watched Gideon sleep. Verah was dead and they were safe, as long as her father couldn't track her during the full moon. Would he be able to find her when they were so many miles apart? She had never heard of a werewolf—even an Alpha—being able to track another wolf when there was so much distance between them, but just because she had never heard of it didn't mean it wasn't possible.

Suddenly restless, she slid out of bed and went into the living room. Drawing back the heavy draperies at one of the windows, she watched the sun rise over the city. It was always a beautiful sight, seeing the way the sky slowly changed from dark to light, the way the sun's light splashed the clouds with streaks of lavender, pink, and crimson. No two sunrises or sunsets were ever quite the same, but they were all beautiful.

Gnawing on her thumbnail, Kay let the drapes fall back into place. In three days, she would have an answer to the question of whether her Alpha would be able to find her.

Three days, she thought, her anxiety growing. Only three days until the moon would be full. Thinking about shedding her human self stirred her anticipation, and even though it was only her imagination, it seemed she could already feel her body changing, her skin tightening, tingling.

Suddenly ravenous, she tiptoed into the bedroom for her clothes. She dressed in the living room, then picked up the key Gideon had given her last night before he fell asleep so she could go out for something to eat.

It had surprised her that he had a key, since she had never seen him use one.

"It came with the apartment," he had explained. "I've just never needed it."

He had also left her seventy dollars cash and his cell phone.

Gideon hadn't wanted her to leave his lair, but she had insisted. She didn't want to spend the day in the apartment; she had been cooped up enough. And she certainly didn't want to wait until he woke to satisfy her hunger, which grew harder to ignore the closer she was to the change.

She locked the door behind her, checked it twice to make sure it was secure, then took the elevator to the ground floor. She paused at the sound of music. Walking down a narrow hallway, she came to a large glass window. Peering inside, she saw a number of girls of various ages wearing leotards and tights. She grinned as she watched a little girl with long red pigtails execute a perfect pirouette. Kay felt like applauding for the child, who couldn't have been more than three or four.

Kay stayed for several minutes, imagining a daughter of her own standing at the barre doing her first *demi-plié*. Did Gideon want children? Was it even possible for the two of them to conceive a child together?

She lingered, watching the dancers, until her stomach growled so loudly she was certain they could hear it over the music.

Outside, she took a deep breath. It was a beautiful day, cool and clear. The scent of food drew her down the street toward a café.

When she went inside, the myriad scents of food and drink, perspiration, cologne, and shampoo, were almost overpowering. Odd, she thought, wrinkling her nose against the onslaught. Of course, she'd always had a good sense of smell, but nothing as acute as this.

She moved along the food tables, filling two plates, one with roast beef, turkey, and ham, the other with mashed potatoes, corn, and a blueberry muffin. She added a carton of milk, a glass of orange juice, and a cup of coffee, then found a seat in the far corner of the room near a window.

She ate quickly, and went back for more ham, turkey, and roast beef. After adding a slice of chocolate cake and a piece of berry pie, she returned to her table. She told herself being this hungry was normal for this time of the month, but she didn't believe it. True, she had always had a healthy appetite, especially before the full moon, but this was over the top. She was eating like her father. . . .

Kay frowned. Thinking of her father brought her mother to mind and she was suddenly ashamed that she hadn't given any thought to her mother since being reunited with Gideon.

Pushing her plate aside, she went in search of a quiet place to make a phone call.

Gideon stirred, his senses telling him that the sun was not yet down, yet something had roused him.

Forcing his eyes open, he saw Kay pacing the floor beside the bed.

"What's wrong?" He sat up, trying to concentrate. When his life was in jeopardy, he woke with all his senses alert; it was hard to remain awake when there was no threat to his continued existence.

"I called my mom this afternoon."

Now he was awake.

"Her phone's been disconnected. There's no new number."

"What are you thinking?" he asked, but he already knew the answer.

"I don't want to say it out loud." She shook her head. "I know it's silly, but I'm afraid putting it into words will make it so. . . ."

"Come here." When she climbed into bed beside him,

Gideon slipped his arm around her waist. "You don't really think your father would hurt her, do you?"

"You've never seen him in a rage. At times like that, he's capable of anything."

"Even murder?"

She nodded. "I've got to go home."

"Are you out of your mind?" He blew out a breath. "I'm sorry. I didn't mean that, but, dammit, you just got away from there."

"I know, but Gideon . . . when she screamed, it didn't sound like she was pretending." Kay scrubbed her hands up and down her arms. "I never should have agreed to let her get involved, but I was so anxious to get away from there, away from Victor." She looked up at Gideon, her eyes tormented. "Back to you."

He swore under his breath.

"I'm not blaming you!" Kay said quickly. "Don't ever think that. I wanted out. But now . . ." She shook her head. Her mother had assured her that Russell was out of the house that night, but what if he had come home early? "I have to know that she's all right."

"Are you sure about this?"

"No." She rested her head against Gideon's shoulder, taking comfort in his nearness, in the easy strength that was so much a part of him. "I could call Greta. She'll know what's going on."

"Will she tell you the truth?"

"I think so."

"I don't like it, but go make your call."

"I'm sorry I woke you."

"It's okay." He slid down onto the bed again, his eyes closing as his head hit the pillow. "Let me know what she says."

Kay felt a rush of tenderness for Gideon as sleep claimed

him once again. After pressing a kiss to his brow, she left the bedroom and closed the door.

In the living room, she picked up Gideon's cell phone, only to stare at it for several moments, wondering if she was doing the right thing. Was it possible for her father to trace the call to Gideon's lair? She wasn't up to speed on all the latest achievements in modern technology.

She hesitated for a few more minutes, debating the wisdom of contacting anyone in the pack, then punched in her aunt's number.

Smart move or not, she had to get in touch with her mother.

The sun was slipping over the horizon when Gideon woke to the muffled sound of crying. He pulled on a pair of sweats. A moment later he was in the living room. He found Kay curled up in a corner of the sofa, her eyes red rimmed, her cheeks soaked with her tears.

She looked at him through haunted eyes for a moment; then, amid a flood of fresh tears, sobbed, "She's . . . dead. My mother's dead."

"Dammit." Moving swiftly across the room, Gideon swept Kay into his arms and held her tight.

"It's . . . it's all . . . all my fault!"

"Shh."

"She said she would provide a distraction so I could get away and . . . and she killed herself, Gideon! She committed suicide . . . hanged herself . . . so I could be free. So I could be with you."

Gideon stroked Kay's hair while he tried to think of something to say that would comfort her, but at the moment, words failed him. He hadn't known Kay's mother well, had seen her only a few times, spoken to her only once or twice, yet because Kay loved him, Dorothy Alissano had gone against her husband's wishes and set him free, had sacrificed her own life so her daughter could be with the man she loved. He had rarely seen that kind of courage and devotion.

"The funeral's on Saturday," Kay said, sniffling. Had her father purposely arranged it then, knowing the moon would be full? Her mother would have hated that.

Gideon nodded. His immediate inclination was to tell Kay she couldn't go, but it wasn't his decision to make.

"You think I should stay here, don't you?"

"Are you reading my mind now?"

"No, just your silence."

"I think it's a big risk. Victor's bound to be there, too."

"I know it's dangerous, but I have to go."

"Kiya, your mother died so you could get out of there. How can you even think of going back?"

"I have to see her one last time. I have to tell her good-bye. I'll never forgive myself if I don't." She stroked his cheek with her fingertips. "The moon will be full. The pack will run that night. I'll slip away and find you like I did before."

"Yeah," Gideon muttered dryly. "I remember how well that turned out."

"Well, we won't be distracted this time."

"Is that what I am to you?" he asked, his voice suddenly husky. "A distraction?"

"Yes, but only in a good way. Oh, Gideon," she sobbed. "I'm going to miss her so! And the funny thing is, we were never that close," she said, sniffling. "I always envied the kind of mother-daughter relationship that Wanda has with her mom. They share everything, spend time together, gossip, go shopping. My mother and I never did anything like that. I hardly ever told her that I loved her, and now it's too late." She looked up at him, her eyes brimming with tears. "Forever too late."

Murmuring her name, Gideon wrapped Kay in his arms again. At times like this, words were useless. He just hoped his being with her was enough.

Kay slept late the next day, and woke feeling as if she hadn't slept at all. Her eyes were swollen and gritty, her throat hurt from all the tears she'd shed. She glanced at Gideon, sleeping beside her, loosed a soul-deep sigh. Life had been a lot less complicated before she met him, but looking at him now, she didn't know what she would do without him.

Or how she was going to live with her guilt.

Swinging her legs over the side of the bed, she stared at the floor. If she hadn't fallen in love with Gideon, her mother would still be alive. She blinked as tears stung her eyes. She told herself she wasn't entirely to blame, that her mother had been unhappy for years, but it didn't help. Her mother was dead and it was all her fault. And even though Gideon didn't want her to attend the funeral, Kay knew she would never forgive herself if she didn't go.

Once the decision was made, she felt a little better. She couldn't change the past, but fear of the future would not keep her from telling her mother good-bye.

Hunger drove her out of the apartment. Emotionally, she didn't feel like eating, but the wolf inside demanded nourishment. She was always ravenous before the full moon. She had asked her father once why that was, and he'd told her it was because it required an amazing amount of physical energy and stamina to shift from human to wolf and back again.

Kay thought about that while she ate, wondering why she was so much hungrier this time than she had ever been in the past. She devoured four double cheeseburgers, two orders of fries, and two chocolate shakes and she was still hungry. She ordered a cheeseburger to go and left the restaurant.

She wandered down one side of the street and up the other

and then, feeling the need to connect with another human being, she ducked into a bookstore and called Wanda, who was her only real friend in all the world.

"Girlfriend!" Wanda exclaimed. "Where on earth have you been? We've all been going crazy around here wondering what happened to you. I thought . . . we thought . . ."

"I'm so sorry," Kay said. "I should have gotten in touch with you sooner to let you know I'm okay, but . . . well, my life has been sort of . . . strange, lately."

"You could have called."

"I know." Kay shook her head. With everything that had been going on, she'd completely forgotten about her job and just about everything else. "I need you to tell Dr. Saltzman that I won't be coming back."

"What? Why not? What's happened? Are you all right? Should I . . . ?"

"One thing at a time," Kay said, interrupting her friend in midsentence. "A lot's happened. I got married. . . ."

"Married!" Wanda exclaimed. "To who? That hot guy you mentioned?"

"Yes. It was kind of sudden. And my mother . . ." Kay swallowed the lump rising in her throat. "My mother . . . she passed away."

"Oh, Kay, I'm so sorry."

"Thanks, Wanda." Kay took a deep breath. "Anyway, I just wanted to say hi."

"I'm glad you called, although I almost didn't answer the phone. Did you get a new number?"

"No, this one belongs to Gideon. Listen, I've gotta go."

"All right. Keep in touch, Kay. I want to hear all about that new husband of yours. And if you ever get back here, stop by and see us, okay?"

"I will. I promise. Take care of yourself, Wanda."

"You, too."

Kay closed the phone, then stared out the window. She could sense the night coming, feel the darkness whispering over her skin in a way she never had before.

Feeling suddenly uneasy, she left the bookstore and hurried back to Gideon's lair.

The sun was setting when she let herself into his apartment.

Chapter 34

Gideon paused in the act of transporting himself out of the apartment when he heard the key in the lock.

He was in her face when she closed the door. "Where in the hell have you been? I was just coming after you."

Kay stared at him, uncharacteristically annoyed by his tone. What was wrong with her? All things considered, it was only natural for him to be worried.

She took a deep breath, stilling the angry words that rose in her throat. "I needed to get out." She ran her hands up and down her arms. "I called my friend."

Gideon nodded. "You needed to talk to someone who's, for want of a better word, normal. I understand."

"You do? Have you ever felt that way?"

"Sure, now and then." He shrugged at her startled expression. "I've had—I guess you could call them lady friends—from time to time in the last few hundred years. Not for prey. Not for sex. Just for companionship. Just for a chance to feel human for a week or two."

He stepped away from her and she moved to the sofa and sat down. "Did you ever love any of them?"

Brow furrowed in thought, he shoved his hands into his

pants pockets. "No, but I cared for them because they served a purpose."

"Did you compel them to be with you?"

"Hey! Don't you think I could get a girlfriend without resorting to tricks?"

"Of course I do. I . . . oh! Very funny," she muttered when she realized he was teasing her. "Did you ever have any men friends?"

He shook his head. "No."

"Why not?"

"I'm not sure. Probably the whole male macho thing. Vampires, especially old ones, are notoriously territorial." Taking a seat beside her, he slipped his arm around her shoulders. "Are you all right?" he asked, feeling the tension humming inside her.

"Of course. Why do you ask?"

"You're lying to me, Kiya. If you don't want me reading your mind, then tell me what's wrong."

"I don't know. I just feel . . . strange."

"Strange how?"

"Just . . . strange." She made a vague gesture with her hand. "Like my skin is too tight. And I'm hungry all the time."

"Nothing strange about that. You've eaten like a truck driver on steroids ever since I met you."

She glared at him.

"Sorry. What else?"

"I just don't feel like me. You don't think it's because I've tasted your blood, do you?"

"No. The little bit you've had wouldn't have any ill effect on you. Might even make you stronger."

She lifted a hand to her brow. "Maybe I'm coming down with something."

"Do werewolves get sick?"

"Rarely."

Gideon eased back a little, his gaze moving over her face. "You look all right to me." Leaning forward, he scraped his fangs over the skin alongside her neck. "You taste the same."

She frowned at him. "Are you telling me you'd know if I was sick?"

He nodded.

"How can you do that?"

"You'd taste different. Smell different."

"Hmm. Maybe I'm just imagining it."

"Probably. I know you're stressed out about going back home. Maybe that's all it is."

"It shows, huh?"

"Oh, yeah." He slipped his hand under her hair and lightly massaged her neck. "Are you sure I can't talk you out of it?"

"I'm sure."

"Maybe a glass of wine and a warm bath would relax you," he suggested.

"It's worth a try."

Moving to the sideboard, Gideon poured a glass of wine for Kay, then went into the bathroom to fill the tub.

Kay sipped her drink, thinking how thoughtful Gideon was and how much she loved him. No one else had ever made her feel the way he did. With him, she felt cherished, protected. Important. But, most of all, he respected her wishes, let her make her own decisions.

She smiled when he appeared in the doorway. "Your bath awaits, my lady," he said, bowing at the waist.

"Thank you, kind sir." Setting her empty glass on the end table, she moved past him and went into the bathroom. She glanced over her shoulder when she realized Gideon was behind her.

"I thought I'd wash your back," he remarked, flashing a smile.

"Why didn't I think of that?"

Gideon stood with one shoulder braced against the doorjamb, watching appreciatively as Kay undressed and stepped into the tub. Venus slipping into the sea.

Kay looked up at him, one brow raised as the deliciously warm water closed over her. "Jasmine bubble bath?" she asked with an impish grin. "Who knew?"

"Very funny, Wolfie. I made a quick trip the drugstore while the tub was filling." Kneeling, he picked up the washcloth and ran it over her shoulders and down her back.

"It's a big tub," Kay remarked.

"Yes, it is."

"Big enough for two."

"Is that an invitation?"

"If you want it to be."

He was undressed and in the tub before she finished the sentence and proved, rather inventively, that the tub was indeed, big enough for two.

Late the next afternoon, Kay went shopping for a dress and shoes to wear to her mother's funeral. She found a simple black jersey knit and shoes to match, along with a black bra, panties, and a silk slip, also black.

She was famished when she left the department store. She ducked into a coffee shop and ordered a turkey club sandwich, a double order of fries, and a large chocolate shake.

She ate quickly, her nerves humming with tension at the thought of going home. Maybe Gideon was right. Maybe she shouldn't go. But staying away wasn't an option. She'd never forgive herself if she chickened out now. She was going and that was that. She would deal with her father and Victor after her mother had been laid to rest.

With her mind made up once and for all, she ordered another shake, strawberry this time. Good thing her werewolf metabolism burned up the calories, she mused as she drained her glass, or she would soon be as big as her horse.

"Barika," she murmured, and wondered who, if anyone, was looking after the mare.

It was near dark when Kay returned to Gideon's lair. More and more, she was keeping his hours—staying up until the wee hours of the morning, sleeping later and later every day. But then, she thought with a grin, it was a small price to pay to spend time with him.

When she went into the bedroom, he was still asleep. Moving quietly, she hung her dress in the closet, put the rest of her things in a drawer, then crawled into bed beside him. Her gaze moved over his face while her fingertips traced lazy eights on his stomach.

She smiled when his hand covered hers and guided it lower.

"What will you do while I'm gone?" Kay asked.

They were lying in bed, wrapped in each other's arms, their bodies still damp from their lovemaking. A fire crackled in the hearth.

"Worry about you," he said. "What else?"

"I'm serious."

"So am I. Besides, I won't be far away." He ran his knuckles along the length of her neck. "Kiya, please reconsider. You know once your father has you back in his control, he'll never let you go."

"I don't want to talk about it."

He had one last argument, one he would never have used if he hadn't been so desperate to keep her from returning to the Shadow Pack's compound. "Your mother sacrificed her life so that you could get away from your father. Would she think it was a good idea for you to put yourself in harm's way again?"

He wanted to take the words back as soon as they left his mouth. Kay stared at him, mute, her eyes dark pools of pain.

"Kiya, I'm . . ."

"Don't talk to me!" She pushed him away and scrambled out of bed, stood with her back toward him, her arms tightly folded over her chest. "Don't you think I've thought of that?"

Sitting up, he raked a hand through his hair. Dammit, why hadn't he kept his mouth shut? Or ripped out his tongue? What kind of heartless, thoughtless monster was he, to say such a thing out loud?

She was crying now, silent tears that wracked her body from head to foot. If she never forgave him, he wouldn't blame her.

Slipping out of bed, he moved up behind her, tentatively placed his hands on her shoulders.

She stiffened at his touch, but didn't move away.

"Kiya, forgive me. That was a rotten thing for me to say. I don't have any excuse, except that I'm worried sick about you going back home."

"I know." She drew in a deep, shuddering sigh, then slowly turned to face him. "But I have to go."

"You're a stubborn woman, Kiya Alissano."

Nodding, she got into bed again.

Gideon stayed where he was, not moving until she held out her hand. Sliding in beside her, he drew her gently into his arms. "I'm sorry," he whispered. "Forgive me?"

"You didn't say anything I haven't thought a hundred times myself."

"That doesn't excuse me."

"I don't know how to explain it, but there's something deep inside me, some kind of pack instinct, that's calling me back home, something besides the funeral. I don't expect you to understand." She shook her head. "I don't understand it myself. I just know I have to go."

"You're a strong woman, capable of making your own decisions. It's one of the things I like best about you. I'll be nearby if you need me."

"I know. Make love to me again. I want to forget everything but you for a little while."

"Always my pleasure, darlin'."

He kissed her then, his hands gently caressing her, arousing her, his own desire growing with the sweet seduction of skin against skin.

Kay raked her nails down his chest, then bit him on the shoulder. She bolted upright when she drew blood. "I'm sorry! I didn't mean to bite you so hard!"

"Hey, don't worry about it. It didn't hurt."

"But . . . you're bleeding all over the sheets."

Swinging his legs over the edge of the bed, Gideon went into the bathroom. After wetting a washcloth, he pressed it over the bite.

He grinned at Kay's reflection in the glass when she came up behind him.

"I'm sorry," she said again.

"It's okay, as long as I get to bite you back."

"Gideon . . ."

Turning, he wrapped his arm around her waist and pulled her close. "Forget it, Kiya. You didn't hurt me."

"But I've never done anything like that before."

"I guess I'm a bad influence on you."

"It's not funny!" she exclaimed.

"It's not the end of the world, either. Lighten up, Wolfie."

She rested her forehead against his chest. "I don't know what's wrong with me."

Gideon stroked her hair. "There's nothing wrong with you, sweetheart. It's natural for you to be upset over your mother's death, and all things considered, I'd be surprised if you weren't more than a little edgy about going back home." He put his hand under her chin and lifted her head. "I won't let anything happen to you, Kiya."

"I love you."

"I know." Cupping her face in his palms, he kissed her gently. "I love you, too, sweetheart. Believe that if you believe nothing else."

"Are you ready?"

Kay closed her suitcase, then looked across the bed at Gideon. "I guess so."

She had put this moment off as long as possible, but it was time to go. Her mother's funeral was tomorrow afternoon. Gideon was going to transport them to their favorite bed-and-breakfast in Bondurant tonight. If they didn't hurry, it would be dawn before they arrived.

They had made love several times last night, clinging to each other in silent desperation. She knew the risk she was taking by returning to the pack, but, regardless of the consequences, it was something she had to do. If she stayed away from her mother's funeral, she knew she would regret it for the rest of her life. But, like she'd told Gideon, it was more than that. It was as if the pack, the land itself, was calling her home.

"Are you sure you won't change your mind?"

"Gideon, we've been over this a dozen times."

"I know." Rounding the end of the bed, Gideon pushed a stray wisp of hair behind her ear. He had tried every argument he could think of, but there was no changing her mind. Resigned, he picked up her suitcase, then drew her body close to his. "Ready?" At her nod, he said, "Here we go."

Kay experienced that odd queasiness in the pit of her stomach, the disorienting sense of moving rapidly through time and space.

Moments later, they were in Bondurant.

"This place is starting to feel like home," Kay remarked, glancing around the now-familiar room.

"Yeah." Gideon put Kay's suitcase in the closet, then drew her into his arms. He hated the idea of her going home, but there was no point in bringing it up again. She knew how he felt.

"When the pack runs, it'll probably be late."

"I'll look for you somewhere in the hills near the river," Gideon said. If her father got her back into the compound, there was no telling if or when she would ever get out again. At least he didn't have to worry about Verah hunting them down this time.

Knowing their time together was growing short, Kay held him tighter. "Where will you spend the day?"

He shrugged. "I'll find a place, don't worry. Promise me you'll be careful."

"I will."

Gideon grasped her arms. "If I had any sense, I'd tie you to that bed and keep you there until tomorrow night."

"Gideon. . . ."

"I can't help it! Dammit, Kiya, this is the stupidest thing you've ever done!"

She glared at him. "I think you'd better go."

With a sigh of resignation, he drew her back into his arms. "All right, you win. But if your father locks you up again, I don't know how the hell I'll get you out of there." Which wasn't entirely true, as long as Kusuma Ila was on his side. If not for the witch's promise of help should he need it, he would have locked Kay up in one of his lairs and to hell with the consequences. He could live with her anger, but he didn't think he could live without her.

Relenting, Kay said, "I'll be fine."

Gideon nodded. Reaching into his pocket, he pulled out a hundred dollars and pressed the bills into her hand. "Go rent a car," he said, smiling. "And buy yourself a big breakfast."

Shoulders slumped, she rested her forehead against his chest. How did you stay mad at such a man?

He glanced out the window, his skin prickling with dawn's approach. "I've got to go."

"Be careful."

"Yeah, you, too."

Drawing her body up against his, he kissed her, a long, slow kiss that made her toes curl inside her shoes.

And then he was gone.

Kay stood there a moment, her fingers pressed to her lips, before changing into her nightgown and crawling into bed. She lay there, staring up at the ceiling for a long time, wondering where Gideon had gone to spend the day.

Wondering if he was right and she was making the biggest mistake of her life.

Chapter 35

Kay took a deep breath as she got out of the rental car and walked up to the entrance of the house. She was surprised by the rush of unease that filled her as she opened the door. For a moment, she was tempted to turn around and drive back to Bondurant just as fast as she could, but the same instinct she had felt before propelled her forward.

She paused in the entryway, listening to the muted sound of voices coming from the living room. She quickly identified them—her father, Greta, Brett, Victor and his parents.

Closing her eyes, she took another deep breath, smoothed her hand over her skirt, and entered the living room.

If she hadn't been so nervous, if the occasion hadn't been so solemn, she would have laughed at the startled expressions on the faces of everyone present—and none more so than her father.

"Kiya." He closed the distance between them, hesitated a moment, and then embraced her. "I knew you'd come to your senses and return home where you belong."

She didn't see any reason to tell him she wasn't there to stay. That news could wait until later. "Where is she?"

Russell inclined his head toward the dining room.

With a nod, Kay went to pay her last respects to her mother.

The casket was white and expensive. A blanket of dark red roses covered the closed portion. Baskets of flowers and plants filled every corner of the room, overpowering the air with their fragrance.

Kay blinked back her tears as she gazed at her mother. How old and frail she looked, her face almost as pale as the white satin lining.

"I love you, Mom," Kay murmured. "I'm so sorry for everything. Please forgive me for coming back here, but I had to see you. I had to say good-bye. I know that you're happier wherever you are now, happier than you ever were here."

She tensed as her aunt Greta came up behind her.

"I'm glad you came home, Kiya. Your father's been worried about you." She paused. "And Victor, too, of course."

Kay dashed the tears from her eyes. "I don't want to talk about Victor. Not now."

"All right." Greta lowered her voice. "Are you sure it was wise to come home?"

Kay looked at her aunt, surprised by her words, but before she could respond, her father entered the room.

"It's time," he said quietly. "The pack is waiting for us at the cemetery."

With a nod, Greta took Kay's hand and led her out of the house and into the backseat of the waiting limo.

Moments later, her father, Brett, and Victor's family joined them in the car.

The drive to the cemetery was silent, save for the sound of Greta's weeping. Kay refused to cry in front of her father for reasons that weren't altogether clear, even to herself.

There had been only a few funerals during Kay's lifetime— one for a woman who had died in childbirth, another for a young boy who had drowned, the last for a baby girl that had lived only a few days. Kay had heard rumors that the baby had been horribly deformed.

The cemetery was located in a meadow ringed by tall cottonwood trees, which were considered sacred—not only by the Lakota, but by other tribes, as well. The Lakota always used a cottonwood tree for their Sun Dance pole. It was said by the old ones that it was from the shape of the cottonwood's leaves that the People learned to make their tipis.

Most of the pack's dead were entombed in the pack vault located several yards away. The graves of those who had been buried were located inside a fenced square of ground not far from the crypt. There were fourteen graves here. The date of the oldest was 1826.

Kay walked carefully between the headstones to the site of her mother's grave. Burials were rare among werewolves; most were cremated. But her mother had requested a Christian burial, and though there was no church service, the minister from the Methodist church in Jackson had agreed to officiate at the graveside service.

Kay listened as the reverend spoke about the afterlife, then read from the Bible, his voice filled with conviction as he said, "'I am the resurrection and the life, he that believeth in me, though he were dead, yet shall he live. And whosoever liveth and believeth in me shall never die.' Let us pray."

Kay bowed her head, finding comfort in the familiar words of the Lord's Prayer.

"'Our Father, who art in heaven, hallowed be Thy name. Thy kingdom come, Thy will be done, in earth as it is·in heaven . . .'"

After the prayer, the members of the pack came by, one by one, to offer their condolences to the family, until only Kay, her father, Greta, and Brett remained.

Kay's tears came as, whispering, "Good-bye, Mom," she laid a bright red rose on the top of the casket.

She flinched when her father put his arm around her.

"I know you're still angry with me," Russell said, "but we need to stick together now, more than ever."

Kay nodded but said nothing.

"I realize that you and Victor have a lot to work out between you. I suggest that the two of you have a long talk after the pack runs tonight."

She nodded again. After the pack ran tonight, she would never see any of them again.

Back in the compound, Kay went straight to her room and locked the door. She removed her shoes and hung the black dress in the closet. She would leave it behind when she left here, because she was never again going to wear it or anything else she had worn to the funeral.

Clad only in her underwear, she glanced around her room, which held little other than her bed, a chair, a desk, and a few stuffed animals left over from her childhood. Some of her things were still at Victor's. Well, they could stay there. She didn't want anything to remind her of him or of this place, either. She would never forget her mother, of course, but she was going to do her best to erase every other memory from her mind. Whatever happiness she had known here had been tainted by her father's treachery and her mother's death.

Standing at the window, she watched the sun set the sky on fire in blazing shades of crimson as it slipped behind the distant mountains. It would be dark soon. In spite of the sorrow that engulfed her, she felt a rush of excitement at the thought of running beneath the moon. Her skin tingled. Her heart beat faster. Even knowing it was impossible, she felt that she could change now, even though the moon had not yet taken command of the sky. What would it be like, to be able to change at will? To run wild and free in the meadows and mountains whenever she wished, the way the Alphas did?

Feeling suddenly fatigued by the day's events, she

stretched out on the bed and closed her eyes. She would rest for just a moment.

She woke to the sound of someone knocking on the door. For a moment, she couldn't remember where she was.

"Kiya?" her aunt Greta called. "We'll be leaving in a few minutes. Are you ready?"

Sitting up, Kay ran a hand through her hair. "I'll be right down."

She removed her bra and stepped out of her panties, her thoughts briefly turning to Gideon. Where had he spent the day? Was he nearby?

Wrapping a towel around her nakedness, she went downstairs to join the others on the patio.

She glimpsed Victor standing to one side. She intended to tell him not to follow her, but, to her surprise, he kept his distance.

While she was puzzling over that odd state of affairs, her father shifted. Kay dropped her towel, her body transforming from human to wolf in the blink of an eye. The suddenness of it took her by surprise. Usually, she had to concentrate for several moments before completing the change, but not tonight.

She ran after her father and sailed cleanly over the fence, her exhilaration growing as she ran through the night, quickly outdistancing the rest of the pack, including her father. She basked in the feel of the damp earth beneath the sensitive pads of her feet, the myriad scents carried to her by the wind, the beauty of the night as seen through the wolf's eyes.

She glanced over her shoulder, her tongue lolling in a wolfish grin. She was in the lead, followed by her father and Victor, who were running side by side. She didn't see any of the other wolves.

What had happened to the rest of the pack?

She slowed when her father and Victor veered to the left and disappeared from sight over a low hill. Her ears pricked forward when a warning bark she recognized as her father's pierced the night. She skidded to a stop when she heard the sharp report of a gunshot followed by a high-pitched whine.

The ensuing silence filled her with apprehension. She lifted her head, her anxiety growing when she scented blood on the wind.

Throwing back her head, she howled for the pack, then raced toward the place where she had last seen her father and Victor.

When she topped the rise, she came to an abrupt halt, unable to believe what she was seeing. Her father, slowly shifting from wolf to human, lay on the ground. Victor knelt beside him, one hand pressed against her father's chest. A few feet away, a middle-aged man lay sprawled on the ground, his throat ripped out. A rifle lay beside him.

Kay ran down the hill, shifting to human form as she went. "What happened?"

Victor looked up at her, his cheeks damp with tears. "I don't know," he said. "It all happened so fast. That man came out of the brush and shot your father. I . . . I killed him before he could fire again."

"My father . . . is he—?"

Victor nodded. "I'm afraid he's gone."

Kay shook her head. "No. No, he can't be." She pushed Victor's hand away, her own searching for some sign of life, and finding none.

She sank back on her heels. She had just buried her mother, and now this. Had she known, on some primal level, that something like this was going to happen? Was that why she'd been drawn home? Because she needed to be here?

Massaging her temples, she closed her eyes. Why did she feel so numb inside, so empty? Her father had just been killed. Shouldn't she be devastated? Railing against fate? What kind of a daughter was she, that she didn't feel anything?

One by one, the pack arrived. Victor searched the dead man's pockets, looking for identification. There was none.

Rising to his feet, he looked at the pack. "You know what to do."

Rising, Kay turned away, unable to watch, as the wolves disposed of the dead man's remains.

It was then that she saw the black wolf standing on the rise, watching her.

Kiya, are you all right? Gideon asked.

Someone just killed my father. I need to be here, with the pack.

I'm sorry, Kiya. Is there anything I can do?

Just stay close.

Count on it. He needed to talk to her, but now wasn't the time.

I have to go.

I'll be here if you need me.

She nodded again. When she turned to face her pack mates, there was no trace of the stranger save for his clothing and a faint smear of blood in the dirt. Three members of the pack shifted to their human forms to help Victor carry their fallen Alpha home. A fourth gathered the dead man's clothes to be burned.

Feeling uncomfortable being naked in front of Victor, Kay shifted back to her wolf form and followed the others back to the compound.

She trailed behind as they carried her father into the house and up to his room where they laid him on the bed.

Kay hurried to her room. After shifting to her human form, she pulled on a pair of jeans and a sweater, then returned to her father's bedroom. Victor, Greta, and Brett were gathered around the bed, their expressions somber. It was obvious they had dressed in haste. Victor wore a pair of sweatpants, Greta had pulled on a bathrobe, Brett wore only a pair of jeans. They all looked up when Kay entered the room.

She moved slowly toward the bed. A sheet covered her father. How could he be dead? He had always seemed so strong, so invincible. And now he was gone.

Greta came around the bed to give Kay a hug. "We have some hard decisions to make," she said quietly.

"And we need to make them right away," Brett said.

"What kind of decisions?" Kay asked, although she was certain she already knew the answer.

"Your father didn't leave a male heir," Brett said.

Greta took Brett's hand in hers. "Which means leadership of the pack falls to me."

"You've always been next in line," Kay said. "So, what's the problem?"

"You know how it is. Word of your father's death is probably already spreading through the werewolf community. We're a small pack."

Kay nodded as she began to see the dilemma. Even though Greta had been born an Alpha, it was rare for females to be pack leaders, mainly because male werewolves tended to be bigger and stronger. When challenged, the females were almost always defeated.

"As long as your father was our leader, we weren't in any danger," Brett remarked. "But now . . ."

"It's come to our attention that the pack in Montana is looking to expand its territory," Greta said.

"Why haven't I heard anything about that?" Kay asked.

"There was no need to worry about it while your father was alive," Greta answered. "He was one of the strongest Alphas our kind has ever had. No one was willing to go up against him."

Brett slipped his arm around his wife's shoulders. "Your aunt doesn't have a reputation like that. I don't want her risking her life."

Greta touched her husband's cheek. "We've already talked about this. I'll do whatever I have to do. And I'll win. I'm not afraid. My biggest concern is that the pack won't accept me. If that happens, we'll have a whole new set of problems."

Kay nodded. A pack without an Alpha didn't survive very long. "So, if you refuse to take over, or the pack doesn't accept you—and I don't see that happening—what then?"

"An Alpha from another pack will issue a challenge. If no one opposes him, our pack will be absorbed into a new one."

"What if we don't want to be absorbed into another pack?" Kay asked.

"Those who refuse will be disposed of."

"Disposed of?" Kay shook her head. How could she have grown up here and never heard about any of this?

"It's a pack thing," Brett said, as if that explained everything.

Which it didn't, at least as far as Kay was concerned.

"We'll have to discuss this with the pack tomorrow night," Greta said. "Right now, we need to get cleaned up and lay our Alpha to rest."

With a worried glance at Kay, Brett followed Greta out of the room.

When Kay started to follow them, Victor took hold of her arm, then closed the door.

Kay stared pointedly at his hand. "Let go of me."

"We need to talk."

"I don't have anything to say to you."

"No? Well, I've got a few things to say to you, *wife*." His hand tightened on her arm when she tried to pull away. "Tomorrow night, when the pack meets to discuss who should take over as Alpha, you will suggest that I take your father's place."

"Like hell I will. You're not even a member of our pack." She flinched as his fingers bit into her arm. "You're hurting me!"

"I'll do worse than that if you don't do as I say. I want this, Kiya. If you're smart, you won't oppose me."

"Are you threatening me?" She stared at him, appalled by a sudden niggling fear that Victor was somehow responsible for her father's death.

"Of course not," he said, his eyes narrowing to mere slits. "But it would be a shame if anything happened to your aunt Greta, her being next to the last of your blood kin and all."

There wasn't a doubt in her mind that Victor would carry through on his threat. Even worse, the suspicion that Victor had killed her father no longer seemed as far-fetched as it had only moments ago. Victor had always been power-hungry. Alpha werewolves lived a long time. She had a horrible feeling that Victor had grown tired of waiting and had decided to hurry things along.

"If you suggest that I take your father's place, the transition will be smooth. No one will get hurt. With your blessing, the pack will agree. After all, I'm your husband and everyone knows how much your father loved me. Who better to take his place?"

"Anyone but you!"

"Think about this, then. If you don't back me, I will challenge Greta for leadership of the pack. Who do you think will win?"

Feeling sick to her stomach, Kay could only stare at him, mute.

"So, do we understand each other?" he asked, his voice a low growl.

She nodded curtly.

"You need to get ready for the funeral. I'll help you dress."

"I don't need any help."

"It's my husbandly duty," he said smugly. Still grasping her arm, he opened the door and escorted her to her bedroom.

When it became obvious he wasn't going to leave, Kay turned her back to him. She longed to take a shower, but it wasn't going to happen with Victor in the room. She quickly pulled on the black dress she had worn such a short time ago, brushed her hair, stepped into her heels.

When she was ready, Victor grabbed her hand and hauled her to the guest room at the other end of the corridor. She moved to the window, staring out into the night while he dressed. She tried to think, but she was numb inside. Empty. Her parents were gone and she hadn't had a chance to tell either of them good-bye. But even worse, she couldn't shake the feeling that Victor was responsible for her father's death. She told herself it was impossible. Her father's death had been an accident. A hunter in the wrong place at the wrong time.

"Let's go."

She turned away from the window, her jaw clenching when Victor again took hold of her arm.

He grinned at her. "I'm not taking any chances on your doing something stupid."

"I already did that when I married you."

She gasped with pain when he struck her across the face, her head snapping back from the force of the blow.

"That tongue is going to get you in trouble one of these days, Mrs. Rinaldi. I'd advise you to choose your words with more care in the future."

Werewolf funerals were always held in the deep woods late at night. Her father's body, tightly wrapped in a wool blanket, was laid out on a bier to be burned. The pack, all clad in unrelieved black, surrounded it.

Shrouded in a long hooded cloak, Greta stood at the head of the bier. "We are met here this night to mourn our Alpha, Nagin Luta. He has served our pack well. We know not whether his death was accidental or provoked, but the man who caused it will slay no more of our kind."

Brett moved up beside his wife. "Nagin Luta was my brother-in-law, and my friend. Under his leadership, the

Shadow Pack knew fifty-three years of peace and prosperity. He will be sorely missed."

One by one, the members of the pack paid their verbal respects to their Alpha.

As his next of kin, it was Kay's duty to ignite the funeral pyre. She stared at the lighter that Brett offered her, then shook her head. "I can't do this."

Without a word, Victor took the lighter from her hand.

Tears flooded Kay's eyes as the hungry flames devoured her father's remains. A morbid part of her mind wondered if fire consumed all preternatural creatures as quickly and completely.

As the flames died away, mournful howls of sorrow rose on the wind.

In the distance, a wild wolf yipped in reply.

Standing a good distance away, Gideon watched the proceedings. He didn't miss the way Victor Rinaldi kept Kay close to his side. Gideon had only to brush her mind to know what she was thinking, feeling. It came as no surprise that Rinaldi had threatened her. What was a surprise was her suspicion that Rinaldi had murdered her father so he could take over as Alpha of the Shadow Pack.

Which was exactly what had happened. Gideon couldn't say for sure what Rinaldi's reasoning had been, but Gideon had seen the whole thing, which had taken only a few moments. Victor had paused at the foot of the rise and Alissano had stopped beside him. The murder itself had happened very fast. Victor shifted to human. A man stepped out from behind a tree and fired once. The bullet struck Alissano in the heart and he went down. Victor had congratulated the shooter on a job well done. Then, in a move quicker than the human eye could follow, he had shifted into his wolf form, ripped out the shooter's throat, and quickly shifted back to human. By the time Kay reached the scene, Victor was kneeling beside Alissano.

The howls died away as the flames consumed the last of Alissano's remains.

Dissolving into mist, Gideon followed Kay and the others back to the compound.

Trying to pass over the fence was like hitting a brick wall. He had hoped the death of the Alpha would allow him to pass, but apparently not.

He waited until the pack members had dispersed to their homes before resuming his own shape. He had to get in touch with Kay and let her know what he had seen and heard, had to warn her that her father's death hadn't been an accident.

Chapter 36

Kay hated to see the pack members return to their own homes after the funeral. So much had happened in such a short time, she would have welcomed their company. . . . Who was she trying to kid? Other than her aunt's family, she had no real affection for any of the people who lived in the compound. The truth was, she was afraid to be alone with Victor, who had stayed downstairs to have a drink. She hoped he drank himself into a stupor.

She tried not to think of the two men who had remained behind in the forest. They would collect her father's ashes, deposit them in a large urn, and take it to the pack crypt where it would be placed on a shelf beside his father's remains. In a few days, she would order a bronze plaque bearing her father's name and the years he had ruled as Alpha so that he would not be forgotten.

She had a bad case of nerves by the time she reached her room. She considered locking the door, but what was the point? Victor would likely just break it down. Going into the bathroom, she changed into flannel PJs, washed her face, and brushed her teeth, constantly glancing over her shoulder for fear Victor would burst in on her and demand his husbandly rights.

When she returned to the bedroom, he was waiting for her.

Nervousness turned to fear when he grabbed both her hands in his. Before she knew what he was up to, he'd handcuffed her to the bedpost. Heart pounding, she stared up at him.

He snorted. "Don't worry. I have no intention of bedding you tonight."

She went weak with relief.

Relief that was short-lived when he leered at her. "There's always tomorrow night. And the night after that. Try not to miss me too much while I'm gone."

Kay closed her eyes after he left the room. She had to get out of here.

Gideon? Where are you?

I'm here. Are you okay?

Yes, for now. I think Victor killed my father.

I know he did. He would have preferred to break the news in person, but she needed to know what Victor was capable of.

Kay felt as though someone had submerged her in ice water. She had suspected Victor of murder, but having her suspicions confirmed by someone she trusted came as a shock.

Kiya, you need to get out of there as soon as you can.

I can't. Victor wants to take over as Alpha. That has to be why he killed my father. The pack is meeting tomorrow night to discuss it. Victor has threatened to kill Greta if I don't support him in his bid to take over. And the thing is, the pack will probably sustain him. Everyone knows that my father loved him like a son.

Gideon considered her words. If what she said was true, then she was safe, at least until the pack had made its decision.

Gideon?

Try not to worry, Wolfie. And whatever you do, don't make him angry.

What are you going to do?

I don't know, but hang tight. I'll think of something.
I miss you.
I miss you, too. When this is over, I'll show you how much.
Promise?
Do you doubt it?
No. I love you.
I know.
Gideon, I . . . oh! He's back!
I'll be in touch. And Kiya? I love you, too.

Kay woke with a groan, thinking that she had spent more comfortable nights in Verah's basement. She had tossed and turned all night long, unable to get comfortable with her wrist secured to the bedpost. Even more unsettling had been sharing her bed with Victor. She had tensed every time he moved, afraid he was reaching for her.

Sitting up, she was relieved to see that his side of the bed was empty, and surprised to find that he had uncuffed her hand.

After taking a quick shower, she dressed and went downstairs. Brett and Victor were sitting at the kitchen table, reading the paper. Greta stood at the stove.

For a minute, Kay simply stood there, watching them. How could they behave as if this was a morning like any other? As if they hadn't just buried her parents?

Approaching the stove, she poured herself a cup of coffee.

"How are you this morning?" Greta asked.

"Fine," Kay lied. "Can I help you?"

"Nope, I'm all done." She handed Kay a platter of bacon. "Just put that on the table and we're ready to eat."

Kay wanted to scream at her aunt, to ask how she could even think about food at a time like this. Instead, she carried the dish to the table.

She took the place across from Victor so she wouldn't have to sit beside him.

The conversation was subdued as Brett and Greta expressed their concerns about finding a new Alpha.

Victor glanced pointedly at Kay several times, but she pretended not to notice.

He glared at Kay when she remained in the kitchen to help Greta tidy up, but there was little he could do about it without making a scene.

Kay breathed a sigh of relief when he followed Brett into the living room. Fighting the urge to cry, she began loading dishes into the dishwasher.

Greta looked up from rinsing the frying pan. "Kiya, how are you, really?"

Kay sank down on one of the chairs. Elbows resting on the table, her chin propped on her folded hands, she shook her head. "Not good. I don't want to be here. I don't want to be married to Victor."

"It's that vampire, isn't it?" Turing off the faucet, Greta took the chair across from Kay. "You really are in love with him, aren't you?"

Kay nodded.

"Your mother mentioned him to me once." Greta smiled. "I can't say as I blame you. He's far and away one of the best-looking men I've ever seen."

"Greta, my mother killed herself to give me a chance to run away with Gideon. Did you know that?"

Greta's eyes widened in surprise. "No. No, I didn't. We all thought . . ." She bit down on her lower lip, then said, "I know your mother wasn't happy here, but I never thought she'd commit suicide. But if she did it for you . . ." Greta shook her head. "You can't blame yourself. She loved you very much. And so do I. If you want to leave Victor, I'll help you in any way that I can."

"No! I can't ask you to do that! I can't lose you, too. You're the only family I've got left."

"Nothing's going to happen to me."

"I know." Reaching across the table, Kay took her aunt's hand in hers and gave it a squeeze. "And I intend to make sure that it doesn't."

Kay sought refuge in the laundry room, hoping Victor wouldn't think to look for her there. While putting another load into the washer, she debated the wisdom of trying to leave the compound, but Victor's threat against her aunt kept her in place as surely as Verah's iron bars. There was always a chance he had been bluffing, but it wasn't a risk she was willing to take.

She schooled her features into a mask of indifference when he tracked her down an hour later.

"How very domestic of you," he remarked, noting the piles of folded laundry she had stacked on the counter. "I don't see any of my clothes there," he said, crowding her into a corner. "Surely, as a devoted wife, you should be doing my laundry and not your uncle's."

When he lowered his head to kiss her, she turned away. She should have known better. He shoved her against the wall, trapping her between his arms, his body holding hers in place.

She glared at him. When he lowered his head again, she started to lift her knee, intending to drive it into his groin, only to stop when she recalled Gideon warning her earlier not to make Victor angry.

She closed her eyes as his mouth covered hers. It was all she could do to keep from gagging. And then she heard her aunt's voice, calling her name. It was the sweetest sound she had ever heard.

"Oh, Kiya, there you are," Greta said from the doorway.

With a low growl, Victor stepped away from Kay. "I'll talk to you later." Nodding in Greta's direction, he left the room.

"Greta, bless you! Your timing couldn't have been better."

To Kay's surprise, her aunt hugged her. "I knew you didn't want to be alone with him, so I've been sort of keeping an eye on the two of you all day."

"Thank you!"

"I had another reason for coming down here. The pack is starting to gather."

"All right." Kay tossed a load of towels into the dryer. "Let's go."

Kay's nerves were on edge as she dressed for dinner that night. She wore all black—black jeans, sweater, boots.

Earlier in the day, Victor had told her exactly what he expected from her and had gone into great detail outlining the consequences should she fail.

She tensed as he entered the bedroom.

Victor lifted a brow as his gaze ran over her. "Did someone die?"

"Only my mother," she retorted. "And my father."

He glared at her as he went to the closet and pulled out a pair of navy slacks and a pale blue shirt. He ran a comb through his hair, then sat on the end of the bed and pulled on a pair of dark gray loafers. He looked so smug, so sure of her, that she wanted to scream. And yet, what could she do to thwart him? She had no doubt he would do exactly as he'd said, and as opposed as she was to having Victor as the Shadow Alpha, she didn't dare object, not when her aunt's life hung in the balance. She had lost her mother and her father. She couldn't lose Greta, too.

Victor stood. "It's time to make our entrance." He took a last look at his reflection in the mirror, nodded, and said, "Let's go."

* * *

Kay kept her gaze on her plate during dinner, surreptitiously listening to the hum of conversation at her end of the table as her pack mates speculated on what it would be like to have a female Alpha. The wolves liked and respected Greta, but she was, after all, a female and not likely to survive a challenge. Kay heard the name of the Montana Pack's Alpha—Simon LeClare—mentioned several times. No one wanted to be absorbed into LeClare's pack, or any other. It would mean leaving the Shadow Pack's compound, adjusting to a new Alpha, a new pack hierarchy. She heard the worry in their voices, saw it in their furrowed brows as those nearest to her contemplated such a drastic change.

Kay glanced at the table where the children were seated. It would be hardest on them, having to leave all they knew. Not every compound was as large as this one, or had swimming pools and ball courts. The children of the pack were schooled here; most of the very young ones had never been outside the fence line.

Tonight, when the pack went out to choose a new leader, those under the age of eighteen would stay here, in the house.

And suddenly, it was time to go. Parents wrapped their young ones in blankets and settled them on the sofa. Some of the kids sprawled on the floor to watch a movie, while the older kids pulled out cell phones and iPads.

Kay's nerves were stretched wire-thin when they reached the gathering place in the woods just outside the fence line. She refused to look at Victor, who stood on her left, his hand squeezing hers. A silent warning, no doubt.

When everyone was present, Greta stepped into the center of the circle. "You all know why we are here tonight. Our Alpha has been killed and we must choose a new leader. As Nagin Luta's sister, and as the only other Alpha of the

Shadow Pack, it falls to me to take his place. If there are any here who will not support me as Alpha, speak now."

Victor nudged Kay. She glanced up at him, into his cold dark eyes, and knew that unless she suggested Victor's name, her aunt's days were numbered.

Torn by guilt for what she was about to do, Kay stepped into the center of the circle. "I know Greta Crayton would be a credit to our pack, and that she has the heart to be our Alpha, but . . ." Kay swallowed hard, fighting down the bile that rose in her throat. "But I don't believe she has the strength to defend us. We are a small pack. News of my father's untimely death has already spread. As you all know, my father trusted my husband, and loved him like his own son. For that reason, I believe that Victor Rinaldi should reign as our new Alpha."

A hum of excited conversation filled the air as Victor, looking properly humble and surprised, took his place beside Kay in the center of the circle.

Greta held up her hand, silencing the crowd. "As is custom, anyone seeking to be accepted as Alpha must shift on a night when the moon isn't full to prove they are able and worthy."

Victor smiled at Greta, then bowed from the waist. "Ladies first."

He was as good as his word. He waited for Greta to begin, but before she finished, he shifted from man to wolf and back again, proving that he was stronger, faster.

Murmurs ran through the pack.

Resuming her own form, Greta made a slow circle, her gaze resting on each man and woman present. "The choice is yours. Those of you who wish to follow Victor, please stand behind him. Those of you who wish to follow me, join me on this side of the circle."

Kay held her breath, wondering what the outcome would

be. Marriages had broken up when couples refused to follow the same Alpha.

Brett was the first one to make a move. He went to stand at his wife's side.

Victor looked at Kay; after a moment, she went to stand beside him. She lowered her head, hands clenched at her sides, unable to meet her aunt's disbelieving gaze.

In a surprisingly short time, the pack had made its decision.

And Victor had lost his bid to be the Shadow Pack's Alpha.

It took all Kay's self-control to keep from smiling. She had done what Victor asked and the pack had rejected him. He couldn't blame her for that, she thought, until she saw his face. His eyes glittered with anger. Tension rolled off him in waves as he fought to keep his wolf in check.

The pack members felt it, too. Their unease was a palpable thing in the taut silence.

Fear's cold, clammy hand curled around Kay's insides. This wasn't over, not by a long shot.

Chapter 37

Victor made a slow circuit around the circle, his gaze resting on the face of each pack member. Most of them held their ground; a few glanced away.

He stopped in front of Greta. "You're not strong enough to hold the Shadow Pack. Either surrender to me, or fight me for it, here and now."

"No!" Brett sprang in front of his wife. "The pack has made its decision, Rinaldi. Go home, where you belong."

"My wife is here," Victor replied with a sneer. "So here is where I belong." His gaze shifted back to Greta. "Surrender or fight?"

Head held high, Greta stepped around her husband. "I will never surrender to you."

Victor smiled as if the fight was already won. "So be it."

Kay placed a restraining hand on her aunt's arm. "Don't do this."

"I have to," Greta said. "To refuse would be to dishonor everything my brother stood for."

Kay nodded. She embraced her aunt, then moved away, her heart aching because she knew Victor was right. There was no way Greta could win.

As Kay walked away, she felt Gideon's presence. Looking

up, she saw a familiar black wolf standing beneath a tree about a hundred yards away. Just knowing he was nearby made her spirits rise. Maybe there was still hope after all.

Silence descended over the pack as Victor and Greta shifted.

Kay felt her heart sink when she glanced from one to the other. Victor was larger, more muscular, easily the stronger of the two.

The wolves faced each other, ears twitching back and forth, nostrils flared. Victor snarled, then lunged forward, his teeth snapping but biting only empty air as Greta spun gracefully out of the way.

Kay watched breathlessly as the two wolves circled and snapped at each other. For a time, neither one did any damage. To Kay's surprise, her aunt drew first blood. Victor howled with rage as Greta sank her fangs into his shoulder, but he shook her off with ease, then sprang forward, his jaws closing on her left foreleg.

Kay flinched when she heard the bone snap.

Victor let Greta go and took a step away, his lips peeled back in a wolfish grin of triumph as she struggled to her feet. Blood dripped from her injured leg.

Kay watched in horror when Victor closed in on her aunt again. Greta tried to defend herself, but it was no use. On three legs, she couldn't outmaneuver Victor; running away was not an option even if she could manage it. Once begun, it was a fight to the death.

Kay's horror turned to fury as she watched Victor viciously attack her aunt again and again. Instead of granting his opponent a swift, clean death, it was obvious Victor intended to torment her, to inflict as much pain and damage as he could before delivering the final, killing blow. What was worse, he was enjoying it.

With a cry of rage, Brett darted forward, only to be pulled back by three other pack members. He struggled against them, but they refused to let go. In his human form, he had no chance against Victor.

Kay's anger grew stronger, harder to control, as Victor sank his fangs into her aunt's shoulder and gave it a sharp twist. If only she could put a stop to it. But there was nothing she could do. . . .

Suddenly, it was too much to bear. She had lost her mother. She had lost her father. She couldn't stand by and let Victor take her aunt from her, as well.

Anger surged up from the very depths of Kay's being and with it a rush of preternatural power that put fear and caution to flight.

Her clothing shredded as, with a feral cry, Kay shifted.

She stood there for a moment, stunned by the realization that she had changed when the moon was no longer full. But there was no time to think of what that might mean, not now, when her aunt's life was in danger.

Not when she was violating pack law.

She growled a challenge low in her throat, sank back on her haunches, then launched herself at Victor's back, her teeth sinking deep into his neck.

Rearing back in surprise, he shook her off, but only for a moment. Regaining her feet, Kay attacked him again and again, her teeth sinking into his side, his shoulder. He was bigger, but she was faster. And as the fight progressed, she proved she was stronger as she drew blood again and again.

A part of her was repulsed by what she was doing, but another part reveled in her newfound strength. Was this how her father had felt? High on the power thrumming through her, she was impervious to the bites Victor managed to inflict on her.

She attacked him again, her teeth tearing a chunk of flesh from his side.

Howling with pain, Victor broke and ran through a break

in the circle, only to come to an abrupt halt when a large black wolf bounded into his path.

Victor tried to dart past the strange wolf, but the creature blocked him at every turn, herding him back toward the circle.

Kay met Victor before he reached the pack. Snarling, she flung herself at him, her teeth clamping down on his jugular. She tore his throat out with one savage shake of her head.

Stepping away from the body, she stared at it, exhilaration and horror warring within her as she watched Victor's body morph from wolf to human.

Panting, her sides heaving, she lifted her head and stared at Gideon, who remained in the shadows, watching her. What would he think of her now? Would he ever look at her the same?

But there was no time to worry about it. The members of the pack were cheering, shouting her name, proclaiming her as their new Alpha.

She glanced over her shoulder to see them running toward her. When she looked back at the place where Gideon had been standing, he was gone.

And then she heard his voice in her mind. *Good job, Wolfie. Go enjoy your victory. I'll see you soon.*

Before she could reply, the members of the pack had surrounded her. Needing to make sure her aunt was going to be all right, she shifted, then stood there, shivering a little as the wind picked up.

Tyler Red Elk broke away from the pack. Removing his shirt, he wrapped it around her shoulders. "You're bleeding."

Only then did Kay become aware of the numerous bites and scratches on her arms and legs, feel the pain from the deep gouge in her right side where Victor's teeth had savaged her. But it was a small price to pay for her aunt's life.

She felt a rush of relief when she saw Brett gently lift Greta into his arms and start toward the compound. Calling, "Wait," she hurried after them.

"Is something wrong?" Brett asked, frowning.

"No." Kay covered her aunt's hand with her own. "I didn't side with Victor because I wanted to. You know that, don't you?"

"It doesn't matter, Kiya," Greta said. "He's . . . he was your husband."

"That had nothing to do with it. I never would have chosen him over you, but he threatened to kill you if I didn't put his name up as Alpha. And I believed him." Kay squeezed her aunt's hand. "There's something else you need to know. My father's death wasn't an accident. Victor hired someone to kill him. Gideon saw it all."

"I don't believe it!" Brett exclaimed. "He wouldn't—"

"He did."

"Kiya, I'm so sorry," Greta said.

"You're our Alpha now," Brett said. "We're behind you all the way." He glanced at his wife, worry lining his brow. "We'll see you back at the house."

Kay nodded. "I'll be along soon."

Bobby One Horse came up beside her. "You need to get up to the house, too," he said. "Those bites need tending."

Kay nodded. Bobby was the pack doctor. "I'll be all right."

"Victor was an Alpha. Those bites won't heal as quickly. I'll feel better once I clean them up."

"All right, but go and take care of Greta first. And have someone dispose of the body."

Bobby smiled at her. "As you wish, Alpha."

Lying on her bed upstairs while the doctor tended her wounds, Kay overheard snatches of conversation from downstairs as the members of the pack rehashed Victor's battle with Greta, and then Victor's battle with Kay. One and all, they agreed that both she and Greta had upheld the honor of the Shadow Pack.

With her wounds tended to, Kay donned a long-sleeved, red silk dress that covered the half-healed wounds on her arms and legs, took a deep breath, and went downstairs where she accepted the congratulations of those present. Then, calling for silence, she stood before all the members of the pack and demanded their fealty.

One by one, each pack member over the age of eighteen came forward and swore allegiance to her, promising to defend her and the Shadow Pack to the death.

It was the most moving night of her life. What would her father think if he could see her now?

Feeling a sudden need to be alone, she slipped out the back door and made her way to the cemetery.

She hadn't gone far when she sensed Gideon's presence. Moments later, he materialized beside her. "Do you want me here?" he asked. "Or would you rather be alone?"

"Stay." She bit down on her lower lip to keep from crying when he took her hand in his and gave it a squeeze.

Side by side, they made their way to the meadow.

Gideon leaned against one of the cottonwood trees outside the fence while Kay went inside and knelt at her mother's grave.

Kay bowed her head in prayer, silent tears tracking her cheeks.

She deserved a good cry, Gideon thought, watching her. She had lost her parents. She had almost lost her aunt. She had killed the man who was her husband. She had taken over the position of Alpha, and all that it entailed.

Looking at her, his heart swelled with sympathy and pride. His wife was a hell of a woman.

His head snapped up as he caught the scent of wolf.

Alpha wolf.

A second breath and he identified the intruder as Victor's

father. Before he had time to consider the man's presence in the vicinity, the wolf vaulted over the fence and knocked Kay to the ground.

Gideon was on the wolf in an instant. His hands locked around the animal's throat. With one quick twist, he broke the wolf's neck, then tossed the carcass aside and reached for Kay.

"Are you all right?" he asked, helping her to her feet.

She nodded, too stunned to speak.

"Are you sure?"

Nodding again, she glanced at the dead wolf, who even now was reverting to his human form. And then she swore softly. "Do you know what this means?" she exclaimed. "I've only been Alpha for a few hours, and we're already on the verge of war."

Gideon opened his preternatural senses, his gaze sweeping the darkness. "You'd better get back to the house," he said. "I don't think there's anyone else out here, but there's no sense taking chances."

"Come with me?"

"You'll have to invite me in again."

"As Alpha, you will always be welcome in my home," she said, kissing his cheek. "This invitation is irrevocable."

"So," Kay said, after explaining what had occurred at the cemetery. "What are our options?"

Sitting in the easy chair beside the hearth, she glanced from her aunt to Brett and back again. Greta sat on the sofa in the living room, her broken leg propped up on a footstool. It would be healed by morning.

Brett sat next to her. Gideon stood beside the hearth. He had carried Diego Rinaldi's body back to the compound, wrapped it in a sheet, and left it in the barn.

Greta shook her head. "If we're careful, we should be able

to avert a war. After all, you defeated Victor fair and square. And Rinaldi attacked you from behind with obvious intent to kill you. They can't blame Gideon for defending you."

Kay shook her head. She hoped Greta was right and that the Green Mountain Pack would realize that Victor's father had transgressed pack law by not openly challenging Kay to a fair fight to redress his grievances, but somehow, she didn't think the wolves of the Green Mountain Pack would see it that way.

"Who'll take over, now that Victor and his father are both gone?" she asked.

"If no one objects, Diego's brother, Rudolfo, is next in line to be Alpha," Brett said. "Do you know him?"

"Not really." She had met Rudolfo once or twice while growing up. Rudolfo was five years younger than his brother. He had been away from home during the short time Kay had lived in the Rinaldi compound. She had no doubt that he would soon return home to avenge his brother and his nephew. For all she knew, he could be there now.

Brett and Greta exchanged glances, and then Brett asked the question on everyone's mind. "Do you think you can take him?"

"I don't know." Rudolfo was taller than Diego, broad-shouldered, with a neck like a bull. He would be in his early forties now. Like vampires, werewolves grew stronger with age. She was deeply afraid that Rudolfo Rinaldi would not be as easy to defeat as Victor had been.

"Well," Brett said, "tomorrow four of our men will take Rinaldi's body home and explain what happened. . . ."

"I should go with them," Kay said.

"No. They know you're in mourning for your parents, and supposedly grieving for Victor, even though he died at your hand. Hopefully, they'll respect that. It might buy us some time. Maybe enough time to cool any thoughts they have of revenge."

Gideon pushed away from the hearth, his hands clenched at his sides. "And if it doesn't?"

"Then she'll have to fight," Greta said quietly.

"No." Gideon shook his head. "She's not risking her life again."

"I'm Alpha," Kay said. "I knew what I was getting into when I killed Victor."

"Dammit, Kay . . ." He raked a hand through his hair. She was right. He knew it. He admired her courage and the strength of her convictions. But he for damn sure didn't have to like it.

Brett and Greta called it a night a short time later.

With a sigh, Kay stretched her arms over her head. She was weary in mind and body. Doubts about her ability to defeat Rudolfo and to take her father's place as Alpha weighed heavily on her mind.

She closed her eyes as Gideon moved up behind her and began to massage her neck.

"That feels wonderful." She smiled when he brushed a kiss across the top of her head.

"Tired?" he asked.

She nodded, her head lolling forward as his fingers worked their magic on the knots in her back and shoulders.

He massaged her for another twenty minutes, then scooped her into his arms and carried her swiftly up the stairs to her bedroom, where he undressed her, slipped a nightgown over her head, and tucked her into bed.

"Sleep tight, Lady Alpha," he said, giving her hand a squeeze.

She clung to his hand. "Don't you want to stay here, with me?"

"Of course I do, but with all that's going on, I wasn't sure how your pack would feel about that, you know? The whole werewolf–vampire thing."

"You're my husband. This is where you belong, unless . . ."

He covered her mouth with his hand, cutting off her next

words. "Don't go there, Wolfie. There's nowhere else I'd rather be, and you know it."

Wrapping her arms around his neck, she murmured, "I've missed you."

"No more than I've missed you."

She scooted over, tugging him down beside her. "Do you think we'll ever have a life together when someone isn't trying to kill one of us?"

"I sure as hell hope so."

"Gideon . . ."

"It's all right. Go to sleep, darlin'. You've earned it."

"You'll stay with me?"

He brushed a lock of hair behind her ear. "Until the sun comes up."

"You won't go far?"

"Not a chance."

"Promise?"

"I promise."

With a sigh, she snuggled up against him, her head pillowed on his shoulder, asleep between one breath and the next.

Gideon inhaled deeply, grateful to have a few hours to hold her close, to run his fingers through her hair, lightly stroke the softness of her skin. Lying there, he wondered what the future held for the two of them. He was a vampire, she was now the Alpha of her pack. He wasn't entirely sure what that entailed, but one thing he did know was that her pack would expect her to live with them from now on, and he wasn't certain how he felt about that. Since werewolves and vampires were natural enemies, there was little chance that her pack would accept him, and he couldn't ask her to leave.

When she murmured his name in her sleep, he kissed her lightly, felt a rush of tenderness when she turned onto her side, her arm stealing around his waist.

"I thought you were out for the night," he remarked.

"I can sleep tomorrow." She looked up at him through heavy-lidded eyes. "Are you tired?"

"It's two A.M., honey. For me, it's the shank of the evening."

He brushed a lock of hair from her forehead, laughed softly when she slipped her hand inside his jeans.

Gathering her into his arms, he murmured, "I think now *you* must be reading *my* mind."

She woke to the sound of someone pounding on the bedroom door. Bleary-eyed, she pulled on her robe and shuffled to the door. "Brett! What are you doing here so early?"

"There's a delegation downstairs from the Rinaldi compound."

Kay glanced at the clock on her bedside table. Six A.M. She didn't have to ask what the members of the Green Mountain Pack wanted, although she was a little surprised they had arrived at such an early hour. "How big a delegation?"

"There's four of them, including Rudolfo."

"Where are they now?"

"Waiting on the patio. I wasn't sure if I should invite them in."

"Tell them I'll be down as soon as I'm dressed."

"Right."

"Call Tyler and ask him to round up one or two others. Tell him to keep out of sight, but to be ready, just in case the Rinaldi delegation has come to do more than talk."

With a nod, Brett went to do as bidden.

Kay stared after him a moment; then, closing the door, she rested her forehead on the wood. It seemed odd to be giving orders. What had she gotten herself into?

Twenty minutes later, she took several deep breaths, then went downstairs. She paused at the back door.

Rudolfo and three other men sat at one of the round, glass-topped tables. Someone had served them coffee.

The men all rose when Kay stepped out onto the patio.

"Good morning, gentlemen," she said.

Rudolfo inclined his head. "Mrs. Rinaldi."

The sound of her married name slammed into Kay like a fist. In the short time she had been married, only Victor had called her that. "Please, be seated," she said, and took the last chair.

Rudolfo remained standing. "You're probably wondering why we've come at such an early hour. . . ."

"I know why you're here," Kay said.

Rudolfo's expression hardened as he waited for her to go on. He was a younger, more handsome version of his brother.

"I intended to call on you later today," she said.

"Indeed?" He resumed his seat.

She didn't miss the skepticism in his voice. "With my father's untimely death, it was necessary for our pack to sustain a new Alpha. My aunt Greta was the natural choice, being the only other Alpha in our pack."

Rudolfo leaned forward. "Go on."

"Victor threatened to kill my aunt if I didn't put his name forward as Alpha. As you know, my father loved Victor so we were both surprised when the pack refused him. Victor challenged my aunt." Kay took a deep breath, willing her voice not to betray her. "My aunt was defeated. It's no secret that I was forced to marry Victor. It was bad enough that he was my husband. I refused to accept him as my Alpha. And I challenged him."

"You? How is that possible?"

"I don't know. I'm not sure exactly what happened after that, or how it happened, but the next thing I knew, I had shifted. . . ."

"You're lying!" Rudolfo exclaimed. "Such a thing is impossible."

Kay met his gaze without flinching. "It's the truth."

Rudolfo shook his head. "It's impossible."

"I fought Victor and I killed him."

"Where is my nephew?"

"I had his body cremated, of course."

"Of course." Rudolfo leaned back in his chair, his elbows resting on the arms, hands folded, fingers entwined. "And where," he asked softly, "is my brother?"

Chapter 38

Kay went still as all four men focused their attention on her.

"My brother," Rudolfo repeated. "Where is he?"

"Dead." There was no point in lying, or delaying the truth. Better to get it out in the open now and face the consequences, though she would have preferred to have Gideon there beside her. "I intended to bring him home later this morning."

"Who killed him?"

"He attacked me from behind while I was visiting my mother's grave," Kay said, her voice devoid of expression. "My . . ." She paused, wondering what to call Gideon. Friend? Acquaintance? *Husband* would never do. "A friend who was with me came to my defense."

Rudolfo's steely gaze bored into hers. "Why should I believe you?"

"Why should I lie?" Kay replied, her gaze meeting his. It was an effort to keep her expression impassive. She didn't know what would happen if he didn't believe her. Would he challenge her to a fight? Attack her here and now? Declare war on the Shadow Pack?

She slid a quick glance at the other three men. The one

on Rudolfo's left was slight of build, with sallow skin and pale gray eyes. She was certain she had never seen him before. She recognized the man on Rudolfo's right, although she couldn't remember his name, only that he was one of Victor's cousins. Both men stared at her malevolently. The third man was the youngest of the four. There was no doubt that he was related to Rudolfo. A son, perhaps.

Kay looked up, relieved, when Brett rounded a corner of the house, followed by Tyler Red Elk, Jared Broken Lance, Steven One Horn, and Joe Yellow Bear. Her backup had arrived.

"You all know my uncle, Brett Crayton."

Rudolfo nodded curtly. "Of course."

"Gentlemen." Brett stood behind Kay's chair. The other members of the pack spread out behind him.

Rudolfo stood. "If you'll be good enough to tell me where my brother's body is, I'll take it home."

When Kay started to rise, Brett placed his hands on her shoulders. "I'll take care of this, Alpha."

Brett moved toward the patio doors, gesturing for Rudolfo and the other three members of his pack to come with him.

Kay frowned. Where was Brett taking them? Curious, she dismissed Tyler and the others, then went into the house.

She followed the sound of voices to the meeting room. Careful to stay out of sight, she peered around the door frame. Someone had covered a long table with a white sheet and laid Diego's body on it. They had washed his face, combed his hair, and covered him with a blanket, as if he were a member of their own pack.

With her curiosity satisfied, Kay quickly returned to the patio.

Brett returned a few minutes later. "Well, they're gone."

Kay nodded. "That was quick thinking, bringing the body in from the barn."

"It was Greta's idea. She thought it might take some of the heat off if we treated their dead with respect. I think it worked." Brett sank down in one of the chairs. "There's no way to be sure, of course. They could still issue a challenge, but I don't think they will. I get the feeling Rudolfo believed you." Brett paused a moment before asking, "Did it really happen the way you said?"

"Yes. Diego attacked me from behind and Gideon killed him."

Brett nodded, then slapped his hands on his thighs. "Okay, then. I'm going up to see if Greta needs anything."

"Tell her I'll be along in a little while."

"Will do," he said, grinning. "She's just milking this, you know. The break and the bites have already healed."

"Well, she deserves a little pampering. It was a brave thing she did, accepting Victor's challenge."

"No braver than what you did." Folding his arms on the tabletop, Brett leaned forward. "How did you do it?"

"I have no idea. I don't even know if I can shift like that again. For all I know, it was a one-time thing."

Rising, Brett gazed down at her. "Your father would have been proud of you."

Kay blinked against the hot rush of tears his words elicited. "Thank you."

Brett winked at her, then went into the house.

Kay sighed, wishing she could stay in Gideon's embrace forever. He had appeared in her bedroom as soon as the sun went down. She had gone into his arms without a word. When he was making love to her, all her fears and worries melted away. But now, lying spent beside him, all her doubts bubbled back to the surface.

She looked at him when he tugged lightly on her hair.

"Do you want to talk about it?" he asked.

"About what?"

"About how you changed when the moon wasn't full. You're worried you won't be able to do it again, aren't you?"

She nodded.

"Have you tried?"

"No."

"Why not?"

"I guess I'm afraid to find out." If she couldn't shift at will, she would have to give up being Alpha.

"Why don't you try it now?" he suggested.

She was going to have to do it sooner or later; might as well be now, when nothing was at stake. Throwing off the covers, she stood beside the bed and summoned her wolf. The change came as quickly and easily as it had the night before.

Gideon grinned at her and she wagged her tail.

Returning to her human form, she slipped back under the covers and snuggled up against his side again. "Why do you think I'm able to do it now?"

"Well," Gideon drawled, lightly stroking her arm, "I think it might have something to do with the fact that you've got a little prime vampire blood running through your veins."

"You're kidding!"

"Nope. I'm dead serious, if you'll pardon the pun."

"But why would it . . . ?" She stopped in midsentence. There was definitely power in Gideon's blood. She had seen it at work on Verah. She had felt the power of it herself. "Will it work on the rest of the pack?"

He shrugged. "I don't know. Why?"

"Brett doesn't think Rudolfo will seek vengeance for Diego's death, but I disagree. I saw the look in his eyes when I told him his brother was dead."

"Why would he come after your pack? I'm the one who killed Diego."

"You're forgetting about Victor. It was his right to challenge Greta. I violated our laws when I interfered."

"In what way?"

"Victor made a legitimate challenge. It's against pack law for anyone to interfere until that challenge has been decided. I should have waited until my aunt was dead, and then challenged him. But I couldn't do that. I couldn't stand there and watch him kill her. I don't know how it happened, but the next thing I knew, I'd shifted."

"And beat the crap out of him," Gideon said, his voice laced with pride.

"I've never killed anyone before," she said quietly. "It was a terrible feeling, and yet I'd do it again to save Greta."

"You'll make a hell of an Alpha," Gideon said, giving her shoulders a squeeze. "I'm glad you're on my side."

"Me, too." She was silent a moment, then said, "Would you be willing to give Brett some of your blood, to see if it works on him, too?"

"Sure," he said with a grin. "Do you think he'd be willing to give me some of his in return?"

As expected, Brett wasn't crazy about the idea of ingesting vampire blood when Kay suggested it to him the following morning at breakfast.

Greta, who had recovered fully from her fight with Victor, looked thoughtful. "You know, if it works on Brett . . ."

"Hey, I never said I was willing to try it!"

"But you will, since your Alpha expects it," Greta said calmly. "So, if it works on Brett, then what? Are you thinking of trying it on the whole pack?"

"I don't know," Kay replied. "I haven't thought that far ahead. Let's see how this works out first. I'm going to call a meeting this evening. I want everyone to be on their guard. I don't want anyone leaving the compound alone. And I want everyone inside after dark."

"Kiya, don't you think that's a little extreme?" Brett asked. "I mean, do you seriously believe Rinaldi's going to jeopardize the peace between our packs by challenging you? You defeated Victor in a fair fight. Gideon killed Diego to save your life. There are really no grounds for revenge."

"Better safe than sorry," Kay replied. She drained her coffee cup and thanked Greta for breakfast. She paused on her way out of the kitchen. "Brett, meet me in the barn at sundown and we'll see what effect Gideon's blood has on you. Oh, there's one more thing. He wants a little of your blood in return," she added, and left before Brett could object.

The meeting didn't take long. Kay explained her reasons for the increased precautions, and when the meeting was over, she gestured for Brett to accompany her.

Gideon was waiting for them inside the barn. He pushed away from the upright he'd been leaning against when they opened the door. Just seeing him made Kay's heart skip a beat. Dressed in ubiquitous black, he looked rugged and handsome as hell. It was amazing to think that he was hers, that she would be alone with him later, free to hold him and touch him to her heart's content.

As if reading her thoughts, which she had no doubt he was, Gideon winked at her.

Brett eyed Gideon warily, like a rabbit confronted by a hawk, then cleared his throat. "So, how does this work?"

"Like this." Gideon rolled up the left sleeve of his T-shirt, bit into his wrist, then held out his arm.

Brett glanced at Kay, then shook his head. "I don't think I can. . . ."

Kay folded her arms across her chest. "Do it, Brett."

Brett nodded. It wasn't his niece asking, it was his Alpha,

commanding obedience. Grimacing, he took hold of Gideon's arm and lowered his head.

Gideon looked up, meeting Kay's gaze, his expression impassive as the werewolf drank.

Do you want to be next?

She licked her lips as Gideon's voice whispered through her mind.

As the scent of blood rose in the air, the horses began to stir restlessly, pacing their stalls, snorting and tossing their heads.

Kay went to stand next to Barika's stall. "Easy, girl," she said, stroking the mare's head. "It's okay."

The horses quieted at the sound of her voice.

After about forty seconds, Gideon said, "That's enough," and withdrew his arm.

Brett lifted his head. Yanking a handkerchief from his back pocket, he wiped his mouth. "Now what?"

"Turnabout is fair play," Gideon said.

Brett looked at Kay. "Don't make me do this."

"Just do it."

Brett glared at Gideon. "Go on then!" he said, thrusting out his right arm. "Get it over with."

Gideon licked the wound in his wrist, sealing it, then rolled his shirtsleeve down. "Forget it."

"What?" Brett's eyes widened in surprise. "But, I thought . . . ?"

"You heard me. Get out of here before I change my mind."

Kay looked at Gideon, one brow raised, as Brett hurried out of the barn. "I thought you wanted a drink in return?"

Gideon shook his head. "Are you kidding me? Werewolf blood is as bitter as gall."

"Really? Then why do you drink mine?"

Wrapping an arm around her waist, Gideon drew her body up against his. "Yeah, well, yours is different."

"It is?"

"Oh, yeah." Lowering his head, he ran his tongue along the side of her neck. "Sweet," he murmured. "Well, not exactly sweet, but satisfying like no other." He brushed a kiss across her lips. "Have you ever made love in a hayloft?"

Kay swayed against him, her fingers threading through the thick ebony hair at his nape. "No, have you?"

"Do I have to answer that?"

"Yes. No." She scowled at him. "But you have, haven't you?"

He shrugged. "Does it count if it was three hundred years ago, give or take a decade or two?"

She huffed a sigh, her expression wistful. "No matter what we do, you'll always have already done it with someone else."

"Ah, darlin'," he murmured, "nothing that happened before I met you has any meaning." He tucked a lock of hair behind her ear. "Don't you know one of the reasons I love you is that, when I'm with you, everything old is new again?"

"Gideon . . ."

He stroked her cheek, his knuckles lightly caressing her skin, as his gaze moved over her face. "It's true, Kiya. You make me feel alive. What's even more amazing is that you make me feel young again."

"I love you, my husband."

"And I love you." Grabbing a horse blanket folded over a stall door, he draped it over his shoulder, then drew Kay into his arms and willed the two of them into the loft.

Setting Kay on her feet, he spread the blanket over a pile of fragrant hay. "Your bed awaits, my lady wife."

Smiling at the endearment, she sank down on the blanket, then reached for his hand and tugged him down beside her. Holding his gaze, she slipped out of her shirt and bra, kicked off her sandals, then slowly wriggled out of her jeans.

He watched her every move, the heat in his eyes bringing a flush of pleasure to her cheeks.

"So," she murmured, dragging his T-shirt over his head and tossing it aside, "who was that woman you ravished in the hayloft three hundred years ago?"

Gideon shook his head. "I forget," he said, his voice thick as he stripped off the rest of his clothing, then tucked her beneath him. "Kiya, my sweet wife, there's never been anyone but you."

Chapter 39

It was nearing midnight when Gideon and Kay left the barn. Hand in hand, they strolled across the yard toward the main house.

"You've got hay in your hair," Gideon remarked.

"And stars in my eyes," Kay said, grinning up at him.

Chuckling softly, he plucked the hay from her hair, then drew her into his arms and kissed her.

She sighed when he released her.

"We haven't talked about where we go from here," he said as they continued toward the house.

"I know." She'd been reluctant to bring it up.

"So?"

"I guess it's up to you," she said.

"I don't think so."

"What do you mean?"

"You're the one with a home and a family. Responsibilities. Not me."

Kay nodded. For the first time, she felt the full burden of being Alpha of the Shadow Pack weighing down on her. She hadn't really considered what it would entail, becoming the Alpha. Her only thought in challenging Victor had been to save her aunt's life.

"So," Gideon said, wrapping his arm around her shoulders. "I guess the question is, what do you want to do?"

"I want to be with you."

"I'm here."

"For how long?" Finally, the question she'd been afraid to ask was out in the open.

"Ah, Kiya, love, I'll be here for as long as you want me."

It was the right answer. The perfect answer. And reminded her, all too clearly, that he had already lived over three hundred years and would likely live three hundred more after she was gone.

It was, she mused, a most depressing thought. But before she could remark on it, something slammed into her left shoulder, followed by a sharp report that echoed off the hills. The next thing she knew, Gideon had pushed her down on the ground.

"Stay there!" he hissed, and vanished into the darkness.

A moment later, she heard a harsh cry of pain, and then only silence.

By now, her shoulder was throbbing and her arm was numb. A warm stickiness told her she was bleeding. Pressing her hand over the wound, she realized with something of a shock that she'd been shot.

A few minutes later, Gideon strode into view.

Kay gasped when she saw him. He was dragging a body with one hand and carrying a rifle in the other. A second body was draped over his shoulder.

Gideon gestured at the body on the ground. "Recognize him?" he asked.

"His first name's Aaron. I don't remember his last name." She turned away, sickened more by the thought that Rudolfo had tried to kill her in the dead of night than by the sight of Rinaldi's assassin with his throat torn out.

Gideon lowered the second body to the ground.

"Bobby!" Kay exclaimed. "He was guarding the fence line."

"Yeah? Well, he didn't do a very good job. Rinaldi's man took him unawares, then broke his neck and ripped out his heart."

Kay covered her mouth with her hand, afraid she might be sick. When the nausea passed, she said, "It's my fault he's dead. I shouldn't have sent Bobby out alone."

Gideon lifted her to her feet, then swung her into his arms. "Self-recriminations are useless. Let's get you into the house before you bleed to death."

"We can't just leave Bobby lying out here in the dirt."

"Yes, we can. You can send someone out to look after the bodies. Right now, we need to get you cleaned up."

Kay swallowed a groan as her aunt washed the bullet wound, doused it with a strong disinfectant, and then bandaged it up tight.

"I don't know why you're making such a fuss," Kay muttered. "It'll be healed by tomorrow."

"Don't be so sure about that," Greta said, tying off the bandage. "The bullet I dug out of you was silver. I don't want to take any chances on an infection."

Silver didn't burn werewolves the way it did vampires, but a silver bullet to the head or the heart was always fatal.

Kay looked up as Gideon and Brett entered her room. "What is it?" she asked, alarmed by their expressions. "What's happened?"

"Gideon thought we should go out and take a look around." Brett cleared his throat. "We found another body by the back fence."

"Killed the same way as the other one," Gideon said.

Her mouth went suddenly dry, making it hard to ask, "Who?"

"Stewart," Brett answered. "I've already notified his family. We'll lay him to rest tomorrow night, along with Bobby."

Kay nodded. She wasn't ready for this, she thought in despair. She had no experience, no training. Her father had been born to be Alpha, like his father and his grandfather before him. From the day of her father's birth, everything he had been taught had been with one thought in mind, that he would one day rule the Shadow Pack. He had grown up on that knowledge; it had colored everything he did.

"Anything you need me to do?" Brett asked.

"I don't know." Kay shook her head. "I need time to think."

Greta looked at Brett, then jerked her head toward the door. Brett nodded, and the two of them left the room, closing the door behind them.

As soon as they were alone, Gideon sat on the bed and drew Kay into his arms, careful not to jar her wounded shoulder.

"Go on and cry," he said. "You've had a rough couple of days."

She shook her head, determined to be strong even though her throat was tight with unshed tears.

"Kiya, everybody needs to cry once in a while."

"Not you," she said, sniffling.

"Even me," he admitted.

She looked up in surprise, her own hurts momentarily forgotten. "I don't believe you."

"Well, it was a hell of a long time ago," he said with a wry grin. "I was still human at the time, and very young."

"That doesn't count," she said with a dismissive wave of her hand. "We all cry when we're young."

"I cried the night I woke up as a vampire. Does that count?"

She blinked at him. It had never occurred to her that vampires cried for any reason.

"It's true," he said. "I woke up alone in Lisiana's house, my stomach cramping, my veins on fire. At first, I thought I had to be dreaming, but the pain was too real. She'd told me what to do, how to survive, but she hadn't told me that I would have to turn my back on everything and everyone I knew. I found that out the hard way, for myself."

"What happened?"

"I went home. My father was there, alone. The smell of his blood drove me wild. I would have killed him if my uncle hadn't come in. He stabbed me in the back. The shock of it brought me up short, made me realize what I was doing. I fled the house and never returned. I killed a man that night. I killed him and I drained him of blood. And I reveled in it. And then I sat down by his body and cried like a baby because I didn't want to be a killer, and I knew he would be the first of many."

"But you learned to control the urge to kill."

"In time. But too many others died along the way."

"What did you do with Lisiana's house?"

"I still have it. I go there from time to time to remind me where I came from."

Kay laid her hand on his arm. It was a sad story. Her childhood had been mostly happy. She had grown up in luxury, her every wish granted. She hadn't had a normal life, but until she moved away from home, it had been a happy one.

"Where were you born?"

"In a small town in France. My parents were shopkeepers."

"Is that where you were turned? In France?"

He nodded.

"You don't have an accent."

"No, I lost it years ago. I left the country soon after I was turned."

"Did you have brothers or sisters?"

"No, there was just me, and I came to them late in life."

"And you never saw your father again?"

"No. By the time I'd learned to control myself, he was dead."

Gideon blew out a breath. "Enough about me, love. What are you going to do about Rinaldi?"

What, indeed? she thought. That was the question, wasn't it? "We'll take the fight to them."

"Smart girl," Gideon murmured. "So, what's your next move?"

"I have absolutely no idea. I was hoping you'd know."

"It all depends on whether you want to attack them in human form or wolf."

"Hmm. I don't know. What do you think?"

"I think we need to do a little reconnaissance over at their compound. See what kind of precautions they're taking, if they've ramped up their patrols. If we can get close enough, we might be able to find out if they're planning another hit."

Kay nodded. He was right. They needed to take action. Two of their people were dead. If she didn't fight back, Rinaldi would take it as a sign of weakness. If it came to a fight, there would surely be more casualties. The thought of going to war was sobering. Intimidating. Frightening.

"You and I should go check things out tonight," Gideon said.

"Just the two of us?" she asked incredulously.

"We don't want so many that we're tripping over each other. We just need to test their defenses, find out if they've increased their security."

That made sense. "Let me change my clothes."

"That's my girl."

Kay changed into a pair of black pants and a black sweater. She pinned her hair up and covered it with a black knit cap, then pulled on a pair of boots.

Gideon tucked a lock of hair under her cap. "You look like a ninja."

Kay laughed. "That's me."

"You ready?" Gideon asked.

She blew out a sigh. "Ready."

Before leaving the house, Kay took a minute to let Greta and Brett know where she and Gideon were going. Brett was against it. Greta wasn't happy about it, but she saw the wisdom in scoping things out.

It didn't take long to reach the border between the two packs. Once there, Gideon suggested they both shift.

He watched the boundary while Kay undressed. He knew by the ripple in the air when she shifted. He joined her moments later. Side by side, they padded through the darkness toward the valley that sheltered the pack's headquarters.

Gideon paused when they reached the fence line. Lifting his head, he sniffed the air. A half-dozen men patrolled the perimeter; two in human form, four in wolf form.

Taking the lead, he trotted along the fence toward where the two humans stood, talking quietly.

"She won't fight Rudolfo," the taller of the two men was saying.

"Why do you say that?" the second man asked. "She killed Victor."

"Don't you know anything? Her father forced her to marry Victor. She hated him."

"What's that got to do with it?"

"She killed him. No divorce necessary. No loose ends."

The second man shook his head. "She'll fight. She doesn't have a choice."

"Then why hasn't she issued a challenge? We've killed two of her pack mates. Tomorrow night, we'll kill two or three more."

"It's obvious Rudolfo's trying to provoke her. She'll either have to fight or back down as Alpha. Rudolfo wants her to fight. He outweighs her by a good sixty pounds. She doesn't have a chance. He'll be able to avenge both Victor and Diego and take over as Alpha of the Shadow Pack all in the same night."

Gideon had heard enough. Nudging Kay's shoulder, he turned and loped back to where she had left her clothing.

She quickly shifted and dressed. "So, Rudolfo's trying to provoke me, is he?" she said, jamming her knit cap on her head. "Well, it's working. When they come tomorrow night, we'll be ready for them."

When they returned to the Shadow Pack's compound, Kay and Gideon met with Greta and Brett in the living room.

"So," Greta said when Kay had finished relaying the conversation she and Gideon had overheard, "where do we go from here?"

"Tomorrow night, I want Jared, Tyler, and Joe to patrol the fence line. I want the rest of the men to take cover on the outside of the fence, in pairs. I don't want Rinaldi's men to know what hit them. They've killed two of ours. I want to even the score."

Brett nodded. "They've got it coming. I'll alert the pack."

"If they decide to attack us in force, do you think they'll wait for the full moon?" Greta asked.

"I don't know. I guess it depends on how anxious Rudolfo is for revenge."

"So, they won't come busting in here with guns blazing?" Gideon asked, glancing at the others.

"I don't think so," Kay replied, grinning.

"Why not?"

Kay stared at Gideon. "Why not?" she repeated, then shook her head. "I don't know. Brett? Greta?"

Brett answered. "It's not our way. We've always done our fighting during the full moon, pack against pack, or Alpha against Alpha. Or on the sly, the way Rinaldi's men killed Bobby and Stewart. As a declaration of war."

Kay mulled that over for several minutes, then pushed it to the back of her mind to reexamine later.

"So, Brett, have you tried shifting yet?" she asked.

"No."

"Try it, now."

Rising, Brett stepped into the middle of the room. He stripped down to his shorts, then took a deep breath, his brow furrowed in concentration. At first, nothing happened; then, little by little, there was a change in the air, a subtle ripple of preternatural power that gradually grew stronger until it raised the hairs along Kay's arms.

A growl rumbled low in Brett's throat and in the blink of an eye, his shorts shredded and a large brown wolf stood before them.

Kay smiled.

Greta clapped her hands. "It works! It really works!"

"I think it would be a good thing if our whole pack could change at will," Kay remarked. "It would give us the upper hand if it comes to a full-scale war. We're stronger in wolf form. Harder to kill. Our senses are sharper."

Gideon shook his head. "Are you sure about this? Won't it make them all Alphas?"

"No," Kay said. Her father had told her that only a few of each generation were born with the Alpha gene. When she had asked why, he had told her that if every pack member carried it, there wouldn't be any werewolves after a while, because they would kill each other off. "That gene is only passed to a few in each generation." She shook her head. She'd had it all this time and never knew. "I'm the last of my father's direct line. The only other pack member who might have the gene is Brett and Greta's son, Isaac."

"So my blood somehow enables them to shift at will and that's all?"

"Well, as far as I know," Kay said. "There's no way to be sure."

"If you decide to go ahead with this, then Isaac should be exempt until we determine whether he carries the gene or not," Greta said. "You know how unpredictable young Alphas can be."

Kay nodded. Young males were never left alone until they learned to control their wolf.

Kay glanced at Brett, who stood in the middle of the room, watching her.

"Now for the hard part," she said. "Brett, can you shift back?"

It took him less time than usual to resume his own form.

"How do you feel?" Kay asked.

"Good," he said, pulling on his pants. "I feel good. Hell, I feel better than good. I feel like I could take on the whole Green Mountain Pack by myself!"

"Any desire to take over our pack?" Kay asked, eyeing him somewhat apprehensively.

Laughing, Brett shook his head. "No. None at all."

Greta picked up his shoes and socks and tossed him his shirt. "Let's go bring the pack up to speed. We'll all need to get a good night's sleep. Good night, Gideon," she said, nodding in his direction. "See you in the morning, Kiya."

Shrugging into his shirt, Brett followed his wife out of the room.

Kay stared after Brett.

"Something wrong?" Gideon asked.

"No. I was just thinking—Brett was able to shift right away. Why did it take me so long?"

"Probably because you're only half wolf. Or maybe because you're female."

She punched him in the arm. "Chauvinist pig vampire!"

"Ouch!"

"You're probably right about the half wolf thing. Even though it didn't happen right away, I could feel it coming," she mused, remembering how her appetite had increased, until it seemed that she was hungry all the time. There had been other symptoms, too, changes in her body that she couldn't explain at the time. She stretched her arms over her head. "I think I'm ready to call it a night," she said, yawning. "Are you ready for bed?"

"I'll be there in a few minutes."

He didn't say so, but she knew he was going out to feed. She kissed him on the cheek. "I'll meet you upstairs."

"Fifteen minutes," he said. "Twenty at the most."

She shook her head as he vanished from her sight. If only he could pass on that ability to vanish at will, she thought, heading for her bedroom. That would really give them an edge.

Thinking of Gideon, she changed into her nightgown, then washed her hands and face, combed out her hair, and brushed her teeth.

When she returned to the bedroom, he was there, lounging against the pillows.

"You look like a sultan awaiting his harem," she remarked.

He jerked his chin in her direction. "Pretty small harem."

"Are you complaining?"

His gaze moved over her, ever so slowly. "Nope. You're all the woman I need."

"And don't you forget it." She climbed into bed beside him and pillowed her head on his shoulder. "So," she asked, a smile evident in her voice, "if we decide to share your blood with the pack, do you have enough to go around? I mean, we never discussed that part of it."

"What do you think?"

"I don't know."

"Don't worry about it. I've got enough." He stroked the side of her neck. "But if you're offering . . ."

"Anytime," she murmured, and closed her eyes when his fangs skated lightly over her skin. Hard to believe she had once thought such a thing repulsive.

She was sorry when he lifted his head. "I'll never understand why that feels so amazing."

"I can make it hurt if you want."

"Are you always so gentle with your prey? Does it feel as good to them as it does to me?"

Gideon dragged his hand over his jaw. Women. They sure asked a lot of difficult questions.

Kay poked him in the side. "Well?"

"In the beginning, I took what I wanted any way I could get it. I didn't worry about those I fed on, or what they were feeling. Later, as I got older, I guess you could say I refined my eating habits. I never thought of myself as being gentle, but . . ." He shrugged. "A lot of vampires get off on causing fear. I did, too, in the beginning. There's a certain thrill in the hunt—you probably know what I mean—but eventually I learned it could be just as satisfying to seduce my prey as it was to scare the crap out of them."

"Go on."

"I don't know if it feels the same to everyone, Kiya. All I know is it's not the same for me. No one's ever made me feel the way you do."

His words filled her with a soft, radiant glow. A glow that quickly sparked to flame when he covered her mouth with his in a long, searing kiss that robbed her of every coherent thought save the burning desire to feel the weight of his body on hers.

He lifted his head, his dark eyes tinged with red, his smile revealing a hint of fang. "There's no hurry, love," he whispered. "We have until dawn."

Her hands moved over him. "I can't wait that long," she replied breathlessly. "Gideon . . ."

"All right," he said, positioning her body beneath his. "A quickie for now."

"And later?" she asked, gasping with pleasure as their bodies became one.

He laughed softly. "I'll surprise you."

Chapter 40

After a late breakfast, Kay decided it was time to tackle a chore she had been putting off—packing up her mother's things. She would have to go through her father's things, too. Not only his personal effects, but pack business, as well. But that could wait for another day.

She paused outside her mother's sitting room, her hand on the knob. Although her parents had shared a bedroom, her mother had insisted on turning the adjoining bedroom into her own private place. It was only fair, she'd once told Kay, since Russell claimed the den as his own. It had been years since Kay had been inside her mother's room.

She took a deep breath, let it out in a long shuddering sigh, and opened the door.

The scent of her mother's favorite perfume lingered in the air. Standing inside the doorway, Kay glanced around the room. A lovely Queen Anne desk and matching chair made of gleaming cherrywood stood before the window that over-looked the backyard. A small bookcase held her mother's favorite books; a curio cabinet held a collection of Royal Doulton figurines. An old-fashioned record player and an iPod sat side by side on a small table beside an antique fainting couch. Another table held a number of framed photographs.

All the pictures were of Kay and her mother, Kay and Mark, or the three of them together. There were no photos of her father.

Murmuring, "Oh, Mom," Kay picked up a photo of herself and Mark. It had been taken in front of the fireplace one Christmas morning. Kay wore a red flannel nightgown and cradled a beautiful ballerina doll in her arms. Mark was strumming a guitar, a huge grin on his face. They had been so happy then, innocent, certain that life would only get better.

Wiping the tears from her eyes, Kay replaced the photograph. She quickly folded up most of her mother's clothes, then left the room to get some boxes.

She wished Gideon was there. She needed to see him, to be near him, even if he was asleep. But, ever cautious, he had refused to spend the day in the house. She supposed she couldn't blame him. Hopefully, when this trouble with the Green Mountain Pack was over, they could have some kind of normal life together, she thought, and then laughed ruefully. There was no way for an Alpha werewolf and a three-hundred-year-old vampire to ever have a normal life, but she would take whatever she could get.

It was near sundown when Kay called the pack together. Briefly, she explained her plan. As expected, not everyone was thrilled at the idea of drinking vampire blood, even if it was just a little. Deciding a picture was worth a thousand words—or, in this case, a demonstration—she asked Brett to shift.

Murmurs ran around the room as several of those gathered thought she was kidding and others scoffed, saying it was impossible for Brett or any of them who weren't Alphas to shift when the moon wasn't full. When it wasn't even fully dark outside.

"Brett." Kay nodded in his direction.

There were gasps of surprise and exclamations of disbelief as Brett shifted, then glanced around the room with a wolfish grin.

Kay looked at Greta. "Wow, I've never seen him shift that fast before!"

"I know. Do you think a little vampire blood would enable me to shift faster, too?"

"I don't know." Kay smiled as she overheard the comments of those closest to her. "But I think the pack's convinced it works."

Tyler and a werewolf named Hatten Red Shirt, scheduled to patrol the outside of the fence line that night, were the first pack members to drink Gideon's blood. The rest of the men came next, then went out two by two to take their places on the outside of the fence. It was decided that the women, who were even less thrilled about drinking Gideon's blood than the men had been, would wait until the following night.

Kay paced the floor. The house seemed too quiet. Brett and Gideon had gone out with the men. Greta was in the kitchen, making coffee. Isaac was in the living room, playing a video game with one of his friends.

Needing someone to talk to, Kay went into the kitchen. "I hate waiting! How long do you think it'll be before Rinaldi's men make their move?"

Greta shrugged one shoulder. "These things are usually done in the wee hours of the morning, you know."

"I know." Kay tapped her fingers on the tabletop. "I should be out there."

"If they need you, I'm sure they'll send for you."

"That's not the point. I'm the Alpha now. My father wouldn't be hiding out in the house."

"You're not 'hiding out,'" Greta said. "You're keeping an eye on the home place in case they decide to try and sneak in here."

"Right."

"The other women and kids are gathered in the clubhouse watching a movie. Do you want to go over there?"

"No, I don't feel like a lot of company." She huffed a sigh. "I wish I knew what was going on out there."

Gideon moved quietly through the night, his feet making no sound as he followed the fence line, checking on the wolves who were lurking in the shadows.

He had circled the perimeter four times when he picked up the scent of a trio of Green Mountain Pack members stealthily approaching from the north.

A thought took him toward that end of the property. Brett was patrolling that section of the fence on the inside; Tyler and Hatten were hidden in the brush on the outside of the fence.

Gideon dissolved into mist, hovering near the branches of a tree. It would have been easy for him to take out the three intruders, but it wasn't his fight. The Shadow Pack hadn't asked for his help, only his blood. Coldhearted as that sounded, he knew this was something Kay's pack needed to handle on their own. If the fight turned against them, then, for Kay's sake, he would interfere.

As it turned out, they didn't need his help. As soon as the intruders approached the fence, Brett shifted and vaulted over the wire.

Taken by surprise, the three men reeled backward.

Brett killed the first one.

On silent feet, Hatten ghosted up from behind and took out the second one, while Tyler finished off the third.

It was over in less than a minute.

Gideon assumed his own form as Brett shifted.

Brett and the other two men grinned at each other.

"All too easy," Brett said, wiping his bloody hands on the dead man's shirt.

Hatten nodded. "Wish I could have seen the looks on their faces when you shifted!"

"It was priceless," Brett said, laughing. He clapped Gideon on the back. "Let's go dump these bodies outside the Green Mountain compound and then go home."

Kay had just poured herself a third cup of coffee when she heard Gideon's voice in her mind, assuring her that the fight, short as it had been, was over and no one had been hurt.

Greta looked at her and frowned. "What are you grinning about?"

"It's over! Our men are dumping the bodies outside the Green Mountain compound and then they'll be home."

"Brett?"

"He's fine."

"Oh, thank goodness." Greta sagged in her chair.

Kay nodded, her relief short-lived as she realized that they'd only won a battle, not the war.

Greta looked up, her expression suddenly grim. "It isn't really over, is it?"

"No. It won't truly be over until Rinaldi calls a truce. Or . . ."

"Or you defeat him," Greta said, finishing Kay's thought.

"Or he defeats me," she said, and saw the truth of it in her aunt's eyes.

Kay tried to put the thought out of her mind when Gideon, Brett, Tyler, and Hatten came into the kitchen, laughing and grinning and high-fiving each other.

"Where are the others?" Kay asked.

"I thought it best if we keep watch the rest of the night," Brett said. "Hatten and Tyler and I will go out and relieve some of the others as soon as we clean up."

"Good idea," Greta remarked, noting the blood stains on their clothing.

Gideon sat at the table, listening as the men bragged about their kills. Greta poured coffee for everyone, including Gideon. She grinned sheepishly when he lifted one brow in amusement.

When Tyler and Hatten finished their coffee, they excused themselves and went to get cleaned up. Brett and Greta followed a few minutes later.

Gideon remained silent as he watched Kay rinse the dishes and load the dishwasher. She wiped off the counter and the stovetop, emptied the dregs from the coffeepot, and refilled it with fresh water.

"Kiya."

"What?"

"Sit down."

"What's wrong?" she asked anxiously.

"Just come and sit down."

She dried her hands, placed the dishtowel on the towel rack, then sat across from him, her hands tightly folded on the tabletop. "What?"

"Do you want to talk about what's bothering you?"

"Nothing's bothering me."

"You can't lie to me, Kiya."

"Then why ask? Just read my mind."

"You've got every right to be worried, and no one would blame you for being afraid. It's not easy, making decisions that affect the lives of people you love, people you're responsible for."

"They could have been killed tonight. All of them. How could I ever face Greta again if Brett had been killed?"

"If your aunt was Alpha, she would have made the same decisions you did."

"How do you know that? Did you read her mind?"

"No, I read Brett's."

"We need to end this now. I don't want it to drag on, never knowing when Rudolfo will strike again. And now that we've killed three of his men, he's going to want vengeance more than ever."

Gideon shook his head. "Don't even think about it."

"It's the only way to end it."

"Dammit, Kiya, you can't challenge Rinaldi! There's no way you can beat him. He's older than you are. He's got years of experience. And he's twice your size."

"Have you got a better idea?"

"Just one," he muttered. But she would never forgive him for it.

As it turned out, they didn't have to wait long. Rudolfo Rinaldi sent a message to Kay the next night. The message was brief and to the point. Either she would fight him to the death on the night of the next full moon, or she would surrender leadership of the Shadow Pack to the Green Mountain Alpha.

Kay read the message three times. She told herself it was what she'd wanted, that if Rinaldi hadn't contacted her, she would have contacted him before the night was out whether Gideon approved or not. But now, seeing the words in print, she knew she wasn't ready to face Rudolfo in a battle to the death. She hadn't planned it ahead of time when she defeated Victor. When she knew that her aunt's life was in danger, instinct had taken over. She had been as surprised as everyone else that she had won the battle. But this, meeting Rudolfo at an appointed time . . . knowing only one of them would survive the fight . . . it was scary beyond words. She wasn't ready for this. She wasn't sure she would ever be ready. Gideon was right. She didn't have the skill or the knowledge to defeat an Alpha werewolf.

"Kiya?"

She looked up to find Gideon watching her. Wordlessly, she handed him Rinaldi's message.

He read it quickly, then crumpled it in his fist. "Looks like you're about to get what you wanted," he muttered.

She didn't say anything, just looked at him, her eyes wide and scared, her face pale.

Muttering under his breath, Gideon drew her into his arms. He had been doing his best not to read her mind. She'd had him convinced that she was itching to take on Rinaldi, that she was confident she would win. But he didn't have to read her thoughts to know she was terrified.

She melted against him, clinging to him as if his arms were the only things keeping her on her feet.

"You were right," she whispered. "I can't do this."

"Does it have to be one-on-one?"

She nodded.

"I don't suppose you'd consider just walking away."

"I can't. It would shame my father. It would shame my pack." She shook her head. "I couldn't live with myself afterward. I brought this on myself and now I'm honor-bound to see it through."

Gideon brushed a kiss across the top of her head. "And I'm honor-bound to protect the woman I love, whether she likes it or not."

"What do you mean?"

"I mean you're my wife and I'm not about to stand by and watch you get torn apart by some werewolf on steroids."

"Gideon . . ."

"There's no use arguing with me, Kiya. We've got a few weeks until the full moon. There's got to be a way to preserve your honor and your life."

"I don't know what it could be."

Gideon grunted softly. Neither did he.

Chapter 41

The night after Kay received Rudolfo Rinaldi's written challenge, Gideon shared his blood with all the female pack members. Kay found it amusing that, from the oldest woman to the youngest, they were all against drinking his blood until he took them in his arms. She fought down a hot rush of jealousy when several of them asked for seconds.

Later, Kay called a meeting of all the adult pack members. Once they were assembled, she read the challenge issued by the Green Mountain Alpha.

When she finished reading the missive, there were numerous responses, mostly from the men. Some thought Kay should surrender to Rinaldi. Others voiced the opinion that she should step aside and let Brett take over as Alpha, citing the fact that he was married to Greta, who shared the Alissano bloodline. A few thought they should all shift at midnight and attack the Green Mountain Pack.

Gideon had a few ideas of his own, but no one asked for his opinion and he didn't offer it. He remained where he was, one shoulder propped negligently against the doorjamb.

He had to admire Kay. He knew she was afraid of facing Rudolfo, but there was no sign of it now. She stood in front of the pack, head high, shoulders back, radiating self-confidence.

Had it been up to him, he would have swept her into his arms and taken her far away from this place, never to return.

He listened intently as Kay dismissed all the ideas that were presented to her. In a clear, calm voice, she reminded all the men and women in the room that there was more to being Alpha than the ability to shift at will.

"Being Alpha isn't something that can be assigned to another," she said. "It's something you're either born with or you aren't. We all know that Alphas are stronger, swifter, and usually larger than other members of the pack. They heal quicker. They live longer."

Murmurs of agreement were heard here and there.

Brett moved up beside Kay when she finished speaking. "So, it looks like we're stuck with you," he said with a wry grin.

Laughter rippled through the pack, easing the tension.

Brett slipped his arm around Kay's shoulders. "Personally, I can't think of anyone more qualified to lead us, except maybe her husband."

All eyes swung in Gideon's direction.

"He's stronger than twenty men, and swift as lightning," Brett went on. "He heals overnight, he's already lived a few hundred years. I imagine he's picked up some wisdom along the way."

Gideon shook his head. "Forget it." He wasn't cut out to play nursemaid to a pack of werewolves. Nor would he shame Kay by stealing her thunder. He had too much respect for her, both as his wife and the pack's Alpha. But if the upcoming fight turned against her, he'd take Rinaldi out, and to hell with the consequences.

The meeting broke up shortly after Gideon's refusal to take over as Alpha.

Later, when he was alone with Kay, he wasn't quite sure what to say. Was she hurt by Brett's suggestion that Gideon take over leadership of the pack? Insulted? Knowing how she felt about facing Rinaldi, he had to admire her courage.

Thinking she might like to be alone with her thoughts, he said, "I need to go out for a while. I won't be long."

"All right."

He kissed her lightly, then left the house. Dark clouds obscured the moon and stars. The rising wind stirred the leaves with a low, keening cry. On foot, he made a slow circuit of the fence line, nodding at the guards he passed. As far as he could tell, Jared, Tyler, Brett, and a middle-aged werewolf named Landon were the only men within several miles.

A thought took Gideon to Bondurant. At this time of night, most of the businesses were closed. Strolling down the street, he heard music emanating from a small nightclub on one of the side streets.

Inside, he went to the bar and ordered a glass of red wine. Standing there, he studied the patrons. Pickings were slim— an old drunk tapping his foot to the beat of the music, a middle-aged man and woman slow dancing on the club's tiny dance floor, or a single man with a bad hairpiece.

With a shake of his head, he drained his glass and decided to look elsewhere.

He'd gone about two blocks when a faint cry reached his ears. Curious, he followed the sound to the edge of town. There, shielded from view by a broken-down wooden fence, he found a woman struggling in the grasp of two men.

From their scent, Gideon knew they were Green Mountain werewolves.

One of them struck the woman when she opened her mouth to scream.

The men were so engrossed in trying to rape the woman, they didn't realize they were in danger until it was too late.

Gideon broke the neck of the first man, tore out the heart of the second.

The woman fainted.

He had just enough time to catch her before she hit the ground. He held her in his arms a moment, then, while she was still unconscious, he lowered his head to her neck and drank. Since he had just saved her life, he didn't think she would mind.

Kay stared at Gideon. "You killed them? What did you do with the bodies?"

"You don't need to know. No one does."

"Rudolfo is sure to come here, asking questions. And even if he doesn't, he'll blame us for their disappearance."

"If he comes here, just tell him the truth. You never saw them. You don't know where they are."

"Like he'll believe me!"

Gideon shrugged. "Only time will tell."

"What do we do until then?"

"You're going into training."

"What?"

"You heard me." He ran his hands along her arms. "We need to put some muscle on you."

"How do you intend to do that?"

"Proper diet and good, old-fashioned exercise."

Gideon was as good as his word. He wrote out a schedule for Kay and enlisted Greta and Brett to make sure she followed it. And the next thing Kay knew, she was spending three hours a day working out—lifting weights, hitting the heavy bag, swimming.

Greta put her on a high-protein diet.

At night, Kay went jogging with Gideon. And each night, she drank a little of his blood. It was like a narcotic—the more he gave her, the more she wanted.

"Lovemaking is the best exercise," she remarked one night after they'd gone to bed.

"Is that right?"

"I read it in a book somewhere. Burns up a lot of calories."

He grunted softly. "Maybe I've been remiss in that area." He rolled her onto her back, then covered her body with his. "After all, we've only been making love once or twice a night."

"Maybe we'd better try for three."

"Whatever you think best."

"Definitely three." Kay waggled her eyebrows at him. "I never realized exercising could be so much fun."

Rinaldi never came snooping around to see if Kay knew the whereabouts of his missing men, which led her to the conclusion that Rudolfo was convinced the Shadow Pack was to blame.

The night before the full moon, he sent her another missive. It was short and to the point. *Meet me in the valley tomorrow night when the moon is high so we can end this once and for all.*

"Well, that's blunt," Gideon said, reading over her shoulder. "Are you ready?"

"It doesn't really matter, does it?" Kay asked, her voice tight. "I'm out of time."

"You won't be alone. We'll all be there with you."

"I'd rather be alone." She didn't want anyone watching her when she met Rudolfo.

"It's in your power to order the pack to stay away if that's what you want," Gideon remarked quietly. "But I'm not letting you go without me."

"I had a feeling you'd say that."

"Are you serious, about not wanting the pack there to back you up?"

She nodded. "I think so. I'm not sure I have the courage to meet Rinaldi." Admitting it out loud made her cheeks burn with shame. "If I chicken out, I'd rather the pack wasn't there to see it. And if I find the courage to fight him and I lose . . ." She made a vague gesture with her hand. "Well, I'd just as soon no one saw that, either."

"Kiya, listen to me. You don't have a cowardly bone in your body. You're the bravest woman I've ever known. You've survived every challenge you've ever faced, and you'll survive this one, too."

Seeing the love in his eyes, hearing the confidence in his voice, gave her just the boost she needed. But later, when they were lying alone together in the dark, her doubts returned.

Wordlessly, Gideon drew her into his arms. Murmuring tender words in her ear, he made love to her until the rising sun chased the darkness from the sky. She waited for him to leave, as he always did, but, to her surprise, he stayed by her side, his arm around her shoulders, his presence comforting her even after he had succumbed to the darkness.

Kay stayed in bed until hunger drove her downstairs. Greta and Brett were in the kitchen. They both looked up when she stepped into the room.

"How are you?" Greta asked.

Kay shrugged, then slid into an empty chair.

"Let me fix you something to eat," Greta offered. "What would you like?"

"I don't care. Whatever you're having is fine."

"Pancakes, eggs, and sausage okay?" Greta's smile looked forced.

"Fine," Kay said.

"Whatever happens, we'll all be there for you," Brett said.

"About that," Kay said. "I'd rather go alone."

"Alone!" he exclaimed. "Why the hell would you want to do that?"

"I have my reasons," Kay said, "and I won't really be alone. Gideon will be there with me."

Brett shook his head. "No way!" Rising, he pushed away from the table. "No way in hell!" he declared, and stomped out of the room.

"Are you sure, Kiya?" Greta asked quietly.

"Yes. I have my reasons."

Greta smiled faintly. "I think I know what they are. Don't worry about Brett. I'll explain it to him."

"Were you afraid when Victor challenged you?" Kay asked.

"Afraid? No." Greta filled a plate with pancakes and eggs and added six sausage links. "I was terrified." She placed the plate and a cup of coffee in front of Kay. "You're your father's daughter, Kiya. Your courage won't desert you."

"I hope you're right," Kay said. "But if you're wrong, I don't want anyone else to witness it." She sighed heavily. "It's bad enough that Gideon will be there."

The hours until the moon rose passed slowly, and yet all too quickly. Kay showered, dressed in a pair of black jeans, then pulled on a bright red sweater to bolster her courage. She tied her hair back in a ponytail, stepped into a pair of black sandals, and she was ready to go.

Gideon, who had been remarkably silent while she got ready, followed her downstairs to where the pack waited.

"Don't worry about me," she said, forcing a confident smile she was far from feeling. "I'll be back soon." Whole or in pieces, she thought morbidly.

Every member of the pack came forward to give her a hug and wish her well, Brett and Greta last of all.

"We'll be with you in spirit," Greta said. "I know you'll make us proud."

Too choked up to speak, Kay nodded and hurried out of the house, with Gideon at her heels.

"Ready?" he asked.

"I have one stop to make," she said.

He didn't question her, merely fell into step beside her.

He waited outside the fence while she went to kneel between her parents' graves, felt his heart constrict as she bid them good-bye.

Returning to where he waited, she said, "Now I'm ready."

The Green Mountain Pack was waiting for her at the appointed place. Head high, shoulders back, she strode toward Rudolfo Rinaldi.

"I'm here."

He glanced around, his eyes narrowed, his nostrils sniffing the wind. "Alone?"

"My husband is here with me. Are you ready?" She was surprised that her voice didn't shake at all, that her hands were rock steady. And even more surprised to discover that she wasn't afraid anymore.

"Where's the rest of your pack?" Rinaldi asked.

"I thought this fight was between you and me," Kay said boldly. "Do I need to call them?"

"No." Rinaldi removed his jacket and tossed it aside, then cracked his knuckles. "You understand this is to be a fight to the death, with no quarter given."

"I understand. If I didn't know better, I'd think you were stalling."

Rinaldi flushed at her accusation.

"Hold on," Gideon said.

Rinaldi frowned as Gideon moved to stand beside Kay.

"I know this is between you and Kiya," Gideon said. "No one will interfere." Holding Rinaldi's gaze with his own,

Gideon bared his fangs, knew his eyes had gone red. "But if Kiya loses, the next fight will be between you and me."

"You have no right to challenge me," Rinaldi said. "You're not pack."

"That's true. But she's my wife and if she dies by your hand, you will die by mine. Just like those two men who disappeared."

"You killed them?"

"I did."

"One of them was my son."

Gideon shrugged. "You should have kept him home nights."

Fury rolled off the werewolf in waves. There was the sound of shredding cloth and in the blink of an eye, an angry brown wolf hurled itself at Gideon's throat.

Sidestepping, Gideon called up his own wolf, spun on his hindquarters in time to fend off Rinaldi's next attack.

Kay stared at the two wolves. They were evenly matched in size. Had it not been for the difference in color, she would have been hard-pressed to know which was Gideon. Light on their feet, their movements quick, controlled, and savage, they drew blood again and again, until the heavy metallic scent of it permeated the air.

Excited by the scent of blood, several of Rinaldi's pack members shifted.

But Kay had eyes only for Gideon. Both wolves were splattered with blood from numerous bite marks. She noticed Rinaldi seemed to be tiring. And then, from the corner of her eye, she noticed one of Rinaldi's wolfs moving closer to the battle, creeping up on Gideon's back, getting ready to spring.

She shifted before she realized what she was doing, a howl of anger rising in her throat as she sprang forward and buried her fangs in the wolf's jugular.

Her cry energized Gideon. Fearing that she was in danger,

he lunged at Rinaldi, his body partially shifting, so that his forelegs became arms. He sank his fangs deep into the were-wolf's throat, then ripped the wolf's heart from his chest.

Before the rest of the Green Mountain Pack could shift, the Shadow Pack emerged from the cover of the trees, hackles raised, fangs bared.

"It's over," Gideon said, assuming his own form again. "Surrender or we'll tear you to pieces."

A young man with a slight build and light brown hair strode toward Gideon. "I am José Rinaldi, the last of my line," he said. "As the next Alpha, I ask that you take my life if you must, but that you spare my pack. This was not their fight. I would not have them punished for my uncle's mis-guided ambition."

"That decision isn't mine to make," Gideon said, but he couldn't help admiring the boy's courage. José couldn't have been more than twenty years old, yet he carried himself with an Alpha's innate pride and heartfelt concern for his people.

"It's my decision," Kay said, coming to stand beside Gideon.

Gideon slid a glance at his wife. Naked and blood-spattered, she was, in his eyes, the most beautiful thing he had ever seen.

"José Rinaldi, I accept your surrender on behalf of the Green Mountain Pack."

José went down on his knees, his head bowed, obviously awaiting execution.

"I'm tired of fighting," Kay said. "I propose a truce be-tween our packs if you will give me your word of honor that you will abide by it."

José looked up. "I swear to you by the life of my mother that I will honor the truce between us. I further vow that anyone who breaks it will be executed immediately."

"I believe you," Kay said. "We're through here. Take your people, and your dead, and go home."

Chapter 42

"It's over." Soaking in a hot tub fragrant with jasmine-scented bubbles, Kay closed her eyes while the words repeated in her mind. *It's over. Over, over . . .*

The tension of the past few weeks drained away, leaving her feeling like a balloon that had gone flat. No more witches. No more fights. No more worries, at least for the foreseeable future.

The future. What did it hold for her and Gideon? For the first time since she'd met him in that dreadful dungeon, she had time to think about it. So, what did she want? What did *he* want?

"He'd like to share your bath."

Startled by his voice, she sat up. "I didn't hear you come in."

He pointed to his chest. "Vampire."

Kay stuck her tongue out at him.

"So?" He glanced at the tub, then back at her.

"Please come in," she invited. "You can wash my back." She batted her eyelashes at him. "And my front."

He was out of his clothes and sitting behind her in the tub in a matter of seconds. Picking up the soap, he worked up a good lather in his hands, and then began washing her shoulders and back, his fingers gently kneading the muscles.

"Oh, that feels wonderful."

Reaching around her, he ran his soapy hands over her breasts and belly.

What happened next was inevitable, but she had no thought to complain as he lifted her from the tub and carried her to bed. It was strangely erotic, making love while they were both soaking wet. The slippery feel of wet skin sliding over wet skin, the slightly soapy taste that clung to him when she bit his shoulder. His body was a welcome weight on hers, his mouth like fire as he covered her face, neck, and breasts with kisses. He took a sip of her blood. She took a sip of his, and the spark between them burned hotter, brighter, consuming them both. Lost in waves of sensual delight, his thoughts hers as hers were his, it became impossible to tell where her body ended and his began.

She cried his name as pleasure engulfed her, felt his fangs at her throat again as his body convulsed deep within her own, carrying them both over the edge.

Later, snuggled up against Gideon's side, his arm curved around her shoulders, Kay asked the question she had been pondering most of the day.

"What are we going to do now?"

"What do you mean?"

She drew a deep breath and let it out in a long, slow sigh. "About our future. We've never really talked about it, you know."

He laughed softly. "When did we have time?"

"We have time now."

"Yeah." He twirled a lock of her hair around his finger. "I guess it's up to you. I don't have any ties anywhere, nothing that needs doing, no place I haven't been, no one's feelings to consider other than yours."

Propping herself up on her elbow, she gazed into his eyes. "Footloose and fancy-free, aren't you?"

"Pretty much, darlin'," he agreed. "So, what do you want to do with the rest of your life? If you want to stay here, we'll stay. If you wanna go . . ." He shrugged. "Just name the place and we're there."

"You make it sound so easy."

"It is, for me." He stroked her cheek, then drew her down into his arms again. "For vampires, life is pretty simple. People come and go. Governments rise and fall. None of it really affects us, as long as we have a safe lair and a meal now and then."

"I think I envy you."

"What do you want, Kiya?"

"I just want to be with you."

"Then I guess the next question is, where are we going to live?"

Gideon's question repeated itself in Kay's mind throughout the next day. She ate breakfast without really tasting it. She cleaned up the kitchen and found herself in the living room, on the sofa, with no real recollection of how she'd gotten there.

Did she want to stay here? Did she want to leave? Did she have a choice?

She was the Shadow Pack's Alpha. How could she leave? And yet, if she was totally honest with herself, she didn't want to stay here. There were too many bad memories.

Soon after the sun went down, Gideon materialized in the living room looking rested and well fed.

He took one look at her face and said, "Still no decision, I see."

"Actually, I think I've made one. I'm just waiting to discuss it with Greta and Brett."

"We're here," Greta said, stepping into the room with Brett at her heels. She hugged Kay, smiled at Gideon. "So, what did you want to talk to us about?"

When everyone was seated, Kay said, "I've decided to leave the pack."

Greta glanced at Brett, then looked at Kay. "Leave? Why? This is your home."

"I don't belong here," Kay said, sighing. "I don't think I ever have."

"But you're our Alpha," Brett said. "You can't just leave."

"By rights, Greta should be our Alpha," Kay said.

Greta shook her head. "I think I proved I'm a failure at that."

"Things are different now. If you think it will help maintain the truce, I'll be Alpha in name only, but you and Brett can run the pack while I'm gone. And I'll come back, from time to time."

"But . . . where are you gonna go?" Brett asked, frowning.

"I'm not sure yet. Gideon and I have a lot of things to work out."

Greta blinked the tears from her eyes. "Do you want to tell the pack your decision, or should I?"

"I should do it," Kay said, though it was the last thing she wanted to do.

"You're right, of course."

"Call the pack together, will you, Brett? I'd like to get it over with."

Nodding, her uncle left the room.

"Are you sure about this?" Greta asked.

Kay nodded. "It feels right."

Thirty minutes later, Kay stood in front of the men and women she had known all her life, and yet, in reality, she didn't really know them at all. Greta and Brett stood beside her.

Kay glanced at Gideon, who waited in the doorway, his arms folded over his chest, a smile of encouragement on his face.

"I've called you here tonight to tell you good-bye," Kay said. "My aunt Greta is the rightful Alpha, and I am reinstating her in that position now. We have decided that, at least temporarily, I'll remain Alpha in name only. I'm grateful to all of you for your help these past few weeks. If ever I'm needed for anything, you have only to call and I'll be here."

Silence hung in the air and then, as one, the pack surged forward, their voices rising as they wished her well.

Kay blinked back her tears, touched by their devotion. One by one, the members of the pack embraced her, then left the room, until only Gideon, Greta, and Brett remained.

Gideon slipped his arm around Kay's waist and gave her a hug. "Are you sure about this? It's not too late to change your mind."

"No, I'm sure it's the right decision."

"Be happy," Brett said, giving her a hug. "Call us if you need us."

Kay nodded. "I will."

Brett stepped back and Greta took his place. "I'll miss you," Greta said, blinking back her tears. "I know this hasn't been easy on you, but I've loved having you here. Please stay in touch. And let us know when you settle somewhere."

"I will," Kay said, blinking back her own tears. "I promise."

After that, there was no more to say. A last hug, a last good-bye, and she was alone in the house with Gideon.

"All the loose ends tied up?" he asked.

"I guess so."

"No regrets?"

"No."

"Glad to hear it. So, Mrs. Marquet, I was thinking we could use a second honeymoon."

"That sounds nice."

"Where would you like to spend it?" Gideon asked, lifting

her into his arms. "On a sandy beach in Hawaii? A five-star hotel in London? Or maybe a villa in Barcelona?"

"Surprise me," she said, wrapping her arms around his neck. "It doesn't matter where we go, as long as we're together."

"How about that beach in Hawaii tomorrow, and my lair in New York for what's left of tonight?"

"Sounds perfect," Kay said.

And it was.

Have you tried these other books by Amanda Ashley?

His Dark Embrace

A Vampire's Kiss. A Woman's Surrender.

Tall, dark, mysterious—and with a faint scar on his cheek that only makes him more gorgeous—Kaiden Thorne is one schoolgirl obsession Skylynn never forgot. Now, returning to her childhood home after eight years, she can't believe her reclusive neighbor is still living across the street—and hotter than ever. Skylynn doesn't know how Kaiden manages to stay so young, virile, and impossibly attractive. But she knows she wants him . . . even if he harbors a fearful secret he refuses to tell her.

When Kaiden sees the beautiful young woman Skylynn has become, he can no longer control the bloodlust that is his true nature. Once he pulls Skylynn into his arms, presses his lips against hers—and accidentally draws blood—he longs for more. Only she possesses what he wants and what he needs. Only she can save him or destroy him. But once Skylynn agrees to help Kaiden battle his darkest desires, there is no turning back . . .

Bound by Night

A Vampire's Kiss Is Forever . . .

Once featured in a horror movie, the crumbling Wolfram estate is said to be haunted by ghosts, witches, and worse. But Elena doesn't believe a word of it—until she spends the night and wakes up in the arms of a compelling stranger . . .

Tall, dark, and disturbingly handsome, Drake is the most beautiful man Elena has ever seen. For centuries, he has lived alone, and Elena is the first woman to enter his lair—and survive. And Drake is the first man to touch her heart and soul. By the time she discovers who he really is—and what he craves—it's too late. Bloodlust has turned to love, and Elena is deeply under Drake's spell. But forever comes at a price for each of them . . .

Bound by Blood

A Vampire's Love Is Eternal

Zack Ravenscroft loves women—all women—and they love him. The irresistibly seductive owner of the hottest casino in Nevada, Zack has tasted every wicked pleasure Sin City can offer. But never in his six hundred years as a vampire has he seen a morsel as delectable as Kaitlyn Sherrad, the mysterious young newcomer in town. Zack knows nothing about her—except that he craves her . . .

Kaitlyn is half vampire, half human—and all woman. As the cherished daughter of the Carpathian Coven's master, she has been given every luxury a girl could desire. Now her only need is for a prince. But though she's ready to gamble her heart on Zack, a powerful enemy stalks their every move . . . watches their every kiss . . . and waits to destroy their undying love . . .

Thrilling Suspense from
Beverly Barton